DELETED

# Face the Fire

# Titles by Nora Roberts

| | |
|---|---|
| HOT ICE | HIDDEN RICHES |
| SACRED SINS | TRUE BETRAYALS |
| BRAZEN VIRTUE | MONTANA SKY |
| SWEET REVENGE | SANCTUARY |
| PUBLIC SECRETS | HOMEPORT |
| GENUINE LIES | THE REEF |
| CARNAL INNOCENCE | RIVER'S END |
| DIVINE EVIL | CAROLINA MOON |
| HONEST ILLUSIONS | THE VILLA |
| PRIVATE SCANDALS | MIDNIGHT BAYOU |

## Anthologies

FROM THE HEART
A LITTLE MAGIC

## The Once Upon Series

*(with Jill Gregory, Ruth Ryan Langan,
and Marianne Willman)*

ONCE UPON A CASTLE
ONCE UPON A STAR
ONCE UPON A DREAM
ONCE UPON A ROSE

## Trilogies

*Three Sisters Island Trilogy*
DANCE UPON THE AIR
HEAVEN AND EARTH
FACE THE FIRE

| | |
|---|---|
| *The Irish Trilogy* | *The Born In Trilogy* |
| JEWELS OF THE SUN | BORN IN FIRE |
| TEARS OF THE MOON | BORN IN ICE |
| HEART OF THE SEA | BORN IN SHAME |
| | |
| *The Chesapeake Bay Trilogy* | *The Dream Trilogy* |
| SEA SWEPT | DARING TO DREAM |
| RISING TIDES | HOLDING THE DREAM |
| INNER HARBOR | FINDING THE DREAM |

# Nora Roberts

# Face the Fire

BOOKSPAN LARGE PRINT EDITION

JOVE BOOKS, NEW YORK

This Large Print Edition, prepared especially for Bookspan, contains the complete, unabridged text of the original Publisher's Edition.

FACE THE FIRE

A Jove Book / published by arrangement with the author

Copyright © 2002 by Nora Roberts.
Cover art and design by Tony Greco and Associates, Inc.

ISBN: 0-7394-2606-0

A JOVE BOOK®
Jove Books are published by The Berkley Publishing Group, a division of Penguin Putnam Inc., 375 Hudson Street, New York, New York 10014.
JOVE and the "J" design are trademarks belonging to Penguin Putnam Inc.

PRINTED IN THE UNITED STATES OF AMERICA

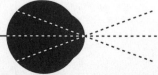

This Large Print Book carries the Seal of Approval of N.A.V.H.

*To lovers,*
*old and new*

O love! O fire! once he drew
With one long kiss my whole soul through
My lips; as sunlight drinketh dew.
                        —ALFRED, LORD TENNYSON

# Prologue

THREE SISTERS ISLAND
SEPTEMBER 1702

Her heart was broken. The jagged shards of it stabbed at her soul until each hour, each moment, of what her life had become was a misery. Even her children—those she had carried in her body, those she carried for her lost sisters—were no comfort.

Nor was she, to her great shame, any comfort to them.

She had left them, even as their father had left them. Her husband, her lover, her heart, had returned to the sea, and the parts of her that were hope and love and magic had died that day.

Even now he would not remember the years they'd had together, the joy of them. He would not remember her, or their sons, their daughters, the life they'd made on the island.

Such was his nature. Such was her fate.

And her sisters', she thought as she stood on the cliffs she loved, above a sea that boiled and bucked. They, too, had been fated to love and to lose. The one who was Air had loved a handsome face and kind words that had disguised a beast. A beast who had shed her blood. He had murdered her for what she was, and she had not used her power to stop him.

And so the one who was Earth had raged and grieved and built her hatred stone by stone until it had become a wall that no one could breach. She had used her power for vengeance, forsaken her Craft, and embraced the dark.

Now the dark closed in, and she who was Fire was alone with her pain. She could fight it no longer, could find no purpose for her own life.

The dark whispered to her in the night, its sly voice full of lies. Even knowing them for what they were, she was tempted by them.

Her circle was broken, and she could not, would not, withstand alone.

She felt it, creeping closer now, sliding along the ground in a filthy fog. It hungered. Her death would feed it, and still she could not face life.

She lifted her arms so the flame of her hair snapped in the wind that she called up with a breath. She had such powers left in her. And the sea howled in response, the ground beneath her shuddered.

Air and Earth and Fire—and the Water that had given her great love, then had stolen it away again.

This last time they were hers to command again.

Her children would be safe, she had seen to that. Their nurse would tend them, teach them, and the gift, the brightness, would be passed down.

The darkness licked along her skin. Cold, cold kisses.

She teetered on the edge, will straining against will as the storm within her, and the storm she'd conjured, raged.

This island, that she and her sisters had conjured for safety from the ravages of those who would hunt and kill them, she thought, would be lost. All would be lost.

*You are alone,* the darkness murmured. *You are in pain. End the loneliness. End the pain.*

And so she would, but she would not forsake her children, or the children who came from them. Power was still in her, and the strength and wit to wield it.

"A hundred years times three, this isle of the sisters is safe from thee."

From her reaching fingers, light whipped, spun, a circle in a circle.

"My children your hand cannot reach. They will live and learn and teach. And when my spell comes undone, three more will rise to form the one. A circle of sisters joined in power to stand and face the darkest hour. Courage and trust, justice with mercy, love without boundaries are the lessons three. They must, by free will, join to face their destiny. If this they fail, one, two, or three, this island will sink into the sea. But if they turn back the dark, this place will never bear your mark. This spell is the last cast by me. As I will, so mote it be."

The darkness snatched at her as she leaped, but could not reach her. As she plunged toward the sea, she hurled her power around the island, where her children slept, like a silver net.

# One

THREE SISTERS ISLAND
MAY 2002

It had been more than ten years since he'd stood on the island. Over a decade since he'd seen—except in his mind—the wedges of forest, the scatter of houses, the curve of beach and cove. And the drama of the cliffs where the stone house stood beside the white lance of the island lighthouse.

He shouldn't have been so surprised by the pull and tug, or by the sheer simplicity of pleasure. Sam Logan was rarely surprised. But the delight in seeing what had changed, and what hadn't, surprised him by its depth.

He'd come home and hadn't realized, not completely, what that meant to him until he'd gotten there.

He parked near the ferry dock because he wanted to walk, to smell the salty spring air, to hear the voices from the boats, to see the life flowing along on the little bump of land off the coast of Massachusetts.

And perhaps, he admitted, because he wanted a little more time to prepare himself before seeing the woman he'd come back for.

He didn't expect a warm welcome. The fact was, he didn't know what to expect from Mia.

Once he had. He'd known every expression on her face, every inflection of her voice. Once she would have been standing on the dock to meet him, her glorious red hair flying, her smoky eyes alight with pleasure and promise.

He'd have heard her laugh as she raced into his arms.

Those days were over, he thought as he climbed the road toward High Street and the stretch of pretty shops and offices. He'd ended them, and had exiled himself, deliberately, from the island and from Mia.

Now, he was deliberately ending that exile.

In the time between, the girl he'd left behind had become a woman. A businesswoman, he thought with a half laugh. No surprise there. Mia had always had a head for business and a view for profit. He intended to use that, if need be, to wheedle his way back into her good graces.

Sam didn't mind wheedling, as long as he won.

He turned on High Street and paused to take a long look at the Magick Inn. The Gothic stone building was the island's only hotel, and it belonged to him. He had some ideas that he intended to implement there, now that his father had finally released the reins.

But business would wait, for once, until the personal was dealt with.

He continued walking, pleased to see that while traffic was light, it was steady. Business on the island, he decided, was as good as reported.

He had a long stride, and it ate up the sidewalk quickly. He was a tall man, nearly three inches over six feet, with a rangy, disciplined build more accustomed in the last years to tailored suits than the black jeans he wore today. The long dark coat he wore against the brisk breeze of early May billowed behind him as he walked.

His hair was black as well and, wind-blown now from the ferry ride from the mainland, swept past his collar. His face was lean, the long bones of his cheeks well defined. The planes and angles were softened somewhat by a full and sculpted mouth, and with those black wings of hair flying back, presented a dramatic picture.

His eyes were alert as they scanned what had been, and would be again, his home. Somewhere between blue and green, they were the color of the sea that surrounded the house, framed by dark lashes and brows.

He used his looks when it suited him, just as he used charm or ruthlessness. Whatever tools came to hand were employed to reach his goal. He'd already accepted that it would take everything at his disposal to win Mia Devlin.

From across the street, he studied Café Book. He should have known Mia would have taken what had been a neglected building and turned it into something lovely, elegant, and productive. The front window held a display of books and potted spring flowers scattered around a lawn chair. Two of her deepest loves, he mused. Books and flowers. She'd used them both in a way that suggested it was time to take a break from the yardwork, sit down, and enjoy the fruits of the labor with a ride in a story.

Even as he watched, a couple of tourists—he hadn't been away so long he couldn't tell tourists from islanders—walked into the bookstore.

He stood where he was, hands in his pockets, until he realized he was procrastinating. There was little more turbulent than Mia Devlin in full temper. He expected her to lash out at him in blistering fury the minute she laid eyes on him again.

And who could blame her?

Then again, he thought with a grin, there was little more arousing than Mia Devlin in full temper. It would be . . . entertaining to strike swords with her again. Just as it would be satisfying to soothe that temper away.

He crossed the street and opened the door to Café Book.

Lulu was behind the counter. He'd have recognized her anywhere. The tiny woman with a gnome's face almost swallowed up by silver-framed glasses had, essentially, raised Mia. The Devlins had been more interested in each other and traveling than in their daughter, and Lulu, the former flower child, had been hired to tend her.

Because Lulu was ringing up a customer's purchases, he had a moment to look around the store. The ceiling was pricked with lights for a starry effect and made the prospect of browsing through the books a festive one. A cozy seating area was arranged in front of a fireplace with a hearth, scrubbed and polished, used as a haven for more spring flowers. The scent of them sweetened the air, as did the pipes and flutes playing softly on the speaker system.

Glossy blue shelves held books—an impressive array, he reflected as he wandered through, and as eclectic as he would have expected of the proprietor. No one would ever accuse Mia of having a one-track mind.

His lips quirked as he saw that other shelves held ritual candles, Tarot cards, runes, statues of faeries, wizards, dragons. An attractive arrangement of another of Mia's interests, he thought. He'd have expected nothing else there, either.

He plucked a tumbling stone of rose

quartz from a bowl, rubbed it between his fingers for luck. Though he knew better. Before he could replace it, he felt a blast of frigid air. Smiling easily, he turned to face Lulu.

"Always knew you'd come back. Bad pennies always turn up."

This was his first barrier, the dragon at the gate. "Hello, Lu."

"Don't you hello-Lu me, Sam Logan." She sniffed, skimmed her gaze over him. Sniffed a second time. "You buying that or do I call the sheriff and have you hauled in for shoplifting?"

He laid the stone back in the bowl. "How is Zack?"

"Ask him yourself, I don't have time to waste on you." Though he had her by a foot in height, she stepped forward, jabbed her finger at him, and made him feel twelve years old again. "What the hell do you want?"

"To see home. To see Mia."

"Why don't you do everybody a favor and go back to where you've been gallivanting these past years? New York City, Paris, and oo-la-la. We've all done fine without you taking up space on the Sisters."

"Apparently." He gave the store another casual look. He wasn't offended. A dragon, in his mind, was meant to be devoted to its princess. In his memory, Lulu had always been up to the job. "Nice place. I hear the café's particularly good. And that Zack's new wife runs it."

"Your hearing's just fine. So listen up. Go on and get."

Not offended, no, but his eyes turned edgy, the green in them deepening. "I came to see Mia."

"She's busy. I'll tell her you stopped by."

"No, you won't," he said quietly. "But she'll know in any case."

Even as he spoke, he heard the sound of heels on wood. It could have been a dozen women, descending the curving steps in high heels. But he knew. As his heart stumbled in his chest, he stepped around the bookshelves and saw her just as she made the last turn.

And the look, that one look at her, sliced him into a thousand pieces.

The princess, he thought, had become the queen.

She'd always been the most beautiful creature he'd ever seen. The transition from

girl to woman had only added polished layers to that beauty. Her hair was as he remembered it, a long tumble of flaming curls
around a face of rose and cream. That skin,
he remembered, was as soft as dew. Her
nose was small and straight, her mouth
wide and full. And he remembered, perfectly
remembered, the texture and flavor. Her
eyes were smoke-gray, almond-shaped,
and watched him now with a studied cool-
ness.

She smiled, and that, too, was cool, as
she walked toward him.

Her dress, a dull gold, clung to her
curves, showed off long, long legs. The
heels she wore were the same tone and
made her look like something glowing with
heat. But he felt no warmth from her as she
arched a brow and looked at him in turn.

"Well, it's Sam Logan, isn't it? Welcome
back."

Her voice was deeper, just a few degrees
deeper than it had been once upon a time.
Sultrier, smokier, silkier. It seemed to wind
its way into his belly even as he puzzled
over her polite smile and detached welcome.

"Thanks." Deliberately, he matched her

tone. "It's good to be back. You look amazing."

"We do what we can."

She tossed back her hair. There were citrine stones at her ears. The details of her, down to the rings on her fingers, the subtle scent that surrounded her, etched themselves into his mind. For an instant, he tried to read hers but found the language foreign and frustrating.

"I like your bookstore," he said, careful to keep his voice casual. "Or what I've seen of it."

"Well, we'll have to give you the grand tour. Lulu, you have customers."

"I know what I've got," Lulu muttered. "It's a workday, isn't it? You don't have time to go showing this one around the place."

"Lulu." Mia merely angled her head, a quiet warning. "I've always got a few minutes for an old friend. Come upstairs, Sam, see the café." She started back up, her hand trailing along the rail. "You may have heard that a mutual friend of ours, Zack Todd, was married last winter. Nell's not only a close friend of mine but she's a spectacular cook as well."

Sam paused at the top of the stairs. It annoyed him that he had to get his bearings, seek his balance. The scent of her was turning him inside out.

The second floor was just as welcoming as the first, with the added enticement of a bustling café on one end and all the wonderful aromas, of spices, coffee, rich chocolate, that wafted from it.

The display glass sparkled in front of a dazzling selection of baked goods and salads. Fragrant smoke streamed from an enormous kettle where even now a pretty blonde ladled out soup for a waiting customer.

Windows on the far wall let in glimpses of the sea.

"It's terrific." That, at least, he could say without qualification. "Just terrific, Mia. You must be very proud of what you've done here."

"Why wouldn't I be?"

There was a bite, a quick, nasty nip, in the tone that had him looking back at her. But she only smiled again, gestured with an elegant hand that sparkled with rings. "Hungry?"

"More than I'd counted on."

A glimpse of that bite snapped, for an instant, in those smoke-gray depths before she turned and led the way to the counter. "Nell, I have a man with an appetite."

"Then he's come to the right place." Nell grinned, her dimples fluttering, her blue eyes friendly when they met Sam's. "Our soup of the day is chicken curry. Special salad is shrimp diablo, and the sandwich of the day is grilled pork and tomato on olive loaf. Plus our regular fare," she added, tapping the counter menu, "with our vegetarian offerings."

Zack's wife, Sam thought. It was one thing to realize that his oldest friend had taken the plunge and another to see the reason why. It gave him yet one more jolt.

"Quite a selection."

"We like to think so."

"You can't make a bad choice when Nell's prepared it," Mia told him. "I'll just leave you in her capable hands for the moment. I do have work. Oh, Nell, I should have introduced you. This is an old friend of Zack's, Sam Logan. Enjoy your lunch," she said, then walked away.

Sam watched surprise race over Nell's pretty face, then every bit of warmth drain away. "What can I get you?"

"Just coffee for now. Black. How's Zack?"

"He's very well, thank you."

Sam drummed his fingers on his thigh. Another guard at the gate, he thought, and no less formidable than the dragon, for all the soft looks. "And Ripley? I heard she got married just last month."

"She's very well and very happy." Nell's mouth formed a firm, unwelcoming line as she set his coffee in a to-go cup on the counter. "No charge. I'm sure Mia doesn't want, or need, your money. They serve a very nice lunch at the Magick Inn, as I'm sure you know."

"Yes, I know." A pretty kitten, and very sharp claws, Sam mused. "Do you think Mia needs your protection, Mrs. Todd?"

"I think Mia can handle anything." She smiled now, thin as a blade. "Absolutely anything."

Sam picked up his coffee. "So do I," he agreed, then wandered off in the direction Mia had gone.

⁂

The bastard. Once she was behind the closed door of her office, Mia let out a splinter of the rage. Even that had books and knickknacks on her shelves rattling and jumping. That he would have the nerve, the insensitivity, the *stupidity* to waltz into her store.

To stand there and *smile* at her as if he expected her to shout for joy and jump into his arms. And to look baffled when she hadn't.

Bastard.

She clenched her fists, and a thin crack snaked across the glass of her window.

She'd known the moment he'd walked in. Just as she'd known the instant he'd come onto the island. It had washed over her, flooded into her, as she'd sat at her desk completing a stock order. Pain, shock, joy, fury, all so intense, all so immediate, she'd been dizzy from them. One stunning emotion slamming into another, leaving her weak and trembling.

And she'd known he was back.

Eleven years. He'd walked away from her, leaving her hurting and helpless and hopeless. It still shamed her to remember the quivering mass of confusion and grief she'd been for weeks after he'd gone.

But she'd rebuilt her life on the ashes of

the dreams that Sam had burned beneath her. She'd found her focus, and a kind of steady contentment.

Now he was back.

She could only thank the fates that her foreknowledge had given her time to compose herself. How humiliating it would have been if she'd seen him before she'd had a chance to prepare herself. And how satisfying it had been to see that flicker of surprise and puzzlement cross his face at her cool and casual greeting.

She was stronger now, she reminded herself. She was no longer the girl who had laid her heart, bleeding and broken, at his feet. And there were more—many more—important things in her life now than a man.

Love, she thought, could be such a lie. She had no place, and no tolerance, for lies. She had her home, her business, her friends. She had her circle again, and that circle had a purpose.

That was enough to sustain her.

At the knock on the door, she blocked her feelings, her thoughts again, then slid onto the chair behind her desk. "Yes, come in."

She was scanning the data on her monitor when Sam stepped inside. She glanced over absently, with just a hint of a frown in her eyes. "Nothing on the menu to tempt you?"

"I settled for this." He lifted the coffee, then pried off the top and set it on her desk. "Nell's very loyal."

"Loyalty's a necessary quality in a friend, to my mind."

He made some sound of agreement, then sipped the coffee. "She also makes superior coffee."

"A necessary quality in a café chef." She tapped her fingers on the desk in a gesture of restrained impatience. "Sam, I'm sorry, I don't want to be rude. You're more than welcome to enjoy the café, the store. But I have work."

He studied her for one long moment, but that slightly annoyed expression on her face didn't waver. "I won't keep you, then. Why don't you just give me the keys, and I'll go off and settle in?"

Baffled, she shook her head. "Keys?"

"To the cottage. Your cottage."

"*My* cottage? Why on earth would I give you the keys to the yellow cottage?"

"Because." Delighted to have finally broken through that polite shield, he drew papers out of his pocket. "We have a lease." He set the papers on her desk, leaning back when she snatched them up to read. "Celtic Circle's one of my companies," he explained as she scowled at the names. "And Henry Downing's one of my attorneys. He leased the cottage for me."

Her hand wanted to tremble. More, it wanted to strike. Deliberately, she laid it, palm down, on the desk. "Why?"

"I have attorneys do all manner of things for me," Sam said with a shrug. "Added to that, I didn't think you would rent it to me. But I did think—was sure—that once a business deal had been made, you'd keep your end."

She drew in a long breath. "I meant, why do you need the cottage? You have an entire hotel at your disposal."

"I don't choose to live in a hotel, nor to live where I work. I want my privacy and my downtime. I won't get either if I stay at the hotel. Would you have rented it to me, Mia, if I hadn't gone through the lawyer?"

Her lips curved now, sharply. "Of course. But I'd have bumped up the monthly rent. Considerably."

He laughed, and more on balance than

he'd been since that first sight of her, drank more coffee. "A deal's a deal, and maybe it was meant to be. Since my parents sold our house to Ripley's new husband, I can't set up housekeeping there. Things usually happen the way they're supposed to happen."

"Things happen," was all she said. She opened a drawer, took out a set of keys. "It's small, and it's on the rustic side, but I'm sure you'll make do with it while you're on the island."

She set the keys on the desk, on top of his copy of the lease.

"I'm sure I will. Why don't you have dinner with me tonight? We can catch up."

"No, thank you."

He hadn't meant to ask, not so soon. It irked him that the words had escaped. "Some other time, then." He rose, pocketed the keys, the lease. "It's good to see you again, Mia."

Before she could evade it, he laid his hand over hers on the desk. Something sparked, visibly. The air sizzled with it.

"Ah," was all he said, and tightened his grip.

"Take your hand off me." She kept her voice low, spoke slowly while looking directly into his eyes. "You have no right to touch me."

"It was never about rights with us, and all about need."

Her hand wanted to tremble. Sheer will kept it steady. "There is no us now, and I no longer need you."

It hurt. A bright, swift pain twisted in his heart. "But you do, and I need you. There's more to be considered than old, bruised feelings."

" 'Bruised feelings.' " She repeated the phrase as if it were a new language. "I see. Be that as it may, you will not touch me without my permission. You don't have it."

"We're going to have to talk."

"That implies we have something to say to each other." She allowed some of the anger to surface and coated it with disdain. "Right at this moment, I don't have anything to say to you. I want you to leave. You have the lease, you have the keys, you have the cottage. That was clever of you, Sam. You always were clever, even as a boy. But this is my office, my store." My island, she nearly said, but bit it back in time. "And I don't have time for you."

When his grip loosened, she slid her hand

free. The air cleared. "Let's not spoil your visit with a scene. I hope you'll like the cottage. If you have any problems with it, let me know."

"I will. Enjoy it and let you know." He turned to the door, opened it. "Oh, Mia, this isn't a visit. I'm here to stay."

He saw, with vicious pleasure, her cheeks go pale just before he shut the door.

He cursed himself for that, and for bungling the first steps. His mood remained foul as he stalked downstairs and out of the store under Lulu's steely stare.

He turned away from the docks where he'd parked, away from the cottage where he would live for a while, and headed toward the police station.

He could only hope that Zack Todd, now Sheriff Todd, would be in. By God, Sam thought, he'd like one person, one goddamn person, to welcome him home and mean it.

If he couldn't count on Zack for that, he was in a very sorry state. He hunched his shoulders against the brisk spring breeze, no longer appreciating it.

She'd brushed him off like a fly. Like a gnat. Not with a slash of temper but with irritation. That snap of connection between them meant something. He had to believe that. But if anyone he knew could hold the line against fate, could press her will against it, it was Mia.

Stubborn, prideful witch, he thought, then sighed. The fact that she was exactly that had always been part of her appeal for him. Pride and power were hard to resist. Unless he missed his guess, she had more of both now than she'd had at nineteen.

That meant he had his work cut out for him, on a number of levels.

He hissed out a breath and shoved open the door to the station house.

The man who sat with his feet on the desk and a phone at his ear hadn't changed much. He'd filled out here, fined down there. His hair was still unruly, still sun-streaked brown. His eyes were the same sharp, pure green.

And they widened as they studied Sam's face.

"Hey, let me get back to you. I'll have the paperwork faxed over by end of day. Yeah. Right. I have to go." Zack swung his feet from desk to floor as he hung up the phone. Then he unfolded himself and stared, grinning, at Sam. "Son of a bitch, it's Mister New York City."

"So, look who's John Law."

Zack crossed the small office area in three strides on battered high-tops and caught Sam in a bear hug.

More than relief rippled through Sam, for here was welcome, and the uncomplicated affection and bone-deep bond that had sprung from childhood.

The years between the boy and the man fell away.

"It's good to see you," he managed.

"Right back at you." Zack eased away, took stock. Pure pleasure flashed in his grin. "Well, you didn't get fat and bald from sitting behind a desk."

Sam shot a look at Zack's cluttered work area. "Neither did you. Sheriff."

"Yeah, so remember who's in charge and keep your nose clean on my island. What the hell are you doing here? Want some coffee?"

"If you're calling what's in that pot coffee, I'll pass, thanks. And I've got business here. Long-term business."

Zack pursed his lips as he poured muddy coffee into a mug. "The hotel?"

"For one thing. I bought my parents out. It's mine now."

"Bought them—" Zack shrugged, eased a hip onto the corner of the desk.

"My family never did run like yours," Sam said dryly. "It's a business. One that my father lost interest in. I haven't. How are your parents?"

"Dandy. You just missed them. They came in for Ripley's wedding and stayed nearly a month. I almost thought they'd decided to move back permanently, but then they packed up their Winnebago and headed up to Nova Scotia."

"I'm sorry I won't get to see them. I've heard Rip's not the only one who got married."

"Yeah." Zack lifted his hand where his wedding ring glinted. "I'd hoped you would make it back for the wedding."

"I wish I could have." That was a real regret, one of many. "I'm happy for you, Zack. I mean that."

"I know it. You'll be happier when you meet her."

"Oh, I met your wife." Sam's smile thinned. "From the smell of that crap you're drinking, she makes better coffee than you."

"Ripley made it."

"Whatever. I'm just grateful your wife didn't pour hers over my head."

"Why would she . . . ? Oh." Zack puffed out his cheeks. "Oh, well, then. Mia." He rubbed a hand over his chin. "Nell and Mia and Ripley. The fact is—"

He broke off as the door swung open. Ripley Todd Booke, vibrating from the brim of her ball cap to the toes of her scarred boots, glowered at Sam. Her eyes, the same green as her brother's, shot arrows of resentment.

"Better late than never," she announced as she started forward. "I've been waiting for this for eleven years."

Zack lunged toward her, caught her around the waist as she swung out. She had, he had reason to know, a keen right cross. "Hold on," he ordered. "Just hold the hell on."

"Hasn't mellowed, has she?" Sam commented. He tucked his hands in his pockets. If she was going to plant a fist in his face, he'd just as soon she get it over with.

"Not a bit." Zack hefted her off her feet while she cursed at him. Her cap fell off, and her long dark hair tumbled over her furious face. "Sam, why don't you give me a few minutes here? Ripley, cut it out!" he ordered. "You're wearing a badge, remember?"

"Then I'll take it off before I punch him." She blew her hair out of her eyes and they scorched the air between her and Sam. "He deserves it."

"Maybe I do," Sam agreed. "But not from you."

"Mia's too much of a damn lady to bust your chops. I'm not."

He smiled now. "I always liked that about you. I'm renting the yellow cottage," he told Zack and watched Ripley's mouth drop open in shock. "Come on by when you have time. We'll have a beer."

He decided the shock was complete when she didn't try to kick him as he walked to the door. He stepped outside again, took another long look at the village.

He'd had a welcome from a friend, even if three women had formed a tight circle of resentment against him.

For better or for worse, he thought, he was home.

# Two

The road to hell, Sam decided, was paved with intentions—and they didn't have to be good.

He'd intended to stride back into Mia's life, face her fury, her tears, her bitterness. She was entitled to all of those, and he would be the last to deny it.

He would have accepted her rage, her curses, her accusations. He'd intended to give her the opportunity to vent every drop of resentment she had harbored for him. And, of course, he'd intended then to sweep them aside and win her over.

A done deal, in his calculations, in a matter of hours at best, days at worst.

They'd been linked since childhood. What was eleven years compared to a bond of blood and heart and power?

But he hadn't intended to face her cool

indifference. Oh, she was angry with him, he thought as he parked in front of the cottage. But overlying the anger was a thick, icy shield. Chipping through that would take more than smiles, explanations, promises, even apologies.

Lulu had blasted him, Nell had slapped at him, and Ripley had bared her teeth. Mia had done none of those things, but her response had leveled him as none of the others' had, or could.

It stung to have her look at him with a kind of studied disdain, particularly since seeing her again had stirred all the memories inside him, churning them with fresh spurts of lust, longing. Love.

He had loved her, obsessively, outrageously. And that had been the root, or one of the many tangled roots, of the problem.

As he turned it over in his mind, he tapped his fingers idly on the steering wheel. He refused to believe she didn't still care for him. There had been too much between them, too much *of* them for there to be nothing left.

And if there'd been nothing, that spark, that one instant of connection when their hands had touched, wouldn't have happened. He was going to hold on to that, Sam thought as his hands tightened and released on the wheel. Whatever else came down, he was holding on to that one spark.

A determined man could build one hell of a blaze from one good spark.

Winning her back, doing what must be done, facing what must be faced, would be a challenge. His lips quirked. He'd always enjoyed one.

He would have to do more than chip through Mia's ice. He'd have to get past the dragon—and Lulu was no pushover. And he'd have to deal with the women who flanked Mia: Nell Todd with her quiet disapproval, and Ripley with her infamous temper.

When a man had to wage a battle against four women, that man had best have a plan. And very thick skin. Or he would be ground to dust in a heartbeat.

He'd work on it. Sam swung out of the car, rounded back to the trunk. There was time. Not as much as he might have liked under the circumstances, but there was time.

He hefted two suitcases out of the trunk, started up the walk. Then stopped and took his first real look at what would be his home for the next weeks.

Well, it was charming, he realized. Neither the photographs he'd studied nor his memory had done the cottage justice. It had been white once, as he recalled, and a bit run-down. The yellow paint warmed it, and the flower beds, just sprouting with spring, cheered it. That would be Mia's doing, he imagined. She'd always had exquisite taste and clear vision.

She had always known precisely what she wanted.

Another tangled root for him.

The cottage was quaint, tiny and private, on a pretty corner lot that bled into a small wood and was close enough to the water that the rumble of the sea played through the greening trees. It had the advantage of quiet solitude and the convenience of being an easy walk from the village.

An excellent investment, Sam thought. Mia would have known that, too.

The clever girl, he mused as he continued up the walk, had become a clever woman. He set his suitcases on the stoop and dug out the house keys.

The first thing that struck him when he

stepped inside was the warmth of welcome, the smooth, open hand of it. Come in and make this home, the room seemed to say. There were no lingering sensations or energy spurts from previous tenants.

That would be Mia's doing as well, he was sure. She'd always been a thorough witch.

Leaving his suitcases by the door, he took himself on a quick tour. The living room was sparsely but prettily furnished, and split logs had already been laid in the hearth. The floors gleamed, and thin, lacy curtains framed the windows. A female ambience, he thought, but he could live with that.

There were two bedrooms, one cozy, the other . . . well, he only needed one. The bath, scrubbed and cheery, was also a narrow box designed to give a tall man with long limbs considerable grief.

The kitchen at the back of the house would more than do for his needs. He didn't cook, and didn't intend to begin. He opened the back door to find more flower beds, an herb garden already thriving, and a tidy patch of lawn that slid right into the spring woods.

He could hear the sea, and the wind, and, if he listened carefully, the hum of a car heading to the village. Birdsong, and the playful yap of a dog.

He was, Sam realized, alone. With the realization, some of the tension that had gathered in his shoulders eased. He hadn't understood just how much he craved solitude. It wasn't a commodity he'd been able to claim in great quantities over the last couple of years.

Nor was it something he'd actively sought in the day-to-day scheme of things. He'd had goals to achieve and points to prove, and such ambitions didn't allow for the luxury of solitude.

He hadn't understood that he needed to find that serenity of aloneness again, almost as much as he needed to find Mia. Once he had had both whenever he wanted them. And once he had cast them both aside. Now the island he'd run from so fast as a young man was going to give them back to him.

He would have enjoyed walking through the woods, or down to the beach. Or driving, he thought, to his old house and seeing his bluffs, his cove, the cave where he and Mia . . . He shook that idea and those memories away. It wasn't the time for sentiment.

There were practical matters to be dealt with. Phones, faxes, computers. The little bedroom would have to suit up as a secondary office, though he planned to base his work at the hotel. He needed supplies, and he knew that as soon as he made his way around the village buying them, word of his return would spread like fire through dry kindling.

He would see what he would see.

Turning from the door, he went back inside to unpack and set his place to rights.

Well-meaning friends, Mia thought, were a blessing. And a curse. At the moment, two of hers were crammed into her office.

"I think you should kick his ass," Ripley announced. "Of course, I thought that ten years ago."

Eleven, Mia corrected silently. Eleven years, but who's counting?

"That would make him too important." Nell stuck her nose in the air. "She's better off ignoring him."

"You don't ignore a blood leech." Ripley

bared her teeth. "You rip it off and stomp it into a quivering pulp."

"What a pretty image." At her desk, Mia leaned back, studied her two friends. "I have no intention of kicking Sam's ass, or of ignoring him. He's taken a six-months' lease on the cottage, which makes me his land-lord."

"You could cut off his hot water," Ripley suggested.

Mia's lips twitched. "How perfectly child-ish—but however satisfying it might be, I've no intention of pulling silly pranks either. If I did, I'd cut off his water altogether. Why stop at hot? But," she continued as Ripley gave a hoot of laughter, "he is my tenant, and that means he's entitled to everything that's spelled out in the lease. It's business, and nothing more."

"Why the hell is he renting anyplace on the Sisters for six months?" Ripley won-dered.

"Obviously he's here to take more per-sonal charge of the Magick Inn."

He'd always loved it, Mia mused. Or so she'd thought. Yet he'd walked away from it just as he'd walked away from her.

"We're both adults, both business own-ers, both islanders. And though it's a small world here, I imagine the two of us can manage to run our enterprises, live our lives, and coexist with a minimum of fuss."

Ripley snorted. "If you believe that, you're delusional."

"I won't let him into my life again." Mia's voice took on an edge. "And I won't let my life be upset because he's here. I always knew he'd come back."

Before Ripley could speak again, Nell shot her a warning glance. "You're right, of course. And with the season coming on, you'll both be too busy to get in each other's way. Why don't you come to dinner tonight? I'm trying out a new recipe, and I could use the feedback."

"You'll get that from Zack. No need to pamper me or soothe me, little sister."

"Why don't we all go out and get drunk and bitch about men in general?" Ripley perked up. "That's always fun."

"As appealing as that sounds, I'll pass. I have a number of things to do at home . . . if I can get my work done here."

"She wants us to clear out," Ripley told Nell.

"I get that." Nell sighed. It was hard, she thought, to want so badly to help and not know how. "All right, but if there's anything you need or want—"

"I know. I'm fine, and I'm going to stay that way."

She scooted them out, then sat—just sat with her hands in her lap. It was self-defeating to tell herself she would work, or to pretend she could move through this particular day as if it were any other day.

She was entitled to rage and to weep, to spit at fate and beat her fists on the face of destiny.

But she would do none of those things, those weak and useless things. She would, however, go home. She got to her feet, gathered her purse and the light jacket she'd brought. And as she passed her window, she saw him.

He stepped out of a sleek black Ferrari, his coat a dark swirl around him. He always did like shiny toys, she thought. He'd changed out of his jeans into a dark suit and tamed his hair, though the breeze was already playing with it. As her fingers once had.

He carried a briefcase and strode toward

the Magick Inn like a man who knew precisely where he was going and what he meant to do.

Then he turned, lifting his gaze unerringly to where she stood in the window. His eyes locked on hers, and she felt the jolt, the punch of heat that would once have melted her knees.

But this time she stood straight, and without a quiver. When enough time had passed for pride, she stepped away from the window and out of his sight.

Home soothed her. It always had. Practically, the big, rambling stone house on the cliff was too much for one woman. But it was, she knew, perfect for her. Even when she'd been a child, the house had been more hers than it had been her parents'. She'd never minded the echoes, the occasional drafts, or the sheer volume of time it took to maintain a house of its size and age.

Her ancestors had built it, and now it was hers alone.

She'd changed little on the inside since the house had come into her care. The furnishings here and there, a few of the colors, some basic modernization of the kitchen and baths. But the *feel* of the house was as it had always been for her. Embracing, warm, waiting.

There had been a time when she'd imagined herself raising a family there. God she'd wanted children. Sam's children. But over the years she had accepted what was, and what wasn't, and had made a nest of contentment.

At times she thought of the gardens as her children. She had created them, taking the time to plant, to nurture, to discipline. And they brought her joy.

And when she needed more than the gentle pleasure they provided, she had the passion and drama of her cliffs, the secrets and shadows of her forests.

She had, Mia told herself, all she needed.

But tonight she didn't wander out to fuss with her flowers or walk to face the sea from her cliffs. She didn't stroll into her forest. Instead, she went directly upstairs, climbing until she was closed inside her tower room.

Here had been refuge and discovery when she was a child. Here she had never felt alone unless alone was what she needed to feel. Here she had learned, and had disciplined, the beams of her own power.

The walls were rounded, the windows tall, narrow, and arched. The late-afternoon sun streamed through them in pale gold to pool on the dark, aged wood of the floor. Shelves curved along one wall, and on them were many of the tools of her trade. Pots of herbs, jars of crystals. Spell books that had belonged to those who'd come before her, and the ones that she'd written herself.

An old cabinet held other objects. There was a wand she'd made herself, from maple that she had harvested on Samhain when she turned sixteen. A broom, her best chalice, her oldest anthame, and a ball of pale blue crystal. Candles and oils and incense, a scrying mirror.

All this and more, carefully organized.

She gathered what she needed, then slipped out of her dress. She preferred, whenever possible, to work skyclad.

And so she cast the circle, calling on her element—fire—for energy. The candles she lighted with a breath were blue, for calm, for wisdom, for protection.

She had performed this ritual before, several times in the past decade. Whenever she felt her heart weaken or her purpose waver. She admitted that if she hadn't done so she would have known Sam was coming back to the Sisters before he'd arrived. So the years of relative peace had their price.

She would block him again—block her thoughts and feelings from him, and his from her.

They would not touch each other, on any level.

"My heart and mind are mine to keep," she began, lighting incense, sprinkling herbs on still water. "When I wake and when I sleep. What once I gave with love and free will, I take back to me, and hold calm and still. Then lovers, now strangers without joined destiny. As I will, so mote it be."

With her cupped palms lifted, she waited for the cool flow of serenity, the stream of confidence that would indicate her ritual was complete. As she watched, the cup of herb-scattered water began to shiver. Water lapped against the rim in quiet, teasing waves.

She fisted her hands, fought back her

own temper. Focusing her energy, she punched magic against magic. "My circle is closed to all but me. Your tricks are foolish and bore me. Do not enter what's mine again without invitation."

At the flick of her fingers, the lights from the candles streamed up, lancing to the ceiling. Smoke from them billowed, spread, and blanketed the surface of the water.

Even then she couldn't find her calm, or get a clean grasp of her temper. He would dare test his power against hers? And in her own home?

So he hadn't changed, she decided. Samuel Logan had always been an arrogant witch. And his element, she thought, hating herself when the first tear escaped, was water.

In her circle, behind the haze of smoke, she lay down and wept. Bitterly.

The island grapevine spread the news fast. By the next morning, the hot topic of Sam Logan had outdistanced every other tendril of gossip.

Conflicting reports had him selling the Magick Inn to mainland developers, expanding it into some fancy resort, firing the staff, or giving everyone a raise.

One thing everyone could agree on was that it was very, very interesting that he was renting Mia Devlin's little cottage. There was no consensus on what it meant, only that it was a puzzler.

Islanders, hoping to gather more nuggets, found reasons to drop into Café Book or stroll into the lobby of the hotel. Nobody had enough gumption to ask Sam or Mia directly, but there was plenty of watching and hoping for some excitement.

It had been a long, slow winter.

"Still handsome as sin and twice as deadly." Hester Birmingham confided this information to Gladys Macey as she bagged Gladys's weekly supply of groceries at Island Market. "Strolled in here big as life and twice as bold, and said hello to me like we'd just seen each other a week ago."

"What did he buy?" Gladys questioned.

"Coffee, milk, dry cereal. Whole wheat bread and stick butter. Some fruit. We got bananas on special, but he passed them up and paid dear for fresh strawberries. Bought himself some fancy cheese and fancy crackers and some bottled water. Oh, and some orange juice in a carton."

"Not planning on doing any cooking or cleaning for himself from the sound of it." Confidentially, she leaned closer to Hester. "I ran into Hank from the liquor store. He says Sam Logan breezed in and bought up five hundred dollars' worth of wine, some beer, and a bottle of single malt scotch."

"Five hundred!" Hester's voice lowered to a hiss. "You think he picked up a drinking problem in New York?"

"Wasn't the number of bottles, but the price," Gladys hissed back. "Two bottles of French champagne, and two of that fancy red wine you-know-who favors."

"Who?"

Gladys rolled her eyes. "Mia Devlin. Heaven's sake, Hester, who do you think!"

"I heard she kicked him out of the bookstore."

"No such thing. He walked in and out again under his own steam. I know that for a fact because Lisa Bigelow was in the café having lunch with her cousin from Portland when he was there. Lisa ran into my daughter-in-law at the Pump 'N Go and told her the whole story."

"Well . . ." Hester liked the first story better. "Do you think Mia will put a whammy on him?"

"Hester Birmingham, you know Mia doesn't do whammies. What a thing to say." Then she laughed. "But it sure will be interesting seeing what she does do. I think I'll go put these groceries away, then go buy myself a new paperback novel and a cup of coffee."

"You call me if anything develops."

Gladys winked as she rolled her loaded cart away. "You can take that to the bank."

Sam was well aware that tongues were wagging. He'd have been disappointed if they hadn't. Just as he'd expected to read trepidation, resentment, and puzzlement when he called a morning meeting with all department heads at the hotel.

Some of the trepidation eased when it became clear that a mass firing was not on the agenda. And some of the resentment increased when it became clear that Sam intended not only to take an active role in the running of the hotel but to make some changes as well.

"In season we run at near capacity. Off season, however, our occupancy rate drops sharply, often dipping to under thirty percent."

The sales manager shifted in his seat. "Business is slow on-island in the winter months. Always has been."

"What's always been doesn't apply," Sam said coolly. "The goal, for now, is to increase the guest rate to sixty-five percent off season within the year. We'll do that by offering more appealing packages to conventions, as well as weekend and weekly getaway packages. I'll have memos regarding my ideas in those areas on your desk by end of week.

"Next," he continued, flipping through his notes, "a number of the rooms require renovation and re-dressing. We'll begin next week, with the third floor." He glanced at his reservations manager. "You'll make the necessary adjustments."

Without waiting for acknowledgment, he flipped another page. "We've had a steady decline in our breakfast and lunch business over the last ten months. Data indicate that Café Book is nipping off our usual business in those areas."

"Sir." A brunette cleared her throat, adjusted the dark-framed glasses on her face.

"Yes? I'm sorry, your name?"

"Stella Farley. I'm the restaurant manager. If I can speak frankly, Mr. Logan, we're never going to be able to compete with the café and Nell Todd. If I could—"

She broke off when he lifted a finger. "I don't care for the word *never*."

She took a deep breath. "I'm sorry, but I've been here the last ten months and you haven't."

There was a deep silence, like a unified holding of breath. After a beat, Sam nodded. "Point taken. And just what have you learned in the last ten months, Ms. Farley?"

"That if we want to bring back business and generate more of it during the breakfast and lunch hours, we should counter-program. The café offers casual and casual gourmet. A relaxed atmosphere and, well, fabulous food. We need to offer an alternative. Elegance, formality, romance, an upscale atmosphere for a business meal or a special date. I sent your father a report and a proposal last fall, but—"

"You're not dealing with my father now." It was said so flatly, so smoothly, none of the resentment showed. "Get a copy on my desk by this afternoon."

"Yes, sir."

He paused. "If anyone else has run ideas or proposals by my father over the last year, they should copy me by end of week. I want to make it clear that I own this hotel now. Own and run. While my word will be final, I expect input from my department heads. I'll have memos to all of you over the next several days, and expect your responses to same within forty-eight hours of receipt. Thank you."

He watched them file out and heard the mumbling start before the door was closed.

One woman remained behind in her seat. Another brunette, she wore a simple navy suit and practical pumps. She was nearing sixty, had worked at the inn for more than forty years. She slipped off her glasses, lowered her steno pad, and folded her hands.

"Will that be all, Mr. Logan?"

Sam lifted an eyebrow. "You used to call me Sam."

"You didn't used to be my boss."

"Mrs. Farley . . ." His eyes cleared. "Was that your daughter? Stella? Jesus."

"Don't swear in the office," she said primly.

"Sorry. It just didn't connect. Congratulations," he added. "She was the only one with guts or brains enough to say anything worthwhile."

"I raised her to stand up for herself. They're scared of you," she told him. Boss or not, she decided, she'd known him since he was a baby. If her daughter could speak her mind, so could she.

"Most of the people who were in this room haven't ever so much as seen a Logan. For better or worse, this hotel's been run by proxy for a decade." There was just enough acid in her voice to let him know her opinion was worse. "Now, you drop in out of nowhere and stir things up. You always were one for stirring things up."

"It's my hotel, and it needs stirring up."

"I won't disagree. The Logans haven't taken enough interest in this place."

"My father—"

"You're not your father," she reminded him. "No point in using him as an excuse when you just finished making sure to get that point across yourself."

That rap on the knuckles made him nod. "All right. Then we'll say I'm here now, I intend to take plenty of interest—and make no excuses."

"Good." She opened her steno pad again. "Welcome back."

"Thank you. So"—he got to his feet, wandered to the window—"let's get started. The flower arrangements," he began.

He put in a fourteen-hour day, eating what passed for lunch at his desk. Because he wanted to keep his business local, he met with an island contractor personally and went over his renovation requirements. He instructed his assistant to order updated equipment for his office, then set up a meeting with the head of Island Tours.

He re-ran figures, reviewed proposals, refined and solidified random ideas. He knew just how much it would cost, in hard capital and in man-hours, to implement his plans. But he was in for the long haul.

Not everyone would think so, he admitted when he came to the surface and rubbed the stiffness out of the back of his neck. Mia wouldn't.

He was grateful he'd had so much on his plate through the day: It had helped keep thoughts of her at bay.

But he thought of her now, and remembered how he had felt the shimmer of her power flutter around the edges of his mind the day before. He'd pressed back at it, poked through it momentarily. And had seen her, clearly, kneeling in her tower room, her body washed by pale gold light, her hair a fiery fall to her shoulders.

Her birthmark, the tiny pentagram high on her thigh, had shimmered.

He had no doubt it had been that momentary jolt of desire that had allowed her to snap the link between them so quickly, so easily.

No matter. It had been wrong of him to intrude on her the way he had. Rude and wrong, and he'd been sorry for it almost as soon as he'd done it.

He would have to apologize for it, of course. There were rules of conduct that neither intimacy nor animosity could excuse breaking.

No time like the present, he decided. He culled the most pressing paperwork and tucked it in his briefcase. He'd speak to Mia, then grab some takeout and finish his work at home over a meal.

Unless he could convince her to have dinner with him, as a peace offering. Then work could wait.

He walked out of the hotel just as Mia stepped out of the bookstore across the street. They stood where they were a moment, each obviously caught off guard. Then she swiveled on her heel and walked toward a spiffy little convertible.

He had to dash across the street to catch her before she slipped into it.

"Mia. A minute."

"Go to hell."

"You can send me there after I apologize." He snagged the car door she'd swung open and closed it again. "I was completely in the wrong. I have no excuse for that kind of discourtesy."

Being surprised didn't mean being mollified. "I don't recall you ever being so quick with an apology before." She gave a little shrug. "Fine. Accepted. Go away."

"Give me five minutes."

"No."

"Five minutes, Mia. I've been cooped up all day, and I could use a walk and some fresh air."

She wouldn't struggle with him for the car door. It would be—and look to the people who were trying to pretend they weren't watching—undignified. "No one's stopping you. There's a great deal of air around here."

"Give me a chance to explain. A casual walk on the beach," he said quietly. "If you blow me off, you're just going to give them more to talk about. And me more to wonder about. A friendly conversation, in public, doesn't hurt either of us."

"All right." She dropped her car keys in the pocket of her long gray dress. "Five minutes."

She took a deliberate step away from him, slid her hands into her pockets, and jingled her keys as they walked along High Street toward the beach.

"Was your first day productive?"

"It was a good start. Do you remember Stella Farley?"

"Of course. I see her quite often. She belongs to the book club at the store."

"Mmm." Another reminder that she'd been here while changes had taken place and he hadn't. "She has some ideas for getting back some of our lunch business that you've been stealing away."

"Really?" Mia asked, amused. "Good luck." She felt people watching them as they turned toward the seawall. She stopped there, sliding out of her shoes before stepping onto the sand.

"I'll carry them."

"No, thanks."

The sea was a warm blue, deeper toward the horizon. Shells heaved up by the last high tide scattered the shore. Gulls circled, wheeled, cried.

"I felt you," he began. "Yesterday. I felt you and I reacted. That's not an excuse, it's a reason."

"I've already said accepted."

"Mia." He reached out, but his fingers only brushed her sleeve as she moved away.

"I don't want you to touch me. That's basic."

"We were friends once."

She stopped to stare at him out of cold gray eyes. "Were we?"

"You know we were. We were more than lovers, more than . . ." Mates, he'd nearly said. "It wasn't just passion. We cared about each other. We shared thoughts."

"Now my thoughts are my own, and I don't need any more friends."

"Lovers? You never married."

She turned that staggering face on him, and her expression was all female and smug. "If I wanted a lover or a husband, I'd have one."

"No question about it," he murmured. "You're the most extraordinary creature. I thought of you."

"Stop," she warned. "Stop now."

"Damn it, I'll say what I have to say. I thought of you." He dropped his briefcase, grabbed her arms, as some of the frustration broke through. "I thought of us. What's happened in between doesn't erase what we were to each other."

"You erased it. Now you have to live with it, as I did."

"It's not just about us." He tightened his grip. He could feel her vibrating and knew she could strike out, woman or witch, at any moment. "You know that as well as I do."

"There *is* no us. Do you think after all this time, after all I've done, all I've learned, I'd let fate toy with me again? I won't be used. Not by you, not by a centuries-old curse."

A single bolt of white lightning speared out of the clear sky and blasted into the sand between his feet. He didn't jerk back, but it was a near thing.

His throat was dry, but he nodded. "You always did have exquisite control."

"Remember that. And remember this: I am done with you."

"Not by a long shot. You need me to break the spell. Are you really willing to risk everything, everyone, for pride?"

"Pride?" Her color drained, and her body went still. "You arrogant jackass, do you think this is pride? You broke my heart."

The words, the way her voice trembled, had him dropping his hands.

"More than broke it. You crushed it into dust. I *loved* you. I would have gone anywhere, done anything for you. I mourned for you, until I thought I would die from it."

"Mia." Shaken, he reached up to touch her hair, only to have his hand slapped aside.

"But I didn't die, Sam. I got over you, and got on with my life. I like who I am now, and there's no going back for me. If you came here thinking differently, you're wasting your time. You won't have me again, and what you won't have—what you tossed aside—would have been the best thing in your life."

She walked away from him in long, un-hurried strides and left him alone to stare out at the sea, knowing she was right.

# Three

"You did what?"

Zack stuck his head in the refrigerator and rummaged for a beer. He knew that tone. His wife didn't use it often, which was why it was so effective.

He took a long time pulling out the beer and made sure his face was relaxed and composed when he looked back at her.

She stood in front of the stove, where something wonderful was cooking. She had a wooden spoon in her fist and her fists on her hips. He thought she looked like an outraged, and very sexy, Betty Crocker.

But he figured it wouldn't be healthy to say so just at the moment.

"I invited Sam to dinner." He smiled when he said it, and twisted the top off the beer. "You know how I like to show off my beautiful wife's incredible cooking."

When she only slitted her eyes, he took a deep gulp from the bottle. "Problem? You never mind company for dinner."

"I don't mind company. But I do mind sleazeballs."

"Nell, Sam might have been a little reckless as a kid, but he was never sleazy. And he's one of my oldest friends."

"And he broke the heart of one of *my* friends—and yours. He left her flat and went off to New York to do God-knows-what for more than ten years. Then—then," she continued, working up a fine rage, "he slithers back on-island and expects everybody to greet him with open arms."

She slapped the spoon on the counter. "I for one am not interested in tuning up the brass band for Sam Logan."

"How about just one trumpet player?"

"You think this is a joke?" She swiveled on her heel and strode to the back door.

He managed to get there in time to brace a hand on the door. "No. Sorry. Nell." He ran his hand over her cap of hair. "Look, I'm sorry about what happened between Sam and Mia. I was sorry then, and I'm sorry now. The fact is, I grew up with Sam, and we were friends. Good friends."

"Isn't 'were' the operative word?"

"Not for me." And for Zack it was just that simple. "Mia matters to me, and so does he. I don't want to be put in the position of taking sides, not in my own home. More than that, more than anything, I don't want you and me at odds over it. But I shouldn't have asked him to dinner without talking to you first. I'll go head him off."

She bit back a sigh, but couldn't quite master the pout. "You're doing that to make me feel small and low."

He waited a beat. "Did it work?"

"Yes, damn it." She gave him a little shove. "Get out of my way. If we're having company for dinner, there's no point in burning it."

But he didn't move aside. Instead he took her hands and squeezed. "Thanks."

"Don't thank me until I've gotten through the evening without giving him hives or warts."

"Gotcha. How about I set the table?"

"How about you do?"

"You want candles?"

"Yeah, black ones." She smirked as she walked over to check her wild rice. "To ward off negative energy."

Zack heaved out a breath. "Should be some evening."

Sam brought a good wine and sunny yellow daffodils. But she wasn't mollified. She was polite, brutally so, and served the wine on the comfortable front porch, with canapés that she'd tossed together at the last minute.

Sam wasn't sure if she meant that to be friendly or to illustrate that he would be admitted to her home in stages.

"I hope you didn't go to any trouble," Sam told her. "Nothing more tedious than unexpected guests."

"No, there isn't, is there?" she replied sweetly. "But then again, I'm sure you're not used to potluck, so we'll all make do."

She swung back into the house, and Sam hissed out a breath. He was sure now. He was getting in, but in painful stages. "This is going well."

"Mia means a lot to her. For a lot of reasons."

Sam merely nodded, wandered to the rail of the front porch. Lucy, Zack's black Lab, rolled over to expose her belly for a rub, batting her tail for a bit of charm. Crouching, Sam obliged her.

He knew the reasons for Nell's fierce loyalty to Mia. He'd made it his business to know what happened on the island over the years. He knew Nell had been on the run when she'd arrived on Three Sisters, escaping an abusive husband. She had faked her own death—and he had to admire her guts for it—and had changed her name and her appearance as she zigzagged across the country, picking up jobs waitressing, cooking.

He'd seen the news reports on Evan Remington, who was now serving time in a prison mental facility.

And he knew that Mia had given Nell a job running the bookstore café, had given her a home. And he suspected, had taught her how to refine the gift.

He'd recognized Nell as one of the three the minute he saw her.

"She's had a rough time, your Nell."

"Very rough. She risked her life to save her life. When she got here, Mia gave her a chance to dig in, put down roots. I've got to be grateful to Mia for that, too. And more," he added, waiting until Sam turned back. "You've heard about Remington."

"Hollywood power broker, wife beater, psychopath." He straightened. "And I know he took a slice out of you trying to get to Nell."

"Yeah." Absently, Zack rubbed a hand over his shoulder where Remington had stabbed him. "He tracked her here, knocked her around before I got to her, then he took me out. Temporarily. She'd run into the woods, knowing he'd come after her and probably not take the time to finish me off." His face went grim at the memory. "When I took off after them, Ripley and Mia were here. They knew Nell was in trouble."

"Yes, Mia would know."

"The son of a bitch had a knife to her throat." Even now, the memory had rage swimming into him. "He'd have killed her. Maybe I could've gotten a shot off, maybe not, but he'd have killed her either way. She's the one who took him out. She gathered what was inside her, what she is, and with Mia and Ripley, turned what he was back on him.

"I watched it happen," Zack murmured. "There in the little wood by the cottage where you're staying now. A circle of light, out of nowhere. Then Remington was on the ground screaming."

"She has courage and faith."

"She does," Zack agreed. "She's everything."

"You're a lucky man." Though his own mind took a smart side step at the thought of a woman, any woman, who could be everything to a man. "Her love for you is a tangible thing. Even when she's pissed," Sam said with a weak smile, "the way she's pissed now that you've invited Judas to her table."

"Why did you do it? Why did you leave?"

Sam shook his head. "A lot of reasons, some I'm still figuring out. When I have them, all of them, I'll tell Mia."

"You're expecting an awful lot of her."

Sam studied the wine in his glass. "Maybe I always did."

※◎

Zack worked hard to keep the conversation light and friendly at dinner. By his calculations, he talked more during that hour at the table than he normally did in a week. But every time he sent Nell an imploring look, she ignored it.

"I can see why the café's taken a bite out of our lunch trade," Sam said. "You're an artist in the kitchen, Mrs. Todd. My biggest regret is that you didn't walk into the hotel instead of Café Book when you came on-island."

"I went where I was meant to go."

"Do you believe in that? In destiny?"

"Absolutely." She got to her feet to clear the table.

"So do I. Absolutely." He rose as well, picked up his plate. When Nell's back was turned he gave Zack a little head signal.

*Make yourself scarce.*

Weighing his wife's ire against the sheer exhaustion of playing buffer, Zack pushed away from the table. "I need to round up Lucy," he said, and using his dog as an excuse, he hurried out.

Nell sent a fulminating look at his retreating back. "Why don't you go on with Zack? I'll make a pot of fresh coffee in a minute."

Absently, Sam reached down to pet the

gray cat that had uncurled from under the table to stretch. It hissed at him.

"I'll just give you a hand," he said after barely saving his hand from a nasty swipe. He saw Nell give the cat he'd heard her call Diego a small, approving nod.

"I don't want a hand."

"You don't want my hand," Sam corrected. "Zack's the best friend I ever had."

Rather than spare him a look, Nell opened the dishwasher and began loading. "You have an odd way of defining friendship."

"However I define it, it's a fact. He matters to both of us. So, for his sake, I hope we can call a truce."

"I'm not at war with you."

He glanced at the cat again. It had plopped down beside its mistress to wash and watch Sam narrowly. "You'd like to be."

"Fine." She slammed the dishwasher door, turned. "I'd like to hang you by your toes for what you did to Mia. And while you're hanging by your toes, I'd like to start a nice, steady fire under you, so you'd roast slowly and in great pain. And while you were roasting slowly and in great pain, I'd like to—"

"I get the picture."

"If you do, you know just how useless it is for you to try to charm me."

"Did you make all the right choices, the best choices, the wisest choices, when you were twenty?"

She slapped on the hot water, squirted soap under the stream. "I never deliberately hurt someone."

"And if you had, deliberately or otherwise, how long would you expect to be punished for it? Damn it!" He swore as she ignored him, then switched the water off himself.

She cursed right back, lifted a hand to turn it on again. Infuriated, he closed his hand over hers.

Light, shimmering blue, sparked between their meshed fingers.

Nell went very still as her anger slid under shock. She left her hand in his as she shifted her body, angling it until they were face-to-face and she could look directly into his eyes.

"Why didn't anyone tell me?" she demanded.

"I don't know." He smiled as the light mellowed to a glow. "Sister."

Baffled now, she shook her head. "There are only three who form the circle."

"Three who came from three. But four elements. Yours is air, and she who was, lacked your courage. Mine is water. You believe in destiny, in the Craft. We're connected, and you can't change that."

"No." But she would have to think about it, hard and long. Slowly, she slid her hand from under his. "I don't have to like it, or you."

"You believe in fate, in the Craft, but not in forgiveness."

"I believe in forgiveness. When it's earned."

He stepped away, jammed his hands in his pockets. "I came here tonight planning on charming you. To scrape away a few layers of your resentment and dislike. Part of that was pride. It's tough having your oldest friend's wife detest you."

He picked up the wine bottle, poured some into the glass she'd yet to clear. "Part of that was strategy." He drank. "I know very well that you and Ripley stand in front of Mia."

"I won't see her hurt again."

"And you're sure that's what I'll do." He brought his glass to the counter. "Then I came into your home, and felt what you and Zack have together. What you've made between you. I sat at your table, and you fed me, though you'd rather have hung me by my toes. So instead of charming, I'm charmed."

He glanced around the kitchen. It had always been a warm and friendly room. Once, he'd been welcome there. "I admire you, for what you made out of your life. And I envy you your clear vision and your happy home. Zack's important to me."

He looked back at her as she said nothing. "It's hard, I imagine, for you to buy that, but it's fact. I don't intend to do anything that complicates his relationship with you. I'll go out the back while he's busy with his Lucy."

Nell dried her hands. "I haven't made coffee yet."

He turned at the door, just looked at her.

And she saw why Mia had fallen for him. Not just the dangerous good looks. But in his eyes she saw so much power, so much pain.

"I'm not forgiving you," she said briskly. "But if Zack considers you a friend, you must have some redeeming qualities. Somewhere. Sit down. We're having trifle for dessert."

She had humbled him, Sam thought later as he walked back to the cottage. The pretty blue-eyed blonde who'd been bitingly polite, then brutally frank, then cautiously understanding all in one evening had brought him to his knees.

It was rare for him to want to earn someone's respect, but he now wanted badly to earn Nell Todd's.

He walked the beach as he had walked it as a boy. Restlessly. And turned for home, as he had as a boy. Without any sense of pleasure.

How could he explain that while he had loved the house on the bluff, it had never been his place? He'd had no regrets when his father had sold it.

The cove, the cave, they had meant a great deal once. But the house itself had just been wood and glass. With so little warmth inside. Demands, yes. To be a Logan, to succeed, to excel.

Well, he'd learned to do all three, but he wondered now what it had cost him.

He thought again of the spirit in the Todd house. He'd always believed houses had spirits, and theirs was warm, affectionate. Marriage actually worked for some people, he decided. The commitment, the unity, and the promise—not just for convenience or status but for heart.

That, in his mind, was a rare, rare gift.

There'd been little affection in his house. Oh, no neglect, no abuse, no meanness. His parents had been partners, but never, in his memory, a couple. And their marriage was as coldly efficient as any merger.

He could still remember being baffled, fascinated, and vaguely embarrassed when he was a boy by the open displays of affection between Zack's parents.

He thought of them now, traveling around in their house on wheels and reportedly having the time of their lives. His parents would be appalled at the idea.

How much, he wondered, did who we came from form us? Did Zack's staggeringly functional childhood predispose him to create his own functional family?

The luck of the draw?

Or was it all, in the end, what we made of ourselves? Each choice leading to another choice.

He paused now, looking out and watching the swath of white light sweep over the water. Mia's lighthouse, on Mia's cliffs. How many times had he stood and studied that hopeful beam and thought of her?

Wanted her.

He couldn't remember when it had started. There were times when he thought he'd been born wanting her. And it had been terrifying, that feeling that he'd been swamped by some tide that had begun forming before his existence.

How many nights had he ached for her? Even when he'd had her, even when he'd been inside her, he'd ached. Love, for him, had been a storm, full of boundless pleasure and abject terror.

For her, it had simply been.

Standing on the edge of the beach, he sent his thoughts winging over the black water, toward the beam of light. Toward the cliffs, the stone house. Toward her.

And the wall she'd built around what was

hers rejected them, bounced them back at him.

"You have to let me in," he murmured. "Sooner or later."

But he left it alone, for now, and continued to walk toward the cottage. The solitude he'd welcomed on his first day pressed down on him now and became loneliness. He shook it off, and instead of going into the house, he moved into the woods.

Until Mia talked to him, he would learn what he needed to learn, see what he needed to see, by other means.

The dark was deep, with a scatter of stars and a thin sickle of moon. But there were other ways to see. He tuned himself to the night. He could hear the babble of a little stream, and knew that wildflowers were sleeping on its banks. There was the rustle of a small animal in the brush, and the plaintive call of an owl. One would feed, the other would perish.

He smelled earth, and water, and knew there would be rain before morning.

And he felt power.

He moved through the dark, through the trees, as confidently as a man walks down

Main Street on a sunny afternoon. Power pulsed along his skin, that awakening thrill of magic.

He saw, where there was only ground scattered with fallen leaves, where the circle had been cast.

The three were strong when linked, he thought. He'd felt that same trickle of energy on the beach and had known that a circle of power had been cast there. But this one had come first, and so he would look here first.

"It would be simpler if they'd just tell me," he said aloud. "But probably not as satisfying. So."

He lifted his hands with palms up, like cups ready to be filled.

"Show me. I call to the three, once and ever a part of me. I use as my mirror the night to bring what transpired to my sight. Show me how and why this circle was cast that I might begin to complete my task. Grant this vision unto me. As I will, so mote it be."

The night thinned, and billowed like a blowing curtain. Parted. Fear, like a rabbit in a trap. Hate, sharp as ravaging teeth. And love, wrapped warm in courage.

He saw what Zack had told him, saw Nell racing through the woods, and her thoughts were clear to him. Fear and grief for Zack, a desperation not only to escape what pursued her but to save the man she loved.

Sam's hands fisted as he saw Remington leap at her, angle the knife at her throat.

Emotions pounded at him. There was Mia, in a black dress scattered with silver stars, and Ripley, holding a gun. Zack, bleeding, his own weapon pointed.

The night was alive with madness and terror.

The magic began to hum.

It pulsed from Nell, who glowed as she rejected her fears. It shimmered around Mia, whose eyes gleamed as silver as the stars she wore. And slowly, almost reluctantly, it sparked from Ripley when she lowered her gun and clasped Mia's hand.

And then the circle burned like blue fire.

The punch of it caught Sam unprepared and pushed him a full two paces back before he regained himself. But he'd lost his hold on the vision, and it wavered, faded.

"The circle's unbroken." He lifted his face, watched clouds stream across the stars.

"You have to let me in, Mia, or this was for nothing."

Late into the night, without plan, without design, he reached out to her in dreams. Floating back in time to when love was fresh and sweet, and everything.

She was seventeen and leggy, with hair a tumble of fire and eyes as warm as summer fog. Her beauty struck him, as always. A fist in the heart.

She laughed as she waded in the cove. She wore trim khaki shorts and a bright-blue top that left her arms and an inch of her midriff bare. He could smell her, over the scents of salt and sea, he could smell that heady, taunting fragrance that was Mia.

"Don't you want to swim?" She laughed again as she splashed up water. "Sad-eyed Sam, what are you brooding about today?"

"I'm not brooding."

He had been. His parents were freezing him out because he'd chosen to work on-island that summer in the hotel rather than in New York. He'd been wondering if he was making a mistake, a terrible mistake, by being so desperate to stay on-island because of Mia.

Because the idea of being away from her month after month was both tantalizing and unthinkable.

Yet he had begun to think it. To wonder about it more and more every time he left the Three Sisters to go back to the mainland and college. He'd begun to consider testing himself by making some excuse not to come back to the island, back to her, some weekend during the semester.

Every time he left the mainland on the ferry, they pulled him back. The island and Mia. Now he was refusing to take the escape hatch that had been tailor-made for him. He needed to think it over again. Reconsider.

But when Mia had come along to his beach, he'd been too crowded with lust and longing to brood or to think about being anywhere but with her.

"If you're not brooding, prove it." She walked backward in the water so that it lapped at her calves, her knees, those long white thighs. "Come in and play."

"Too old for games."

"I'm not." She slid into the water,

skimmed through it like a mermaid. And when she surfaced, water raining from her hair, her shirt clinging seductively to her breasts, he thought he'd go mad. "But I forgot. You're nearly nineteen. Too dignified to splash around in the water."

She did a surface dive and streaked through the dark blue water of the cove. When he grabbed her ankle, she kicked and came up laughing.

Her laughter, as always, bewitched him. "I'll give you dignity," he said, and dunked her.

It was innocent. Sun and water, the bright beginning of summer, the slippery edge between childhood and the future.

It couldn't stay innocent.

They splashed, warred, swam as sleekly as dolphins. Then came together as they always did, lips meeting first under the surface, then clinging when they burst through into air. Need rose with them, strong and urgent, so that she trembled as she wrapped herself around him. Her lips, warm and wet, parted for his with a trust and acceptance that shook him to the bone.

"Mia." Knowing that he would die wanting her, he pressed his face into the wet ropes of her hair. "We have to stop. Let's go for a walk." Even as he spoke, his hands were moving over her. He couldn't help himself.

"I dreamed last night," she said softly. Cradled in his arms, she sighed. "Of you. It's always of you. And when I woke, I knew it would be today." She dipped her head back, and he all but fell into those great gray eyes. "I want to be with you, and no one else. I want to give myself to you, and no one else."

His blood pounded for her. He tried to think of right and wrong, of tomorrow. But could only think of now. "You have to be sure."

"Sam." She traced kisses over his face. "I've always been sure."

She slid away from him, but only to take his hand. It was she who led him out of the water and to the cave tucked into the bluff.

The cave was cool and dry, high enough at its heart for him to stand upright. He saw the blanket spread near the far wall, and the candles scattered over the floor. And looked at her.

"I told you I knew. This is our place." Watching him, she reached for the tiny buttons running down the front of her shirt. And he saw her fingers tremble.

"You're cold."

"A little."

He stepped to her. "And afraid."

Her lips curved. "A little. But I won't be either for long."

"I'll be careful with you."

She let her hands fall to her sides so that he could finish unbuttoning her shirt. "I know. I love you, Sam."

He lowered his lips to hers as he peeled the cotton away. "I love you."

The little niggle of fear inside her vanished. "I know."

He'd touched her before, and been touched. Glorious, frustrating caresses, too often hurried. Now as they undressed each other, the candles flickered into life. As they lowered to the blanket, a thin film seemed to coat the mouth of the cave, closing them in.

Their mouths met, sweet and hot. Even as her pleasure began to rise, she sensed him holding back. His fingers, sometimes unsteady, skimmed over her as if he feared she would vanish.

"I won't leave you," she murmured, then gasped when his mouth, suddenly urgent, found her breast.

She arched beneath him, hands stroking,

body as fluid as the water that scented it. When he looked at her, her hair damp and tumbled on the blanket, her eyes clouded with what he brought her, he shuddered with power.

And made her fly. She cried out, a long, full-throated sound that rippled through him and made him feel invincible. When she opened for him, offering him her innocence, he trembled.

Through the rage of blood, the pound of need, he struggled to be gentle. Still, he saw the flicker of shock.

"Only for a minute." Delirious, he ran kisses over her face. "I promise. Only for a minute." Then he surrendered to the demands of his body and took her.

Her hands fisted on the blanket, and she bit back the first cry. But almost as soon as the pain began, warmth replaced it.

"Oh." Her breath shuddered out again, on a sigh. "Of course." She turned her lips to the side of his neck. "Of course."

And began to move under him. She rose and took him deeper, fell and drew him with her. When warmth simmered to heat, their bodies grew slick. Clinging, they took each other.

When she lay wrapped in his arms, half dreaming, the candlelight burned gold.

"This is where she found him."

Sam traced his fingers over her shoulders. He couldn't stop touching her. The lazy sexual haze clouded his mind so he forgot all he'd thought of on the beach. "Hmm?"

"The one who was Fire. The one who's mine. This is where she found her silkie, in human form, and fell in love while he slept."

"How do you know?"

She started to say she'd always known, but shook her head instead. "She took his pelt and hid it away so she could keep him. For love. It couldn't be wrong when it was for love."

Basking in the afterglow, Sam nuzzled her neck. He wanted to be here, with her. He wanted nothing, no one else. Never would. Never could. Now, the realization steadied rather than unnerved him.

"Nothing's wrong when it's for love."

"But she couldn't keep him," Mia said quietly. "Years later, after they'd had children, after she'd lost her sisters, her circle, he found his pelt. He couldn't stop what he did. It was his nature. Once he'd found his pelt, nothing, not even love, could make him stay. He left her, went into the sea, and forgot she existed. Forgot his home, and his children."

"It makes you sad to think of it." He held her tighter. "Don't be sad now."

"Don't leave me." She buried her face against his shoulder. "Don't ever leave me. I think I'd die, as she died, alone and heartbroken."

"I won't." But something went cold inside him. "I'm right here. Look." He shifted so that they faced the cave wall. Lifting a finger, he laid it on the stone. Light sparked from his fingertip and etched words into rock.

She read the Gaelic and her eyes misted. " 'My heart is your heart. Ever and always.' "

She lifted her own finger, carved a Celtic knot beneath the words. A promise of unity.

She turned those swimming eyes up to his. "And mine's yours."

Alone in her house on the cliff, Mia turned her face into her pillow. And murmured his name in her sleep.

# Four

The rain, a steady, drumming splatter, began before morning. It rode on a kicky little wind that had the tender green leaves shivering and foamed the surf. Throughout the day it continued to blow and spit, until the air was raw with damp, the sea as unremittingly gray as the sky. It showed no signs of abating by evening.

It was good for the flowers, Mia told herself as she stood at the window and stared at the unbroken dullness of the gloom. The earth needed a good soaking, and despite the chill, there would be no frost to damage delicate buds.

The first fine day, she would take off work and spend hours gardening. An entire, precious day with no company, and no demands but her flowers.

That was the beauty and privilege of owning her own business.

The occasional privilege helped balance out the weight of responsibility. Of business, and of magic.

She had a dozen things to do in the store that day. It didn't matter that she'd slept poorly, tossed in her dreams, or that her mood was so low she'd wanted nothing so much as to bury herself under the blankets. The fact that she'd considered it, even briefly, had been sufficiently appalling to get her up and out.

Then she'd forgotten, and she *never* forgot anything, that Nell and Ripley were coming to the house. At least they were a distraction, something to keep her mind off her memories and dreams, unwelcome intruders into the disciplined order of her life.

He'd snuck into her dreams. The bastard.

"Would you rather do this another time? Mia?"

"What?" Frowning, she looked up. Blinked. By the goddess, she wasn't even paying attention to her distraction. "No, no. Sorry. The rain's making me edgy."

"Right." Ripley slouched in her chair,

hooked a leg over its arm. There was a bowl of popcorn in her lap, and she popped pieces in her mouth quickly, carelessly. "Like it's a weather pattern that got under your skin."

Saying nothing, Mia walked to the sofa, curled up. Tucking her bare feet under the spread of her skirt, she flicked a finger at the stone fireplace across the room. The logs burst into snapping, sizzling flame.

"There, that's better." She plumped one of her velvet pillows as if she had no concern other than her own comfort. "Now, Nell, what did you want to talk to me about before we discuss our plans for the solstice?"

"Get her." Ripley gestured with her wine-glass, and dumped a neat fall of popcorn in her mouth with her free hand. "Sounds like the chairwoman for some ladies social club."

"Not so far off. Club, coven. But anytime you want to take charge, Deputy Fife—"

"Okay." Nell held up a hand for peace. It seemed she was always calling for peace when Mia and Ripley spent more than ten minutes together. There were times when she thought it would be simpler to just knock their heads together. "Why don't we move beyond the insult portion of our program? I wanted to say that I thought the first meeting of the cooking club went well."

Mia steadied her temper. Nodded. She leaned over, contemplated the glossy purple grapes she'd arranged on a pale green dish. Selected one. "It did. It was a terrific idea, Nell. I think we'll find it brings business into the store, and the café. We sold a dozen cookbooks that night, and a dozen more since."

"I was thinking after we give it a couple of months to see if interest holds, we might want to plan a combination event with the book club. Maybe around Christmas. I know that's a long way off, but—"

"But it never hurts to plan," Mia finished and, nipping into a second grape, leveled a smirk in Ripley's direction. "There are a number of novels that have food playing a major role, and some even have recipes. We might suggest one for the book club, then the cooking club could prepare the dishes. Everybody has fun."

"And you sell books," Ripley pointed out.

"Which, oddly enough, is the primary function of Café Book. Now—"

"There's something else."

Mia paused, lifted an eyebrow at Nell. "All right."

Nervous, Nell pressed her lips together. "I know selling books is the primary function, but, well, I had this idea a while ago. I've been playing with it in my head, trying to see if it would work, or be worthwhile. You may think it's out of line, but—"

"Oh, for heaven's sake, Nell." Out of patience, Ripley shifted in her chair and set the bowl of popcorn aside. "She thinks you should expand the café."

"Ripley! Would you just let me tell it my way?"

"I would, but I don't have a week to spare before I get home."

"Expand the café?" Mia interrupted. "It already takes up nearly half the square feet on the second level."

"Yes, the way things are now." After shooting Ripley a hot look, Nell turned back to Mia. "But if you took out the windows on the east side, added a terrace of, oh, say six feet by ten feet, used atrium or sliding doors leading out to it, you'd have more room for seating, and the benefit of alfresco seating in good weather."

Because Mia said nothing, just lifted her

glass from the table, Nell rushed on. "I could extend the menu here and there, adding more entrée selections for a nice, casual dinner during the summer evening hours. Of course you'd have to take on more help, and . . . and I should mind my own business."

"I didn't say that." Mia leaned back. "But it is a complicated idea. There's zoning, and building codes. Then there's cost, and the ratio of profit projection against that cost. The potential loss of business during that kind of remodel."

"I've, um, looked into it. A little." With a quick, sheepish smile, Nell pulled a stack of papers out of her satchel.

Mia stared, then sat back with a long laugh. "You've been busy, little sister. All right, let me look it all over, think about it. It's intriguing," she murmured. "More seating, entrée selections . . . I imagine, if successful, it would nip into the hotel's dinner business, at least during the season."

At Mia's small, satisfied smile, Nell felt a wave of guilt. "There's one more thing. We had Sam Logan over for dinner," she blurted out.

Mia's smile slipped away. "Excuse me?"

"You had that rat bastard at your table!" Ripley popped out of her chair. "You fed him a meal? Did you at least poison him while you were at it?"

"No, I didn't poison him. Damn it, I didn't invite him, Zack did. They're friends." Nell sent Mia a look filled with misery and guilt. "I can't tell Zack who he can or can't invite to the house."

"Just let Booke try asking some traitorous son of a bitch to leach off us." Ripley bared her teeth as if she was ready to take a bite out of her new husband whether he had the thought or not. "Zack always was stupid."

"Now, just a minute."

"He's been my brother longer than he's been your husband," Ripley shot back. "I can call him stupid, especially when he is."

"There's no point in this," Mia said quietly and drew both Nell's and Ripley's attention. "No point in casting blame or in recriminations. Zack's entitled to choose his friends, and to have them in his home. That's nothing Nell should feel guilty over. What's between Sam and me is between Sam and me, and it doesn't affect anyone else."

"Doesn't it?" Nell shook her head. "Why didn't anyone tell me he was one of us?"

"Because he's not." It all but exploded out of Ripley. "Sam Logan isn't one of us."

"I don't think Nell was implying he's a girl," Mia said dryly. "Or even an islander. Though, of course, since he was raised here he'll always be considered an islander." She waved her hand as if brushing that aside. "The fact that he has the gift has nothing to do with us."

"You're sure of that?" Nell demanded.

"We are the three." In the stone hearth, flames rose and snapped. "We make the circle. It's for us to do what must be done. Just because some—what was that lovely term of Ripley's—oh, yes, just because some rat bastard has magic doesn't change anything."

Deliberately calm, she stretched out her hand for another grape. "Now, about the solstice."

She wouldn't let it change anything. She would do what had to be done, alone or with her sisters. But she wouldn't allow anyone into their circle. Or into her heart.

In the deepest part of night, while the island slept, she stood on her cliffs. The cold rain poured and the black sea lashed at the jagged rocks as if it would, in one night, wear them to nubs. All around her the irritable wind swirled, snapping at her cloak until it billowed up like wings.

There was no light, no relief from the black except the single circling blade from the white tower behind her. It cut over her, the cliffs, the sea. Then left her alone in the dark again.

*Fly,* the canny voice whispered. *Fly out and let go, and it will all be over. Why do you fight the inevitable? Why would you live with the loneliness?*

How many times, she wondered, had she heard that voice? How many times had she come here, testing herself against it? Even when her heart had been shattered, she'd come. And had won. She would never give in.

"You won't beat me." She felt the cold as the dirty fog slithered over ground and rock. Felt it like icy fingers wrapping around her ankles, where it could tug, and tempt. "I'll never give up." She raised her arms, spread them wide.

And the wild, whirling wind she called tore the fog to tatters.

"What's mine I serve and protect and keep." She lifted her face to the rain, let it wash over her like tears. "Whether I wake or whether I sleep, to what I am I will be true in what I say, in what I do."

Magic poured into her and pulsed like a heart.

"This vow I make, and will not break: I will meet my destiny. As I will, so mote it be."

With her eyes closed, she fisted her hands as if she could beat against the night. As if she could use them to rip through the veil that blinded her from what would come for her.

"Why don't I *know*? Why can't I feel? Why can't I do anything but feel?"

Something shivered on the air, like warm hands brushing her cheeks. It wasn't comfort she wanted, or the urges to be patient. So, she turned from them, from the cliffs, and the sea. Her cloak whipped behind her as she ran toward the lights of home.

While Mia wrapped herself in isolation, cocooned in the house on the cliff, Lulu was propped in bed with her third glass of wine, her latest true crime book, *Diary of an American Cannibal*, and a bag of cheese-and-garlic potato chips. Across the room, the bedroom TV blasted out gunfire as Mel Gibson and Danny Glover kicked ass in *Lethal Weapon*.

It was, for Lulu, her Saturday-night ritual.

Her nightclothes consisted of ratty shorts, a T-shirt that announced it was better to be rich than stupid, and a book light fastened to a ball cap.

She munched, sipped, divided her attention between the book and the video, and considered herself in her own personal heaven.

Rain drummed outside the windows of her colorful little saltbox, and the breeze rattled the love beads that dangled in lieu of curtains. Content, marginally tipsy, she sprawled under the spread she'd quilted from squares of madras, paisley, and tie-dyed scraps.

You could take the child out of the sixties, but you couldn't take the sixties out of this child, she often thought.

The words on the page began to blur, so she adjusted her glasses, boosted herself up in bed a little more. She just wanted to finish one more chapter and find out if the young prostitute was going to be stupid enough to get her throat slit and her internal organs gutted.

Lulu was banking on it.

But her head dipped. She jerked it back up. Blinked. She could have sworn she heard someone whisper her name.

Hearing things, she thought in disgust. Getting old was God's big rip-off.

She polished off the glass of wine, glanced toward the TV.

And there was Mel, his pretty face filling the screen, his eyes brilliantly blue as they grinned at her. "Hey, Lu. How's it going?"

She rubbed her eyes, blinked rapidly. But the image was still there. "What the hell?"

"That's what I say! What the hell!" The image drew back, far enough for her to see the gun. Its barrel looked to be the size of a cannon. "Nobody wants to live forever, right?"

The explosion boomed out of the set, flashed hot red light into the room. The sharp pain in Lulu's chest had her crying out, frantically pressing her hands between her breasts. Chips flew as she scrambled up, looking for blood.

She found nothing but her own wildly beating heart.

On the screen Mel and Danny were arguing about police procedure.

Shaken, and feeling like an old fool, Lulu staggered to the window. A little fresh air, she thought. Clear her head. Must've fallen asleep for a minute, she decided as she pushed the rattling beads aside and shoved her window all the way up.

She shivered. It was cold as winter— colder, she realized, than it should have been. And the mists swirling out of the ground had an odd tone to them. Like floating bruises, all dull purples and sickly yellows.

She could see her calliope of flowers, and the moonball rising up through them. Her rude little gargoyle who stuck his tongue out of a grinning mouth at passersby. The rain sounded icy now, and when she reached out the window, cold, sharp shards of it stabbed into her palm.

Her glasses slid down as she jerked her hand back. And when she shoved them back into place, she'd have sworn the gargoyle was closer to the house, turned so that instead of his profile she could see three-quarters of the homely face.

Her chest began to hurt from the racing of her heart.

Need new glasses, she thought. Eyes are going.

As she stared, frozen in shock, the gargoyle swiveled to face her. And bared long, vicious teeth.

"Jesus H. Christ!"

She could hear them, actually hear the greedy snap of them as he inched through the fog toward the house. Toward the open window. Behind him, the little flute-playing frog she'd bought the week before began to hop closer. And the flute he held was now a long, jagged-edged knife.

"Nobody will care."

Reeling, she snapped her head around. On TV a huge cartoon snake with Mel Gibson's handsome face leered at her.

"Nobody will give two good shits if you're dead. You've got nobody, do you, Lu? No man, no kid, no family. Nobody to give a rat's ass about you."

"That's bull!" Terror screamed through her as she saw that the gargoyle and his companion had come within a foot of the house while she was looking away. Teeth snapped—a hungry sound, and the knife swished through the thick fog like a deadly metronome.

"That's just horseshit." Her shaking hands fumbled at the window, her breath panting out in puffs as she fought to find a grip on the sash.

As she slammed it down, she fell backward and hit the floor with a jar of her bones.

She lay there, struggling to catch her breath, struggling to find her nerve. When she managed to get to her knees, she crawled whimpering toward her sewing basket and grabbed two knitting needles as weapons.

But when she managed to find the courage to go back to the window, the rain was falling warm and gentle, the mists had cleared. And the gargoyle, homely and harmless, squatted in its usual spot, ready to insult the next visitor.

Lulu stood in the bedroom while another firefight broke out on television. She rubbed her hand over her clammy face.

"That must've been some bottle of chardonnay," she said aloud.

But for the first time since she'd moved into the little house, she—armed with her needles—walked through it locking all the doors and windows.

A man, however dedicated, was entitled to some time off. That's what Sam told himself as he drove away from the village. He'd spent hours at his desk, in meetings, doing inspections, reading reports. If he didn't clear his mind, it was going to fry.

And it was Sunday. The rain had finally blown out to sea, leaving the island sparkling like a jewel. Getting out, seeing what on this little clump of land had changed, and what hadn't, was as important to his business as ledgers and projections.

That sensibility, he knew, had skipped a generation in the Logan family. He'd always been aware that his parents had viewed the twenty-odd years they'd spent on Three Sisters as a kind of exile. Which, he imagined, was why they'd found excuses to leave it so often during that period—and then to pull up stakes permanently when his grandfather had died.

It had never been home for them.

Coming back had proved that to him, just as it had proved the island *was* home for him. One answer he'd come back to find was clear to him now. Three Sisters was his.

Pleasure boats were skimming along the water, motors humming or sails fat with wind. It brought him a steadying kind of pleasure to see them. Buoys bobbed, orange, red, white, against the cool blue surface. The land jutted or curved or tumbled out to meet the water.

He saw a family clamming and a young boy chasing gulls.

There were houses that hadn't been there when he'd left. And the time between came home to him as he noticed the weathered silver of cedar and the thick clumps of vegetation. Growth, he thought. Man's and nature's.

Time didn't stand still. Not even on Three Sisters.

As he approached the north point of the island, he turned onto a narrow shale road, listened to his wheels crunch. The last time he'd driven this stretch he'd had a Jeep, with its top off so the air had streamed over him. And his radio had been going full blast.

He had to smile at himself as he realized that while he might be in a Ferrari, he had still put the top down. And turned the stereo up to scream.

"You can take the boy off the island," he murmured, then pulled off the side of the road opposite the bluffs and the house that rose from them.

The house hadn't changed, he decided, and wondered how long it would take the islanders to stop referring to it as the Logan place. Two stories, it rambled over the bluff, jutting out, shooting up as if on its own whim. Someone had recently painted its shutters a dark blue to contrast with the silvered wood.

The screened porch and the open decks offered stunning views of the cove, and the sea. The windows were wide, the doors glass. He remembered that his room had faced the water, and how much time he'd spent staring out at it.

How often its changing and unpredictable moods had reflected his own.

The sea had always spoken to him.

Still, the house didn't bring him any tug of sentiment, or any lovely haze of nostalgia. The islanders could call it the Logan place for another decade, but it had never been Sam's. It was, in his opinion, a good property in a prime location that had been well maintained by its absentee owners.

He hoped the man who owned the Land Rover parked outside it felt he'd gotten his money's worth.

Dr. MacAllister Booke, Sam thought now, of the New York Bookes. A man with a brilliant mind, and an unusual bent. Paranormal science. Fascinating. He wondered if Booke had felt like a round peg in the square hole of his family, as he himself had.

Sam got out of his car, walked toward the bluff. It wasn't the house that called him, but the cove. And the cave.

It pleased him, more than he'd expected, to see a bright-yellow sailboat tied to the dock below. And it was a honey, he mused, studying its lines. He'd had a boat tied there too. For as long as he could remember. For that, at least, he felt the tug, the soft haze.

Sailing had been the single real interest that father and son had shared.

The best times he'd had with Thaddeus Logan, the only times there had ever been that click of kinship between them, Sam remembered, had been when they were sailing.

They'd actually communicated, connected, during those hours on the water, not just as two people who happened, through circumstance, to occupy places in the same family, the same house. But as father and son who shared a common interest. It was good to remember that.

"Pretty, isn't she? I just got her last month."

Sam turned and, through the lenses of his shaded glasses, watched the man who had spoken walk toward him. Dressed in faded jeans and a gray sweatshirt ragged at the hem, he was tall, with a strong, lean face shadowed by a night's growth of beard. Dark blond hair blew in the frisky breeze, and friendly brown eyes squinted against the flash of sunlight. He had a tough, disciplined build that Sam could admit he hadn't expected from a scholarly spook hunter.

He'd imagined a thin, pale, and nerdish bookworm. Instead, he thought, amused with himself, he was getting Indiana Jones.

"How's she handle in the rough?" Sam asked.

"Oh, like a charm."

They spent a few minutes, thumbs tucked in front pockets, admiring and talking about the boat.

"I'm Mac Booke." Mac held out a hand.

"Sam Logan."

"Thought so. Thanks for the house."

"It wasn't mine, but you're welcome."

"Come on inside, have a beer."

He hadn't intended to socialize, but the offer was so easy and unstudied that Sam found himself heading toward the house with Mac. "Ripley around?"

"No, she's on duty this afternoon. Did you want to see her about something?"

"Absolutely not."

Mac only laughed, and after they climbed the steps to the main deck, opened the door. "I guess that feeling's going to be mutual for a while. Until it all settles in."

The deck led into the living room. Sam remembered it as being polished, full of pastels and pale watercolors. Time hadn't stood still here, either, he mused. The colors were bold and bright, the furnishings tailored for comfort. There were homey, untidy piles of newspapers, books, shoes.

One of which a busy puppy was currently gnawing.

"Damn it!" Mac leaped in, tripped over the unmauled mate of the sneaker, and made a grab for the other. The pup was faster, and with the shoe in his mouth he scrambled for cover.

"Mulder! Give me that."

Sam angled his head as man and pup went into a little tug-of-war. The pup lost, but didn't look put out by it.

"Mulder?" Sam asked.

"Yeah, you know—*X-Files* guy. Ripley said she named him after me. Her little joke." He heaved out a breath. "She's not going to think it's a joke when she sees her shoe."

Sam crouched, and the pup, thrilled at the prospect of company, raced over to leap and lick. "Pretty dog. Golden retriever?"

"Yeah. We've only had him three weeks. He's smart, and mostly housebroken, but he'll chew through rock if you don't watch him, which I wasn't." Sighing, Mac scooped the pup up and went nose to nose. "You know who's going to take the heat for this, don't you?"

The puppy wriggled in delight and licked Mac's chin. Giving up on the lecture, Mac tucked Mulder under his arm. "Beer's in the kitchen." He led the way back, got two bottles out of the fridge. On the table sat a number of electronic devices, one of which seemed to be gutted.

Idly, Sam reached over to pick one up, and set off a series of beeps and blinking red lights.

"Sorry."

"No problem." Mac's eyes narrowed, a speculative look. "Why don't we take these out on the deck? Unless you want to look around. You know, the old homestead and whatever."

"No, thanks anyway." But as they started back out, Sam glanced toward the stairs, imagined his room as it had been, and himself watching the sea, or watching for Mia, out the window.

From the second floor a new beep sounded.

"Equipment," Mac said easily, and had to squelch the urge to dash upstairs and check readings. "I've got my lab set up in one of the extra bedrooms."

"Hmmm."

Once outside, Mac set Mulder down, and he immediately bounded down the steps and began to sniff along the yard. "Anyway . . ." Mac took a swig of beer, leaned on the rail. "Ripley didn't mention that you were a witch."

Sam opened his mouth, closed it again, then just shook his head. "What, am I wearing a sign?"

"Energy readings." Mac gestured toward the house. "And actually, I'd wondered about it, as I've done a lot of research on the island, the families, the bloodlines, and so on. Did you practice in New York?"

"Depends on your definition." It wasn't often that Sam found himself being studied like a science experiment, or that he would have allowed it. But something about Mac appealed to him. "I've never neglected the Craft, but I don't advertise either."

"Makes sense. So what do you think of the legend?"

"I've never considered it a legend. It's history, and fact."

"Exactly." Delighted, Mac lifted his bottle in a kind of toast. "I've done a time line, projecting the spin, you might say, of the cycle. By my calculations—"

"We have until September," Sam interrupted. "No later than the equinox."

Mac nodded slowly. "Well, bingo. Welcome home, Sam."

"Thanks." He sipped his beer. "It's good to be back."

"Are you going to be open to working with me?"

"It'd be stupid to turn down the input of an expert. I've read your books."

"Yeah?"

"You have an open and flexible mind."

"Someone else said that to me, once." Mac thought of Mia, but was tactful enough not to mention her name. "Can I ask you a personal question?"

"Yes, as long as I can tell you to mind your own business as an answer."

"Deal. If you knew September was a kind of deadline, why did you wait so long to come back?"

Sam turned his head, looked out on the cove. "It wasn't my time. This is. Now let me ask you one. In your expert opinion, with your research, your calculations, your projections, am I necessary to the Three Sisters?"

"I'm still working on that. I do know you're part of what's necessary to Mia's role in it—the third step."

"Her acceptance of me." When Mac frowned, drummed his fingers on the deck rail, Sam felt unease slither into his belly. "You don't agree."

"Her choice, when it comes, has to do with her own feelings. Accepting them, and what's right for her. That might mean accepting you, or it might mean resolving her emotions by rejecting you—without malice." Mac cleared his throat. "The last step has to do with love."

"I'm fully aware of that."

"It doesn't require her to . . . it doesn't mean, in my opinion, that she'll be obliged to love you now, but that she accepts what she once felt, and that it wasn't meant. To, well, let you go without resentment and cherish what used to be. Anyway, it's a theory."

The hem of Sam's coat snapped in a stray gust of wind. "I don't like your theory."

"I wouldn't like it either from where you're standing. The third sister killed herself rather than face her lover's desertion. Her circle was broken, and she was alone."

"I know the goddamn story."

"Just hear me out. Even then, she protected the island, and her bloodline and the line of her sisters. As far as she could with what she had left. But she couldn't—

or wouldn't—save herself. Couldn't or wouldn't live without the love of one man. That was her weakness, and her mistake."

It was direct enough to follow. It was logical. It was maddening. "And Mia's lived without me very well."

"On one level," Mac agreed. "On another, and in my opinion, she's never resolved her feelings, never forgiven you or accepted. She'll have to, one way or the other, and with a whole heart. If she doesn't, she'll be vulnerable, and as the protective spell weakens, she'll lose."

"And if I'd stayed away?"

"The logical conclusion is you weren't meant to stay away. And the presence of more magic on the island . . . well, it can't hurt."

He'd never thought it could. But his conversation with Mac had put doubts in his mind. He'd come back to the island with no questions about what needed to be, and would be done.

He would win Mia again, and once things

were as they had been between them, the curse would be broken. End of story.

End of story, he thought now as he walked the beach by the cove, because he hadn't wanted to look beyond it. He wanted Mia, was ready for Mia, and that was that.

He'd never once entertained the notion that her not wanting him, not loving him, might be the answer.

He looked toward the mouth of the cave. Maybe it was time to explore that possibility, and face his ghosts. As he walked toward the cave, his heart beat too fast. He stopped, waiting until he'd controlled it, then ducked into the cave's shadows.

For a moment, it was filled with sound. Their voices, her laughter. The sighs of lovers.

And of weeping.

She'd come here to cry for him. Knowing it, feeling it, sliced him with sharp stabs of guilt.

He willed them clear, then stood in the silence, with only the backdrop of the surf lapping at the shore.

When he'd been a boy, the cave had been

Aladdin's, or a bandit's hideout, or whatever he and Zack and other friends had made it.

Then he'd no longer been a boy, or not quite a boy, and it had been Mia.

His legs felt weak as he moved to the far wall, knelt and saw the words he'd carved for her. She hadn't scored them out. Until that moment, until a fist released its squeezing grip on his heart, he hadn't realized he'd been afraid she might. That she could. And if she could, that her heart would be lost to him.

Ever and always.

He reached out, and light filled the words, seemed to drip from them like tears of gold. He felt in that light everything the boy had felt when he'd carved them, with magic and utter faith.

It rocked him, staggered him that there had been so much bursting inside that boy that the man he was could still reel from it. And ache for it.

The power was still there. Why would it be, if it meant nothing? Was it only his will, his wish, that brought back to life what had been?

They'd loved here, so wrapped up in each other that the world could have ended without them knowing, or caring. They'd shared bodies, and hearts. And magic.

He could see her now, rising above him, her hair like wildfire and her skin golden. Her arms lifted as she rode them both past reason.

Or curled against him in sleep with her mouth curved in contentment.

Or sitting close while they talked, her face alight with excitement, so full of plans. So young.

Was it his fate to let her go, before he had her again? To be forgiven, then forgotten?

The idea stabbed at him, left him shaken as he got to his feet. Unable to bear the press of memories any longer, he turned away from them and walked out of the cave.

Into the sunlight, a flash like fire, where she stood with her back to the sea.

# Five

For a moment he could only look at her as old memories and old needs tangled with new. Time hadn't stood still for them. She wasn't the coltish young girl who would splash headlong into the water with a dare. The woman who watched him now with cool, measuring eyes had a layer of polish and sophistication the girl had lacked.

The breeze had her hair dancing in fiery spirals. That, at least, hadn't changed.

She waited with every appearance of calm as he walked to her, but he neither saw nor felt any welcome.

"I wondered how long it would take you to come here." Her voice was low, as measured as her gaze. "I wasn't sure you'd have the nerve."

It was difficult, horribly, to speak rationally when the emotions and images from the cave still churned inside him. "Do you ever come back here?"

"Why would I? If I want to look at the ocean, I can stand on my own cliffs. If I want the beach, it's a short walk from my store. There's nothing here to warrant the trip."

"But you're here now."

"Curiosity." Her head tilted to the side. The dark blue stones at her ears caught the light and glinted. "And did you satisfy your own?"

"I felt you in there. Felt us in there."

It surprised him when her lips curved, almost affectionately. "Sex has strong energy, when it's done correctly. We never had a problem in that area. As for me— well, a woman has a certain sentimental vision of the first time she gave herself to a man. I can remember that particular event fondly, even if I came to regret my choice of partner."

"I never meant to—" He broke off, swore.

"To hurt me?" she finished. "Liar."

"You're right. Absolutely." Whatever came from this point on, if he was indeed fated to lose her, he could and would be honest about this one thing. "I did mean to hurt you. And I'd say I did a damn good job of it."

"Well, you surprise me at last." She turned away because it hurt to look at him, to see him stand there with his back to the shadowed mouth of the cave that had been theirs.

To feel the echoes of that boundless, consuming love she'd once felt for him.

"A clear truth, after all these years."

"Meaning to do something at twenty doesn't mean I can't, and don't, regret it now."

"I don't want your regrets."

"What the hell do you want, Mia?"

She watched the water tease the shore in its endless flirtation. She heard the edge in his voice, knew it as a sign of a rising and reckless mood. And it pleased her. The more unsettled he was, the more she could feel in control.

"A truth for a truth, then," she said. "I want you to suffer, to pay, and to go back to New York or to hell, or wherever you choose, so long as it isn't here."

She looked back over her shoulder at him, and her smile was cold as winter. "It seems so little to ask, really."

"I mean to stay on Three Sisters."

She turned back to him. He looked dramatic, she thought. Romantic. Dark and broody. Full of anger and turmoil. Because of it, she indulged herself and gave him yet another push.

"For what? To run a hotel? Your father managed to run it for years without being here."

"I'm not my father."

The way he said it, that small, verbal explosion, triggered more memories. He'd always had to prove himself, to himself, she thought. The constant internal war of Samuel Logan. She shrugged.

"Well, in any case, I imagine you'll be bored with island life soon enough and escape. As you did before. 'Trapped,' I believe was your term. You felt trapped here. So, it's just a matter of waiting you out."

"You'll have a long wait," he warned. He hooked his hands in his pockets. "Let's get something straight, so we can avoid going around the same loop again and again. I have roots here, just as you do. The fact that you spent your twenties on-island and I didn't doesn't change the fact that we both come from the same place. We both have businesses here, and beyond that we have a purpose, one that goes back centuries.

What happens on and to Three Sisters matters to me as much as it matters to you."

"An interesting speech from someone who walked away so casually."

"There was nothing casual about it," he began, but she had already turned her back on him, was already striding toward the bluff.

Let her go, his mind ordered. Just let her go. If this is fate, it can't be beaten. Shouldn't be, for the good of the whole, fought against.

"The hell with that." The words ground between his teeth as he went after her. He grabbed her arm, spun her around so quickly their bodies collided. "There was *nothing* casual about it," he repeated. "Nothing impulsive, nothing careless."

"Is that how you justify it?" she tossed back. "Is that how you make it right? You left because it suited you, and you come back because it suits you. And because you're here, why not see if you can stir up some old flames?"

"I've been pretty restrained in that area." He yanked his sunglasses off, threw them on the ground. His gaze was burning, blistering green. "Up till now."

He crushed his mouth to hers, let himself take, let the storm of emotions that had shadowed him since he left the cave break over both of them. If he was to be damned, he'd be damned for taking what he wanted, not for letting it go.

The unique flavor of her seared through him, sizzling the nerves, smoking the senses. His arms tightened so that her long, lean body was molded to his, and against his heart her heart kicked and galloped until the paces matched. Exactly.

The scent of her, darker than he remembered and somehow forbidding, slithered into him, twining through his system until it was tied in knots. The memories of the girl, the reality of the woman—both blurred together and became one. Became Mia.

He said her name once, his lips moving against hers, then she broke free.

Her breathing was as uneven as his. And her eyes were huge, dark, unreadable. He waited to be cursed, and counted it worth the price of that one taste of heaven.

But she moved to him in one quick stride. Locking her arms around his neck, pressing her body to his, she took from him as he had taken from her.

Her mouth was a fever, and the ache of it throbbed through her. He was the only man who'd ever brought her pain, and the only man who'd ever brought her true pleasure. Both edges of that keen sword stabbed, and still she took.

She had pushed him, plucked at the ragged threads of his temper with one underlying purpose. This. Just this. Whatever the risks, whatever the price, she'd had to *know*.

She remembered the taste of him, the texture, the way it felt when his hands slid up from her waist to fist in her hair. She relived all of that now, and experienced the new.

He nipped her bottom lip, just one quick bite before his tongue slicked over the same spot to soothe and to entice. She changed the angle of the kiss, daring him to follow, to circle the slippery rim of that well of need.

Someone trembled. She wasn't sure who, but it was enough to remind her that a misstep could lead to a tumble. And the fall was long.

She drew back, then away, as the reverberations of that mating of mouths tossed her emotions.

So she knew. He was still the only one who could meet and match her passions.

His voice was hoarse, and far from steady when he spoke. "That proves something."

It helped, somehow, knowing he was as undone as she. "Proves what, Sam? That we still have heat between us?" She waved her hand, and a duet of clear blue flames danced on her palm. "Fire is easily lit." She curled her fingers, opened them again, and her palm was empty. "Easily extinguished."

"Not so easily." He took her hand, felt the pump of energy. And knew she felt it, too. "Not so easily, Mia."

"Wanting you with my body means so very little." She drew her hand from his, looked toward the cave. "It makes me sad to be here, to remember how much more we both expected of each other, and our-selves, once."

"Don't you believe in fresh starts?" He reached out to touch her hair. "We've both changed. Why not take the time to get to know each other again?"

"You just want to get me into bed."

"Oh, yeah. That goes without saying."

She laughed, surprising them both. "More honesty. Soon I'll be speechless."

"I'd seduce you eventually, but—"

"Seduction's overrated," she interrupted. "I'm not a jittery virgin. If I decide to sleep with you, then I'll sleep with you."

He blew out a breath. "Well, then. It so happens I have an entire hotel at my disposal."

" 'If' is the key word," she said mildly. "On the occasion 'if' becomes 'when,' I'll let you know."

"I'll stay available." To give himself a moment to steady, he bent down to pick up his sunglasses. "But what I was going to say, was that while I'd seduce you eventually, I'll settle for a friendly dinner."

"I'm not interested in dating you." She turned to walk back up the bluff, to the road, and he fell into step beside her.

"A civilized meal, intelligent conversation, that chance to see who we are. If you don't like calling it a date, we can call it a meeting of two of the island's prominent business owners."

"Semantics don't change reality." She stopped beside her car. "I'll think about it."

"Good." He opened the car door for her, but blocked her from getting in. "Mia—"

Stay with me, he wanted to say. I've missed you.

"What?"

He shook his head, stepped back. "Drive safe."

She went straight home, ruthlessly keeping her mind turned off as she changed into gardening clothes. Her large black cat, Isis, ribboned between her legs as she headed outside. In her greenhouse she babied and fussed over her seedlings, selected flats to set out in the sun to help them harden off before planting later in the month.

She gathered tools and set to work prepping soil.

Her daffodils were already up and dancing, and the hyacinths perfumed the air. Warm weather was beginning to tease her tulips open, and soon she imagined they'd be parading in their candy colors.

She had manipulated him into kissing her, Mia admitted as she turned the earth. Once a woman knew a man's buttons, she didn't forget where to push.

She'd wanted him to hold her, she'd wanted to feel his mouth on hers.

It wasn't a crime or a sin, or even a mistake, she thought now. She'd had to know. And now she did.

There was still a charge between them. She couldn't claim it surprised her. Between the last kiss and this, no man had truly moved her. There'd been a time when she'd wondered if that part of her had simply died off. But the years had coated the wound, and she had recognized, even appreciated, her own sexuality.

There had been others. Interesting men, amusing men, attractive men. But none who tripped that switch inside her, opened her to that rush of feeling.

She'd learned to be content without it.

Until now.

And now what? she wondered, studying the wisteria, just greening, that scrambled over one of her arbors. Now she wanted, and had tested and believed—needed to believe—that she could take her pleasure on her own terms. And protect her heart.

She was human, wasn't she, and entitled to basic human needs?

This time she would be careful, she

would be calculating, and in control. Better, always, to face a dilemma head-on than to turn your back on what wouldn't be ignored.

Her wind chimes jingled, and the tune struck her as faintly mocking. She glanced over to where Isis lay sprawled in the sun, watching her.

"And what would happen if I let him drive this train?" Mia demanded. "I wouldn't be sure of the destination, would I? But if I choose the track, *I* choose the station."

The cat made a sound between a purr and a growl.

"So you say," Mia muttered. "I know exactly what I'm doing. And I believe I will have dinner with him. Here, on my turf." She stabbed her garden spade into the soil. "When I'm damn good and ready."

Isis rose, stuck her tail meaningfully in the air, then stalked over to watch the fish swim in gold flashes in the lily pond.

For the next few days, Mia had too much to do to think about critical cats, or having dinner with Sam, or potentially taking him to her bed. Lulu was distracted and cranky. Crankier than normal, Mia corrected. They'd squabbled twice over petty bookstore business.

Which forced Mia to admit she was a bit cranky herself. In any case, Nell's expansion proposal had lighted a fire under her and provided her with an outlet for the energy that had pumped through her since the moment on the bluff with Sam.

She met with an architect, with a contractor, with her banker, and spent several hours running figures.

It didn't please her that the contractor she wanted had already committed the bulk of his time over the next few months to Sam and his renovation of guest rooms at the Magick Inn. But she tried to take it philosophically. Sam had, damn it, gotten there first.

Both the renovation and her expansion, she reminded herself, were good for the island.

As the weather continued warm, she spent her free time in the gardens at home and in the beds she'd planted behind the bookstore.

"Hey." Ripley wandered to the back garden of the store from the road. "Looks nice," she commented, scanning.

"Yes, it does." Mia continued to plant. "The moon's been warm and yellow all week. We won't have another frost."

Ripley pursed her lips. "Do you make that stuff up?"

"I'm setting in my cosmos, aren't I?"

"Whatever that means. Mac's got this itch to plant some stuff around the house. He's been researching the soil and the local flora and blah, blah. I told him he should just ask you."

"He's welcome to."

"He's going to be coming into the village sometime soon to interview Lulu for his books and stuff. He can catch you then."

"All right."

"I had the weirdest dream about Lu the other night—something to do with Mel Gibson and frogs."

Mia paused, looked up again. "Frogs?"

"Not your lily pad variety. A big, spooky frog." Ripley furrowed her brow, but could bring the dream back only in vague and disjointed pieces. "Something about the stupid gargoyle thing of hers, too. Weird," she said again.

"Lulu might be interested—if Mel was naked."

"Yeah, well. Anyway." Ripley stuck her hands in her pockets, shifted her feet. "Anyway, I guess you know Logan came over to the house a few days ago."

"Yes." Mia said a mental charm as she set a plant. "It's natural he'd want to see the house again."

"Maybe so, but that doesn't mean Mac should let him inside and give him a damn beer. Believe me, I skinned him over that one."

"Ripley. There's no reason Mac should've been rude, and no way his nature would allow him to be."

"Yeah, yeah." Which was, she thought, just where her argument with him had ended up. "But I don't have to like it. He's got this whole mumbo about Sam's place in the destiny deal, and your step toward holding the circle intact."

Mia's stomach clutched, but her hands remained steady as she selected another plant. "I've never considered Mac's theories or opinions mumbo."

"You don't live with him." But on a sigh, Ripley crouched down beside Mia.

There was a time, not so long before, when such a gesture would have come hard to her. It still took her a moment to find what she wanted to say, and how she wanted to say it.

"Okay, Mac's stupendously smart, and he's thorough, and nine times out of ten, he's right, which is really irritating in the day-to-day course of things."

"You're crazy about him," Mia murmured.

"Well, sure. Sexiest geek on the planet, and all mine. But even the amazing Dr. Booke has to miss sometime. I just want to say I don't figure Sam Logan has to have anything to do with anything."

"Succinct, and sentimental."

"Well, why the hell should he?" Ripley lifted her hands, let them fall in frustration. "You two had a thing when you were practically kids still, and it cut you up when he ended it. But you've been handling the way he came back, going about your business and pretty much keeping your distance. You've blown him off, and lightning hasn't shot out of the sky."

"I'm going to sleep with him."

"So I say chances are he's irrelevant to your part of the . . . What? *What?*" Ripley's mouth dropped open as she goggled. "Sweet Jesus Christ."

Even as Mia's lips twitched, Ripley leaped to her feet and headed into a full-blown rant.

"What are you thinking? Have you lost your mind? Sleep with him? You're going to give the guy sex as a reward for dumping you?"

All amusement fled. Carefully tugging off her gloves, Mia got slowly to her feet. "I'm thinking I'm an adult and capable of making my own decisions. That I'm a single, healthy, thirty-year-old woman who is free to have a physical relationship with a single, healthy man."

"It's not a man, it's Logan!"

"Perhaps you could shout just a little louder. I don't believe Mrs. Bigelow across the street heard you clearly."

Ripley set her teeth, rocked back on her heels. "I gave you too much credit, I see that. I figured you'd kick his ass, one way or the other. Then dust your hands off and walk away. I don't know why I thought you had it in you. You never did."

"What does that mean?"

"Just what I said. You want to cozy up with Sam, go right ahead. Don't look for me to pick up the pieces when he breaks you again."

Mia bent to set down her garden trowel. Even a controlled and civilized woman had to take care when she had a weapon in her hand. "You needn't worry. I've had experience in that area with you. You cut me off every bit as coldly, as completely as he did. Cut yourself off, for ten years, from the gift we share and all its joys and responsibilities. Yet I still manage to join hands with you when it's necessary."

"I didn't have a choice."

"Convenient, isn't it, how when one devastates another, it's always because there wasn't a choice."

"I couldn't help you."

"You could've been there. I needed you to be there," Mia said quietly, and turned to go.

"I couldn't." Ripley took her arm, wrapped her fingers tight. "It's his goddamn fault. When he left you all you did was bleed, and I . . ."

"What?"

Ripley dropped her hand. "I don't want to get into all this."

"You kicked in the door, Deputy. Have the guts to step through it."

"Fine, great." She paced away, paced back. Temper still stained her cheeks, but her eyes were bleak. "You walked around like a zombie for weeks, barely functioning. Like somebody who hadn't quite recovered, and never would, from some horrible illness."

"It probably came from having my heart ripped out."

"I know it, because I felt it too." Fisting a hand, Ripley tapped it on her chest. "I felt what you felt. I couldn't sleep, I couldn't eat. I could barely get out of bed most days. It was like dying from the inside out."

"If you're talking about complete empathy, I've never—" Mia stammered.

"I don't know what you call it," Ripley snapped. "I experienced, physically, what you experienced. And I couldn't stand it. I wanted to do something, wanted you to do something. Pay him back, make him hurt. And the longer it went on, the more angry I got. If I was mad, it didn't hurt as much. I couldn't think past the fury."

She drew a breath. "I was standing outside, behind the house. Zack had just come in from a sail. Minutes before. And all this rage just rose up. I thought about what I wanted to do, what I could do. It was inside me to do it. I pulled lightning out of the sky. A black bolt. And it struck the boat where Zack had just been. A few minutes earlier, and I might have killed him. I couldn't control it."

"Ripley." Shaken, appalled, Mia reached out to touch her arm. "It must have terrified you."

"A few giant steps beyond terrified."

"I wish you'd talked to me. I could've helped."

"Mia, you couldn't even help yourself." Sighing as the weight slid off her shoulders, Ripley shook her head. "And I couldn't take the chance of hurting someone. I couldn't handle the—I don't know—the intimacy of my link with you. I knew if I told you, you'd talk me out of giving up the Craft. I saw only one way out, and that was to pull back from you. From all of it, before I did something I couldn't take back."

"I was furious with you," Mia countered.

"Yeah." Ripley sniffled, but she was only marginally embarrassed. "I got mad back, and it got easier, maybe more comfortable for me, to be at odds with you than it had been to be your friend."

"Maybe it got easier for me, too." It was difficult to admit, after all the years when casting blame had helped soothe the hurt. "Sam was gone, but you were still here. Needling you whenever possible was some small satisfaction."

"You were really good at it."

"Well." With a little laugh, Mia brushed back her hair. "Just one of my little gifts."

"I always loved you, even when I called you nasty names."

Tears threatened. A stone that had been in her heart for so long dissolved in an instant. She took the two steps that separated them, slid her arms around Ripley's waist and held on. Held tight.

"Okay." Mia's voice caught. Ripley patted her back. "Okay."

"I've missed you so much. So much."

"I know. Me, too." She let out an unsteady breath, then blinked when she saw Nell standing just outside the door, crying silently.

"Sorry I came out in the middle of that, and, well, by the time I'd decided whether I should mediate or just slip back inside, I was caught up." She handed tissues all around. "I'd apologize for eavesdropping, but I'm just so happy."

"What a trio." Ripley sniffled. "Now I'm going to finish my rounds with red eyes. It's embarrassing."

"For heaven's sake, do a glamour and get rid of them." Mia finished wiping her eyes, then closed them, murmured a chant. When she opened them again, they were sparkling and clear.

"Always the show-off," Ripley muttered.

"I still can't do it that quickly," Nell began. "Do you think if I—"

"Let's not get into a damn coven here." Ripley waved a hand. "Since you're here, Nell, I need some weight. Get this. Mia's going to shag Sam."

"You have such a way with words," Mia said. "It never fails to impress me."

"The point is, whatever you call it, it's a mistake." Ripley gave Nell a little poke on the arm. "Tell her."

"It's none of my business."

"Cop-out," Ripley stated, with a sneer.

"To spare you from the insults, and from

biting your own tongue, I'll ask for your opinion." Mia raised her eyebrows. "If you have one on the subject."

"My opinion is it's your decision. And if," Nell continued over Ripley's snort, "you're considering going to bed with him, then you're still attracted enough for it to be an issue. You don't do things on impulse or recklessly. It seems to me that until you either get Sam out of your system or resolve your feelings, you'll be conflicted and unsettled."

"Thank you. Now—"

"I'm not quite finished," Nell told Mia, then cleared her throat. "Physical intimacy will resolve only one level of your conflict, and probably the easiest one. What happens after will depend on whether you open yourself or close yourself. That'll be your decision, too."

"I'm considering it finishing up old business. Until I do, I can't know, clearly, what step it is I'm meant to take."

"Then just look," Ripley said impatiently. "You were always a whiz with visions."

"Do you think I haven't tried?" Some of the pent-up frustration snapped out. "I can't see my own. I see her, standing on the cliffs, with the storm raging, the fog creeping. I feel her strength and her despair. And in that instant before she jumps, she seems to reach out to me. I can't tell if it's to pass that last link to me, or to pull me over with her."

Her eyes blurred, and the air thickened. "Then I'm alone, and I feel the dark pressing in. Close, tight. And so cold it seems the night should crack from it. I know if I can get to the forest, to the clearing and the heart of the island, we'll make the circle and that dark will break apart, once and for all. But I don't know how to get there."

"You will." Nell took her hand. "She was alone. You aren't and never will be."

"We haven't come this far to lose now." Ripley took her other hand.

"No." Mia drew strength from the circle. She needed it. For even there, in the sunlight, with her sisters beside her, she felt alone in the dark.

# Six

A mist blanketed the island, as thin and luminous as the skin of a pearl. Trees and rocks rose up from it, humps and towers in a soft white sea.

Mia left the house early. On the slope of her lawn, she stood for a moment, absorbing the serenity, the stillness that was the Sisters on a lovely spring morning.

Her spread of forsythia was a golden fan of color through the morning fog, her daffodils a band of sunny trumpets. She could smell her hyacinths, damp and sweet. It seemed to her that the earth was waiting to awaken, to throw off all memories of winter and burst into life.

She could appreciate the sleepy before as much as she would the beauty of what was to come.

She opened her car, her satchel of paperwork on the seat beside her, and started down the long and curving road to the village.

There were several routine chores to deal with before the store opened. She enjoyed that, too—the relative quiet, the repetition, the freshening of stock—as much as she did the business hours with customers breezing in and out, lingering, browsing. And, of course, buying.

She loved being surrounded by books. Uncarting them, shelving them, designing displays. She loved the smell and the texture and the look of them. And the surprises uncovered when she flipped one open at random and saw the play of words on paper.

The bookstore was more than a business to her. It was a deep and steady love. But she never forgot it *was* a business, one she ran efficiently, and profitably.

She'd come from money, and as a result had never had to work for a living. She'd had to work for her own gratification, her own sense of ethics. Her financial base had allowed her to choose the course of her career and establish a business that reflected her interests. Those ethics, and her own skills, effort, and shrewdness had made the business flourish.

She was grateful, and always would be, for the Devlin money. But it was, to her mind, much more exciting and satisfying to make her own.

And to risk her own.

That was precisely what she would be doing by following through with Nell's idea. Expanding the café would change things. As much as Mia trusted and respected tradition and continuity, she was also a proponent of change. As long as the change was smart. And this one, she thought as she wound her way through the mist, could be.

Expanding the café could mean tucking in a more appealing, and roomier, event area. Her monthly book club was popular on the island, and the new cooking club already showed potential. The trick would be to make the best use of space and still maintain the intimacy the store was known for.

But since Nell had planted the seed in her mind, the idea had taken hold. Mia could see exactly what she wanted, and how it would be. When it came to Café Book, she knew precisely what she was doing.

Too bad she wasn't quite as confident at the moment about the rest of her life.

It was as if a curtain had been lowered, dead center of her vision. She could see peripherally, but straight ahead was blocked. It worried her more than she was willing to admit.

Behind the curtain were choices, she understood that. But how could she make the right one if she didn't know the options waiting for her?

One of the choices was Sam Logan. But to what extent did she trust her instincts there, weighing them with logic and past history? Balancing them against a primal sexual attraction that tended to cloud logic.

A misstep with him could crush her a second time. She might not survive it whole. More, the wrong choice could doom the island she loved and was sworn to protect.

Once another woman had chosen death rather than bear the pain of loneliness and heartbreak. She had flung herself into the sea, after the lover who had deserted her. And had woven the last threads of the web about Three Sisters.

Hadn't she herself, by choosing to live, to find contentment, even to flourish, already countered that act?

Nell had chosen courage, and Ripley true justice. And so their circle held. And she had chosen life.

Perhaps the curse had already been broken, and the dark that hovered in wait around the island had already been banished.

Even as the thought, and the hope of it, ran through her mind, the mist boiled up from the roadbed. A jagged lance of lightning crashed beside her car with an explosion of dirty red light and the stink of ozone.

In the center of the road, an enormous black wolf snarled.

Instinctively she slammed on the brakes, jerked the wheel. The car skidded, spun, giving her a dizzying view of rocks, fog, and the dull glint of the guardrail that stood between the narrow edge of road and the sheer drop to the sea.

Fighting back the panic that gushed into her throat, she yanked the wheel again. The eyes of the wolf glowed like embers, and its teeth were long. On its muzzle was a white pentagram, sliced through the black hide like a scar.

Her mark—and her heart slammed painfully against her ribs at the sight of it.

Through the roar of blood in her head, over the scream of her own tires, she felt the cold of its breath on the back of her neck. She heard the sly, coaxing voice whispering, whispering in her mind.

*Let go. Just let go, and you won't be alone. It's so hard to be alone.*

Tears blurred her vision. For a moment, her arms went weak, trembling as the urge to let it end nudged at her will. In that moment she saw herself, quite clearly, flying over the edge of the cliff.

She bore down even as she struggled to control the car, and pulled her power up from the gut. "Go back to hell, you son of a bitch."

As the wolf threw back its head to howl, she spun the car forward, punched the gas. And drove through it.

She felt the shock, not from impact but from the explosion of greed that pounded the air as her car rammed through the image.

The fog lifted, and the mist, thin and pearly in the strengthening sun, sparkled over Three Sisters.

Mia pulled over to the side of the road, laid her forehead on the wheel, and gave in to the shakes. Her own breathing was too loud in the closed car, so she fumbled for the window control. The cool, damp air and the steady chant of the sea revived her.

Still she closed her eyes, made herself sit back until she began to calm again.

"Well, I guess that answers my question about this being over and done." She inhaled, exhaled slowly until her chest no longer hitched with every breath. Then opening her eyes, she scanned the road behind her in the rearview mirror.

Her tires had left wild, sinuous trails over the pavement—trails, she noted with one quick shudder, that had veered perilously close to the edge.

The wolf was gone, and the mist was already as sheer as gauze.

"An obvious ploy," she said aloud for herself and whatever listened. "Black wolf, red eyes. Obvious and clichéd."

And, she thought, very, very effective.

But he'd borne her mark, the mark she'd

put on him when he'd worn another form. He hadn't been able to disguise it, and that gave her some comfort. Much-needed comfort, she admitted, for the ambush had very nearly succeeded.

She eased the car back on the road, and her hands had almost stopped trembling by the time she parked her car in front of Café Book.

He'd been waiting for her. It had been easy enough to time his arrival at the hotel to match hers at the store. She wasn't like clockwork, Sam mused as he strolled across the street. But sometime between eight-forty-five and nine-fifteen she parked her pretty little car and unlocked the store.

She wore one of her long, thin dresses today, the kind of dress that made a man want to offer thanks to the gods of spring. It was a soft, pale blue, the color of quiet pools, and skimmed fluid as water down her body.

She wore sexy high-heeled sandals, hardly more than a series of buff-colored straps and a long, thin spike.

He'd had no idea shoes could make the mouth water.

She'd tied her hair back, his only complaint about her appearance that morning. He liked it best wild and loose, but the binding did leave an intriguing spill of red down the center of her back.

He'd like to lay his lips there—beneath the spill of hair, beneath the soft, thin dress, and onto the smooth skin at the center of her back.

"Good morning, gorgeous."

She jerked when he spoke and turned away from the door. His opening grin faded instantly, and his eyes went dark at the shock still mirrored in hers.

"What is it? What happened?"

"I don't know what you're talking about." Damn it, her hands were going to shake again. "You startled me." She angled her body enough to hide the tremor in her hand as she unlocked the door. "Sorry, Sam, no time for a neighborly chat. I have work."

"Don't pull that on me." He moved through the door with her before she could attempt to shut it and lock it in his face. "I know you."

"No, you don't." Her voice wanted to rise,

and she refused to allow it. As casually as possible, she set her satchel on the front counter. "You don't know me."

"I know when you're upset. Christ, Mia, you're shaking. Your hands are like ice," he said as he snatched one and held it between his own. "Tell me what happened."

"It's nothing." She'd thought she was calm. She'd thought she was steady again. But her legs wanted to give. Pride made her lock them stiff. "Damn it, let me go."

He nearly did. "No," he decided, moving closer. "I did that once. Let's try something new." He scooped her off her feet.

"What the hell do you think you're doing?"

"You're cold, and shaking. You need to sit down. Put on a little weight, haven't you?"

She sent him one withering look. "Oh, really?"

"It looks good on you." He carried her to the sofa, set her down. He pulled the bright throw off the back and tucked it around her.

"Now. Tell me."

"Don't sit on the—" She bit off a sigh because he'd already lowered himself to the coffee table facing her. "I see you never have figured out the difference between a table and a chair."

"They're both in the furniture family. There, you've got some color coming back. Good thing I came along to annoy you."

"Just my lucky day."

He took her hand again, warming it in his. "What scared you, baby?"

"Don't call me that." He had only used that term, she remembered, when he was being particularly sweet. She let her head rest back against the cushions. "It's just . . . I had a near miss on the drive down. A dog jumped out in the road. The roads were damp with the mist, and I skidded."

His grip tightened on hers. "I don't think so."

"Why would I lie?"

"I don't know." He held on until she stopped trying to pull her hand free. "But something's off. I imagine I could find out for myself if I took a drive up the coast road."

"Don't." Fear grabbed her by the throat so that the single word was thin and urgent. "Don't," she repeated with more control. "It isn't for you, but at this point I can't be sure it won't take what it can get. Let go of my hand, and I'll tell you."

"Tell me," he countered, knowing the

value of the link, "and I'll let go of your hand."

"All right," she managed after a vicious internal struggle. "Your way. This time."

She told him, sparing none of the details but keeping her tone even, almost conversational. Even so, she saw his expression change.

"Why aren't you wearing protection?" he demanded.

"I am." She lifted the trio of crystals dangling from a star-shaped pendant. "It wasn't enough. He's strong. He's had three centuries to gather his forces, nurse his powers. Even so, he couldn't cause me real harm. He can only play tricks."

"This trick might've caused you to have an accident. You were probably driving too fast."

"Please, you'll force me to pull out the old pot calling the kettle."

"I didn't nearly drive off a cliff." He pushed to his feet, paced away the terrifying image of Mia doing exactly that.

He hadn't anticipated this kind of direct, frontal attack on her. And, he thought, neither had she. Confidence in their own powers, he realized, had blindsided them.

"You'd have taken extra precautions with your home."

"I protect what's mine."

"You neglected your car," he said, tossing a look over his shoulder and having the satisfaction of seeing her flush.

"I certainly did not neglect it. I have the standard charms—"

"Standard isn't enough, as you've just discovered."

Her teeth clenched at being told how to conduct herself, but she nodded. "Point taken."

"Meanwhile, I'd prefer to give him back some of his own rather than constantly taking the defense."

She got to her feet. "This isn't for you, isn't about you."

"No point in wasting time arguing that point, as we both know I'm part of it."

"You're not one of the three."

"No, I'm not." He stepped back to her. "But I'm *of* the three. My blood and your blood, Mia, spring from the same pool. My power and your power feed from the same source. It links us, however much you might prefer otherwise. You need me with you to finish this."

"What I need isn't yet clear."

He lifted a hand, grazing a knuckle over the line of her jaw. An old gesture. "And what you want?"

"Wanting you sexually isn't life and death, Sam. It's scratching a vague itch."

"Vague?" Amusement brightened his face as his hand slid around to cup the back of her neck.

"Vague," she repeated and let his mouth come to hers, let it rub teasingly. And entice. "Slight."

"I was thinking more . . ." He danced the fingers of his free hand up and down her spine. "Constant. Chronic." Nibbling on her, he eased her closer.

She kept her gaze on him, her arms at her sides. "Desire's only a hunger."

"You're right. Let's eat."

He ravished her mouth, shifting so swiftly from gentle warmth to raging heat that she had no choice but to plunge with him.

Her hands gripped his hips, squeezed, then ran roughly up his back to hook like talons over his shoulders. If he would push her to the brink, she thought, she would push him harder—and further.

She let her head fall back, not a gesture

of surrender but one of demand. *Take more, if you dare.* When he dared, she purred in pleasure.

Her scent seemed to pour over him, into him, until his belly ached and his head spun. In one desperate move he dragged her closer and prepared to fall with her onto the couch.

The front door opened. The cheerful jingle of bells might as well have been sirens.

"Go rent a damn room," Lulu snapped and let the door slam behind her. It gave her dark satisfaction to watch the two of them spring apart. "Or at least crawl into the backseat of a car if you're going to act like a couple of horny teenagers." She slapped her enormous purse on the counter. "Me, I've got a business to run around here."

"Good point." Sam slipped an arm possessively around Mia's waist. "We'll just take a walk across the street."

It was another old gesture, Mia remembered. Once she would have hooked her arm around him in turn and leaned her head against his shoulder. Now, she simply stepped away.

"That's a charming offer, really, but I'll

just take a rain check. The business that Lulu so helpfully pointed out needs to be run is mine. And we're opening in . . . less than an hour," she said after a glance at her watch.

"Then we'll make it fast."

"Another delightful offer. Isn't that sweet, Lu? It's not every day a woman gets an invitation for a quick roll before operating hours."

"Adorable," Lulu said sourly. She felt sour—and preferred blaming it on Sam rather than on not being able to sleep well since her Saturday-night hallucination.

"But be that as it may . . ." Mia patted Sam's cheek absently, then started to turn away.

He took her chin in a firm grip. "You're playing me," he said softly. "You want to make this a game, then I should warn you. I don't always play by the rules now."

"Neither do I." She heard the back door open, close. "Ah, there's Nell. You'll have to excuse me, Sam. I have work. As I'm sure you do."

She nudged his hand away, then walked over to meet Nell as she came in. "I'll take that up." Mia scooped the first box of baked goods out of Nell's arms. "Smells fabulous." She sailed up the stairs with the scent of cinnamon rolls floating behind her.

"Um." Nell cleared her throat. Walking into the tension had been like walking into a wall. "Hello, Sam."

"Nell."

"Well, I've got . . . more," she managed, then escaped out the back again.

"In case you haven't noticed," Lulu said, "we're not open for business. So get."

He could still taste Mia. With his mood hot and ripe for trouble, he walked to the counter and leaned over close to Lulu's scowl. "I don't give a damn if you approve or disapprove. You won't keep me away from her."

"You did a good job of that yourself these past years."

"Now I'm back, and we're all just going to have to deal with it." He strode to the door, yanked it open. "If you want to play guard dog, there's something a hell of a lot more dangerous than me you should be snapping at."

Lulu watched him stalk across the street.

She wasn't sure there was anything more dangerous to Mia than Sam Logan.

*No family.* The wine-and-junk-food-induced hallucination had been wrong about that, she thought. She had family. She had a child. Lulu glanced up the stairs where Mia had gone.

She had a child, she thought again.

He canceled his first meeting. A man had priorities. He drove up the coast road. Through sheer will he held his temper and his speed in check.

But he could do nothing about the shock and horror that careened through him when he saw the skid marks. Inches, he thought as he got out of his car on rubbery legs, just inches more and she'd have been into the guardrail. The right speed, the right angles, and her little car would have toppled right over it and down the unforgiving face of the cliff.

He followed the pattern, scanning the road, scenting the air for anything that lingered. He knew she liked to drive fast, but she'd never been reckless. To go into a spin such as the one indicated by the tire marks smeared over the pavement, she'd have had to be doing ninety.

Unless she'd had help.

Cold fingers ran over his spine because he was certain now that was what had happened. Something had shoved that spin along, pushing her toward the edge.

If she hadn't been strong enough, smart enough, fast enough, she might not have come out of it whole.

He studied the roadbed where a black scar marred it, like an old, festering burn. It oozed, like oily blood, as he watched. And as he watched, he felt the dark energy that emanated from it crawl over the air.

Mia had been more shaken than either of them had realized, he thought, to have left this.

Going back to his car, he popped the trunk, selected what he needed. With his tools in hand, he took a long look up and down the road. It was deserted. A plus, he thought, as what he needed to do would take a little time.

He circled the scar three times with sea salt, and the ooze smoked where it spilled into the ring. With his power cold and clear inside him, he used a birch wand for cleansing. As he sprinkled both bay and cloves for protection, the scar bubbled and hissed. And began, slowly, to shrink.

"No one who passes now need fear. You can do no more harm here. Dark back to dark as light breeds light. Safe passage here by day and night." He crouched as the scar closed in on itself. "I will guard what is dear to me," he whispered. "As I will, so mote it be."

He returned to his car and drove over the shadow of the scar toward Mia's house.

He'd needed to see it, and had resisted. But he couldn't afford to wait for her invitation now.

It was so much what it had been, he thought as he studied the gorgeous ramble and spears of stone. And so much more. More Mia, he realized as he again got out of his car.

The flowers, the budded shrubs and great trees. The gargoyles and faeries. The breeze stirred wind chimes and strings of crystal into constant music. The white tower of the lighthouse stood like an ancient sentinel, guarding both island and house. And she'd planted purple pansies at its feet.

He followed the winding path of stepping-stones around the side of the house. The sea beating on the rocks drew both his mind and his heart toward the cliffs and made him remember how many times he'd stood on them with her. Or come upon her standing there alone.

But as he walked he glanced around, then stopped, staggered.

Her gardens were a world. Arches and arbors, slopes and flows. Stone paths softened by moss spreading through the cracks meandered through rivers and floods of flowers. Some were tender with spring, some already reigned.

Not just blooms, he realized, but the green. There were so many tones and textures of it that each spill or shimmer of pink or white, yellow or blue against it added a wonder.

There were pools of water, the glint of copper from a sundial, the charm of a dancing faerie twirling in the shrubbery. He could see benches tucked here and there, some in sun, some in shade, inviting visitors to sit, to enjoy.

He couldn't imagine what it would be like when the young plants burst into full summer bloom, when the vines finished their climb up the arbors. Couldn't conceive of the color and shape, the perfume.

Unable to resist, he wandered along some of the stone paths, trying to imagine how she had done it. How she had turned what had been a pretty, if pedestrian, garden, a stretch of manicured lawn, and the single formal terrace he remembered into a celebration.

And he wished, foolishly, that he could sit and watch while she tended one of her beds.

The house had always been beautiful, he thought now. And she had always loved it. But he remembered it as somewhat staid, and very formidable. She had made it a place of pleasure and beauty, warmth and welcome.

And standing in the midst of Mia's personal Eden, with the fragile scents, the trill of birds, the thunder of the surf, he understood what she had created, and what he had never found.

Home.

He had had the luxurious, the adequate,

the tasteful, and the efficient. He had looked for, but had never found, his place. Until now.

"A hell of a note, isn't it?" he murmured. "To realize she had hers, and mine, all along."

Since he didn't know what to do about it, he went back to his car to finish what he'd come to do. He would add his own charms of protection to Mia's, and make her—and hers—doubly safe.

He'd just finished when he spotted the island's patrol car coming up the road. Watching it, he dropped a small silk bag of crystals back into his coat pocket. His initial pleasure at the prospect of seeing Zack flipped over to irritation when Ripley got out of the car.

"Well, well, isn't this interesting." Simmering, and delighted to be so, she tucked her hands in her back pockets and swaggered toward him. The bill of her cap was angled low over dark glasses.

But he didn't need to see the whole of her face to know it was hard as stone.

"Here I am, on routine island patrol, and what do I find but a nefarious character. And find him skulking around on private property." Smiling fiercely, she unhooked her cuffs from her belt.

Sam eyed them, eyed her. "Not that I don't have a soft spot for a little bondage now and again, Rip, but you're a married woman." When her lips peeled back to show her teeth, he shrugged. "Okay, bad joke. But so are those."

"The law isn't a joke, hotshot. You're trespassing, and I imagine I could make an attempted daylight B and E stick." The cuffs jingled in her hand. "Either way, trying is just going to make my day."

"I didn't go in the damn house." He'd just been considering it. "And if you think you're going to arrest and cuff me for trespassing—"

"Goody. I can add resisting."

"Cut me some slack."

"Why the hell should I?"

"I didn't come up here to poke around." Though he had poked, a bit. "I'm just as concerned about Mia as you are."

"Too bad being a lying sack of shit isn't against the law."

"How about this for truth?" He leaned over until they were nose to nose. "I don't give a rat's ass what you think of or about me. I'm going to make damn sure this house and the woman who lives in it are protected, especially after what nearly happened to her this morning. And if you think you're going to get those fucking cuffs on me, sweetheart, you'd better step back and think again."

"It's not your job to protect this house. And if I want these cuffs on you, city boy, you'll be flat on the ground eating dirt while I secure them. What the hell do you mean, 'after what happened this morning'?"

He started to spit something back at her, but then his gaze narrowed in speculation. "Mia didn't tell you? She tells you every damn thing. Always has."

Ripley's color came up a little. "I haven't seen her today. What happened?" Then the color drained away again as she gripped his wrist. "Is she hurt?"

"No. No." His temper ebbed, leaving only frustration. He raked his fingers through his hair. "But she could've been. Nearly was."

He relayed the story, appreciating when Ripley swore impressively and stalked around the front yard as if looking for something handy to kick.

It reminded him why he'd always liked her.

"I didn't see any skid marks."

"I vanished them after I cleansed the area," he explained. "I thought it would upset her to see them again. God knows, it bothered me."

"Yeah, well." Her voice dropped to a mutter. "You're right."

"Excuse me? I don't believe I caught that."

"I said you're right. Don't milk it. You took care of things here?"

"Yeah. Just added a layer over what she's done. She's stronger than she was," he said half to himself. "And she's thorough."

"Obviously not thorough enough. I'm going to talk to Mac about it. He has all sorts of ideas."

"Yeah, he's full of them," Sam said sourly, then shrugged his shoulders when Ripley scowled at him. "I liked him. So congratulations and best wishes on your marriage, and all of that."

"Gee, thanks, that was so heartwarming."

That made him smile. "Maybe it's just hard for me to imagine Let-It-Rip cozied up in connubial bliss."

"Shut up. That was high school."

"I liked you in high school." Because he

had, he tried again. "I'm glad you and Mac bought the house. It's a great spot."

"Yeah, we think so. No hard feelings your old man sold it out from under you?"

"It was never mine."

She opened her mouth, shut it again. For a moment he'd been the lost and restless boy she remembered. And had cared for. "You messed her up, Sam. Seriously messed her up."

He stared at the cliffs that rose over the sea and spilled down to it. "I know it."

"Then I messed her up."

Puzzled, he looked back at Ripley's face. "I don't understand you."

"She didn't tell me about this morning because we're just getting back on even ground again, after a long time. I dumped her just as hard as you did, so I'm thinking . . ." She drew a breath. "I'm thinking I don't have any right to take shots at you, when part of it's just to ease my own conscience. You knocked the ground out from under her, but I didn't stick around to help break her fall."

"You want to tell me why you didn't stick?"

She sent him a hard, level look. "You want to tell me why you didn't?"

He shook his head. "No. Why don't we start dealing with now? I'm part of this, and I'm sticking this time around."

"Fair enough," she agreed. "I say we can use all the help we can get, from whatever the source."

"I'm going to do whatever I can to convince Mia to let me back into her life."

"I'll wish you luck." At his surprised glance she smirked. "But until I make up my mind about you, pal, I won't say whether that's good luck or bad."

"Reasonable." He held out a hand, and after a moment's hesitation she took it.

Heat shimmered and sparked. "Figures," she said in a dour voice.

"Connections." He gave her hand a friendly squeeze before releasing it. "What can you do?"

"I'll let you know when I figure it out. I have to finish my patrol." She waited a beat, inclined her head. "After you." She jerked a thumb at his car. "And keep that phallic symbol on wheels under the speed limit."

"Oh, absolutely, Officer Friendly." He

sauntered back to his car. "One more thing? Let's not mention my little visit here to Mia. She'll just get pissy about me questioning her skills."

Ripley snorted as she climbed into her own car. She had to give Sam credit for one thing. He still knew his woman.

# Seven

She wouldn't tell Mia, but Ripley didn't consider that her discretion was required to extend to Mac. She was pretty sure there was some loophole in the confidentiality law that applied to spouses.

The way she looked at it, if you loved someone enough to promise them a lifetime, you got to tell them all your stuff and listen to all of theirs. It was a side benefit and balanced out having to share closet space.

Though they lived together, slept together, woke together, they met for lunch a few times a week at Café Book. The few times a week Mac wasn't so buried in his work that he remembered what time it was. The lunch date, she decided, was as long as she could hold out before she spilled her news.

She itched to relay the story to Nell, but after a complex internal debate, she decided Nell cut too close to Mia and didn't come under the dispensation rule.

Mac would have to do.

"So," she continued as she plowed through a grilled tuna and avocado salad, "he stood there, all handsome and brooding—it was still cool and misty, so he had on this long dark coat and it was all, you know, billowy. Perfect tortured-hero look. So he's like that, on her front lawn with that big old house behind him and the mists just burning off, until I made him leave."

"He vanished the remnants on the road?" It wasn't easy to get a word in when Ripley was on a roll, but Mac had carved out one salient point.

"Yeah—poof. It can be a pretty intense spell, depending on the, you know, quality and complexity of the evil and stuff." She jerked a shoulder and grabbed her coffee. "But I didn't see a trace of it, and I stopped and took a good look on the way back, just in case he'd missed something."

"Had he?"

"Nope. Not even a stray vibe left, which means he swept it clean."

"I wish he'd talked to me first," Mac complained. "I could've gotten some on-site readings and taken a sample for lab tests."

She sat back, shook her head at him. "Oh, yeah, just what I want my guy to have his fingers in, some evil black ooze."

"It's what I do." Mac sulked about it for a minute, then decided he might as well take a drive out and see if some of his more sensitive equipment could pick up anything.

"So let's backtrack a minute," he continued. "He told you that Mia told him she'd seen a large black wolf with the pentagram mark on his muzzle."

"That's the manifestation. Black wolf, red eyes, big fangs. Her mark on it. Had to be a hell of an image to shake the queen of weird."

"An image is just the point," Mac said. "Not an actual wolf. No living creature was possessed this time out. Could have something to do with her branding it last winter. But it was still potent enough to send her into a skid. That's interesting."

"And a bad one, from the way Sam was shaken up. I'll tell you what else is interesting." She leaned forward, hunching over what was left of her lunch and lowering her voice. "The guy sweeping up behind her, standing there looking at her place like some contemporary version of Heathcliff looking over the moors for Catherine—"

"Good one."

"Hey, I read. Anyway, him standing there, emotions all swirling—and trying to act all cool and casual about it. That's interesting."

"From what you told me, they had a very intense relationship."

"Had," Ripley confirmed. "I could see him being all moony if she'd dumped him way back when. But he's the one who pulled stakes."

"Doesn't mean he got over her."

"Guys don't carry torches for a frigging decade."

Smiling, Mac rubbed his hand over the back of hers. "I'd carry one for you."

"Get out." But she turned her hand over, linked her fingers with his. "Anyway, he doesn't want her to know he went out there. He says she'd be ticked if she knew he'd backed up her charms. And she would. But if you ask me, there's another layer. He doesn't want her to know he's stuck on her. It'd be funny if it wasn't so complicated, and if there wasn't so much at stake."

"Whatever was between them, is between them—or isn't—plays into what happens next. I've got some theories."

"You've always got some theories."

He smiled, inched forward. "We need to have a meeting. All parties."

"I figured." Like his, her voice was a whisper now. To the casual observer, it might have appeared they were flirting, or plotting an insurrection. "Let's have it at Zack's. Nell'll cook. We're scraping the bottom of the leftover barrel at home."

"Good thinking. How do we handle how much we know, and who told us what who doesn't want somebody else to know we know?"

"Jesus, I understand that." She grinned at him. "It must be love."

"Well, if it isn't Bill and Coo." Mia stepped up to the table, ran an affectionate hand over Mac's shoulder. "Don't the two of you look adorable?"

"Yeah, we're thinking about entering a contest." Ripley eased back, studied Mia's face. She had to give the woman credit, nothing showed but bone-deep beauty. "So what's up with you?"

"Oh, this and that." Mia left her hand on

Mac's shoulder. Something about him always comforted her. "Actually, there is something I need to speak with you about—and Nell."

A shadow of worry crossed her face as she glanced back at the café counter. "It'll have to wait a bit, though," Mia decided. "She's pretty tied up with customers at the moment."

Ripley considered how to play it, then went with instinct. "If this is about your dances with wolves, I know about it."

It was a toss-up, she thought, who looked more stunned, Mia or Mac. But at least Mia didn't kick her under the table. She shifted, which gave her the opportunity to kick Mac back as she reached toward a neighboring table and dragged over a third chair.

"Sit down a minute."

"I think I will." Struggling to settle, Mia slid into the chair, folded her hands. "I didn't realize you and Sam were such confidants."

"Oh, can it." Ripley pushed what was left of her lunch aside. "I ran into him out on the coast road." Which was true, Ripley thought. Mia's house was on the damn coast road. "He cleaned up the little mess you left behind."

"The . . ." She trailed off, paled. My God, how could she have been so careless! She hadn't so much as thought of the smear of power that might have stained that section of the island.

"Give yourself a break," Mac said gently. "You had to have been badly shaken."

"It doesn't matter. It was my responsibility."

"You don't get it, professor." Casually, Ripley broke off a piece of the éclair Mac had picked out for dessert. "Ms. Perfect here isn't allowed to make mistakes like the rest of us lesser beings."

"I should've cleaned the area," Mia repeated, and gave Ripley a genuine jolt of concern when she didn't snap back.

"Well, you didn't. He did, and all's well. Anyway, while I was ragging on him and threatening to haul him in on some trumped-up charges just to brighten my morning, he filled me in. I've filled Mac in, so you just have to bring Nell up to speed when she's off her shift."

"Yes, all right." Mia rubbed at the vague pounding in her temple. She couldn't remember the last time she'd had a headache. And her stomach was queasy.

She'd have to take the time to balance her chakras so she could think clearly.

"I would like to go over it with you in more detail, Mac. I tend to believe it was nothing but a scare tactic, but I don't want to shrug it off and miss something critical."

"You're right, and as it happens Ripley and I were just saying we should have a meeting. Why don't we see if we can get together at Nell and Zack's tonight?"

"At dinnertime," Ripley chimed in and made Mia smile.

"Yes, why waste time or an opportunity for a free meal? I'll speak to Nell." Mia got to her feet, then looked down at Ripley. "I intended to tell you about it myself. I just needed to clear my head first. I don't want you to think I was keeping secrets. It's past time for that between us."

Ripley suffered a pang of guilt over Sam, but sucked it in. A deal was a deal. "Don't sweat it. Besides, it gave me a chance to needle the pretty boy."

"That's something, then. I'll see you later."

When she walked toward Nell and was out of earshot, Mac leaned forward again. "You're good, Deputy. Really good."

"Did you doubt it? Now I've got to make tracks and get to Sam, let him know what I told her and what I didn't, before she gets to him and everything's screwed."

"I'll do it." He shoved his éclair in front of her as he rose. "I want to talk to him anyway. I need to document all of this."

"Hey, good deal." She plucked up the pastry.

"And you get to buy lunch."

"Always a catch," she muttered with her mouth full.

Mac had only been able to wheedle an hour out of Lulu, and that was just as well now, he thought. He still had to drive back home, meet up with Ripley again, and drive back for the newly arranged dinner meeting at the Todds'.

But for now he had his tape recorder and notebook, and had primed Lulu with a box of Godiva.

"Really appreciate this, Lulu."

"Yeah, yeah." She drank coffee, black, with the candy. She was giving wine a little rest. "I told you I don't much like this interview crap. Reminds me of being hauled in by the cops for protesting."

"What were you protesting?"

She sent him a pitying look. "Come on. It was the sixties. What wasn't I protesting?"

It was a good place to start, he decided. "You lived in a commune, right?"

"For a while." She shrugged. Might as well get it done. "I flopped here, or there. Slept in parks, on beaches, whatever was handy. Saw a lot of the country you're not going to see if you're in the family minivan and stopping at the Holiday Inn."

"I bet. How'd you end up here? On Three Sisters?"

"Heading east."

"Lulu . . ." he pleaded.

"Okay, don't give me that puppy-dog look." She made herself more comfortable on the sofa. "I hit the road when I was about sixteen. Didn't get along with my family." She leaned over, plucked out another chocolate.

"Any particular reason for that?"

"You name it. My old man had a narrow mind and a hard hand, and my mother danced to his tune and played with the ladies auxiliary. Couldn't stand it. I lit out first chance I got, and I'd been such a pain in their asses, they didn't go to much trouble to find me."

He found the offhanded way she spoke of her parents' disinterest sad and telling. But knowing Lulu, the slightest inkling of sympathy would earn him a kick in the teeth. "Where were you going?"

"Anywhere that wasn't there. Ended up in San Francisco for a while. Gave my virginity in a nice marijuana haze to a sweet-faced boy named Bobby."

She smiled at that, as despite the years and the circumstance, it was a nice memory. "I made love beads, sold them for food, listened to a lot of music, solved all the world's problems. Smoked a lot of joints, dropped a little acid. Cruised around New Mexico and Nevada with a guy named Spike—can you beat that—on his Harley."

"At sixteen?"

"Might've been seventeen by then. You only get to be sixteen for a year. Liked being a gypsy, as I had itchy feet." She wiggled her toes in her ancient Birkenstocks. "I planted them now and then. The commune in Colorado for one. I learned to plant a garden, how to cook what I planted. Learned how to knit there, too. But . . ."

Behind her lenses, her eyes sharpened. "You want the weird stuff, right? Not the hippie-trippie memoirs."

"I'll take what I can get."

"I had dreams. Not like goals," she added. "Didn't have an ambition to my name back then. But I had dreams of this place—The Sisters. The house on the cliff, and a woman with long red hair."

Mac had been sketching Lulu's face on his notepad, but now he stopped and looked up. "Mia."

"No." Because it reminded her of the old days, Lulu lighted a cone of vanilla incense. "She'd cry in the dreams, and tell me I had to tend her children."

Mac made a quick notation. There had been a nurse, and the one called Earth had left the children with her before leaping from the cliffs. "Reincarnation?" He scribbled. "A link within the circle?"

"Whenever I had the dream, I just had to move again, just had to leave where I was and move on. Long story short, I ended up in Boston, broke. But I didn't mind being broke back then. Somebody always knew somebody who had a pad you could crash in. One day this girl who called herself Buttercup—Jesus—said how we should all take the ferry over to Three Sisters Island. She liked to think she was a witch, but as I remember she was the daughter of some rich lawyer whose money she was pissing away in college. She could pay the freight to get us all over and back with daddy's allowance money. I went along because, hey, free ride. They made the round-trip. I stayed."

"Why?" Mac asked her.

She didn't answer for a moment. Despite her relationship with Mia, with Ripley and Nell, and the island itself, Lulu didn't talk much about her own brushes with magic.

It always made her feel a little silly.

But Mac was watching her in that quiet way he had. And she was damn fond of him.

"I knew it was my place, as soon as I saw it coming up out of the water. I was high," Lulu continued. "We all were. Buttercup was a moron, but she always had prime weed. I saw the island like it was in crystal, everything so vivid and clear. Maybe it was the pot, but it was the most beautiful thing I'd ever seen. I looked up and saw the house on the cliffs, and I thought—well, shit, there it is. That's where I'm supposed to be. I walked away from Buttercup and the rest as soon as we hit the docks, and never gave them another thought. Wonder what the hell ever happened to her."

"You went to work for Mia's grandmother."

"Not right away. I wasn't looking for gainful employment. Too establishment for me." She took off her glasses to polish the lenses. "I camped out in the woods a while, ate berries or what I'd liberated from people's vegetable gardens. I think I was going through a vegetarian stage," she mused with a little frown of concentration.

It was interesting to look back and see herself—young, careless, smooth.

"Didn't last long. Born a carnivore, die a carnivore. So . . . one day I was hiking and this woman came by in a fancy car. Stopped. She leaned out, looked me up and down. I guess she was on the shy side of sixty, but when you're figuring thirty's the end of it all, that's really old."

She stopped, laughed now as she put her glasses on. "What the hell, I'm having a glass of wine. Want one?"

"No thanks. I've got driving to do."

"You're a real straight arrow, aren't you, Mac?" She headed off to the kitchen, shouting back. "I never was much to look at, and after camping a couple weeks, I'd've been a little ripe. Had long hair then, wore it in braids. What was I thinking? The woman, she was old to me, but she was a looker. Dark red hair all done up, lady suit on like she'd just come from teatime. She had dark, dark eyes, and when they latched on to mine, I swear I heard waves crashing on rock, storms, I *felt* the wind blow over me though the day was hot and still. I heard a baby crying."

Wineglass in hand, Lulu clumped back in, dropped back on the colorful, well-sprung sofa. "She told me to get in, just like that. And I did, just like that. Never thought about it twice. Mrs. Devlin, she had power, just like her granddaughter does. I didn't know what it was then, I just knew *it* was. She took me to the house on the cliffs.

"I loved her." Lulu allowed sentiment to fill her throat along with the wine. "I respected her, and I admired her. She was more family to me than my own blood. They'd never given much of a damn about me, and I'd gotten used to that. But she taught me. Passed on her love of reading, trusted me. Made me work for my keep—goddamn, she expected you to pull weight! I cleaned that big-ass house so many times I could've done it in my sleep."

"You didn't know she was a witch?"

Lulu considered. It wasn't something she had given a great deal of thought to. "It was kind of gradual. I think she saw to that so it'd be a natural thing for me to accept. Maybe it was easier seeing as how I was into all that hippie-metaphysical-nature-is-our-mother business."

"When did you learn about the legend?"

"That was a gradual thing, too. It's part of the Sisters, so you hear this, read that. Working for Mrs. Devlin, I became part of the island before I realized it."

"Then by the time Mia came along, it was natural for you to accept power in her."

"If I had to analyze it, I'd say Mrs. Devlin saw to that, too. She knew the way things would be before they were. When Mia was born, her son and his wife moved into the house. I figured out pretty soon they'd done it so they'd have themselves a couple of live-in sitters. Selfish twits."

She paused, took a deep gulp of wine. "The night they brought her, they went down to the hotel to have dinner, and Mrs. Devlin took me into the nursery. Mia was a beautiful baby—red-headed, bright-eyed. Long arms and legs. Mrs. Devlin, she picked her up out of the crib, cuddled her for a minute, then she held her out to me. Scared me boneless. It wasn't just that I'd never held a baby before, or that this one looked like something made of precious glass. It was that I knew. I knew she was giving her to me, and nothing would ever be the same for me again. You ever want something so bad you could taste it, but the idea of taking that first sip makes your belly jump?"

"Yeah." He set his notebook aside now and just listened. "Yeah, I have."

"It was just like that. We stood there, her holding Mia out, me with my arms crossed over my chest with my heart beating like a hammer inside it. And a storm came up out of nowhere, just like in my dreams. Wind whipping the windows, lightning flashing. It was the first and last time I saw her cry.

" 'Take her,' she said to me. 'She needs love and care, and a firm hand. They won't give it to her, they can't. And when I'm gone, she'll only have you.' I told her I didn't know how to take care of a baby, and she smiled at me, and just kept holding Mia out. Mia started to squirm and fuss, shake her fists, and before I knew it, I was taking her. Mrs. Devlin stepped back. 'She's yours now.' I'll never forget that. 'She's yours now, and you're hers.' And she left me to rock Mia to sleep." Lulu sniffled. "Wine's making me sloppy."

Touched, Mac leaned over, closed a hand over hers. "Me, too."

Sheriff Zachariah Todd emptied the dishwasher—one of the few tasks he was allowed to attempt in his own kitchen. "Okay, let me see if I got this straight. Mia told Sam what happened out on the coast road this morning. Ripley, who didn't know what happened, found Sam up at Mia's house and he told her, Ripley—but she promised she wouldn't tell Mia he'd been there, so *she* told Mia—when Mia was going to tell her—Jesus—about what happened; that she, and that would be Ripley, ran into Sam on the road when he was cleansing the area."

"You're doing great," Nell encouraged as Zack took a breath and she checked on the progress of her lasagna.

"Don't throw me off the track. Then Mac told Sam what Ripley had told Mia while Mia was telling you what happened this morning. Then Ripley told you the rest of it, which you told me. For reasons that escape me."

"Because I love you, Zack."

"Right." He pressed a fingertip dead center of his forehead. "I think I'll just keep my mouth shut altogether. No way to wedge my foot in there that way."

"Never a bad choice." She heard Lucy's sudden and joyful barking. "Someone's here. You go, take the tray on the third shelf. I'm experimenting with canapés for the Rodgers's wedding I'm catering next month. Put them up where Lucy can't get them," she called as he started out, then glanced down at Diego. "Men and dogs," she said, and clucked her tongue. "You have to watch them every minute."

And because she did, Nell took the time to shift all the utensils Zack had put away into their proper slots before she grabbed a bottle of wine and went out to greet her guests.

Mac and Ripley had brought the puppy along, which sent Lucy into spasms of delight and terror, and had a miffed Diego stalking upstairs to sulk.

Mia arrived with a bouquet of freshly clipped daffodils, and helped herself relax by sitting on the floor playing tug-the-rope with Mulder.

"I think of getting a dog now and then." She laughed as Mulder lost his toothy grip on the rope and went tumbling ears over tail. "Then I think about my gardens." She snatched the puppy up, holding him high. "You'd just love digging up all my flowers, wouldn't you?"

"Not to mention chewing on your shoes," Ripley said sourly. "Of course, you've got a hundred pair to spare."

"Shoes are a form of self-expression."

"Shoes are to walk in."

Mia drew the puppy down, rubbed noses. "What does she know?"

That's how Sam saw her when he came to the door, sitting on the floor, laughing while a fat yellow puppy licked her cheeks.

His gut clenched, and his throat snapped shut.

She looked so carelessly happy with her skirts spread out on the rug, her hair tumbling down her back, and her eyes bright with pleasure.

There, in that outrageously beautiful woman, was the shimmer of the girl he'd left behind.

Then Lucy barked, Mulder leaped, and Mia stopped laughing as her gaze snapped to the doorway.

"Lucy!" Zack called to the dog, then grabbed her collar as he opened the screen door for Sam. "No jumping," he ordered as Lucy's muscles bunched for a joyful leap. "Either of you." He said it under his breath. A blind man could have seen that hungry look on Sam's face.

"She's all right." Sam skimmed a hand over Lucy's head and she collapsed onto her back. He passed the wine he'd brought to Zack before crouching down to rub her exposed belly. The puppy gamboled over, wanting his share.

"What are you doing here?" Mia demanded.

Sam lifted his eyebrows at her tone, but

before he could respond, Mac stepped in. "I asked him to come." Mac nearly flinched at Mia's quick, accusing stare. "We're all part of this, and everyone here has something to contribute. We need to cooperate with each other, Mia."

"You're right, of course." The carefree woman was gone. In her place was one with a cool voice and a polished smile. "So rude of me, Sam. I apologize. This has been our little club for some time now, and I wasn't expecting a new member."

"No problem." He picked up the rope Mulder dropped hopefully at his feet.

"Dinner will just be a few more minutes." Smoothly Nell moved into the tense air. "Can I get you a glass of wine, Sam?"

"Love one, thanks. Does your little club have any initiation rite I should know about?"

"Just the little business where we shave all the hair off your head and body." Mia sipped her own wine. "But that can wait until after dinner. I think I'll wash up."

Before she could get to her feet, Sam was on his, a hand held down to her.

Whether it was a test or a peace offering, Mia blocked herself so that when she took his hand it was nothing more than palm meeting palm. "Thanks."

She knew the house as well as she knew her own, but headed up the stairs rather than using the more convenient powder room on the first floor.

More distance, she thought. More solitude.

She slipped inside, shut the door. Leaned back against it. It was ridiculous. Absurd for the man to affect her the way he did. It was all right, or nearly so, when she was prepared, but when she saw him at those odd moments—those moments when too much of her was already open—he just filled her up.

She wanted to blame him for it, but it was foolish, and foolhardy, to keep picking at an old wound. What was done was done.

She stepped to the sink, studied her face in the mirror. She looked tired, a little pale and drawn. Well, it had been a difficult day. And the shell, at least, was simple to mend.

She washed her hands, then ran water in the sink. Bending, she scooped it, cool and fresh, onto her face. In the normal scheme of things, she enjoyed using cosmetics. The pencils and tubes and brushes were amusing, and there was something reassuringly female about using them.

But for now, this was simpler, and certainly quicker.

She dabbed her face dry, weaving the glamour spell. Then she looked critically in the mirror again. Much better, she decided. She looked rested, with the subtle bloom of healthy color in her cheeks. More color, not quite so subtle, slicked her mouth.

Then with a sigh for her own vanity, she traced a fingertip over the curve of her eyelid, as a woman might use eyeshadow and a brush to define them. The contour deepened.

Satisfied, she gave herself another moment to smooth out her emotions. And went back down to join the others.

A close-knit group, Sam thought as he ate Nell Todd's truly amazing lasagna. The body language, the looks, the half-finished thoughts one would complete for another all told him these were five people who'd bonded like glue.

By his time line, Nell had been on the island slightly less than a year, and Mac only since the past winter. Yet they'd been absorbed in a way that made them all very much a single unit.

A common enemy was part of the answer. But he saw more here than what he perceived as a kind of wartime intimacy.

There was something in the way Mia warmed when she spoke to or listened to Mac, the amused affection on her face. It was love he saw there, not the sort that sprang from passion, but something deep and true.

He saw byplay like that all around the table.

Nell scooped up a second helping for Mac before he'd asked for one. Zack tore off a hunk of bread and passed it to Mia while he continued to hold a heated debate with his sister on the pitching depth of the Red Sox. Nell and Mia exchanged looks in an unspoken joke that had them both chuckling.

And all of it, all the ease, made it clear to Sam that building a bridge over his years away would take more than time and proximity.

"I think my father and yours played in the

same foursome for some charity golf tournament," Mac commented. "Just last month, in Palm Springs, or Palm Beach. Or something with a Palm in it."

"Really?" Sam had never been interested in his father's pseudo charity events. And it had been years since he'd had to bow to the pressure of participating in any of them. "I met your parents at various functions in New York."

"Yeah, same circles."

"More or less," Sam agreed. "I don't recall meeting you at any of those various functions."

Mac only grinned. "Well, there you are. So . . . do you play golf?"

Now, Sam smiled. "No. Do you?"

"Mac's pretty much a spaz," Ripley put in. "If he tried to tee off, he'd probably slice his big toe into the woods."

"Sad, but true," Mac agreed.

"Last week he tripped going down the deck steps. Six stitches."

"The dog tripped me," Mac said in his own defense. "And it was only four stitches."

"Which you could've avoided if you'd come to me instead of going to the clinic."

"She rags on me every time I get a bump or a bruise."

"Which is daily. On our honeymoon—"

"We're not getting into that." The flush started creeping up Mac's neck.

"When we were using taking a shower as an excuse to have some hot, steamy sex—"

"Cut it out." Mac spread his hand over Ripley's face and gave it a nudge. "And that towel bar was not properly installed."

"He ripped it right out of the wall in the throes." She batted her lashes at him. "My hero."

"Anyway," Mac said on a long breath. "Seeing as you're in the hotel business, Sam, you might want to make sure your towel bars are secure."

"I'll make a note, particularly if the two of you decide to take a weekend at the Magick Inn."

"Well, if Nell and Zack make a reservation," Ripley continued, "you'd better check the stability of the bathroom sinks. They knocked the one upstairs out of alignment when—"

"Ripley!" Nell hissed it, horrified.

"Do you have to tell her everything?" Zack demanded.

"Not anymore." Ignoring Ripley's laughter, Nell pushed to her feet. "I'll get dessert."

"I had no idea bathrooms had become such erogenous zones," Mia commented as she rose to clear her plate.

"I'll be happy to show you mine," Sam said, and was given a shrug as she strolled into the kitchen.

"She didn't eat. She only pretended to." Sam kept his voice low.

"She's tense," Mac added.

"There's no point in my being here if it closes her off."

"The world doesn't revolve around you." Ripley snagged her glass and drank.

"Rip." Zack's voice was a quiet warning. "Let's just see how it goes from here."

With a nod, Sam picked up his own plate. "She trusts you," he said to Mac.

"Yes, she does."

"Maybe that balances things out."

Sam had nerves of his own when they settled back in the living room. What he was had never been an issue for him. It simply was. But neither was his gift something he discussed. He joined no coven. And though only four out of the six there were hereditary witches, it was very much a kind of coven.

"We all know the legend," Mac began.

The historian, Sam thought. The scientist. The detail man with the facile mind.

"During the Salem witch trials, the three who were known as Fire, Earth, and Air conjured what became Three Sisters Island as a haven against persecution."

"While innocents were hunted and murdered," Ripley added.

The soldier. Sam idly stroked the cat, who had deigned to join him on the sofa. A woman with grit. The earth.

"They couldn't have stopped it, or if they'd tried," Zack said, "others might have died."

And here, Sam decided, was reason and authority.

"Change one angle of destiny, change all." Mac nodded, continued. "The one called Air fell in love, married a merchant who took her back to the mainland. Bore his children, kept his home. But he could never accept what she was. He abused her, and ultimately killed her."

"She blamed herself, I think, for not being

what he wanted. For not staying true to herself, and choosing poorly."

Nell, the nurturer, Sam thought when she spoke. The cat stretched under his hand, as if agreeing. She was the air.

"She saved her children, sent them back to her sisters. But the circle was diminished. Weakened. And the horror of it, the fury of it," Mac went on, "festered in the one known as Earth until she surrendered to the anger, the rage, and the need for revenge."

"She was wrong," Ripley said now. "I understand what she felt, why she felt it, but she was wrong. And she paid. Using her power to kill the one who'd killed her sister destroyed her, and came back threefold. She lost her husband, a man she loved; was never able to see her children again; and shattered what was left of the circle."

"There was one left." Mia's voice was clear, her gaze level. "One left to hold it."

Intellect, pride, and passion. Was it any wonder that she stirred him? Sam thought. She was the fire.

"Despair can crush even the strongest." Nell laid a hand on Mia's. "But even alone, even heartbroken, she wove a web of protection. Three hundred years strong."

"She made certain her children were taken care of." Mac thought of Lulu. "Which brings us to now." He frowned into his coffee. "A still unbroken circle."

"You're worried I'll fail when my time comes. Nell faced her demons, and Ripley hers." In what seemed an idle gesture, Mia stroked Mulder with the side of her foot. "Of the three of us, my knowledge and practice of the Craft is the most extensive."

"Agreed. But—"

She lifted a brow at Mac. "But?"

"I wonder if, on the other side of the scale, what you'll have to deal with is more, well, insidious. Nell had Evan Remington, a man."

"He was a piece of shit," Ripley corrected.

"Be that as it may, he was human. She had to find the courage to face him, to defeat him and embrace her gift. I'm not saying any of that was a walk on the beach, but it was pretty tangible. If you're following me."

"A man with a knife." Sam spoke for the first time since Mac had begun, and drew everyone's attention. "A sociopath, psychopath, whatever the term might be for that kind of evil, in the woods, in the dark of the moon. No, not a walk on the beach. It took great courage, deep faith, and a formidable power to do what Nell did. But it was an evil whose face she knew."

"Exactly." Mac beamed as if Sam were a prized student. "In Ripley's case—"

"In Ripley's case," Ripley repeated, "I had to accept a power I'd rejected, and walk the line when part of me wanted to cross it."

"Emotional turmoil," Sam agreed. "It can affect the tone of power in the same way it can affect the tone of your voice, the tone of your actions. The gift doesn't protect us from flaws, or mistakes. That kind of turmoil was tailored toward you, and Nell's was turned toward her as a potent weapon. With—"

He broke off, glanced at Mac.

"No, keep going." Mac waved a hand. "It's good to hear it from someone else's point of view."

"All right. The force that was unleashed centuries ago used Remington as a conduit and fed itself into the reporter who followed Nell's cross-country route to the Sisters."

"You've kept up," Mia said quietly.

"Yeah. I've kept up. Holding the line, power against power, without crossing that line isn't a simple matter. It requires conviction, compassion, strength. Even so, in the end Ripley, like Nell, faced a man. Whatever was inside him, he was flesh and blood."

"It looks like Sam and I have circled around to the same theory."

"Then why the hell don't you punch through to the point of it and stop circling?" Ripley complained.

"Okay." Since Sam gestured the go-ahead, Mac took over. "What came at Mia today wasn't flesh and blood, not a living thing, but a manifestation. That tells me a couple of things. Maybe, just maybe, because the circle's intact, because twice now it's been defeated, its power's diminished. It can't possess, but can only deceive."

"Or it hordes its strength. Waiting for its time, and its place."

"Yes." Mac nodded at Sam. "Waiting for the right circumstance. There isn't that much time—when you measure by three centuries—left on either side. It's going to keep pushing, trying to weaken the circle, and Mia most specifically. Undermining the bedrock of your power. It'll use your fears, doubts, any weaknesses that trickle through the chinks. Tailored to you," he added with a nod to Sam. "That's just exactly right. It'll try to prey on you as it did on her three centuries ago. Through her loneliness and loss, her despair at the thought of living without the people she loved, and needed most."

"I'm aware of that," Mia acknowledged. "But I'm not lonely, and I've lost nothing. My circle holds."

"Yes, but . . . I don't believe the circle can be considered complete, and whole, until your step is taken." Since this was tricky ground, Mac took his time. "Until then, there's a vulnerability, and that's where the pressure will be the greatest. It only needed to break Nell, and it failed. To seduce Ripley, and it failed. With you . . ."

"It needs to cause my death," Mia finished calmly. "Yes, I know. I've always known."

When she started to leave, Nell held on to her.

"Don't worry so, little sister." Mia pressed her cheek to Nell's hair. "I know how to protect myself."

"I know. I just wish you'd stay. I know how stupid that sounds, but I wish you'd stay with one of us until this is really over."

"I need my cliffs. I'll be fine, I promise." She gave Nell one last squeeze. "Blessed be."

She'd lingered longer than the others, hoping to avoid any more conversation. But when she stepped outside, she saw Sam leaning against her car.

"I walked over. How about a lift back?"

"It's a pleasant night for a short walk."

"Give me a lift, Mia." He took her wrist as she started to move past him. "I want to talk to you, for a minute anyway. Alone."

"I suppose I owe you a favor."

"Do you?"

She circled the car, slipped in behind the wheel. She waited until she'd started the car. "For cleaning up my mess on the coast road this morning," she said as she eased into a U-turn. "Ripley told me she ran into you. Thank you."

"You're welcome."

"Well, that didn't hurt too much. Now, what did you want to talk to me about?"

"I wondered about you and Mac. There's something there."

"Really?" Deliberately she took her attention away from the road long enough to bat her lashes. "Do you think I'm trying to tempt my sister's husband into a wild, illicit affair?"

"If you were, he'd already be there."

She laughed. "What a lovely compliment, even if you're wrong. He's sweetly, madly in love with his wife. But you're right about one thing, there is something between us. You've always been good at picking up atmosphere and emotion."

"What is it?"

"We're cousins."

"Cousins?"

"It happens that the granddaughter of the first sister married a MacAllister—Mac's mother's side of the family."

"Ah." Sam did his best to stretch out his legs in the little car. "So he's of the blood. That explains a number of things. I felt a connection the minute I met him, but couldn't pin him down. Just as I felt one for Nell, even when she wanted to drop me into a dark pit and leave me there to rot. I like your friends."

"Well, I'm so relieved."

"Don't snipe at me, Mia. I meant it."

Because she knew it was true, she sighed. "I'm tired. It always make me cross."

"They're worried about you. How you'll handle things."

"I know. I'm sorry about it."

"I'm not worried." He paused when she pulled up in front of the cottage. "I've never known anyone, witch or woman, more vital than you. You won't give in."

"No, I won't. But I won't say I don't appreciate the confidence, particularly after a long, difficult day. Good night, Sam."

"Come inside."

"No."

"Come inside, Mia." He slipped a hand through her hair to rub the back of her neck. "And be with me."

"I'd like to be with someone tonight," she continued, "to be comforted and soothed. To be touched and taken. So I won't."

"Why?"

"Because it wouldn't make me happy. Good night, Sam."

He could have pressed, they both knew it. But some of her glamour had slipped, and he saw fatigue breaking through to haunt her face. "Good night."

He climbed out, watched her drive away. And kept her in his mind until he knew she was safely inside the house on the cliffs.

# Eight

It was all a matter of strategy. In business, Sam thought. In relationships. And sometimes in just surviving the day. He checked the progress on the rehab and was pleased that the work was proceeding on schedule.

He knew something about building and design. There had been a time, years before, when he'd considered breaking with Logan Enterprises and building his own hotel. He'd taken some extra college courses in architecture and design and had even spent a summer working as a laborer on a construction crew.

That had given him some practical knowledge, an elementary skill, and a healthy respect for manual labor.

But his plans to build his own had faded as every design he attempted or imagined turned into a mirror image of the Magick Inn.

Why replicate what already was?

Once he'd realized he wanted the hotel, the rest was a matter of patience, canniness, and careful strategy. It had been important not to let his father know that the Magick Inn was the single family asset he coveted.

It would have come to Sam through inheritance in any case, but had Thaddeus Logan realized it had become a kind of Holy Grail to his son, he would have felt obliged to nudge it out of reach, thereby pressuring his son and heir to take more personal interest in other areas of the family empire.

The carrot would have dangled at the end of a very long, very thorny stick during his father's lifetime. It was, Sam knew, how his father operated. He was not a man who rewarded; he was one who withheld. A philosophy that garnered results and never concerned itself with affection.

Despite that, Sam hadn't been willing to perch like a vulture on a tree branch, waiting for his own father to die before he claimed what he wanted.

For nearly six years, he had held his desire for the hotel close to the vest. He'd worked, he'd learned, and whenever he'd managed to carve out room, he had implemented some of his own ideas, establishing a few profitable offshoots to Logan Enterprises.

In the end it had come down to deflecting his father's attention, waiting him out, then broaching the deal at the right moment and meeting the cost.

Historically, the Logans were staunch believers in the adage that nothing comes free—unless, Sam thought, it was their own trust funds. So he had paid fair market value for his father's share of the hotel.

Sam didn't count the cost, not when he had what he wanted.

He was going to try not to count the cost with Mia.

He intended to be patient—within reason. He would, of course, be canny. But he had yet, he was forced to admit, to outline a clear-cut strategy.

His direct approach—Honey, I'm home!— hadn't worked. And why he'd been brainless enough to think it would was currently beyond him. Let's kiss and make up hadn't done much better. She wasn't freezing him out at every opportunity, but neither was she softening.

He wanted her safe. He wanted his island secure. And he wanted her back.

The idea that he might not be able to have all three didn't sit well with him. But the fact was that the responsibility of cleaning up a disaster three hundred years in the making was in their laps. And it couldn't be ignored.

Mac hadn't mentioned his theory in the meeting at the Todds' the other night. But Sam imagined he had discussed it—or would—with Mia in private. In the end, rejecting him might be her answer. Might be *the* answer.

But going down without a fight went against nature.

So . . . strategy, he thought, and scanned the parlor area of the currently empty suite where the walls had been newly papered in pale green moiré silk and the woodwork sanded down to its natural oak and varnished golden.

Thinking, he wandered through the bedroom and to a doorway where a second bedroom had been sacrificed to expand the bath and the master closet space. The fixtures had yet to be installed, but he'd selected the generous jet tub himself, the ripple glass on the multi-head shower unit, the curving ribbon of counters.

He'd used warm colors, a lot of polished granite and copper. Luxurious amenities in old-fashioned apothecary jars.

A blend of tradition, comfort, and efficiency.

Just the sort of thing, he mused, that appealed to Mia. Business, steady profit, and exquisite service.

He smiled to himself as he took his cell phone out of his pocket. Then just as quickly replaced it. A personal call wasn't the way to conduct some business discussions.

He headed down to his office to tell his assistant to get Ms. Devlin on the phone.

He puzzled her. The boy she'd thought she knew so well had become a man full of unexpected turns and missing pieces. A business dinner? Mia mused when she hung up the phone. At her convenience. She frowned at the receiver she'd just replaced. And he'd sounded as if he meant it. Very cool, very professional.

A business meeting, over dinner at the hotel, to discuss a proposal he hoped would be of benefit to both of their establishments.

Just what did the man have up his sleeve?

Sheer curiosity had pushed her to agree to the meeting, though she was wily enough not to be available the same night. She graciously agreed to rearrange her schedule to fit him in the following evening.

It wouldn't hurt to see if there was anything she should be ready for. She took a ball of crystal from her shelf and set it at the center of her desk.

With her hands cupped around it, she focused her mind, gathered her power. The glass began to warm. Mists swam inside it, shimmering with a light that seemed to come from deep within the globe.

Visions swirled into the mists, and into her eyes.

She saw herself as she had been, young—so young—lying naked in the cave, wrapped only in Sam's arms.

"Not yesterday," she whispered. "But tomorrow. Clear the future from the past so I can see what may be."

Her garden, lush with summer, under a bright white moon. As she looked, the air in her office was perfumed with the vanilla scent of heliotrope, the spice of dianthus. She wore white, a long flow of it, to echo the moon.

He stood with her in that ocean of flowers and held out a hand. In his palm he held a star, a slice of colored light that beat like a pulse.

He was smiling when he tossed it high, when a shower of light and color exploded over their heads. As it streamed down, she felt the thrill, the utter joy that the woman inside that ball of glass felt.

It swelled inside her own heart, like a song.

And in a flash, she was alone on the cliffs while a storm screamed. Lightning struck around her, burning arrows of it. Her island was enveloped by a fetid fog. The chill of it reached out to where she stood in her quiet office and iced her bones.

Out of the dark, the black wolf leaped. His jaws were still snapping at her throat as they fell toward the raging sea.

"Enough." She passed a hand over the globe, and it was only a pretty glass ball.

She replaced it, and sat. Her hands were steady, her breathing even. She had always known that looking into what might come could mean seeing her own death. Or worse, the death of a loved one.

It was the price that power demanded. The Craft didn't ask for blood, but still it squeezed the heart to a throbbing bruise at times.

So, she thought, which would it be for her? Love or death? Or, by taking the first, would she ensure the second?

She would see. She'd learned much in thirty years as a witch, Mia thought as she turned back to her computer, back to the work of the day. And one thing she knew. You did what you could to protect, to respect, taking the joys and the sorrows. Then, in the end, you accepted your destiny.

"I thought you said it wasn't a date."

Mia secured the back of her earring. "It's not a date. It's a business dinner."

Lulu sniffed. Loudly. "If it's a business dinner what're you doing wearing that dress?"

Mia picked up her second earring, let it dangle in her fingers a moment. "Because I like this dress."

She'd known it was a mistake to bring the change of clothes to work rather than going home. But this saved time, and energy. Besides there was nothing wrong with the little, very little, black dress.

"Woman puts on a dress like that because she wants a man to think about what's under it."

Mia merely fluttered her lashes. "Do tell."

"And don't you get smart with me. I can still give you a good whap when you need one."

"Lu, I'm not ten anymore."

"If you ask me, you're showing less sense than you had when you were."

A long-suffering sigh wouldn't work. Pointing out that she *hadn't* asked would only lead to an argument. Since it was impossible to ignore the scowling woman jammed in the bathroom with her, Mia tried another angle.

She turned. "I've finished my homework and cleaned my room. Please can I go out and play?"

Lulu's lips twitched, but she managed to

get them back into a thin, flat line quickly enough. "Never had to nag you to clean your room. I used to worry because you were too damn neat for a kid."

"You don't have to nag me about this either, because I know how to handle Sam Logan."

"You figure squeezing yourself into that dress and showing half your boobs is handling him?"

Mia glanced down. Her boobs, in her opinion, were nicely, even elegantly, displayed. As were her legs, clear up to midthigh. "Oh, yes, indeed."

"Are you wearing underwear?"

"Oh, for God's sake." Mia yanked the black jacket off the padded hanger.

"I asked you a question."

Searching for patience, Mia put on the jacket. Its hem grazed an inch above the bottom of the skirt, turning the sexy little dress into a sexy little suit. "I find that an odd question coming from a former flower child. You probably didn't even own any underwear from 1963 to 1972."

"Did so. I had a very pretty pair of tie-dyed panties for special occasions."

Undone, Mia leaned back on the seat and

chuckled. "Oh, Lu. What an image that creates in my feverish little brain. Just what sort of special occasion called for tie-dyed panties?"

"Don't change the subject, and answer the question."

"Well, I don't own anything quite that festive, but I'm wearing underwear—after a fashion. So if I'm in an accident, I'm safe."

"I'm not worried about an accident. I'm worried about on purpose."

Straightening, Mia leaned down, cupped Lulu's homely face in her hands. She hadn't had to search for patience after all, she realized. She'd only had to remember love.

"You don't have to worry at all. I promise."

"My job is to worry," Lulu muttered.

"Then take a break. I'm going to have a lovely dinner, find out just what business it is Sam's cooking up, and enjoy the side benefit of driving him crazy."

"You've still got a thing for him."

"I never had a thing for him. I loved him."

Lulu's shoulders drooped. "Oh, honey." She lifted a hand, fussed with Mia's hair. "I wish he'd stayed in goddamn New York City."

"Well, he didn't. I don't know if what I'm

feeling now is just left over from what I felt then, or if it's because of now, or all the years between. Shouldn't I find out?"

"Being you, you have to. But I wish you'd kick his ass first."

Mia turned, slipped on a hammered-gold necklace that dripped a slim column of pearls between her breasts. "If this dress doesn't kick his ass, I don't know what will."

Lulu curled her lip, angled her head. "Maybe you're not so stupid."

"I learned from the best." Mia colored her lips in murderous red, shook back her wild cloud of hair, turned. "So, how do I look?"

"Like a man-eater."

"Perfect."

Mia thought she timed it perfectly as well. At precisely seven, she strolled into the lobby of the Magick Inn. The young desk clerk glanced over, goggled, then dropped the sheaf of papers in his hand. Pleased, she shot him a killer smile, then breezed into Sorcery, the hotel's main dining room.

There was a moment of surprise as she scanned the room and saw the changes.

Sam had been busy, she realized, and felt an unwilling tug of pride.

The standard white tablecloths had been replaced by rich midnight-blue ones, the china on them a moon-bright contrast. The old clear glass vases had been removed, and now brass and copper pots rioting with white lilies formed ribbons of glint and fragrance. The crystal glassware had a heavy, almost medieval look.

Each table was graced with a small copper cauldron. Candlelight flickered through cutouts in the shapes of stars and crescent moons.

For the first time in her memory, the room reflected, and honored, its name. Impressed, approving, she stepped in. And experienced a fast, hard jolt.

There on the wall was a life-size painting of three women. The three sisters, backed by the forest and the night sky, looked down at her from a frame of ornate antique gold. They were robed in white, and the folds of those robes, the tendrils of their hair, seemed to move in an unseen wind.

She saw Nell's blue eyes, Ripley's green ones. And her own face.

"Like it?" Sam said from behind her.

She swallowed so that her voice would be clear. "It's stunning."

"I had it commissioned nearly a year ago. It just arrived today."

"It's beautiful work. The models . . ."

"There were no models. The artist worked from my descriptions. From my dreams."

"I see." She turned to face him. "He or she is very talented."

"She. A Wiccan artist living in SoHo. I think she captured . . ." He trailed off as he shifted his gaze from the portrait to Mia. Every thought in his head scattered in pure, primal lust. "You look amazing."

"Thank you. I like, very much, what you've done with the restaurant."

"It's a start." He started to take her arm, then realized his palms had gone damp. "I'm having new lighting designed. Something in brass, more lanternlike. And I want—well, why don't we sit before I bore you with all my plans."

"On the contrary." But she let him guide her to an intimate corner booth where, she noted, a bottle of champagne was already chilling.

She slid in, then deliberately slipped out

of her jacket. She watched his eyes blur, but to his credit, his gaze stayed primarily on her face. "Warm in here," she said, then nodded to the waiter when he poured her champagne. "What are we drinking to?"

Sam sat, picked up his own glass. "One question before we get to that. Are you trying to kill me?"

"No. Just kick your ass."

"Done. I don't think a woman's made my hands sweat since, well, since you. Now if I can just get some of the blood back into my head." When she laughed, he tapped his glass to hers. "To mutual business."

"Do we have any?"

"That's what this is about. First, regarding dinner. I pre-ordered. I think I remember your taste. If that doesn't suit you, I'll get you a menu."

Smooth, she thought. Very smooth. The man had learned how and when to polish over all those dangerous edges. When it suited him.

"I don't mind the occasional surprise." She sat back, let her gaze drift around the room. "Business is good."

"It is. And I intend for it to get better. The

first-floor renovations should be complete in another two weeks. The new presidential suite rocks."

"So I hear. Your contractor is my contractor."

"So *I* hear. When do you plan to start your expansion?"

"Soon." She glanced at the variety of appetizers placed on the table by silent waiters. She sampled a bit of lobster paté.

"I hope to keep the inconvenience to my customers at a minimum. Still, during the main part of the work, I imagine you'll pick up some of my lunch crowd." She paused for a beat. "Temporarily."

"Improvements to your business only benefit mine, and vice versa."

"I can agree to that."

"Why not exploit it? I want to stock some local-interest books, maybe some current bestsellers, in the luxury suites. A discreet card or bookmark could advertise your store."

"And?" She waited for the catch.

"You get a lot of day-trippers. Again, using the local-interest angle, what if they bought a particular book you've selected— a book on the island's history, whatever. A purchase of that book gives them a chance to win a free weekend's stay at the hotel. They fill out a form with their name and address, we pull a ticket once a month during the season, and somebody gets lucky."

"And we have all those names on our mailing list."

He topped off their champagne. "I knew you'd follow me. You sell books, I get a few more tourists into the hotel, and we both add to our potential customer base. Vacations," he continued, selecting a delicate crab puff. "Hotels, beach reading. Then there's business travel. Same deal. I'm working on pulling in more conventions. I get them in and part of the welcome package is a discount coupon for Café Book, which gets them into your place across the street."

"Which, if they fill out the prize form, gets them back into your place on a weekend vacation."

"Bull's-eye."

She considered as fresh field-greens salads were served. "The cost to each of us is negligible. Some paperwork. It's simple enough. In fact, much too simple to warrant a business dinner to discuss it."

"There's more. I've noticed you don't, as a rule, do author events."

"One or two a year, local interest again." She shrugged her shoulders. "Sisters and Café Book are well off the beaten path for book tours and standard book signings. Publishers don't send authors to remote islands off the New England coast, and most authors aren't going to pay to come here and work."

"We can change that."

He had her interest now. She accepted the bread he'd buttered for her, unaware that he'd been nudging food on her since she'd sat down. "Can we?"

"I made a number of contacts in New York. I've still got some buttons to push, but I'm working on convincing a few key people that sending a touring author to Three Sisters would be well worth the time and money. Particularly since the Magick Inn will offer a generous corporate rate and first-class accommodations. Then there's the convenience of having a classy independent bookstore right across the street. What you have to do is put together a proposal detailing just how Café Book would host an author, how you'd pull in the warm bodies and have books moving out the door. We pull it off once, just once, and others will be hopping on the ferry."

She felt the quick twist of excitement at the idea, but weighed it from all angles. "Filling a room a few times a year at a corporate rate will hardly make a difference to you."

"Maybe I'm just trying to help my neighbor. So to speak."

"Then you should know your neighbor isn't gullible or naive."

"No, she's just the most beautiful woman I've ever known."

"Thank you. Now. What's the point in these ideas for the hotel?"

"Okay, so much for charm." He leaned toward her. "There are a lot of publishers with a lot of authors with a lot of books to hype. That's one. Two, publishers have sales conferences. If I snag the interest of one publisher because of a successful author event, it's going to add to the weight I'm putting on to cop a major conference. I get that, I'm going to get in a lot of repeat business." He lifted his water glass. "So will you. If you can handle an author event."

"I know how to host a signing." She ate

without thinking because her mind was already on the details. "If you can push those buttons for, say, July or August, even into September the first time around, I'll get plenty of warm bodies. Give me a novel, a mystery, a romance, a thriller, and we'll sell a hundred minimum on the event day, and half that many during the follow-up week."

"Write the proposal."

"You'll have it tomorrow, by the close of the workday."

"Good." He ate some salad. "How would you like John Grisham?"

Enjoying herself, enjoying him, she picked up her glass again. "Don't toy with me, smart guy. He doesn't tour, his books come out in February, not the summer. And even you aren't that good."

"Okay, just testing. How about Caroline Trump?"

Mia's lips pursed. "She's very good. I've read her first three books. Solid romantic thrillers. Her publisher's been building her well, and they're moving her into hardcover this summer. A July release," she considered, studying Sam's face. "Can you get me Caroline Trump?"

"Get me the proposal."

She sat back again. "I misjudged you. I imagined you used business as an excuse to get me in here. I figured you'd have some little scheme to spring off a seduction attempt, but nothing really viable."

"If I hadn't had something viable, I'd have settled for a scheme to get you here." He brushed his fingers over the back of her hand. "Even if it only meant I could look at you for an hour."

"And I thought," she continued, "that sometime during the conversation you'd remind me that you had a number of rooms upstairs, and why didn't we make use of one."

"I thought about it." He remembered what she'd said to him as they'd sat in her car outside of the yellow cottage. "But it wouldn't make you happy."

Her breath caught for an instant. "Oh, I wish I knew if that was sincere, or just fucking clever."

"Mia—"

"No. I don't know what's between us. I can't see it, and I've tried to. Why is it that, even knowing better, we can fool ourselves into believing we'd be all right if we just knew what happens next?"

"I don't know. I can't see it either." When she looked at him, he nearly sighed. "I was never as good as you at clearing away the now to see the what-ifs, but I had to try."

She looked to the portrait of the sisters. "The only thing set in stone is yesterday. I can promise you I have no intention of letting what they began be destroyed. This is my home. Everything that matters to me is on this island. I'm more than I was when you left, less than I will be when I'm done. That, I do know."

"Do you think being with me diminishes that?"

"If I did, I wouldn't be sitting here now." Her lips curved as their entrées were served. "I was going to sleep with you."

"Christ." He pounded a fist on his heart. "Medic."

Her laugh was low and intimate. "I imagine, before we're done, I will. But since we're being so friendly, I'll tell you frankly, I want you to suffer first."

"Believe me," he said with feeling, and reached for his water glass. "Let's go back to business before I whimper and lose the respect of my restaurant staff."

"All right, tell me about your other plans for the hotel."

"I want it to matter. I want people who stay here to take away an experience. I spent six months in Europe a few years ago, touring and studying and dissecting the smaller hotels. It's about service first, but overall, it's about the details. Color schemes, the thread count on the sheets. Can you reach the phone without getting out of bed? Can I get a damn sandwich at two in the morning, or get this spot cleaned off my tie before my afternoon meeting?"

"How thick are the towels," Mia commented. "How firm is the mattress."

"And so on. In-room faxes and Internet access for the business traveler. Complimentary champagne and roses for the honeymooners. A staff that clues in and greets guests by name. And fresh flowers, fresh linens, fresh fruit. I'm going to hire a *maître d'etage* to butler the luxury suites."

"Well, well."

"And every guest, on arrival, will have an amenity delivered. From a fruit plate and sparkling water to champagne and caviar, depending on the price level of the room.

Every room will be rehabbed before we're done, and every one will be personalized and unique. I'm naming them, so guests will stay in the Rose Room or the Trinity Suite, and so forth."

"That's a nice touch," she told him. "More personal."

"Exactly. We already have a data bank, but we'll put it to better use for repeat guests. That way we can do our best to put them back in a favorite room. We'll bump up the level of their amenities with recurring visits, maintain a file on their preferences. And in the health club . . ." He trailed off. "What?"

"Nothing." But she couldn't help smiling at him. "Go on."

"No." He laughed a little. "I get caught up."

"You know what you want, and how you intend to go about it. It's very attractive."

"It took me a long time to get there. You always knew."

"Maybe I did. But wants and intentions change."

"And sometimes they circle back around."

He laid his hand on hers, and then she

gently slid hers free. "And sometimes they just change."

He went back to work after she'd left the restaurant. But he couldn't concentrate. He went home, but he couldn't settle.

Being with her was both torture and pleasure. Watching the expressions cross her face when she became interested enough not to close herself off from him, pure fascination.

Wanting her was like a drug in his bloodstream.

In the end, he changed and walked into the dark woods. He went unerringly to the circle where he could feel the shimmer of her magic rise up and merge with Nell's, with Ripley's.

Preparing himself, he stepped into its center, and let their power, and his own, wash over him like water.

"What is mine, I add to yours. With power shared, the link endures." The light grew, spreading around the ring as strong as the sun. "To win your heart, I'll face the fire, and all that the fates conspire. By earth and air, by fire and water, I will stand by the sisters' daughter. Yet I wait for her to come to me, that we might make our destiny."

He breathed deep, spread his arms. "Tonight while the moonlight streams, she is safe within her dreams. Here to me I call out of the night that which feeds on pain and blight. Know I join the sisters three and dare to show yourself to me."

The earth trembled and the wind whipped. But the fire that ringed the circle ran straight and true toward the night sky.

And outside the circle, a dark mist fed along the ground, and coalesced into a wolf with a pentagram-shaped scar on its snout.

So, Sam thought, let's understand each other.

"To him who seeks her life to take, within this ring this vow I make. By all the power that lives in me, from your hand she will be free. I will crush you into dust by all means fair or foul or just."

Sam watched while the wolf paced around the circle, snarling.

"Do you think I fear you? You're nothing but smoke and stink."

Sam waved a hand, and the light around the circle lowered. In challenge, he stepped clear of the protection. "Power to power," he murmured while the air outside the circle swirled filthy and foul.

Sam watched the wolf gather, the ripple and bunch of muscle. It leaped for his throat. The weight of it was a shock, as was the quick, sharp pain in his shoulder where claws dug.

Using both muscle and magic, he flung the wolf aside, then yanked the ritual knife out of his belt. "Let's finish it," he said between his teeth.

This time when the wolf charged, he pivoted and raked the knife over its side.

There was a sound, more scream than howl. Black blood dripped onto the ground, sizzling into it like hot oil. And wolf and mist vanished.

Sam studied the fresh scar on the earth, then the blackened tip of his blade. Absently, he ran a hand over his shoulder where his shirt and flesh had been ripped.

So, they'd both bled. But only one had screamed and fled. "Round one goes to me," he murmured, then prepared to cleanse the ground.

# Nine

By ten the next morning, Mia was already polishing up her proposal for an author event. She'd worked off considerable sexual frustration the night before by diving straight into the project and sticking with it until after midnight.

Then she'd sprinkled ginger and marigold over the rough draft for success in business ventures. With rosemary under her pillow to aid in a restful sleep, she'd tuned out the nagging need.

She had always been good at channeling her energies, at focusing them on the task that needed attention. After her initial mourning period for Sam, that strength of will had gotten her through college, into business. Into life.

It had, for years, kept her moving forward with matters both practical and pleasurable when she was fully aware that the web of protection around her home was thinning.

Yet despite that will she'd dreamed. Of Sam, and of being with him then. Of being with him now. The physical ache of it had her tossing until she was tangled in the sheets.

She dreamed of the marked wolf, stalking through the woods. Howling from its perch on her cliffs. And once she'd heard it scream, in pain and rage. And in sleep, she called Sam's name like a chant.

Still, she had slept, and she woke to a brilliant sunrise that promised a perfect day.

She tended her flowers first while the sky shimmered with the reds and golds of dawn. She paid her respects to the elements that gave her the beauty of her gardens and the gift of her power.

She brewed a cup of mint tea, for money and luck, and drank it while standing on her cliffs with the sea raging against the rocks below.

She felt closest to her ancestor there, and could always sense the iron core of strength as well as the bitter, rending loneliness.

Sometimes, when she'd been very young, she'd stood here looking out to sea and hoping to see the sleek head of a silkie bobbing in the waves. Once, she'd believed in happily-ever-after and had woven the tale in her head of how the one who was called Fire's lover had come back for her and how their spirits had found each other. Loved each other. Ever and always.

She no longer believed that, and was sorry for it. But she'd learned, and learned well, that there were some losses that sliced you to bits, shattered the spirit into dust. And still you went on, you remade yourself, mended your spirit. You lived. If not happily ever after, then contentedly enough.

It had been on those cliffs that she had sworn an oath to protect what had been entrusted to her. She had been eight, full of pride in what she was. And every year since, on the nights of the summer and winter solstices, she stood on those cliffs and renewed that vow.

But this morning, Mia stood on the cliffs and simply gave thanks for the beauty of the day, then went in to dress for work.

She didn't shudder when she drove the curves of the cliff road. But she watched.

At her desk, she read over her proposal, searching for mistakes, any detail she might have overlooked. Her brow furrowed at the knock on her door. Though she ignored it, deliberately, Ripley strode in.

"I'm busy. Come back later."

"Something's up." Never one to stand on ceremony, or to be put off by a less than warm welcome, Ripley came in, dropped into a chair.

That annoyed Mia enough to have her looking up. She saw Nell in the doorway.

"Nell. Isn't it your day off?"

"Do you think I'd've dragged her in here on her day off," Ripley said before Nell could answer, "if it wasn't important?"

"All right." With sincere regret, Mia set her work aside. "Come in, close the door. Did you have a vision?"

Ripley grimaced. "I try not to, and no, this has nothing to do with woo-woo stuff. Not directly, anyway. I heard Mac talking on the phone this morning, trying *not* to let me hear him talking on the phone."

"Ripley, I really can't meddle in your domestic disputes during working hours."

"He was talking to Sam. Well, that woke you up," she commented.

"It's hardly surprising that they'd have a conversation." Mia picked up her proposal, frowned at the bullet points, then gave up and set it down again. "All right. What were they talking about?"

"I don't know exactly, but something. Mac was really interested. He even walked outside with the phone, casual-like. But I know it was because he didn't want me to hear him."

"How do you know it was Sam?"

"Because I heard him say, 'I'll come by the cottage this morning.' "

"Well, why . . . can't you just get to the point?"

"I'm getting to it. So he scoots me out to work, trying not to make it obvious he's rail-roading me along. Kiss, kiss, pat, pat. Shove, shove. But I go, because I'm thinking *I'll* just run by the cottage myself once I'm on patrol. But first I check in at the station house, and Zack's on the phone. And he stops talking in the middle of a sentence when I walk in, then says hello to me, using my name really definitely."

Her scowl deepened at the memory. "So I know he's talking to either Mac or Sam. *Then* he starts giving me all this grunt work to do, crap jobs that'll keep me tied to the station house for two or three hours. Says he's got to do stuff. I wait until I'm sure he's gone, then I drive by the cottage and what do you think I see?"

"I hope," Mia said, "you're about to tell me and put an end to this play-by-play."

"The patrol car and Mac's Rover," Ripley announced. "I grabbed Nell, and now I'm grabbing you, because I'm telling you, they're not playing poker or watching dirty movies in there."

"No, they're putting something together without us," Mia agreed. "Too manly for the little women."

"If they are," Nell said, "Zack's going to be very sorry."

"Let's just go find out, shall we?" Mia yanked her car keys out of her desk. "I'll tell Lulu I've got to go out, and I'll be right behind you."

Mac hunkered down on the ground, ran his portable scanner. "Positive energy all the way," he muttered. "Any negativity has been thoroughly cleansed. Next time call me first. I could really use a sample."

"It was a little late for science experiments," Sam told him.

"Never too late for science. Can you sketch the manifestation?"

"I can't sketch a stick figure. It was the same image Mia described. The black wolf, massive size, with the mark of the pentagram."

"It was smart to brand him when they had him down on the beach last winter." Mac sat back on his haunches. "Makes ID simple—and it's diminished his power."

Sam rolled his shoulders. "Sure as hell wasn't any pussycat last night."

"He sucked the extra punch out of something, probably you. Bet you were pissed, huh?"

"The fucker tried to drive Mia off a cliff. What do you think?"

"I think the emotional turmoil we discussed the other night is a primary element of the equation. If you'd—"

"I think," Zack interrupted, "Sam should get that shoulder looked at. Then we should stop jerking off with theories and go after this bastard. If it can hurt Sam, it can hurt somebody else. I'm not having it run loose on my island."

"You're not going to be able to track it

down and shoot it like a rabid dog," Mac told him.

"I can sure as hell try."

"It won't go after anyone who's not connected." Sam frowned at the unscarred ground. He'd spent most of the night thinking it through. "Fact is, I don't think it can."

"No, exactly." Mac straightened. "This entity needs to feed off the power and the emotions of those of us who are tied to the original circle."

"A lot of islanders have ties to the original circle, however diluted," Zack pointed out.

"Yes, but it doesn't want them. Or need them."

"He's right," Sam told Zack. "It has only one focus, one purpose now, and it can't waste time or energy by scattering it. Its magic is limited, but it's canny. It fed on Ripley's emotions before. This time it fed on mine. It won't happen again."

"Oh, yeah, you've always been a real even-tempered sort," Zack muttered. "You wanted it to go for you."

"It worked," Sam pointed out. "The thing is, I didn't hurt it that bad. It should've come at me again. Another charge and I could've gotten it into the circle. I could've held it there."

"It's not for you," Mac said simply.

"Fuck that. I'm not standing back while it waits for a chance to go for Mia's throat. That's what it wants, that's what I felt from it. It'll have to get through me first, and that's not going to happen. She can make whatever the hell choice she's going to make, but in the meantime, I'm going to rip its goddamn heart out."

"See," Zack said after a beat. "Real even-tempered."

"Kiss ass."

"Okay, okay." Mac stepped between them, patted the tensed shoulders of each man for peace. "Let's just keep our heads."

"Isn't this sweet?" Mia's voice dripped honey. "The boys are out playing in the woods."

"Shit," Zack muttered after one look at his wife's angry eyes. "Busted."

Ripley hooked her thumbs in her belt, tapped her fingers on her pockets, and strode forward. And got up in Mac's face. "Lucy, you got some 'spaining to do."

"No point in hassling them. I asked them to come."

"Oh, we'll get to you," Ripley promised Sam, "but there's a natural pecking order here."

Mia stepped forward, and felt the ripples of power. "What happened here?"

"You might as well spill it," Zack advised Sam. "Take my word for it. I've dealt with these three more than you have."

"Let's go inside and—"

Mia simply slapped a hand on Sam's chest before he could move past her. "What happened here?" she repeated.

"I took a walk in the woods."

Her gaze shifted, rested briefly on the ground. "You used the circle."

"It was there."

Part of her resented that he'd been able to use what was hers, what belonged to the three. It tightened the connection, made his link to her—to Nell and Ripley—unarguable. "All right," she said calmly enough. "What happened?"

"I ran into your demon wolf from hell."

"You—" She held up a hand, more to stop herself than to keep Sam silent. Because her first reaction was gut-wrenching fear. She willed it aside—not away, that was beyond her—and made herself think. And felt fury rise up and strangle fear.

"You called him. You came out here in the middle of the night, alone, and called him out like some swaggering gunslinger."

He hadn't known she still had that much temper in her. Or that it could, as always, trigger his own. "I like to think it was more Gary Cooper-esque."

"This is a joke to you, a *joke*?" Fury all but swallowed her whole. "You would dare call up what's mine? You can stand between me and what's mine to do while I—what—shrink aside wringing my hands?"

"Whatever it takes."

"You're not my shield, not my savior. What's inside me isn't less than what's in you." She shoved him back a step. "I won't tolerate your interference. You're meddling because it makes you feel like a hero, and—"

"Take it easy, Mia." Even as Zack spoke, the keen edge of her gaze cut to him, raked over his face. Recognizing a woman ready to bite out a man's heart, Zack merely held up both hands, stepped aside.

Sam, he decided, was on his own.

"Do you think I need your help?" She rounded on Sam again, drilling a finger into his chest.

"Stop jabbing at me."

"Do you think because I lack a penis I'm incapable of fighting for what's mine? So you pull your idiotic, manly display, then call your idiot men friends so you can discuss how to protect the helpless women?"

"I've never seen her like this," Nell whispered and watched, fascinated, as Mia shoved Sam back another step.

"Doesn't happen often." Ripley spoke out of the corner of her mouth. "Really cool when it does." She glanced up as clouds, black as a fresh bruise, boiled into the sky overhead. "Man, she is supremely pissed."

"I said stop jabbing at me." Sam curled his fingers around the fist she was currently slapping against his chest. "If you're finished with your snit . . . Careful," he warned as thunder bellowed.

"You arrogant, stupid, insulting . . . I'll show you a snit." She used her free hand, intending to shove him again. And saw the wince of pain as she bumped his shoulder. "What have you done?"

"We've just covered that."

"Take off your shirt."

He worked up a leer. "Well, baby, if you want to finish things that way, I've got no problem with it. But we've got an audience."

She solved the matter by reaching up and ripping his shirt open.

"Hey." He'd forgotten how fast she could move. A mistake.

The claw marks on his shoulder were raw and angry. With a little sound of distress, Nell started forward before Ripley stopped her.

"She'll handle it."

"You moved out of the circle." Fear shuddered back to twist painfully with temper. "You deliberately opened yourself to attack."

"It was a test." With sorely bruised dignity, Sam yanked what was left of his shirt back in place. "It worked."

She spun away from him, and since Zack was the closest, he took her first swipe. "Do you forget that it was Nell who brought madness to its knees, even when it held a knife to her throat?"

"No." He spoke quietly. "It's not something I'll ever forget."

"And you." She rounded on Mac. "You watched Ripley wage her war against the dark, and beat it back."

"I know." Mac shoved the sensor her angry energy had fried into his pocket. "No one here underestimates what any of you are capable of."

"Don't you?" Her eyes scorched each one of them in turn before she stepped back to stand with Nell and Ripley. "We are the Three." She threw up her hands, and light, bright as fire, shot from her fingertips. "And the power here is beyond you."

She turned on her heel and strode away.

"Well." Mac blew out a breath. "Wow."

"Real scientific, ace." Ripley tucked her hands into her pockets and nodded at Sam. "You got her stirred up, so you'd better find a way to smooth it out. If you're stupid enough to do what you did last night, then you're stupid enough to go after her when she's shooting live ammo."

"I guess you're right."

She'd nearly reached the edge of the woods when he caught up to her. "Just wait a damn minute." Sam reached for her arm, then hissed as the electric shock stung his fingers. "Cut it out!"

"Don't touch me."

"I'm going to do a hell of a lot more than touch you in a minute." But he kept his hands to himself until she'd reached her car.

She yanked the door open. He slammed it shut.

"Taking off isn't going to solve anything."

"You're right." She tossed back her hair. "That's your usual solution."

Pain kicked in his gut, but he nodded. "And you've just recently demonstrated that you're so much smarter and more mature. Let's finish this out away from innocent by-standers. Let's take a drive."

"You want to take a drive. Fine. Get in."

She pulled the door open again, slid be-hind the wheel. When he was beside her, she eased onto the road.

She kept her speed down as she cut through the village. And the minute she hit the coast road, she let it rip.

She wanted speed, and wind, and the keen edge of danger. All of those things would help carve away some of the anger and help her find her center again.

Her tires squealed as she shot into turns. And because she felt Sam tense beside her, she poured on more speed. She whipped the wheel, and the car shuddered as it clung to the road inches from the edge of the island.

He made some sound in his throat. Deliberately she sent him an icy look. "Problem?"

"No." Not, he thought, if you considered driving at ninety on a road that curved off into nothing, with a very pissed-off witch behind the wheel, your idea of fun.

As the road climbed, he kept his eyes trained on the stone house on the cliff. It was, at the moment, his nirvana. All he had to do was live to get there.

When she pulled into the drive, he had to take a few deep breaths to get his lungs working again.

"Point taken," he said, and resisted wiping his damp hands on his jeans. "You're capable of handling yourself, even when your control meter's shaky."

"Thank you so much." Sarcasm dripped like acid as she stepped out of the car. "Come inside." She snapped it out. "That wound needs tending."

Though he wasn't sure it was wise to put his flesh and blood in her hands at the moment, he followed her up the walk. "The place looks great."

"I'm not interested in small talk."

"Then don't say anything back," he suggested. He went inside with her. The colors
were rich, the wood polished. And the air
alive with warm, fragrant welcome.

She'd made changes, he noted. Subtle
ones. Mia ones. Mixing elegance with
charm. Exquisite taste with simplicity.
Though she strode straight back toward the
kitchen, he took his time.

It might give both of them a chance to
cool off.

She'd kept the heavy carved furniture that
had been passed down for generations. But
she'd added plush, sink-in textures. There
were rugs he didn't recognize, but their age
told him they'd been rolled up in some attic
and had been unearthed when the house
had come under Mia's control.

She used candles and flowers generously. Bowls of colored rocks, chunks of
glittering crystals, and the canny little mys-
tical figures she'd always collected. And
books. There were books in every room he
passed.

When he stepped into the kitchen, she
was already taking jars out of a cupboard.
There were gleaming copper pots, hanks of

drying herbs in their delicate faded tones and scents. The broom by her back door was very old, the restaurant-grade range very new.

"You had some work done in here." He tapped his fingers against the surface of the dove-gray counter.

"Yes. Sit down, take off your shirt."

Instead, he walked to the windows, looked out over her gardens. "It's like an illustration out of a book of fairy tales."

"I enjoy flowers. Sit down, please. We both have work to get back to, and I'd like to see to this."

"I did what I could with it last night. It just has to heal."

She merely stood, staring at him, a jar the color of poppies in her hand.

"All right, all right. Maybe you'll rip a bandage off your petticoat."

With little grace, he shrugged out of his torn shirt and sat at her kitchen table.

The sight of those raw wounds knotted her stomach. She hated seeing anything, anyone, in pain. "What did you use on it?" She bent down, sniffed. Wrinkled her nose. "Garlic. Obvious."

"It did the trick." He'd have sawed his

tongue in half before admitting the wound was throbbing like a bad tooth.

"Hardly. Be still. Open up," she ordered. "I've no intention of hurting you until *after* I've healed you. Open."

He did what she asked and felt her magic slide inside him, even as he felt her fingers, coated with soothing balm, slide over his abraded flesh.

He could see it, the warm red of her energy. Taste it, sharp and sweet, like the first bite of a succulent plum. The heavy scent of her, of poppies, clouded his senses.

Drifting, he heard her quiet chant. Without thinking, he turned his head, rubbed his cheek against her forearm.

"I see you in my sleep. I hear your voice inside my head." As he slid along the silk of her power, he spoke in Gaelic. The language of his blood. "I ache for you, even when I'm with you. Always you."

When he felt her slipping out of him, he struggled to hold on. But she slid away, and he was left blinking in confusion and swaying in the kitchen chair.

"Ssh." Her fingers were gentle as she stroked his hair. "Take a moment."

As his mind cleared, he fisted his hands

on the table. "You took me under. You had no right—"

"It would've been painful otherwise."

She'd never been able to stand back from someone's pain. Turning from him, she capped her jars carefully, gave herself time to settle. Easing his pain had brought on her own. His Gaelic words had bruised her heart.

"And you're hardly one to throw rights in my face now. I can't fully erase the wounds. That's beyond my capabilities. But they'll heal quickly enough now."

He angled his head to look at his shoulder. He could barely see the marks, and there was no discomfort. The surprise of that had him studying her. "You've improved."

"I've spent considerable time exploring and refining my gifts." She replaced her jars, then simply lowered her hands to the counter. "I'm so angry with you. So . . . I need the air."

She crossed to the door and walked outside.

She went to the pool, watched the fish dart gold beneath the lily pads. As she heard him come up behind her, she cupped her elbows with her hands.

"Then be angry. Spit and swear. It won't change a thing. I have a part in this, Mia. I am part of this. Whether you like it or not."

"Impulse and machismo have no part in this. Whether you like it or not."

If she thought he would apologize for what he'd done, she was going to have a long wait. "I saw an opportunity, a possibility, and I took a calculated risk."

She spun around again. "It's my risk to take. Mine, not yours."

"So damn sure of everything. You've always been so damn sure. Don't you ever consider there might be another way?"

"I don't question what I know here." She pressed fists to her belly. "And what I know here." And to her heart. "You can't take what's mine to do, and if you could—"

"If I could?"

"I wouldn't permit it. It's my birthright."

"And mine," he countered. "If I had been able to end it last night, Mia, it would be done."

She was more weary than angry now. "You know better. You *know*." She pushed at her hair, wandered away down a garden path where spearing blades of iris fanned out, waiting for the blooming time. "Change one thing, potentially change a thousand others. Move one piece of the whole indiscriminately, and destroy the whole. There are rules, Sam, and reasons for them."

"You were always better at rules than I was." There was a sting of bitterness in the words, and she could taste it even as he did. "How can you expect me to stand to the side? Do you think I can't see you're not sleeping or eating well? I can feel you fighting off the fear, and it rips at me."

She'd turned back as he spoke. How well she remembered that dark anger in him, that restless passion. It had drawn her to the boy. And, God help her, it drew her to the man.

"If I wasn't afraid, I'd be stupid," she pointed out. "I'm not stupid. You can't go behind my back this way. You can't challenge again what comes for me. I want your word."

"You can't have it."

"Let's try to be sensible."

"No." He took her arms, yanked her against him. "Let's try something else."

Hot, and nearly brutal, his mouth took hers. And it was like a branding. She'd pushed and scraped at his feelings even as she'd eased his wound. She'd opened him, tangled herself inside him only to leave him empty again. Now he needed something, would take something back.

His arms pinned hers, leaving her unable to struggle or accept. Leaving her helplessly trapped in a kiss that was all hunger, little heart. The thrill of that, her own pleasure in it, shocked and shamed her.

Still, she could have stopped him. She needed only her mind for that. But it was so crowded with him, just as her body was crowded with need.

"I can't stand it." He tore his mouth from hers to race his lips over her face. "Be with me or damn me, but do it now."

She lifted her head until their eyes met. "And if I told you to go? To take your hands off me and go?"

He ran his hand up her back, into her hair. Fisted it there. "Don't."

She'd thought she wanted him to suffer. Now that she could see he was, she couldn't bear it. For either of them.

"Then come inside, and we'll be with each other."

# Ten

They made it to the kitchen before they dived at each other. Pressed against the back door, she let her system rage under his hands.

Oh, to be touched again, stroked by hard hands so foreign and familiar. The wild and wicked freedom of it gushed into her, flooded away questions, worries, doubts. To be wanted like this again, devoured by desperation. To have her own needs matched by equally insatiable ones.

She pulled his tattered shirt aside and filled her own hands with hot, smooth flesh. She bit at him, craving the taste. Fueling herself on it, she whispered half-crazed demands as they stumbled out of the kitchen.

Something fell, a musical tinkle of glass, as they bumped a table in the hall. Little shards of what had been a crystal faerie's wings were crushed to glittery dust under his feet.

She couldn't breathe, couldn't think. Her lips skimmed over the wounds on his shoulder. Neither of them noticed when the marks faded away. "Touch me. Don't stop touching me."

He'd have cheerfully died first.

He filled his hands with her—curves, slender lines, felt his own primitive thrill when she quivered against him. His blood surged, a primal beat, when her breath caught, then released on a moan.

He slid his hands up her legs, groaning at the glorious length of them, at the heat that gathered around the witch mark that rode high on her thigh. With no thought of finesse, he tugged impatiently at the thin barrier of silk.

"I have to—" And plunged his fingers into her. "Oh, God. Sweet God." His face was buried in her hair when she erupted. "Again, again, again." Savagery took over so that he fixed his teeth on her throat, driving her while her body bucked and shuddered.

Impossibly hot, wonderfully wet, gloriously soft. He found her mouth again, swallowed her sobbing breaths.

They dragged each other up the stairs. With fast and urgent fingers, he fumbled with, tore at the tiny buttons that ranged down the back of her dress. Snapped threads, exposed flesh.

"I need to see you. To see you."

The dress slithered to the floor and was left behind. At the top of the steps, he started to pull her to the right.

"No, no." Nearly sobbing with desperation, she dragged at the button of his jeans. "This way now."

She circled him to the left, shivering when he snapped open the clasp of her bra. When he filled his hands with her breasts. Soon his mouth, hot and hungry, replaced his hands.

"Let me. Just let me." Half mad with her, he pulled her arms over her head. Feasted.

Mia let her head fall back and relished the helpless and heavy sensation of being ravished. Alive—she was so brutally alive. Even as her heart raged against his greedy mouth, her body wept for more.

When he gripped her hips, her arms locked around him in taut, possessive ropes. The bed was steps away, but it might have been miles. His eyes, pure green, burned into the dark smoke of hers. For an instant it seemed the world went still.

"Yes," she said. "Yes."

Then he drove himself into her.

They took each other where they stood, and took hard and fast. The race through pleasure, toward bliss, stole breath and reason as they mated with a kind of willful violence. Her nails scored his back, his fingers dug bruises on her skin, and still they pushed each other for more. Their mouths met, a wild and frenzied feeding, and their bodies plunged relentlessly.

The climax raked her like claws. One long swipe that sliced through her system and laid her bare. Helpless against it, she surrendered. And felt him plunge after her.

Sweaty, weak, quivering, they held each other up. They swayed there, slick, bruised flesh to flesh. Lowering his forehead to hers, Sam struggled to draw in air. His body felt as if it had fallen off a mountain and landed in a pool of hot, melted gold.

"I'm a little dizzy," she managed.

"Me, too. Let's see if we can get to the bed."

They stumbled through the haze and fell on Mia's ancient four-poster together. Lying flat on their backs, they both stared, dazed, at the ceiling.

It wasn't, he realized, precisely the sexual reunion he'd envisioned for them. His fantasy had involved seduction, sophistication, and a great deal more finesse on his part.

"I was in a little bit of a hurry," he told her.

"No problem."

"You know the weight I mentioned you'd put on?"

"Hmmm." The sound was a low warning.

"It really works for me." He shifted his hand just enough to skim the side of her breast. "I mean, it really works."

"You filled out a bit yourself."

He let himself float, studied the mural on her ceiling. In the night sky, stars glowed and faeries flew. "You moved your bedroom."

"Yes."

"Good thing I didn't follow the impulse to climb up the trellis the other night."

Because the image brought her back to nights he'd done just that, she sighed.

It had been a long time, a very long time, since her body had felt so loose, so *used*. It made her want to curl up like a cat and purr.

She would have done so once with him.

Once they would have turned to each other and, tangled together, would have slept like kittens after a romp.

Those days were over, she thought. But as romps went, they'd done very, very well. "I have to get back to work," she said.

"So do I."

They turned their heads, looked at each other, and grinned. "Do you know the beauty of owning your own business?" she asked him.

"Yeah." He rolled over until his mouth hovered a breath from hers. "Nobody can dock our pay."

But that didn't mean you got off scot-free.

When Mia strolled back into the bookstore, Lulu took one look at her and knew. "You did it with him."

"Lulu!" Hissing, Mia scanned the area for customers.

"If you think it's not going to show, and people aren't going to gab about it, then sex gave you instant brain damage."

"Be that as it may, I'm not going to stand here and discuss it at the cash register."

With her head high, she started toward the stairs and was immediately waylaid by Gladys Macey.

"Hello, there, Mia. Don't you look pretty today?"

"Hello, Mrs. Macey." Mia angled her head to read the titles of the books Gladys had picked up. "You'll have to let me know what you think of that one." She tapped a finger against a current bestseller. "I haven't read it yet."

"I'll be sure to do that. I heard you had dinner over at the hotel." Gladys beamed into Mia's face. "Sam Logan's making some changes over there, I'm told. The food as good as ever?"

"Yes, I enjoyed it."

Then Mia looked over her shoulder at Lulu. Considering Lulu's voice and Gladys's ears, there was no doubt the opening comment had been heard and digested.

"Would you like to know if Sam and I had sex?" she asked pleasantly.

"Now, honey." Gladys gave Mia a motherly pat. "Don't get all dandered up. Besides, it's hard to look at you and not see right off you've got a nice, healthy glow about you. He's a handsome boy."

"Troublemaker," Lulu muttered under her breath, and proved that Gladys's ears were well tuned.

"Oh, now, Lu, that boy never caused any more trouble than any of the others around here, and less than some."

"The others didn't come sniffing around my girl."

"Well, they certainly did." Gladys shook her head, calling back to Lulu as if Mia was invisible—or deaf. "There wasn't a boy on the island who didn't sniff around her. Fact is, Sam was the only one who had her sniffing back. I always thought they made a pretty couple."

"Excuse me." Mia held up a finger. "I'd like to remind both of you that the boy and the girl who did the sniffing are now full-grown adults."

"But you still make a pretty couple," Gladys insisted.

Giving up, Mia leaned over, brushed her lips over Gladys's cheek. "You have a sweet heart."

And a wagging tongue, she thought as she walked up to her office. Word would spread like a rash over the island that Sam Logan and Mia Devlin were at it again.

Since she didn't know how she felt about that, but could do nothing to circumvent it, Mia put the matter in a corner of her mind and went back to work on her proposal.

By four, ignoring the stares, she sailed across the street and into the hotel, where she dropped the envelope containing her proposal at the lobby desk, with a request that it be delivered to Mr. Logan as soon as possible. Then she sailed out again.

To make up for the time she'd lost, she closed herself in the stockroom and concentrated on business. She organized, rearranged, and put together a list of inventory that needed replenishing. The solstice always brought a flood of tourists to the island. It paid to be ready for them.

Armed with the stock list, she rose. Then quickly sat again as a wave of dizziness swamped her. Foolish, she berated herself. Careless. She'd had nothing but a half a muffin all day. She got to her feet, thinking she'd pick up a bowl of soup in the café. And an image swam into her brain.

Evan Remington stood by a barred window, smiling. And his eyes were as empty as a doll's. But he turned his head, slowly, so slowly, and those eyes began to glow red and filled with something that wasn't human.

She had to force herself not to run, to pull her calm around her like a cloak. As the image faded, she left her work behind.

"I have an errand," she told Lulu as she breezed out of the store. "I'll be back when I can."

"Going and coming," Lulu muttered.

Mia walked straight down to the station house, pausing when she had to exchange a word with an acquaintance. The streets, she noted, were already full of tourists. They strolled and shopped, cruised the island looking for the perfect picnic spot, a new vista. They would crowd into the restaurants at night or go back to their rental houses to cook up fish brought fresh from the docks.

Shops were running spring-into-summer sales, and the pizza parlor was offering two free toppings with the purchase of a second large pie. She watched Pete Stubens drive past in his pickup with his beloved dog riding shotgun.

Ripley's young cousin Dennis flashed by on the opposite sidewalk, hanging ten on his skateboard. His Red Sox jersey flapped like a flag.

It was all so normal, she thought. So easy and right and real.

She was going to do everything in her power to keep it that way.

Zack was at his desk when she walked in, and immediately sprang to his feet. "Now, Mia," he began.

"I'm not here to pin your ears back."

"That's a relief. Nell already took care of that." To prove it, he rubbed them. "I would like to say we weren't going behind your backs. We were just looking into a situation. It's my job to deal with trouble on the island."

"We can debate that later. Can you check on Evan Remington?"

"Check on?"

"Make sure he's where he's supposed to be. What the progress of his treatment is, the prognosis, his recent behavioral patterns."

He started to ask her why, but the look on her face told him to answer first, then ask questions. "First I can tell you he's still locked up and he's going to stay that way. I make it my business to call a couple of contacts of mine every week." He angled his head. "I assume you don't consider that little chore out of my scope."

"Don't get snotty. Can you get progress reports?"

"I don't have access to his medical records, if that's what you mean. I'd need a warrant, and cause to request one. What's the problem?"

"He's still part of this, padded cell or not."

Zack was around the desk in two strides, and had his hand wrapped firm on Mia's arm. "Is he a threat to Nell?"

"No." What was it like to be loved so utterly? she wondered. Once, she'd thought she knew. "Not directly. Not like before. But he's being used. I wonder if he knows it?"

It was essential to find out.

"Where's Ripley?"

"Out doing her job." His grip tightened. "Is she in trouble?"

"Zack, both Nell and Ripley have done what they were meant to do. But I need to talk to them. Would you tell them both to come up to the house tonight? By seven if they can."

Now Zack's grip lightened to a caress and ran up to her shoulder. "You're in trouble."

"No." Her voice was clear and calm. "I'm in control."

She believed it absolutely. Just as she understood the value of that faith, and that sense of self. Doubts, questions, fears would only diminish power when she needed it most.

The vision had come unbidden, and with some physical distress. She wouldn't take such a thing lightly.

She prepared carefully. It was not a time for rash behavior or showmanship, though she often appreciated the flash and the flare.

It seemed now that much of what had happened that day had been meant to prepare her. Her purging of temper that morning, the fasting, and yes, the sex. Ridding the body of frustration and celebrating one of its more joyful purposes would only aid her in what was to come.

The herbs and oils for her ritual bath were chosen with deliberation. Rose for psychic power and divination. Carnation for protection. Iris for wisdom that she might understand what was shown to her.

By the light of candles inscribed for her quest, she immersed herself, washing body and hair, cleansing her mind.

Using creams she'd made herself, she coated her skin before slipping into a long, loose robe of white. She selected her charms and pendant carefully. Dendritic agate for protection in travel, amethyst to sharpen her third eye. She hung malachite from her ears, for vision questing.

She gathered her tools, her divination wand with moonstone at the tip. Incense and candles, bowls and sea salt. Knowing that she might need it, she selected a tonic for restorative energy.

Then she went into her garden, to gather peace and wait for her sisters.

They came together and found her sitting on a stone bench beside a bed of nodding columbine.

"I need your help," she said. "I'll tell you on the way to the clearing."

They were barely into the forest, the light dimming with dusk, when Ripley stopped.

"You shouldn't be the one to do this. A flight leaves you too open, too vulnerable."

"Which is why I need my circle," Mia countered.

"I should do it." Nell touched Mia's arm. "Evan's most directly connected to me."

"Which is exactly why you shouldn't do it," Ripley argued. "The connection's too close. I've already done this once, so I should do it again."

"You flew without preparation, without protection, and you were harmed." Reminding herself that there was patience in reason, Mia continued to walk. "The vision came to me, unbidden. This is for me to do, and I'm fully prepared. You don't have enough control as yet," she said to Ripley. "And you, little sister, not enough experience. Even disregarding both those facts, this is for me. We all know it, so let's not waste any more time."

"I don't like it," Ripley said. "Especially after what happened to Sam last night."

"Unlike some men, I don't have to prove my heroism. My body stays within the circle."

She set her bag down in the clearing and began to cast the circle.

Nell lit the candles. She was calm because calm was needed. "Tell me what to do if something goes wrong."

"Nothing will," Mia assured her.

"If."

"If, then. You pull me back." She looked up and saw the glow in the trees as the moon began its rise. "We'll begin."

She disrobed, standing in the arms of the young night in nothing but crystals. Holding out her hands for her sisters', she began the chant that would free her consciousness from the shell of her body. And let her fly.

"Open window, open door. I seek to see, I seek to soar. Over sea and into sky, my spirit lifts, my senses fly. It is within my gift of power to command this airy hour and to ask that what I see bring no harm to them or me. As I will, so mote it be."

There was a slow and lovely sense of weightlessness, of lifting out of the shell that held the spirit bound to the earth. She floated free of it, a bird rising on the wing. And, for a moment only, allowed herself to embrace the glory of it.

Such a gift was golden, but she knew the ribbons that tethered her to the earth could be carelessly snapped. Even for the thrill of flight, she wouldn't trade her reality.

She beamed over the sea where the starlight was reflected like bits of sparkling glass scattered on black velvet. From deep within its depths came whale song, and the music carried her to the far shore.

The buzz of traffic, conversations within houses, the scent of trees and of dinners cooking all swirled below her as life drove forward.

She heard the outraged cry of a newborn pushed into life. And the last sigh of the dying. The quick, soft brush as souls passed on their way. She kept the light of them around her, and sought the dark.

He had such hate in him. The breadth of it was infinite, and layered, and not, she realized as she drew closer, all his own. What was in Evan Remington was a rancid mix, one that offended the senses. But she could see as she watched the orderlies, the guards, the doctors move through the facility where Remington was imprisoned, that none of them caught the underlying stench.

She let the thoughts, the voices of the others bleed away, and focused on Remington and what used him.

He was in his room for the night, a cell far removed from the plush surroundings he'd once commanded. She saw he had changed considerably from the night in the woods when Nell had defeated him.

His hair was thinner, his face rounder, with the jowls beginning to sag beneath deep, sharp lines of dissipation. No longer handsome, no longer smooth, his face had begun to mirror what he'd hidden inside him for so many years.

He wore loose orange coveralls and paced his cell like a soldier on sentry duty.

"They can't keep me here. They can't keep me here. I have work. I'm going to miss my plane. Where is that bitch?" He spun away from his cell door, and his pale eyes searched the small space. His mouth folded down as if in mild annoyance. "She's late again. I'll have to punish her. She leaves me no choice."

Someone from outside shouted at him to shut the fuck up, but he continued to pace, continued to rant.

"Can't she see I have business? I have responsibilities? She's not going to get away with it. Who the hell does she think she is! Whores, every one of them whores."

Suddenly, like a puppet on a string, his head jerked up, and his eyes were madness slicked thin over hate. Madness began to glow red.

"Don't you know I see you, whore-bitch? I'll kill you before it's done."

The blast of power slammed into her, a fist in the belly. She felt herself waver, then bore down. "You're pathetic. You use a madman to horde your power. I need only myself."

"Your death will be slow and painful. I'll keep you alive long enough so that you see it all destroyed."

"We've already beaten you twice." She sensed the next whip of energy and deflected it. But it took all of her strength, and she felt her link shudder as Remington's head changed into that of a snapping wolf. "And the third time's the charm," she finished; and pulled herself back.

She poured back into her body, staggered, and might have fallen if Nell and Ripley hadn't supported her.

"Are you hurt?" At the urgency in Nell's voice Mia struggled to settle again. "Mia?"

"No, I'm not hurt."

"You were gone too damn long," Ripley told her.

"Just long enough."

"So you say." Still gripping Mia's hand, Ripley jerked her head. "We've got company."

As the visions cleared out of her mind, Mia saw Sam standing just outside the circle. He wore black, the long coat swirling in the night air.

"Finish it, and close the circle." His voice was brisk, businesslike. "Before you collapse."

"I know what to do." She reached for the tonic Nell was already pouring into a cup. Because she was not yet steady, she took the cup with both hands. And she drank until she no longer felt as if her body was a mist ready to be swept away by the wind.

"Close the circle," Sam demanded. "Or I come in, regardless."

Ignoring him now, she offered thanks for a safe flight and, with her sisters, closed the circle.

"It continues to use Remington." She slipped into her robe and belted it, though her skin felt as thin, as fragile, as the silk. "More like a vessel than a source, but still some of both. It fills him up with hatred of women, of female power, then uses the mix to feed its own energy. It's potent, but not without vulnerability."

She reached down for her bag, and when she straightened, swayed.

"That's enough." In one motion, Sam swept her into his arms. "She needs to sleep this off. I know what to do for her."

"He's right." Ripley put a hand on Nell's shoulder as Sam carried Mia out of the clearing. "He knows what she needs."

Mia's head spun, infuriating her. "I just need to get my balance. I can't get it unless I'm on my feet."

"There was a time you weren't so twitchy about needing help."

"I wouldn't be twitchy if I needed help. And I don't need you to—" She bit off the words. "I'm sorry, and you're right."

"Boy, you must be shaky."

She let her head rest on his shoulder. "I'm queazy."

"I know, baby. We'll fix it. How's the headache?"

"It's not bad. Really. I'd have come back sturdier, but I had to come back fast. Damn it, Sam, this dizziness is . . ." Gray began to swim at the edges of her vision. "It's not passing off. I'm going under."

"That's all right. Go ahead."

For once she did exactly as he suggested and didn't argue. When she went limp in his arms, he continued to carry her toward the house. He would curse her later, he told himself, when she could fight back. For now, he took her inside and up to her bed.

Knowing she had to sleep long and deep didn't make it any easier for Sam to see her, so pale, so still in the shadowy light of her bedroom. He knew what could be done, and tending to her at least helped keep his mind on the practical.

He knew what protective oils and creams she'd used. He could smell them on her skin. After he laid her in bed, he gathered the proper incense and candles to bolster what she'd already used.

She always had been an organized soul, he thought as he checked the shelves and cupboards in her tower room for the supplies he needed.

Even here she had flowers—clay pots of violets—and books. He scanned the books, selected one on healing spells and charms in case he needed to refresh his memory.

In her kitchen he found the herbs he needed, and though it had been some time since he'd practiced any kitchen magic, he steeped a pot of rue tea to aid her in spiritual cleansing.

She was deeply asleep when he returned. He lighted the candles and incense, then sitting beside her, slid his mind into hers.

"Mia, you need to drink, then you can rest."

He trailed his fingers over her cheeks, then brushed his mouth over her mouth. Her eyes opened, but the gray was blurred. She was limp as water as he lifted her head and put the cup to her lips.

"Now you drink and heal in sleep. Dreams will take you far and deep. Through the night and into the light."

He brushed the hair from her face as he eased her down again. "Do you want me to come with you?"

"No. I'm alone here."

"You're not." He lifted her hand to his lips as her eyes closed again. "I'll wait for you."

She let go of him, and slid into dreams.

She saw herself, a child, sitting in the rose garden her parents had neglected. Butter-flies fluttered in the palms of her upturned hands as if her fingers were petals.

She and Ripley, so young and eager, lighting the Beltane fire in the clearing.

Sprawled on the floor in front of the fire while Lulu sat in a chair, knitting.

Walking on the beach with Sam on a hot, close summer night. And the beat, beat, beat of her heart as he drew her up, drew her in. The world standing still, holding its breath in that magical instant before their first kiss.

The feel of tears, the hot flood of them as they'd gushed out of her shattered heart. He'd walked away so carelessly, left her broken and grieving as she stood by a pretty pool of early spring violets.

*I'm not coming back.*

With that one statement, he'd broken her to pieces.

Dreams floated in and out, and she with them. She saw herself standing in her sum-mer garden, teaching Nell how to stir the air. She felt the joy of clasping hands, at last, with both of her sisters in a circle of unity and power.

She saw the soft colors and sweetness of Nell's wedding, the bright promise of Ripley's. She watched as they began yet another circle without her, as was meant to be.

And she was alone.

"Fate moves us, and then we choose."

She stood on the cliffs now, with the one who was called Fire. Mia turned, looked into the face so like her own.

"I regret no choice I've made," Mia said.

"Nor did I. Nor can I now."

"To die for love is a poor choice."

The one called Fire lifted her brows, and there was an innate arrogance in the gesture. In the night wind, her hair streamed like flames. "Yet it was mine. If I had chosen differently, daughter, perhaps you would not be here now. Would not be what you are. So I have no regrets. Will you say the same at the end of your time?"

"I cherish my gift and bring no harm. I live my life, and live it well."

"As did I." She spread her arms. "We hold this place, but the time grows short. See." She gestured to where the fog boiled along the edge of the rocks. "It craves most what it cannot have, and what it cannot have will, in the end, defeat it."

"What is there to do that I haven't done?" Mia demanded. "What's left for me?"

"Everything." With that last word, she vanished.

And Mia was alone.

Lulu was alone. Sleeping deeply under her hodge-podge quilt, floating on dreams. Unaware of the dark mists gathering outside her house, rising up to slither around her windows. And through the cracks.

She stirred, she shivered, when that cold mist slid over her, snuck under the covers to crawl over her skin. With a little sound of protest, she burrowed deeper under the quilt, but found no warmth.

She heard the baby crying, long wails of misery. In a mother's automatic response, she tossed the covers aside, rose in the dark, and started out of the bedroom.

"Okay, okay, I'm coming."

In the dream she walked, sleepily, down the long corridor of the house on the cliff. She felt the smooth wood under her feet— and not the rough grass of her own yard as she left her house, moving through the thickening fog. Her eyes were open, but she saw the door to the baby's room, and not the street where she walked, the quiet houses she passed.

She didn't see or sense the black wolf stalking behind her.

She reached out, opened the door that wasn't there as she trudged around the corner toward the beach.

The crib was empty, and the baby's wails became screams of terror.

"Mia!" She ran, hurling herself across High Street, which was a maze of corridors in her mind. "Where are you?"

She ran, breath heaving, fear rising as she pounded on locked doors and raced toward the sound of the baby's cries.

She fell, scoring her hands on the sand of the beach and feeling her fingers dig into thick carpet. She was weeping, calling for her baby as she pushed herself to her feet, swayed, then raced on. In the dream she flew down the main staircase and out into the black night, then plunged into the sea.

The surf knocked her back, knocked her down, but in a blind fury to find and protect her child, she fought her way up again, pushed her way through the waves.

Even as the water closed over her head,
her eyes were open, and the baby's
screams pounded in her ears.

There was a great weight on her chest, and
the sharp taste of vomit in her throat. She
gagged, heaved again.

"She's breathing. It's okay, Lulu, take it
easy."

Her eyes burned, refused to focus.
Through the haze over them she made out
Zack's face. Water dripped from his hair and
onto her cheeks.

"What the hell is this?" she demanded,
and her voice came out in a croak that hurt
her throat.

"Oh, God, Lulu." Nell knelt on the sand
beside her, grabbed her hand and pressed
it to her own cheek. "Thank God."

"She's still in shock." Ripley nudged her
brother aside and spread a blanket over
Lulu.

"Shock, my ass." Lulu managed to sit up,
coughed violently enough that she considered passing out. But she bore down and
stared at the faces surrounding her. Nell

was weeping openly, and Mac, soaking wet, crouched beside her. Ripley sat on the sand now, and with her brother's help, arranged the blanket over Lulu's shoulders.

"Where's Mia?" she demanded.

"She's at home, she's with Sam," Nell told her. "She's safe."

"Okay." Lulu began to draw slow and careful breaths. "What the hell am I doing out here, soaking wet, in the middle of the night?"

"Good question." Zack considered a moment, then decided flat truth was best. "Nell woke up and knew you were in trouble."

"So did I," Ripley added. "I'd barely fallen asleep when I heard you shouting in my head, for Mia. Then the vision hit like a freight train." She glanced at Nell then. "I saw you walking out of your house, saw the fog closing in."

"And the black dog," Nell murmured, and waited for Ripley to nod. "Stalking you. I was afraid we wouldn't get to you in time."

Lulu held up a hand a moment, trying to clear her head. "I walked into the water? For Christ's sake."

"It lured you there," Mac replied. "Do you know how?"

"I had a dream, that's all. A nightmare. Walked in my sleep."

"Let's get her home, and warm," Nell said, but Ripley shook her head.

"Not yet. You damn near drowned in your sleep." Her tone turned sharp and angry. "So don't pull the stubborn crap on me. If Nell and I hadn't linked in, we'd have found you dead in the morning, washed up in the fucking tide."

Because Ripley's voice broke, she clenched her teeth and spoke through them. "My brother and my man pulled you out, and Zack pumped the life back into you. Don't you dare brush this off."

"Stop it now. Stop that crying." Shaken, Lulu gave Ripley's arm a little shake. "I just had a bad spell, that's all. Nothing more than that to it."

"It lured you here," Mac repeated.

"That's just bull." But she started to shiver again, from a cold inside her bones. "Why would this thing want to hurt me? I've got no power."

"It hurts you," Mac said, "it hurts Mia. You're a part of her, Lu, so you're part of this. What would've happened to the is-land—to the children the sisters left behind—if they hadn't had the nurse to tend them? And we should've taken that into account before. It was stupid not to. Careless."

"We won't be careless anymore." Nell wrapped her arm around Lulu's shoulders. "She's cold. We need to get her home."

She let herself be carried, let herself be pampered, even tucked into bed. She felt her age, and then some, but she wasn't done yet.

"I don't want Mia to know about this."

"What?" Ripley jammed her fists onto her hips. "A near-death experience rattle your brain?"

"Think about what your man said back on the beach. Hurt me, hurt her. If she's worried about me, she's distracted." With her glasses back in place, she turned to Mac and saw him clearly. "She needs all her strength, all her wits to finish this. Have I got that right?"

"She needs to be strong, but—"

"Then why muck her up?" There was nothing—nothing—more vital than Mia's well-being. "How do we know this didn't happen tonight just to make her upset and worried about me so she's vulnerable?

What's done's done, and telling her doesn't change it."

"She could help protect you," Nell put in.

"I can take care of myself." The minute the statement was out, she caught Zack's lifted eyebrows. And huffed out a breath. "Been doing it for longer than any of you've been alive. Added to that, I've got me a big strong sheriff, a smart scientist, and a couple of witches looking out for me."

"She may be right about this." Ripley thought of how pale, how fragile Mia had been when she'd come back from the flight. "Let's at least agree to keep it to ourselves until telling Mia has a purpose. Nell and I can put protection around the house."

"You go right ahead," Lulu invited.

"I can set up a sensor," Mac put in. "So if there's any energy change, you'd be alerted."

"Sounds like a plan." Lulu firmed her jaw. "Mia's the target. Nothing and no one's going to use me to hurt her. That's a promise."

# Eleven

The candles burned low, and the air was full of fragrance and soft light when she woke. She felt him there almost before she felt herself. The warmth of his hand over hers, the weight of his worry.

For an instant only, the years vanished and her heart was light with love. What she'd felt once, what she felt now, collided and dissolved before she could hold either.

"Here, drink this." As he had hours before, he lifted her head, held a cup to her lips.

But this time she sniffed speculatively before she sipped. "Hyssop. Good choice."

"How do you feel?"

"Well enough. Better, I'd say, than you. There was no need for you to sit up all night." The cat that had curled beside her now slithered under her hand for stroking. "What time is it?"

"Sunrise." Sam rose now, began to extinguish the candles. "You only had about nine hours. You could probably use more."

"No." She sat up, shook back her hair. "I'm awake. And starving."

He glanced back. She sat in the old bed, her face flushed with sleep, the black cat in her lap.

He wanted to slide into bed with her. Just to hold, just to rest. Just to be. "I'll fix you something."

"You'll cook breakfast?"

"I can manage eggs and toast," he answered as he stalked out of the room.

"Cranky," Mia said to Isis. The cat swished her tail, then leaped off the bed to trot out after Sam.

He brewed coffee first in hopes that a strong shot of caffeine would clear his head and improve his mood. He didn't question the fact that his tender feelings, his steady concern of the night, had jumped straight to annoyance the minute she'd awakened and looked at him.

A man needed some defense.

While the coffeemaker grumbled, he turned on the cold water tap in the sink and dunked his head under the flow. And rapped his head smartly against the faucet when the cat brushed up against his legs.

He saw stars, swore, then smacked the water off and came up dripping.

When Mia walked in, he was standing, glaring at the cat, with water running down his face. She picked up a fresh dish towel and passed it to him.

"You're welcome to use the shower if you'd like to do more than soak your head." After exchanging a decidedly female glance with the cat, Mia opened the door to let her out.

Rather than trust himself to speak, Sam wrenched open the refrigerator, took out a carton of eggs. Mia reached down to get a skillet out of a cupboard, then held out a hand. "Why don't I take care of this?"

"I said I'd fix some damn eggs, so I'll fix some damn eggs."

"All right." Complacently, she set the skillet on a burner before moving over to get down two mugs. She poured, trying to keep her lips from twitching while Sam slammed around her kitchen. But the first sip of coffee made her eyes water.

"God. Well, this is strong enough to go ten rounds with the champ."

Sam slapped an egg on the side of a bowl. "Any other complaints?"

"No." She decided to be broad-minded and not mention the bits of shell that had gone into the bowl along with the egg. Sipping delicately, she wandered to the back door again, and opened it to the morning air. "It's going to rain."

Barefoot, her white robe billowing, she stepped outside to look at her garden and leave Sam to brood. Wind chimes tinkled as she wound along the paths. There were always surprises. A new bloom just opened, a bud just hazed with color. The blend of continuity and change was one of the great appeals of the garden for her.

She glanced back toward the kitchen. The boy she'd loved was now the man fixing her breakfast. Continuity and change, she thought with a sigh. She supposed, under it all, that was one of Sam Logan's great appeals for her.

And because she remembered he'd held

her hand while she slept, she broke off a tightly budded peony. Curving her hand over it, she encouraged the bud to unfurl and free its soft, fragrant pink petals.

Brushing it against her cheek, she went back to the house.

He was at the stove, looking wonderfully out of his element. His legs were spread, and the spatula held like a weapon in his hand. He was burning the eggs.

Foolishly moved, she crossed to him and gently turned off the flame. She kissed his cheek, handed him the flower. "Thank you for watching over me."

"You're welcome." He turned away to reach for plates, then simply laid his forehead against the glass doors of her cupboard. "Damn it, Mia. Damn it! Why didn't you tell me what you were going to do? Why didn't you call me?"

"I've gotten out of the habit of calling you."

He straightened, a mix of anger and hurt enveloping him.

"I don't say that to hurt you." She spread her hands. "I don't. It simply is. I'm used to doing things my way, and on my own."

"Fine. Fine." But it wasn't. He rattled

plates as he dragged them out of the cupboard. "When it's you, it's just being who you are and doing what you do. But when it's me, I'm going behind your back."

She opened her mouth. Then was forced to close it again and clear her throat. "You have a point." She walked by him to get jam out of the refrigerator. "However, what you did on your own was step into my territory, risk bodily harm, then call out the troops."

"Your territory isn't exclusive. And you risked bodily harm."

"That's a matter of debate. I didn't do this behind your back, not deliberately. In hindsight, I'll admit your presence in the circle would have been valuable." She set the toast, stone-cold and crisp at the edges, on the table. "You're a better witch than you are a cook."

"You're a hell of a lot cockier than you used to be," he countered. "And you always were cocky."

"Confident," she corrected. "*You* were cocky."

"A fine distinction." He sat with her, scooping half the eggs onto his plate, half on hers. The peony lay pretty and pink be-

tween them. He took his first bite. "These
are terrible."

She sampled, tasting scorched egg and
bits of shell. "Yes, yes, they are."

When he grinned at her she laughed and
went right on eating.

He took her up on the shower and ran the
spray hot to ease muscles stiff from the
night's vigil. He supposed they'd called a
truce, a moratorium of sorts over lousy eggs
and cold toast. Maybe, he thought, they'd
taken a tentative step toward being friends
again.

He'd missed that part of them, too. The
easy silences, the shared laughter. He'd
known when she was sad, often before she
knew it herself. He'd felt the thousand little
pinpricks of her hurt whenever her parents
had blithely, benevolently, ignored the child
they'd made between them.

Even before he and she had become
lovers they'd been a part of each other. And
how could he explain to her that it had been
the link, the absolute and unquestioned link

in the chain of their destinies, that had driven him to break the tie?

She didn't ask, and he didn't say. He thought that was for the best, at least for now. At least until they were friends again.

The muscles in his belly contracted when she stepped in behind him, slipped her arms around him, pressed her wet body against his back.

"I thought you might share." She nipped playfully at his shoulder.

This time, they were fated to reverse the process. Lovers first.

He turned, and fisting his hands in her hair, dragged her with him under the pounding spray.

"You have the water too hot," she told him, turning her head as his mouth rubbed along the side of her throat.

"I needed hot."

She picked up a bottle, squirted some of the pale green liquid over both their heads.

"Wait! What is that? Girl stuff?"

Amused, she reached up to lather it in his hair. God, she'd always loved his hair. So black and thick and untamed. Wet, it fell nearly to his shoulders, a dark rain of silk.

"My own blend. The rosemary promotes

hair growth, not that you need it, and smells good. Even for manly men."

He worked it into her hair as well. Sniffed at it. "It's not just rosemary."

"Not just. Some calendula, linden flowers, nasturtium."

"Girl stuff." Suds slid down their bodies, slicking them. "It works on you."

"So do you," she said when his mouth covered hers again.

Steam, fragrant with herbs and flowers, rose as they washed each other. Teased each other. Slippery hands over slippery skin aroused in slow beats that savored each moment, each touch and taste.

Long, lazy strokes coaxed the pulses to quicken and low, lingering moans to mix with the sound of drumming water.

Her mouth was wet and warm, and with restless nips and nibbles grew eager under his. She deepened the kiss as her body rubbed and rocked against his. Invitation, demand, delight. And every breath he took was full of her scent.

As the air turned sultry, he turned her so that he could trace kisses over her back, so that he could mold and cup her breasts. His thumbs scraped her nipples, tortured the hard points while her back arched in plea-sure.

When his hands skimmed lower, she reached back, hooking her arms around his neck and holding on to him when he sent her flying.

"Now." She turned to him. "Fill me now."

He slid into her, achingly slow. And she felt herself open, and give. She gripped his shoulders while the water sluiced over them, tuned her body to his.

Long, silky strokes so that pleasure was a low, sustained beat. Everything she was fo-cused on the need to prolong, to hold this moment like a jewel. Shining and rich. Her blood pulsed, seemed to sing under her skin until the beauty of it wept inside her.

She crested, an endless, warm wave, and her mouth pressed to his as she rode it.

They ended up on the bed again, flat on their backs.

"We never seem to make it here for the first round," Sam managed.

"Be that as it may, round two will have to

be postponed on account of working for a living."

"Yeah. I've got an eleven o'clock meeting."

She stirred enough to twist for a look at the clock. "You've got some time yet. Why don't you stay, get a little sleep?"

"Huh."

She rose, raked her fingers through her damp hair. "I'll set the alarm for ten."

He grunted again, and didn't move a muscle.

Nor had he moved when, thirty minutes later, she was groomed and dressed for the day. Obligingly, she set the alarm clock, tugged the sheet over him.

Then just stood looking at him.

"How did it happen you've ended up sleeping in my bed again?" she wondered aloud. "Does it make me weak, stupid, or just human?"

With no answer, she left him sleeping.

Nell pounced the minute she walked in the door. "You're all right? I was worried."

"I'm fine."

"Don't look any the worse for wear," Lulu commented after a careful study. All the tension balled in her stomach loosened and smoothed out.

"I told Lu," Nell explained and struggled with the hitch in her conscience. She wasn't being as forthcoming with Mia as she was about her. "I . . . thought I should."

"Of course. Is the coffee up? I'm desperate for a decent cup. And to economize time and effort, we'll go upstairs and have some while I save the two of you the trouble of poking at me about what happened."

"You were so pale." Nell went up the steps first. "Ripley and I were about to pull you back when you came on your own. But you were as white as a sheet."

Guarding her province, Nell hurried behind the counter to pour the coffee. "You were gone for nearly an hour."

"An hour?" Mia was surprised. "I didn't realize. It didn't seem like . . . His power's crafty," she said quietly. "He blocked my sense of time. I wasn't prepared to stay so long, which explains why I was so weak when I came back."

She took the coffee Nell offered, sipped,

considered. "It won't do to forget that a second time. You look a little peaked, Lu. Aren't you well?"

"Up late watching a Charles Bronson marathon," Lulu lied glibly, and behind the counter Nell flushed with guilt. "That Logan boy took good care of you?"

"Yes, Lulu. That Logan boy took good care of me. You sound like you're catching a cold."

The surefire way to distract her girl, Lulu knew, was to poke at her. "I didn't see his fancy car in front of the cottage this morning."

"Because it's still parked in my driveway. He sat up all night with me, then fixed me a nearly inedible breakfast this morning, after which I seduced him in the shower. As a result I'm feeling very rested, very serene, and just a little hungry. Nell, how about one of those apple muffins?"

"He sold his condo in New York City," Lulu stated, and had the satisfaction of seeing Mia blink.

"Really?"

"I keep my ear to the ground. Signed the papers on it just yesterday. Got a bunch of stuff going into storage. Doesn't sound like he's planning on going back there anytime soon."

"No, it doesn't." She couldn't think about that, Mia told herself. Not just now. "And as fascinating as that is, we've more immediate concerns than where Sam stores his living room furniture."

"Smart money says he sells it."

"Hmm. In any case," Mia continued, "we have to decide what to do, if anything, about Evan Remington. I don't think the authorities would sanction a coven of witches attempting a casting out on an inmate."

She nibbled her muffin as she considered. "And to be honest, I don't think it would work, not the way it did with Harding last winter. Harding was a pawn, unaware and largely unwilling. Remington isn't unwilling, and my sense is that he knows. He not only accepts, but revels in what comes into him. He welcomes it."

"I could get in to see him." Nell waited for Mia to look back at her. "He would agree to that. I might be able to reach him."

"You couldn't." Mia reached out to squeeze Nell's hand. "You're part of his catalyst. More important, Zack would have my head, and rightly so, if I encouraged you to

try. Another face-to-face encounter between you and Remington is too dangerous
under any circumstances, but it might be
harmful for the baby."

"I wouldn't try to . . ." Nell's eyes went
wide. "How did you know about the baby? I
took a home pregnancy test at dawn." She
pressed a hand to her belly. "I'm going to the
doctor this afternoon to back it up. I haven't
even told Zack. I want to be sure first."

"Be sure. I felt it when I took your hand."
Joy swam into Mia's heart, over her face.
"New life. Oh, Nell."

"I knew, the night . . . when I conceived, I
knew. I felt a light inside." Tears spilled over.
"I was afraid to believe it, to get my hopes
up. We're having a baby!" She pressed her
hands to her cheeks, spun in a circle.
"We're having a baby! I have to tell Zack."

"Go, tell him now. Right now. We can handle things here until you get back, can't we,
Lu? Lu?" Mia turned, saw Lulu digging a tissue out of her pocket.

"Got allergies," Lulu announced in a
strangled voice. "Go on." She waved a
hand at Nell. "Go tell your man he's going to
be a daddy."

"A daddy!" Nell danced around the

counter, threw her arms around Lulu's neck, then around Mia's. "Oh, I can't wait to see his face. Oh, oh, and Ripley's! I won't be long. I'll be back." She raced for the stairs, then spun around with her face glowing. "I'm having a baby."

"You'd think no one ever managed to get knocked up before." After a last sniff, Lulu stuffed the tissue back in her pocket. "Guess I'll have to knit some booties. A blanket." She shrugged. "Somebody has to step in and play grandma."

Mia slid her arm around Lulu's waist, rested her cheek on the older woman's hair. "Let's sit down a minute and have a good cry."

"Yeah." Lulu dragged the tissue back out. "Good idea."

Nothing, Mia was determined, was going to smear this window of joy. Not a three-hundred-year curse, not the inconvenience and confusion brought on by the early stages of expansion. And most certainly not her own prickles of envy.

Whatever had to be done, Nell would

have these thrilling days of happiness and discovery.

Because of the hammering and the blocked view from what had been the café windows, the lunch crowd had dwindled down to the adventurous ones and the diehards. To Mia's way of thinking, the timing couldn't have been better. The smaller crowds allowed Nell a few more hours off a week and the luxury of being distracted.

By the solstice, the bulk of the job would be done. And if the café wasn't yet picture perfect, her customers would be able to dine alfresco on her new little terrace.

From the sidewalk outside the bookstore, Mia measured the progress. The cantilevered overhang would, when all was said and done, blend well with the rest of her building. She intended to hang baskets of flowers from either end. She'd already ordered the curving ironwork for the banister and had selected the slate for the terrace floor.

She could visualize it completed, decked with café tables, pots of summer flowers. And paying customers.

"Coming right along." Zack stopped beside her.

"Better than I could have hoped. We'll try it out during solstice week and be a hundred percent by the July Fourth holiday." She let out a deep, satisfied breath. "How are you, Sheriff Daddy?"

"Couldn't be better. It's been the best year of my life."

"You'll be a good father."

"I'm going to work hard to be."

"You will," she agreed. "But the core of it will just be there. Do you remember when we were kids and I used to come to your house?"

"Sure, if you weren't there with Rip, she was up at your place."

"I always loved coming there, watching your family. Sometimes I'd pretend they were mine." She leaned into him when he stroked her hair. "Just wondering what it would be like to have that kind of focus, I suppose, from my parents. That interest and amusement and pride. All those things that were so much a part of your house."

"I guess they were."

"Oh, Zack, sometimes I'd see your mother look over at you, or Ripley, and just grin. I could hear her thinking, just look at those kids. Aren't they great? And they're mine. Your parents didn't just tend you, didn't just love you. They enjoyed you."

"We were lucky. We enjoyed them right back."

"I know. Lulu gave me that, so much of that. So did my grandmother when she was alive. So I understood what it was. And because I did, my parents' innate disinterest in me was such a puzzle. In some ways it still is."

"Well." Because he thought she needed it, he pressed a kiss to her hair. "There were times growing up when I'd think you were lucky because you could get away with more than I could. You just had Lu running herd on you, and I had two people."

"She did the work of two people," Mia said dryly. "Two sneaky people. She would always let me run right to the end of the tether, then, when I thought I'd get away with it, she'd yank me right back."

"She's still running herd on you."

"Don't I know it. Anyway, to circle back to where we were before this ramble turned around to be about me, I wanted to say you're going to be a terrific father. You come by it naturally."

"There's nothing I won't do to protect Nell

and the baby. I need to ask you straight out if anything the three of you plan to do can hurt the baby."

"No." She framed his face with her hands. "No, I promise you. And I'll give you my word, my vow, that I'll protect her child, your child, as I would my own."

"Okay, then. Now I'm going to ask you one more thing. You trust me."

"Zack, I already do."

"No." He curled his fingers around her wrists, surprising her with the sudden intensity. "You trust me to do my job, and that job is to protect the people on my island. You trust me to care about you, to stand for you the same way I would my sister. You trust me to help you when it comes time to finish this. You trust me enough for that."

"For all of that," she told him. "And more. I love you."

Sam stepped onto the curb in time to hear her say it. And hearing it, he felt a twinge in his gut. Not in jealousy—he knew better—but in envy that another man could draw such absolute trust and warmth from her. That another man could hear that quiet and heartfelt declaration, even as a friend.

It took all his willpower to work up a sneer. "Greedy son of a bitch." Sam punched Zack lightly on the shoulder. "Haven't you already got a woman?"

"Seems I do." Still, Zack leaned down, kissed Mia on the mouth. "In fact, I think I'll go on up and see what she's up to. Nice kissing you, Ms. Devlin."

"Nice kissing you, Sheriff Todd."

"Looks like I have to do better than nice." To work off some of the frustration, Sam spun her around, caught her up, and gave her a long, sizzling kiss that had a trio of women across the street breaking out in applause.

"Well." Mia caught her breath and tried to uncurl her toes. "I suppose that was a few levels above nice. But then, you always were competitive."

"Take an hour off with me and I'll show you some competition."

"That's such an interesting offer. But—" She put a hand on his chest and eased back. "We're just a little pressed with the remodeling. I've already used up my break kissing the sheriff."

"Why don't you serve me lunch? I thought I'd scope out your menu."

"Your patronage is appreciated. The violet-and-herb salad is getting raves today." She walked to the door and opened it.

"I'm not eating flowers."

"I'm sure Nell has something suitably manly to offer you. Like a raw, meaty bone."

"Phone's for you," Lulu called out as Mia started up the stairs.

"I'll take it in my office." She glanced back at Sam. "You know the way to the café."

He did indeed. He settled on the Cajun chicken sandwich and an iced coffee. And watched the workmen.

It had been to his benefit as much as Mia's for him to spring the crew for a few weeks. His season was underway, and the guest rooms already rehabbed were fully occupied. After the Fourth, he intended to put the workers on half days so as not to disturb his guests during the early-morning or early-evening hours.

That would take them into September. And by September, he thought, he'd know what to do with the rest of his life.

She wasn't letting him get any closer. She welcomed him into her bed—but wouldn't sleep in his. She would talk about work, about the island, about magic. But she'd made it clear that an entire decade of their lives was off-limits.

Once or twice he'd tried to bring up his time in New York, but she'd simply closed down, or walked away.

Though they were both aware that everyone on the island knew they were lovers, she wouldn't go out with him. She hadn't had dinner with him in public since that first business meeting. His suggestions that they take an evening on the mainland and have dinner or go to the theater had been brushed away.

The underlying message came through clear enough. She was telling him she would sleep with him, enjoy him, but they weren't a couple.

Brooding over his sandwich, he wondered how many men would celebrate finding themselves in his position. He had an extraordinarily beautiful woman who was willing to share sex with him and expected—indeed permitted—little else. No strings, no expectations, no promises.

And he wanted more. That, he admitted, had been the root of the problem from the beginning. He'd wanted more, but he'd been too young, too stupid, too stubborn to see that the more was all Mia.

When she sat down across from him, he found his heart was in his throat and ready to spill out. "Mia—"

"I got Caroline Trump." She snatched his iced coffee, drank deep. "I just got off the phone with her publicist. I have her for the second Saturday in July. You should've heard how cool and professional I was on the phone. She'd never have guessed I was turning cartwheels."

"In that dress?"

"Ha ha. Sam." She reached over to take his hands. "I know your influence is largely responsible for this. I'm grateful. I want you to know how much I appreciate you putting in a good word for the store."

"That part was easy. Now don't screw up."

"I won't. I already designed the ad, in anticipation. I have to talk to Nell about food." She started to spring up, then hesitated. "So, do you have any plans for the solstice?"

He met her gaze, kept his voice as casual

as hers. Though they both knew she was offering to take another step. One that was,
for her, a big one.

"No, no formal plans."

"You do now."

# Twelve

Mia closed and locked the door behind the last straggle of customers. Then leaned back against it and looked at Lulu. "Long day."

"I thought that last group was going to make camp in here." Lulu shut down the cash register for the night, then zipped the cash bag. "You want to take this moola home, or should I make a night deposit?"

"How much moola?"

Because they both enjoyed it, Lulu unzipped the bag, pulled out the stack of bills, and flipped her thumb over the ends. "Lots of cash customers today."

"God bless them every one. I'll do the deposit. Credit card receipts?"

"Right here."

Rolling her shoulders, Mia crossed over, scanned the stack. "Business is good."

"Solstice week, sucks them right in. I had two teenagers in here today, summer girls. Wanted to know if they could see the witch and get some love potion."

Amused, Mia leaned on the counter. "And what did you tell them?"

"I told them sure, and how well the beauty potion worked for me. That sent them scurrying."

"Well, they have to learn not to look for life cures in a pretty bottle of potion."

"You put out some fancy jars full of colored water during solstice week, and customers would trip over themselves to buy them. Mia's Magic Mix, for love, beauty, and prosperity."

"Terrifying thought." Mia angled her head. "In all these years, Lu, you've never once asked me for a spell or a charm. For luck, love, fast money. Why is that?"

"I get on well enough on my own." Lulu hauled her enormous purse from behind the counter. "Besides, don't think I don't know you look out for me anyway. Better start looking out for yourself."

"What an odd thing to say. I always look out for myself."

"Sure, you've got your house, and you

live well. Live the way you see fit to live. You've got your looks, and you're healthy. Got more shoes than a Vegas chorus line."

"Shoes separate us from the lower mammals."

"Yeah, yeah. You just like having men look at your legs."

Mia trailed a hand through her hair. "Well, naturally."

"Anyway." Lulu focused in. She knew her girl, and she knew when that girl was trying to distract her. "You run things pretty much as you want to. Got good friends. And you've made this place into something you can be proud of."

"We made it," Mia corrected.

"Well, I didn't sit on my hands, but this is your place." Lulu gave a decisive nod that took in the entire store. "And it shines."

"Lu." Touched, Mia brushed Lulu's arm as she came around the counter. "It means a lot to me that you'd think that, say that."

"It's fact. And there's another fact, one that worries me some nights. You're not happy."

"Of course I am."

"No, you're not. And worse, you don't think you're ever going to be. Not deep-down-in-the-gut happy. You want to give me a spell, you fix that. That's all I have to say. Now I'm going to go put my feet up and watch my video of *Die Hard.* I like seeing Bruce Willis kick ass."

With no comeback, Mia simply stood there while Lulu strode through the store and out the back. Unsettled now, she took the cash and receipts and wandered through the store. It did shine, she thought. She had put a great deal of energy and imagination to use here. Financial resources and intellect, long, hard hours and eclectic taste.

And nearly seven years of her life.

It made her happy, she insisted as she walked up the stairs. It challenged and fulfilled her. That was enough. She'd made it be enough. Maybe she had once assumed she would have a different kind of life. A life that included a man who loved her and the children they made together.

But that had been a young girl's fantasy, and she had put away such dreams.

Just because she didn't have those things didn't mean they were missing, she thought as she went into her office to fill out the deposit slips. It only meant she'd taken

another path, ended up at a different destination.

In-the-gut happy, she mused, and sighed.
How many people were, when it came right
down to it? Wasn't it just as important to be
satisfied, fulfilled, successful? And wasn't it
essential to any level of happiness to feel in
control of your life?

She heard, as clearly as fingernails scraping against glass, the dark pressing against
her windows. She looked outside. The sky
was still glowing with the light of a summer
evening. But the dark was there, just at the
edges, trying to find a crack, a chink in her
will.

"You won't use me to destroy." She said
it clearly, so her voice carried through the
empty store. "Whatever else I do in my life,
I won't be used. You are not welcome here."

And there at her desk, with the day's receipts and paperwork neatly stacked, she
spread her arms, palms up, and called the
light. It shimmered in her hands like gilded
pools, then flowed out in golden rivers. As it
spilled from her, the dark slithered back.

Pleased, she gathered what she needed
to make the deposits.

Before she left the store, she detoured to her new terrace. The doorwalls had been installed that day, and she unlocked the glass, slid it open. Stepped out into the evening.

The ironwork railing was exactly as she'd wanted. Fussy and female. She laid her hands on it, gave it a quick, testing shake, and was satisfied at its unyielding strength. Beauty, she thought, never had to be weak.

From her vantage point she could see the curve of beach, the roll of the sea. And the first sword of white from her lighthouse as dusk faded toward night. The dark that crept in now was benign, full of hope.

Below her, High Street was still busy. Tourists were out for strolls, wandering into the ice cream parlor for a treat. The air was so clear she could hear bits of conversation and the shouts and squeals of young people on the beach.

As the first stars glimmered to life, she felt her throat go tight with a longing that she refused to recognize, and couldn't resolve.

"If you had a trellis, I'd climb up."

She looked down and there he was. Dark and handsome, and just a little dangerous.

Was it any wonder the girl she'd been had fallen so pathetically in love with Sam Logan?

"Climbing up into business establishments after hours is discouraged on the island."

"I've got pull with the local authorities, so I'd risk it. But why don't you come down? Come out and play, Mia. It's a hell of a night."

There had been a time when she would have run to him. Because she remembered just how easy it had been for her to forget everything and anything but him, she simply leaned out over the railing. "I have an errand to do and another long day tomorrow. I'm going by the bank, then home."

"How can anyone so beautiful be so stuffy? Hey"—he grabbed the arm of one of three men walking by, then pointed up—"isn't she spectacular? I'm trying to hit on her, but she's not cooperating."

"Why don't you give the guy a break?" one of the men called to her, only to be elbowed aside by one of his companions.

"The hell with him. Give *me* a break." He laid a hand dramatically on his heart. "I think I'm in love. Hey, Red."

"Hey, yourself."

"Let's us get married and move to Trinidad."

"Where's the ring?" she demanded. "I don't move to Trinidad unless I have a big fat diamond on my finger."

"Hey." The man jabbed one of his friends. "Lend me ten thousand dollars so I can buy a big fat diamond and move to Trinidad with Red."

"If I had ten K, *I'd* move to Trinidad with her."

"Now see what you've done." Sam chuckled. "Destroying friendships, inciting riots. You'd better come down here and go with me before my new pals and I have to beat the crap out of each other."

Amused, she laughed, stepped back, and shut the doors.

He waited for her. When he'd seen her standing on the terrace, he'd been staggered. She'd looked so enchanting, and so sad. Heartbreaking. He'd have done anything in his power to lift that quiet sorrow. And anything, nearly anything, to reach past that thin shield she kept between them. He wanted to see what was in her mind. In her heart.

Maybe the key, at least for one precious evening, was to keep things simple.

He stood on the sidewalk when she came out and locked the front door behind her. She wore a slim dress that flowed around her ankles and was scattered with tiny yellow rosebuds. Her shoes were a series of slender crisscrossing straps and a high wedged platform. He found the thin chain of gold around her left ankle ridiculously sexy.

She turned, hitched the strap of her bag onto her shoulder, then scanned the sidewalk. "Where did your friends go?"

"I bribed them with free drinks at the Coven." He jerked his head toward the hotel.

"Ah. Replaced by a cold beer."

"Want to go to Trinidad?"

"No."

He took her hand. "Want an ice cream cone?"

She shook her head. "I have to go to the bank, make a night deposit. Which, I'll point out, isn't being stuffy but responsible."

"Uh-huh. I'll walk with you."

"What are you doing in the village?" she asked as they started toward the bank. "Working late?"

"Not particularly. I went home about an hour ago. I was restless." He shrugged his shoulders. "Came back." And, he thought, had timed it exactly as he'd planned. Just as she'd be closing.

He glanced over, studied a small group of people on the opposite side of the street. They were decked in flowing robes and weighed down with silver chains and crystal pendants.

"Amateurs," he commented.

"They're harmless."

"We could call up a storm, turn the street into a meadow. Give them a real thrill."

"Stop it." She drew out her key for the deposit slot.

"See—stuffy." He heaved a sigh. "It's painful to see such a bright hope turn into a rule book."

"Really." Efficiently, she made her deposit, tucked her copy of the transaction into her cash bag. "I don't recall you ever so much as looking at a rule book."

"When they look like you, I study them in depth."

His moods, she thought, were many and varied. Tonight's seemed to be foolish.

She could do with some foolishness.

And as the group of would-be witches approached a window box filled with struggling dahlias, she gave a graceful turn of her hand. The flowers sprang up like jewels, full and bright.

"And the crowd goes wild." Sam acknowledged the reaction across the street, the shouts, the gasps. "Nice touch."

"Stuffy, my butt. I'll take that ice cream now."

He bought her a frothy swirl of orange and cream and talked her into enjoying it during a walk on the beach. The moon was nearly full. It would be fat and round by the weekend, and the solstice.

And a full moon on the solstice meant bounty, and promise. And the rites of fertility that lead to harvest.

"Last year I went to Ireland for the solstice," he told her. "There's a small stone dance there, in County Cork. It's more intimate than Stonehenge. The sky stays light until nearly ten, and when it begins to fade, toward the end of the longest day, the stones sing."

She said nothing, but paused to look out to sea. Over it, she thought, thousands of miles away, was another island. And the stone circle where he had been a year ago.

She had been here, where she always was. A solitary witch. A solitary celebration.

"You've never gone," he said. "Never gone over to Ireland."

"No."

"There's magic there, Mia. Deep in the soil, bright in the air."

She continued to walk. "There's magic everywhere."

"I found a cove, on the rocky western coast. And a cave, nearly hidden by the tumble of the rocks. And I knew it was where he'd gone when he left her here."

He waited until Mia stopped again, turned to him. "Three thousand miles across the Atlantic. He'd been pulled back by his own blood. I knew how it felt, to be pulled that way."

"Is that why you go to Ireland? You're drawn by your blood?"

"It's why I go there, and why I came back here. When you've done what you need to do, I'd like to take you. To show you."

She licked delicately at her ice cream. "I don't need to be taken anywhere."

"I'd like to go with you."

"You learn fast, don't you?" Mia said. "I may go one day." She shrugged and wandered closer to the surf. "We'll see if I want company. I will say, though, you were right about one thing. It's a hell of a night."

She threw back her head, drank in the stars and sea air.

"Take off your dress."

She kept her head back. "Excuse me?"

"Let's go swimming."

She nipped into the cone. "I realize it may seem fussy to a sophisticated urbanite like yourself, but there are laws against nude swimming on the public beach in our little world."

"Laws—that would be the same as rules, right?" He scanned the beach. They weren't alone, but there was hardly a crowd. "Don't tell me you're shy."

"Circumspect," she corrected.

"Okay, we'll preserve your dignity." He spread his hands and conjured a bubble around them. "We see out, but nobody sees in. It's just you and me in here."

Stepping to her, he reached around, slowly lowered the zipper in the back of her dress. He could see her thinking, considering, as she finished off the cone. "A moonlight swim's a nice way to cap off the evening. Haven't forgotten how to swim, have you?"

"Hardly." She slipped out of her shoes, then let the dress slither down. She wore nothing but amber beads and a glitter of rings. Turning, she strolled into the surf, then dived into the dark sea.

She swam strong, cutting cleanly through the breakers and reveling in the sensation of streaking through the water as unencumbered as a mermaid. Until her spirit began to hum—with pure joy—she hadn't realized how much she'd needed this.

Freedom, fun, and foolishness.

She circled a buoy, listening to its hollow clang, then rolled over to float lazily on her back under a bejeweled sky. The water lapped gently over her breasts as he swam to her.

"You ever beat Ripley in a swim race?"

"No. Much to my regret." Mia trailed her fingers through the water. "Putting her in water's like putting a bullet in the air."

"I used to watch the two of you in the inlet over at the Todds'. I'd be hanging out with Zack and pretending not to notice you."

"Really? I never noticed you."

It didn't surprise her to find her head underwater. She'd expected it. And because she had, she turned like an eel in the water and jerked him under by the ankles.

She surfaced, slicked back her hair. "You always were a sucker for that move."

"It got your hands on me, so who's the sucker?" He treaded water in circles around her, his hair black and glossy as a seal. "I remember the first time I maneuvered you into wrestling with me wet. You had on this blue number, cut so high up on the hips that I speculated your legs went clean up to your ears. That sexy pentagram birthmark like gold on your thigh, driving me nuts. You were fifteen."

"I remember the suit. I don't recall being maneuvered."

"You were cooling off with Rip in the water. Zack was fooling around with his boat at the dock. He'd just gotten that boat. Fast little fourteen-footer."

She remembered that well enough. Remembered perfectly how her heart had slammed into her ribs when Sam, long and tanned a summer gold, had sauntered out onto the dock wearing nothing but cutoffs and a teenage smirk.

"There were a number of times I swam with Ripley in the inlet while Zack tinkered with his boat. And you came along."

"This particular day," Sam continued, "I bided my time, fiddling on the boat with Zack, plotting out my moves. I got him to take a break, and in we went. That meant a lot of splashing, which meant you and Ripley had to bitch about being splashed. And doing so, you fell right into my clever hands."

Like Sam, Mia began to tread and circle. She'd always enjoyed him in these playful moods. They'd been rare in his youth. She imagined they were rare still.

"I believe you have delusions of grandeur in your faulty memory."

"Memory's clear as a bell on this one. I egged Zack into challenging Rip to a race, which left the two of us bobbing around. Which meant, naturally, I could challenge you to a race."

"Oh, yes. I do seem to recall something of that sort."

Perfectly. She remembered perfectly, the

nervy thrill of floating in the water with him, of having him focus on her with those sea-toned eyes. And the longing that had swept through her like a summer storm.

"Of course, I held back, paced myself so it was close, so I beat you by only a stroke."

"Held back?" She dipped back her head, studied the stars. "Please."

"Oh, yeah, I knew what I was doing. You said it was a tie, and I said I'd crushed you. When you got huffy, I dunked you."

"When I protested your bad call, you dunked me," she corrected.

"You retaliated, as I'd anticipated, by locking your arms around my knees and hauling me under. Whereby, I could engage you in the sort of battle that allowed me, at last, to get my hands on your excellent young ass. It was a moment for me. Then you giggled."

She made a derisive sound. "I've never giggled in my life."

"Oh, yeah, you did. You giggled and squirmed and wriggled around until I was so worked up I thought I'd explode."

She let her feet come up and floated again. "Foolish, foolish boy. When you wrestle naked with a female, she's bound to discover just where your brain cells have gathered."

"You were fifteen. What did you know?"

Now she smirked. "Enough to wriggle and squirm until I obtained a satisfactory result."

"You did it on purpose?"

"Of course. Then Ripley and I discussed it in some detail."

"That better be a lie." He reached across the water, grabbed a handful of her hair.

"We were both fascinated and amused. And if it soothes your ego, I'll finish this walk down memory lane by telling you I had hot, disturbing, and imaginative dreams for a week afterward."

He tugged at her hair until their bodies bumped. Then he skimmed his hand over the wet white slope of her breast. "So did I." He trailed a fingertip down her torso, back up again. "Mia?"

"Mmm."

"I bet I can still make you giggle."

Before she could evade, he nipped her by the waist and turned her facedown in the water. Taken by surprise, she flailed for a moment, then rolled when his fingers moved unerringly up her ribs.

"Stop it." Her hair was in her face, saltwater in her eyes.

"Giggle," he insisted, tickling ruthlessly. "And squirm and wriggle."

"You idiot." She couldn't see or catch her breath. Despite her struggles the helpless and foolish laughter escaped. It rolled out of her and over the waves as she slapped at him and tried to wiggle free.

She managed to get a grip on his hair and yank, while trying to shove her own out of her face. But he only rolled them over and over into the waves until she was dizzy, disoriented, and brutally aroused.

"Damn octopus." His hands were everywhere.

"You've got a hell of a squirm. And it still works. Only this time"—he gripped her hips—"why just dream?" And plunged into her.

He went home with her, and they ate bowls of cold pasta like ravenous children. With hunger unabated, they fell into bed and fed off each other.

Tangled with him, she slipped into sleep,

and into dreams of floating in a dark sea as peacefully as the moon sailed the night sky. She drifted on her own pleasure, the water cool, the air sweet. In the distance, the shadows and shapes of her island rose out of the sea. It slept, with only the beam from the cliff light guarding it from the dark.

The music of the waves lulled her until she, too, slept.

And the stars erupted into bolts of lightning, stabbing down at the shadows and shapes of her island. Around her the sea began to thrash and heave, pulling her helplessly away from home.

She fought, striking out with hard, desperate strokes toward the fog that had begun to build a dirty wall at the shore. Waves swamped her, spun her into that breathless black, slapped her back, dragged her under.

Roaring filled the night, and the screams that followed it ripped at her heart. With what strength she had left, she reached for the fire inside her. But she was too late to beat the dark.

She watched the island fall into the sea. Even as she wept, it pulled her down with it.

She woke curled away from Sam, drawn

into a tight ball and clinging to the edge of the bed. Trembling, she rose, walked to the window to soothe herself with the view of her garden, of the steady beam of the island light.

Would it come to that? Would she do everything that could be done, and have it still not be enough?

Through the night she heard the long, triumphant howl of a wolf. Knowing that it wanted her to cower, she stepped out onto her little balcony.

"I am fire." She said it softly. "And what's in me will, one day, purge you."

"Mia."

She turned and saw Sam sitting up in bed. "Yes, I'm here."

"What is it?"

"Nothing." She came back in, but left the doors open to the night. "Just restless."

"Come back to bed." He held out a hand. "Let me help you sleep."

"All right." She slid in beside him, turned her body to his. Invitation.

But he only drew her close, stroked her hair. "Close your eyes. Let your mind go. Let it go for one night."

"I'm not—"

"Let it go," he repeated, and stroking her hair, he charmed her into a deep and dreamless sleep.

# Thirteen

"This," Mia said as the sun broke the sky in the east with an arrow of fire, "is for us. The Midsummer sabbat, the celebration of the earth's coming bounty, the warmth of the air, and the full power of the sun. We are the Three."

"Yeah, yeah." Ripley yawned hugely. "And if we can get on with this, I might be able to get home and catch another hour's sleep."

"Your reverence is, as always, inspiring."

"You'll remember, I voted against standing around up here at dawn. Since it's Sunday, both of you can go back to bed. I'm on duty all day."

"Ripley"—Nell managed to make her voice mild and patient—"it's the solstice. Celebrating the longest day should begin when the day begins."

"I'm here, aren't I?" Ripley scowled at

Nell. "You're awfully bright and chipper for a pregnant woman. Why aren't you flat out with morning sickness?"

"I've never felt better in my life."

"Or looked happier," Mia said. "We'll celebrate fertility today. The earth's and yours. The first balefire has burned since sunset. The dawn fire is for you to light."

She lifted a circlet she'd woven from lavender and set it on Nell's head. "You're the first of us to carry life, and to take what we are to the next generation. Blessed be, little sister."

She kissed Nell's cheeks, then stepped back.

"Okay, that gets me misty." Ripley moved up, kissed Nell in turn, then linked her hand with Mia's.

Nell lifted her arms and let the power ripple into her. "From dawn until the day is done, this fire we make glows bright as the sun. As light grows strong across the sky, I call the flames from air to fly. Burn no flesh, no feather nor tree. As I will, so mote it be."

Fire spewed up from the ground, bright as gold.

Mia lifted another circlet from the white cloth on the ground. Set it on Ripley's head.

Though she rolled her eyes for form, Ripley lifted her arms. The power was warm, and welcome.

"In the earth we sow our seed that she may grant us what we need. Across her breast the dawn brings light, all through this day to shortest night. We celebrate her fertility. As I will, so mote it be."

Wildflowers sprang up through the earth to ring the circle.

Before Mia could reach for the third circlet, Ripley picked it up, and kissed her. "Just to make it official," she said and settled the flowers on Mia's hair.

"Thanks." She, in turn, lifted her arms. Power was like breath. "Today the sun holds its full power. Its strength and light grow hour by hour. Its bright fire warms the air and earth. Its cycle sustains us birth to death to birth. I celebrate the fire in me. As I will, so mote it be."

From her fingertips beams shot, to the sun, and from the sun to her. Until the circle in the clearing shimmered with the birth of the day.

She lowered her arms, joined hands with Nell, with Ripley. "He watches," she told them. "And he waits."

"Why don't we do something about it?" Ripley demanded. "The three of us are here, and like both of you keep hammering home, it's the solstice. That's a lot of punch."

"It isn't the time to—" Mia broke off when Nell squeezed her hand.

"Mia. A show of force, of solidarity and strength. Why not make a point? Our circle is whole."

A point, Mia thought. Perhaps the unbroken circle was the point. At least for the moment. She could feel, through the link, Nell's determination, Ripley's passion.

"Well, then, let's not be subtle."

She gathered herself, and the pooled strength of her sisters.

"We are the Three and of the blood," Ripley began, moving like her sisters in a ring within the ring. "From us the force and light will flood."

"With might that strikes the waiting dark." Nell's voice rose to echo on the air. "An arrow of light toward what bears our mark."

"Here we stand so you can see." With hands still joined, Mia lifted her arms. "And beware the wrath of the sisters three."

Light spewed up from the center of the circle like a funnel, whirling, roaring as it geysered up. Like the arrow Nell had called, it shot out of the circle, out of the clearing, and into the shadows of the summer trees.

From those shadows came a single furious howl.

Then there was only the quiet breeze and the musical call of crystals hanging from branches.

"So he slinks away," Mia remarked.

"That felt good." Ripley rolled her shoulders.

"It did. It felt positive." Letting out a long breath, Nell looked around the clearing. "It felt right."

"Then it was right. Today, he can't touch us or ours." Whatever came after, Mia thought, they had made a stand. They had made their point. She lifted her face to the sun. "It's a beautiful day."

She intended to spend it in her garden, away from the crowds that would pack into the village and the traffic that would stream along the roads. She intended to spend it on simple things, the tasks that gave her pleasure.

A day without worry, she thought. A clean and clear day with all shadows brushed away like dust with a broom.

She gathered the herbs and flowers she'd selected for her midsummer harvest with a bolline, the curved white-handled knife she saved for that purpose alone. The scents and shapes and textures never failed to delight her, the variety of their uses never failed to satisfy.

Some she would dry by hanging them in her kitchen, some in her tower room.

She would make charms from some, potions from others. From soaps to creams to healing balms and divination aids. And some would simply be sprinkled into sauces and salads for flavor, or mixed into a potpourri to scent the air.

Just before twelve she stopped to light the noon balefire. She set it on her cliffs, like a beacon. And stood for a time watching the sea and the pleasure boats that skimmed over it.

Now and then she saw the glint of binoculars and knew she was watched as she watched. There! the summer people would say. Up on the cliffs. She's supposed to be a witch.

Such attention would once have caused her to be hunted and hanged. Now, Mia thought, the possibility of magic brought people to the island and into her store.

So the wheel ran, she mused. A circle spinning.

She went back to her garden. When her herbs were tied and hung, she used the sun to brew a small pot of chamomile tea. She had it iced with a hint of fresh mint when Sam stepped onto her path.

"Traffic's a bitch," he said.

"Midsummer and Mabon draw the most tourists." She poured the tea into a glass. "Tourists who are interested in such things," she added. "Did you light your balefire?"

"This morning, near your circle in my woods. Your woods," he corrected when she arched her eyebrows. Absently, he reached down to pet Isis, who had come to rub against his legs. He noted the new collar and the charm hanging from it, a pentagram carved on one side, a sun wheel on the other.

"New?"

"For the Midsummer blessing." She cut a slice of bread from a fresh loaf, drizzled it with honey, and offered it to him. "I made more than the faeries need."

He took a bite, but she noticed that his restless gaze roamed her garden. It was rich and ripe with summer, the tall spires dancing in the breeze, the mobs of color tumbling over the ground. He watched a hummingbird flash by, then drink from the long purple bells of foxglove.

Roses, red as passion, climbed up the trellis to her old bedroom window as he had once climbed, risking flesh and bone to reach her.

The scent of summer roses could still make his heart ache.

Now he sat with her, in the sun and dappled shade of her garden. Adults with more weighing on them than the girl and boy could have imagined.

She wore a sleeveless dress, green as the lush leaves that surrounded them. And her face, beautiful and calm, told him nothing.

"Where are we, Mia?"

"In my midsummer garden, having tea with bread and honey. It's a lovely day for it." She lifted her cup. "But judging from your mood, perhaps I should have served wine."

He rose, paced away. He would, she knew, tell her what was on his mind soon enough. Whether or not she wanted to hear it. Only a few nights before, he'd been light-hearted and playful enough to coax her into a swim. But today there was a cloud around him.

He'd always been a moody creature.

"My father called me this morning," he told her.

"Ah."

"Ah," Sam repeated, and managed to make the syllable a bite. "He's 'displeased with my performance.' That's a direct quote. I'm putting too much time and money into the hotel here."

"It's your hotel."

"I pointed that out. My hotel, my time, and my money." Sam rammed his hands into his pockets. "I might've saved my breath. I'm told I'm making rash and dangerous financial and career decisions. He's pissed off that I've sold my place in New York, annoyed that I've budgeted so much for the rehab at the hotel, and irked that I sent a proxy rather than attending the June board meeting personally."

Because she felt for him, Mia rose and

rubbed his stiff shoulders. "I'm sorry. It's difficult ramming up against parental disapproval. It doesn't matter how old we are, it stings when they don't understand us."

"The Magick Inn is our first and oldest asset. He's figured out that I finessed it from him. Now it's like a bone he wants to drag back from me."

"And you're just as determined to keep your teeth in it."

He shot a furious look over his shoulder. "Damn right. He'd have sold it to strangers years ago if he hadn't been legally bound to keep it in the family. He sold it to me happily enough, but now he's realized I intend to make something of it, so he's irritated. It's a thorn in his side. So am I."

"Sam." For a moment she pressed her cheek against his back. And for a moment she was sixteen again, and comforting her unhappy, moody love. "Sometimes you just have to take a step away, and accept what is."

"What is," he agreed, turning to her. "He never could. Neither he nor my mother ever accepted what I am. It was something not to be discussed, as if I had some sort of embarrassing condition."

Furious, as much because of letting himself be sucked in again as by the facts themselves, he strode down the path, through an arbor where morning glory vines were busily tangling.

"It's in his blood as much as mine." He saw her start to speak, then stop herself. "What? Just say it."

"All right, then. It's not the same for him. You respect what you have, you celebrate it. For him it's a . . . well, a pesky inherited trait: He's not alone in that. And because of it, you have more—are more—than he can ever have or be."

"He's ashamed of it. And me."

"Yes." Her heart wrung with pity. "I know. It hurts you. It always has. You can't change what he thinks or feels. You can only change what you feel."

"Is that how you handle your family?"

It took her a moment, and that was a jolt, to realize he meant her parents and not Lulu, or Ripley and Nell. "I used to envy you on some level. Just the fact that your parents worked up the interest and energy to push at you. Even if it meant pushing you in the wrong direction. We never argued here."

She turned back to study the house she

loved. "They never noticed if I was angry. My rebellions were completely wasted on them. There came a point when I had to accept that their disinterest wasn't personal."

"Oh, for Christ's sake."

She nearly laughed at his impatient explosion. "It was healthier, and more practical, and certainly more comfortable all around. What was the point of breaking my heart over it, when they wouldn't have noticed? Or if they had, it would have baffled them. They're not bad people, just careless parents. I'm who I am because they were what they were. That's enough for me."

"You always were sensible," he replied. "I could never figure out whether I admired that or found it annoying. I still can't."

"You always were moody." She sat on the bench by the arbor. "And the same goes. Still, it's a shame the call put a blight on your holiday."

"I'll get over it." He slipped his hands into his pockets again, fingering the tumbling stones he'd forgotten he carried. "He expects me back in New York within the month, to resume my proper place in the company."

Her world tilted. She gripped the edge of

the bench to balance herself, then forced herself to her feet. Forced shut that piece of her heart she'd allowed to be touched by his pain. "I see. When will you leave?"

"What? I'm not going back. Mia, I told you I was here to stay. I meant it, no matter what you think."

With a careless shrug, she turned to start back to the house.

"Damn it, Mia." He grabbed her arm, pulled her back.

"Watch your step." She said it coldly.

"Are you just waiting for me to pack up and go?" he demanded. "Is that where we are?"

"I'm not waiting for anything."

"What do I have to do to get us past this?"

"You can start by letting go of my arm."

"Letting go is just what you expect." To prove her wrong he took her other arm so they were facing each other in the dappled shade of the path. "So you won't let me touch you, not where it matters most. You'll take me to your bed, but you won't come to mine. You won't so much as sit and have a meal with me in a public place, unless it's under the guise of business. You won't let me talk about the years without you. And you won't share magic with me when we make love. Because you don't trust me to stay."

"Why should I? Why should I do any of those things? I prefer my bed. I don't choose to date. I'm not interested in your life off-island. And to share magic during the physical act of love is a level of intimacy I'm not willing to explore with you."

She shoved his hands aside and stepped back. "I've given you cooperation in business, some friendly companionship and sex. This is what suits me. If it doesn't suit you, find someone else to play with."

"This isn't a goddamn game."

Her voice was sharp. "Oh, isn't it?" He stepped toward her, and she held up her hands. Light, spitting red, shot between them. "Be careful."

He merely held up his own hands, and a wash of searing blue water struck the light until there was nothing but the sizzle of vapor between them. "Was I ever?"

"No. And you always wanted too much."

"Maybe I did. The problem was I didn't know what I wanted. You always did. It was always so fucking clear to you, Mia. What you needed, what you wanted. There were times when your vision choked me."

Stunned, she dropped her hands to her side. "Choked you? How can you say that to me? I loved you."

"Without questions, without doubts. It was as if you could see the rest of our lives in this pretty box. You had it all lined up for me. Just the way my parents did."

Her cheeks paled. "That's a cruel thing to say. And you've said enough." She hurried back down the path.

"It's not enough until I'm done. Running away from it doesn't change anything."

"You're the one who ran." She whirled back, and the pain of it crashed through all the years and struck her with a fresh blow. "It changed everything."

"I couldn't be what you wanted. I couldn't give you what you were so sure was meant to be. You looked ahead ten years, twenty, and I couldn't see the next day."

"So it's my fault you left?"

"I couldn't be here. For God's sake, Mia, we were hardly more than children and you were talking marriage. Babies. You'd lie beside me when my head was so full of you I couldn't think and talk about how we'd buy a little cottage by the woods and . . ."

He trailed off. It seemed to strike both of them at once. The little yellow cottage by the woods—where she hadn't come since he'd moved in.

"Young girls in love," she said, and her voice trembled, "dream about marriage and babies and pretty cottages."

"You weren't dreaming." He walked to her table again, sat and dragged his fingers through his hair. "It was destiny for you. When I was with you, I believed it. I could see it, too. And at that point it smothered me."

"You never said it wasn't what you wanted."

"I didn't know how, and every time I tried, I'd look at you. All that confidence, that utter faith that this was the way it would be. Then I'd go home and I'd see my parents and what marriage meant. I'd think of yours and what family meant. It was hollow and air-less. The idea of the two of us moving in that direction seemed insane. I couldn't talk to you about it. I didn't know how to talk to you about it."

"So instead, you left."

"I left. When I started college, it was like being torn in two. The part that wanted to be there, the part that wanted to be here. Be with you. I thought about you constantly."

He looked at her now. He would say to the woman what he'd never been able to say to the girl. "When I'd come home on weekends, or breaks, I'd be half sick until I'd see you waiting on the docks. That whole first year was like a blur."

"Then you stopped coming home every weekend," she remembered. "You made excuses for why you needed to stay on the mainland. To study, to go to a lecture."

"It was a test. I could go without seeing you for two weeks, then a month. Stop thinking about you for an hour, then a day. It got easier to convince myself that staying away from you, and the island, was the only way I was going to escape being trapped into that box. I didn't want to get married. I didn't want to start a family. Or be in love with one girl my entire life. Or root myself on a little island when I'd never really seen the world. I got a taste of the world in college, the people I met there, the things I learned. I wanted more."

"Well, you got more. And the lid's been off the box for a number of years. We're in different places now, with different goals."

He met her eyes. "I came back for you."

"That was your mistake. You still want more, Sam, but this time I don't. If you'd told me this eleven years ago, I would have tried to understand. I would have tried to give you the time and the room you needed. Or I'd have tried to let you go, without bitterness. I don't know if I would have succeeded, but I know I loved you enough that I would have tried. But you're not the center of my life any longer—you haven't been for some time."

"I'm not going away, or giving up."

"Those are your decisions." Ignoring the headache brewing, she gathered up the tea things. "I enjoy having you for a lover. I'll regret having to end that, but I will if you insist on pressing for a different dynamic in our relationship. I think I'll get that wine after all."

She carried the dishes inside, rinsed them. The headache was going to plague her, so she took a tonic before selecting a bottle of wine, taking out the proper glasses.

She didn't allow herself to think. Couldn't allow herself to feel. Since there was no going back, no crisscrossing over paths that were already long overgrown, the only direction was forward.

But when she stepped outside, he was gone.

Though her stomach fluttered once, she sat at the table in her midsummer garden and toasted her independence.

And the wine was bitter on her tongue.

He sent her flowers at the bookstore the next day. Simple and cheerful zinnias, which in the language of flowers meant he was thinking of her. She doubted he knew the charming meaning of a bouquet of zinnias, but puzzled over them nonetheless as she selected a suitable vase.

It wasn't like him to send flowers, she mused. Even when they'd been madly in love, he'd rarely thought to make such romantic gestures.

The card was explanation enough, she supposed. It read:

*I'm sorry.*
*Sam*

When she found herself smiling over the flowers instead of getting on with her work, she carried the vase downstairs and set it on the table by the fireplace.

"Aren't those sweet and cheerful?" Gladys Macey slipped up beside her to coo over the bouquet. "From your garden?"

"No, actually. They were a gift."

"Nothing perks a woman up more than getting flowers. Unless it's getting something sparkly," Gladys added with a wink. She slid a discreet glance over to Mia's left hand. But not discreet enough.

"I've found that a woman who buys herself something sparkly ends up with something that suits her own taste."

"Not the same, though." Gladys gave Mia's arm a quick squeeze. "Carl bought me a pair of earrings on my last birthday. Ugly as homemade sin, no question about it. But I feel good every time I put them on. I was just on my way up to the café to see how our Nell's getting on."

"She's getting on beautifully. When she

tells you she thinks she's started to show, just go along with her. It makes her happy."

"Will do. I just pre-ordered Caroline Trump's new book. We're all excited about her coming here. I've been delegated by the book club to ask if she would agree to doing a book discussion just before the official signing."

"I'll see if I can set it up."

"Just let us know. We're going to give her a real Three Sisters welcome."

"I'm counting on it."

Mia made the call to New York herself. Once the wheels were set in motion, she checked her book orders, called her distributor to nag about a delay in a selection of note cards, then picked up the newest batch of e-mail orders.

As Lulu was busy, Mia filled them herself, slipping in the notice that signed copies of Trump's book would be available. Then she carted them down to the post office.

She ran into Mac as she came out again. "Hello, handsome."

"Just the woman I was looking for."

Smiling, she slid her arm through his. "That's what they all say. Are you on your way to the café to meet Ripley for lunch?"

"I was on my way to the bookstore to talk to you." He glanced down, noted that she was wearing heels. "No point asking you to take a walk on the beach with me."

"Shoes come off."

"You'll ruin your stockings."

"I'm not wearing any."

"Oh." He flushed a bit, delighting her. "Well, let's walk, then, if you've got a few minutes."

"I always have a few minutes for attractive men. How's your book going?"

"Fits and starts."

"When it's finished, I expect Café Book to host your first signing."

"Nonfiction books with academic bents on paranormal science don't exactly draw in the crowds for book signings."

"They will at Café Book," she retorted.

They crossed the street, winding through the pedestrian traffic. Families returning from the beach, their skin pink, their eyes blurry from the sunlight, trudged into town for lunch or a cold drink. Others, loaded with coolers, umbrellas, towels, sunscreen, walked toward the sand and surf.

Mia slipped off her shoes. "By the time the solstice crowd thins out, the Fourth of

July crowd will stream in. We're having a good summer on the Sisters."

"Summers go fast."

"You're thinking of September. I know you're concerned, but I have it under control." When he didn't speak, she tipped down her sunglasses and peered over the tops. "You don't think so?"

He struggled with the guilt of keeping Lulu's incident from her, weighing it against her peace of mind. "I think you can handle just about anything that gets tossed at you."

"But?"

"But." He laid a hand over the one she'd curled around his arm. "You play by the rules."

"Not honoring the rules is what put us here."

"Agreed. I care about you, Mia."

She leaned her head on his shoulder. Something about him made her want to cuddle. "I know you do. You added to my life when you came into it. What you and Ripley have together adds to it."

"I like Sam."

She retreated, lifting her head. "Why shouldn't you?"

"Look, I'm not prying. Okay," he corrected, "I'm prying, but only for practical and scientific purposes."

"Bullshit," she said, laughing.

"All right, mostly for those purposes. If I don't know where the two of you stand, I can't weigh my theories and hypotheses. I can't calculate what we might need to do."

"Then I'll tell you we're, for the most part, enjoying each other. Our relationship is primarily comfortable and largely superficial. As far as I'm concerned, it's going to stay that way."

"Okay."

"You don't approve."

"It's not for me to approve. It's for you to choose."

"Exactly. Love, consuming and obsessive, destroyed the last sister. She refused to live without it. I refuse to live with it."

"If that was enough, it would be over."

"It will be over," she promised him.

"Look, Mia, there was a time when I believed it could be that simple."

"And now you don't?"

"Now I don't," he confirmed. "I was up at your place this morning. You said I could go up and take readings after the solstice."

"And?"

"I went up, took Mulder with me so he could get some exercise. To keep it simple, I'll say I started getting snags in the readings right at the edge of your front lawn. Positive and negative spikes. Like a . . ." He slammed the heels of his hands together to demonstrate. "One ramming against the other. I got similar readings around the verge, straight toward the cliffs on the other side of the lighthouse, and into the forest."

"I haven't been lax in protection."

"No, you haven't, and it's a damn good thing. We followed the readings away from the clearing, away from the heart. My sensors started going wild, and so did Mulder. He damn near snapped the leash. There's a path of negative energy. I could follow it, the way it circled around, like an animal might stalk prey."

"I know it's there, Mac. I don't ignore it."

"Mia, it's gaining strength. There were places along that path where everything was dead. Brush, trees, birds. The pup stopped straining at the leash and just curled up, crying. I had to carry him, and he didn't stop shaking until we'd come out again. We came out, following that path, at the north end of your cliffs."

"Have Ripley do a cleansing spell on the puppy, and on you. If she doesn't remember the ritual—"

"Mia." Mac grabbed her hand in a tight grip. "Don't you understand what I'm saying? It has you surrounded."

# Fourteen

"What did she say when you told her?"

As Sam paced his office, Mac lifted his hands. "That it has surrounded her all her life, but is just being more blatant about it now."

"Yeah, I can just hear her saying that. When we were—before I left the island, we talked about it a couple of times. She'd read up on it more than I had at that point. That's probably still true. The woman can absorb a book before most of us get to chapter two. She was so confident about it all. Good would overcome evil as long as good was strong and faithful."

"She's both of those. What I didn't tell her was that my readings picked up several different—let's call them fingerprints—on her side of the line. I'm assuming they'd be yours."

"Just because she doesn't want my protection doesn't mean she isn't going to get it."

"Whatever you're doing, keep it up."

Sam wandered to the window, looked out on the new terrace across the street. She had taken in the tables she'd put out for the weekend, and the crew was setting the slate in place. "How did she look today?"

"Spectacular."

"You should see her when she uses real power." Then he glanced back at Mac. "But I suppose you have."

"Late last winter—a call to the four elements. It took me half a day to come to my senses. I wonder if she uses the Wiccan equivalent of a dimmer switch on that face of hers for the everyday."

"No. The power punches it up, as if it wasn't enough already. Beauty like that blinds a man, muddles the brain. I've asked myself if it's that that pulls me to her."

"I can't answer that."

"I can now. I've loved her all my life. Before I knew what love meant, after I tried to redefine it. It's a nasty blow to finally understand that now, when she doesn't love me. Or won't."

He turned back, eased a hip onto the edge of his desk. "All right, scientifically speaking—or theoretically, academically, whatever you like—is my being here—no, loving her now—putting her at greater risk?"

"Your feelings don't count." As soon as he said it, Mac winced. "I didn't mean that the way it sounded."

"I get it. It's her feelings that tip the scale, one way or the other. In that case, I'm going to assume that trying to rekindle her feelings, or change them, won't hurt her. If you think otherwise, I'll hold off on that until after September."

"I can't tell you."

"Then I'm going with the gut. If nothing else, I intend to be as close to her as I can when it comes to the sticking point. Even the circle can use a guard dog."

He called her that night, at home, just as she was settling in with a book and a glass of wine.

"I hope I'm not catching you at a bad time."

"No." Mia pursed her lips as she studied

the play of light and liquid in her glass. "Thank you for the flowers. They're lovely."

"I'm glad you liked them. I am sorry we argued yesterday. That I took my mood out on you."

"Accepted."

"Good. Then I hope you'll have dinner with me. We can call it a business meeting, to discuss the details of Caroline's tour stop. Would tomorrow night suit your schedule?"

So pleasant, she thought. So smooth. That was when you had to watch him most carefully. "Yes, I suppose."

"I'll pick you up, then, say seven-thirty?"

"There's no need. I can easily walk across the street."

"I had somewhere else in mind and you usually take the late afternoon and evening off on Tuesdays. No point in you changing your routine just for this. I'll pick you up. We'll keep it casual."

She'd nearly asked for specifics before she decided he wanted her to. "Casual's just fine. I'll see you tomorrow."

She hung up, went back to her book. But found it hard to concentrate.

The day before, she thought, they'd raked

up the past with all its wounds and bitterness. Had she trapped him by being so blindly in love, so sure of her own feelings and so confident of his? Could he have been so selfish, so cold, that he had cast her aside rather than share his own mind and heart, rather than give her a chance to understand?

How foolish and shortsighted of both of them, she thought now.

Still, blame, excuses, reasons, none of that changed what had happened. None of it changed, nor would she have it change, who each of them had become. It was best to bury it again and go on as they were. Cautious friends, careless lovers, with no plans to be more.

From his current attitude, it seemed he agreed with her on that one point.

And yet . . .

After setting it aside, Mia said to her cat, "He's up to something."

On the other side of the village, Sam made a hurried second call. "Nell? It's Sam Logan.

I have an emergency. A confidential emergency."

It was a matter of sharpening the details. To hone some of them, he had to wait until Mia left the store the next afternoon. He also concluded that the only way to deal with Lulu was to be direct. Inside Café Book he gestured her over to a display of CDs. A CD titled *Forest Serenity* was tucked in a slot labeled *Playing Now.*

"Which one's her favorite?"

Lulu adjusted her glasses. "Why?"

"Because I'd like to buy her favorite."

Always ready for a sale, Lulu ran her tongue around her teeth. "You buy five, you get the sixth half price."

"I don't need half a dozen—" He broke off, hissed. "Okay, I'll buy six. Which *ones* are her favorites?"

"She likes them all or they wouldn't be in here. It's her store, isn't it?"

"Right." He started to pluck some at random.

"Don't be in such a damn hurry." She

brushed his fingers aside. "When she gets in before me, she tends to put one of these three on."

"Then I'll take these three. And these."

"We sell books, too."

"I know you sell books. I'm just . . . What would you recommend?"

She hosed him, but Sam decided it was money well spent. Or well enough. It wasn't as if he couldn't use a hundred-dollar coffee table book on Renaissance art, or this week's top ten bestsellers. Or the six CDs, and the three audiotapes. And the rest of it.

At least when Lulu had rung him up, she'd laughed. And meant it.

He left Café Book several hundred dollars poorer, and with a great deal left to do in a short amount of time.

Despite that, he arrived at Mia's door at exactly seven-thirty.

She was just as prompt, and stepped out carrying a slim file.

"Notes," she said. "On the event. And copies of the flyer that went out, the store's newsletter, and the ad that will run for the next two weeks."

"Can't wait to see them." He gestured toward his car. "Want the top up?"

"No, let's keep it down."

She noted he'd meant casual. He wore dark trousers and a blue T-shirt. Once again, she had to suppress the urge to ask him where they were going for dinner.

"By the way"—he gave her a light kiss before he opened the car door for her—"you look wonderful."

All right, she thought. Smooth and lightly flirtatious. She could play that game.

"I was just thinking the same thing about you," she replied as she slid into the car. "It's a lovely evening for a drive down the coast."

"My thoughts exactly." He walked around to the driver's side, got behind the wheel. "Music?"

"Yes."

She settled back, calculating how much time she would allow him to seduce her, then lifted her eyebrows in surprise as flutes played on the speakers. "An odd choice for you," she commented. "You were always more fond of rock, particularly if it was loud enough to slam the eardrums."

"No harm in changing the pace now and then. Exploring different avenues." He lifted her hand, kissed it. "Broadening horizons. But if you'd prefer something else . . ."

"No, this is fine. And aren't we accommodating?" She shifted, her hair flying around her face. "The car handles well."

"Want to try it out?"

"Maybe on the way back." Deciding against trying to puzzle him out, for now she sat back to enjoy the rest of the ride.

And when he drove through the village without stopping, she tensed up again.

She studied the yellow cottage when he parked in front. "Odd, I didn't realize you'd turned this into a restaurant. I believe that's a violation of your lease."

"It's temporary." He got out and came around the car for her. "Don't say anything yet." Again, he lifted her hand, brushed his lips over her knuckles. "If you decide you'd rather go somewhere else, we'll go somewhere else. But give it a minute first."

Still holding her hand, he led her around the house rather than into it.

On the freshly mowed lawn a white cloth was spread. It was surrounded by candles not yet lit, and pillows in rich colors and fabrics. Beside it was a long basket overflowing with lilacs.

He lifted it. "For you."

She studied the flowers, then his face. "Lilacs are out of season."

"Tell me about it," he said, holding the basket out to her until she took it. "You always liked them."

"Yes, I've always liked them. What is all this, Sam?"

"I thought we'd have a picnic. A compromise between business and pleasure, public and private."

"A picnic."

"You always liked them, too." He leaned forward to brush his lips over her cheek. "Why don't we have a glass of wine, and you can think about the idea?"

To refuse would be both cold and ungracious. And, she admitted, cowardly. Just because she'd once imagined them happily married and having picnics on the lawn by their own little cottage was no reason to slap at him for trying to give her a pleasant evening.

"I'd love some wine."

"I'll be right back with it."

She let out a little sigh when he was out

of earshot, and when the back door swung shut behind him she lifted the basket of lilacs and buried her face in them.

Moments later, she heard the music of harp and pipe drifting from the house. With a shake of her head, she sat down on one of the pillows, put the basket of flowers beside her, and waited for him to come back.

He brought not only wine but caviar.

"Some picnic."

He sat, and in an almost absent gesture, lit the candles. "Sitting on the grass doesn't mean you can't eat well." He poured the wine, tapped his glass to hers. *"Slainte."*

She nodded in acknowledgment of the Irish toast. "You've been tending the little garden."

"In my limited capacity. Did you plant it?"

"Some of it, and some is Nell's doing."

"I can feel her in the house." He heaped beluga on a toast point. "Her joy in it," he said and offered the caviar to Mia.

"Joy is one of her greatest gifts. When you look at her, you don't see the horror she's been through. It's been an education to watch her finish discovering herself."

"How do you mean?"

"With us, it always was. The knowing.

With Nell it was finally unlocking a door, then stepping through it and finding a room full of fascinating treasures. The first magic I showed her was how to stir the air. Her face when she did it . . . it was wonderful."

"I never taught anyone. I did attend a weekend seminar on Wicca a few years ago, though."

"Really?" She licked caviar off her thumb. "And how was that?"

"It was . . . earnest. I went on impulse, and actually met a few interesting people. Some of them with power. One of the lectures dealt with the Salem trials, and segued into Three Sisters Island."

He helped himself to the caviar. "They had most of the facts, but not the spirit. Not the heart. This place . . ." He skimmed the woods, listened to the beat of the sea. "It can't be summed up in a fifty-minute lecture." He looked back at her. "Will you stay?"

"I've never left."

"No." He brushed her hand with his. "For dinner."

She picked up another toast point. "Yes."

He topped off her wine before he rose. "It'll take me a minute."

"I'll give you a hand."

"No. It's under control."

Under control, he thought as he went back to the kitchen, thanks to Nell. Not only had she prepared everything and delivered it, but she'd left him a detailed list of instructions—one, he'd discovered, that even the culinary retarded could follow.

Blessing Nell, he managed to serve the tomato slices in oil and herbs and the cold lobster.

"It's lovely." Mia stretched out comfortably as she enjoyed the meal. "I had no idea you were such a whiz in the kitchen."

"Untapped talents," he said and smoothly changed the subject. "I'm thinking of buying a boat."

"Are you? John Bigelow still makes wooden boats to order. Though he only does one or two a year now."

"I'll go see him. Do you do any sailing now?"

"Occasionally. But it was never a passion of mine."

"I remember." He touched her hair. "You preferred watching boats to being on one."

"Or being in the water rather than on it." She glanced over as a group of teenagers raced by, using the shortcut from one of the neighboring summer rentals to the beach. "Mr. Bigelow rents boats, too, but if you want to try your hand again before you buy, you're better off talking to Drake at Seafarer. He's built up a very nice rental business."

"Drake Birmingham? I haven't seen him since I've been back. Or Stacey. How are they?"

"They're divorced. She took the kids— they had two—and moved to Boston. Drake remarried about six years ago. Connie Ripley. They have a little boy."

"Connie Ripley." Sam flipped through mental images as he tried to place her. "Big brunette with a lot of teeth."

"That would be Connie."

"She was just ahead of me in school," he recalled. "Drake must be at least—"

"He's on the other side of fifty." Mia twirled her wineglass by the stem. "The age difference, and the speculation about a blistering affair between them causing the marriage to break up, was the hot topic on-island for a good six months." She plucked up another bite of lobster. "Nell really outdid herself. The lobster's delicious."

He winced. "Tagged. Do I lose points?"

"Not at all. By hiring Three Sisters Catering, you show wisdom and good taste. Now." She crossed her legs, picked up her file.

"I love looking at you." He traced a fingertip over her ankle. "Any light, any angle. But just now, when the sun's going down, and the candles are tossing light, I love looking at you."

It fluttered in her blood. The words, the tone, the look in his eyes as he shifted toward her. Lightly, his hand cupped the back of her neck. Sweetly, his lips rubbed against hers.

The flutter turned to a melting. She breathed him in, along with the scent of lilacs and candle wax. And her head took one long, lazy spin.

"Sorry." He pressed a kiss to her forehead, then eased back. "There are moments when I can't keep my hands off you. Let's see what you've got here."

What she had was a case of weak knees and dizzy confusion. He'd kissed her bones away one moment and was now briskly reviewing her file.

"What is this about, Sam?"

"Business and pleasure," he said absently and skimmed his hand down her back before taking out her copy of the upcoming ad. "This is great. Did you design it?"

Settle down, she ordered herself. "Yes."

"You should send a copy to her publicist."

"Done."

"Good. I've already seen the flyer, but I don't think I told you how effective it is."

"Thank you."

"Problem?" he asked nonchalantly.

She felt her teeth clench at his mild question. Irritated that she *was* irritated, Mia composed herself. "No. I appreciate your input." She took a deep breath. "I really do. This is a big event for the store. I want it done not just right, but perfectly."

"I'm sure Caroline's going to enjoy herself."

There was something, some subtle something in the way he said the name. "You know her personally?"

"Hmm. Yeah. This is a nice touch, having Nell make a cake that reproduces the book jacket. The flowers. You may want to change them to pink roses. I seem to recall she prefers those."

"You seem to recall."

"Uh-huh. I see here you're planning to have champagne and chocolate in her suite as a welcome gift from the store. I'd suggest, since the hotel would already provide this amenity, that we add a couple of things and combine it. From the hotel and the store."

Mia tapped her fingers on her knee, then made herself stop. "That's an excellent idea. Perhaps some candles, a book on the island, that sort of thing."

"Perfect." He skimmed through the e-mail and faxed correspondence between Mia and the publicist, nodded. "I can't see you've missed a trick. So . . ." He laid the folder aside, leaned toward her again.

When his mouth was a breath from hers, she pressed a hand to his chest. Smiled. "I'd like to freshen up."

She got to her feet, took her wine with her, and walked into the house.

Once in the kitchen, she took a good look around. It was admirably tidy, but then she doubted if he used it except for brewing his first hit of coffee in the morning. He'd always been a cliché in the kitchen. The man who could burn water.

She saw Nell's instruction sheet lying on the counter, and softened.

She wandered into the living room, pursing her lips in consideration when she spotted the coffee table book. There were candles here as well, and he used them. It made her wonder what rituals and meditation techniques he practiced when he was alone.

Like her, he'd always been a solitary witch.

There were no photographs, but she hadn't expected them. The pair of lovely watercolors on the wall was unexpected. Garden scenes, she mused. Soft and serene. It surprised her that he hadn't selected more dramatic and bold images.

Other than the candles and paintings, and the obviously new and unread book, there was little of Sam Logan in the living area of the cottage. He hadn't surrounded himself with the bits of comfort that were so essential to her.

No flowers or little pots of plants, no bowls of colorful stones or glass.

Since she had pried this far—and she reminded herself she was both his lover and his landlord—she didn't scruple to walk into his bedroom.

There was more of him here—the scent, the feel. The old iron bed she'd bought for the cottage was made up in an almost militarily efficient dark blue spread. The floors were bare. But there was a book on his nightstand, a thriller that she'd enjoyed herself, marked with one of his business cards.

The single painting here was bold and dramatic. An old stone altar rose out of rocky ground into a sky vivid with the triumphant red streaks of sunrise.

On his dresser was a large and lovely chunk of sodalite that she imagined he used for meditation. His windows were open, and she could smell the lavender she'd planted herself.

Because it made her yearn—the simplicity, the fragrance, that almost ridiculously masculine sense of him—she turned away from it.

In the tiny bathroom, she freshened her lipstick, dabbed the perfumed oil she had made herself on her throat, her wrists. Since Sam was priming her for a seduction, she would accommodate him. But not until she was home again, on her own ground.

She could play toy and tease just as skillfully as he.

When she came back out, he'd already switched the dinner service for glass bowls filled with ripe red strawberries and rich whipped cream.

"I wasn't sure if you wanted coffee, or more wine."

"Wine." A confident woman, she thought, could afford to be just a bit reckless.

Night was sliding in. She sat beside him, letting her fingers dance through his hair before she reached for a berry. "I had no idea . . ." Deliberately, watching him, she ran her tongue over the berry, then nipped in. "That you were interested in Renaissance art."

Some circuit in his brain seemed to cross wires. He could almost hear it fizzle. "What?"

"Renaissance art." She dipped her finger into the cream, licked it off. "The book in your living room."

"The . . . oh." He managed to tear his gaze away from her mouth. "Yes. It's a fascinating period."

She waited until he'd coated a berry with cream, then leaned over playfully and took a bite of it. "Mmm," she purred and slid her tongue over her top lip. "Do you prefer Tintoretto's depiction of the Annunciation, or Erte's?"

Another circuit snapped. "Both are brilliant."

"Oh, absolutely. Except, of course, Erte was a sculptor, Art Deco, and born centuries after the Renaissance."

"I assumed you were referring to Giovanni Erte, an obscure and impoverished Renaissance artist who died tragically of scurvy. He was very unappreciated."

The laugh rolled out of her and tightened every muscle in his stomach. "Oh, *that* Erte. I stand corrected." This time she nipped his bottom lip instead of a berry. "You're awfully cute, aren't you?"

"I paid through the nose for that book. I imagine Lulu's still cackling about it." He let her feed him a berry. "I went in to buy some music and came out with fifty pounds of books."

"I like the music." She lay back across the white cloth, her head on an emerald-green pillow. "It relaxes me. Makes me think about floating in a warm river in a shady wood. Mmm. My head's full of wine."

She stretched, lazily so the thin fabric of her dress slithered over her curves. "I don't suppose I'll be able to drive your sexy car tonight after all."

She waited for him to tell her she could drive it in the morning, to ask her to come inside, to stay with him. And when he lay beside her, traced a fingertip down her throat, over the rise of her breasts, she smiled.

"We can take a walk, let the sea air clear your head a bit." He caught the flicker of surprise on her face just before he lowered his mouth to hers.

He nibbled, nipped, let his hands roam. He felt her yield, the softening of her body, the quickening of her pulse. To torment them both, he trailed his fingers along her leg, skimming them under her dress to the warm, silky skin of her thigh, circling the witch mark.

"Unless . . ." He slid a finger under the edge of her panties at the hip. Closed his teeth, lightly, lightly, over her breast through the soft cotton of her dress. "You're not in the mood for a walk."

She felt more than reckless now, and arched her hips in invitation. "No, a walk isn't what I'm in the mood for."

"Then . . ." He bit, just a little harder. "I'll drive."

And when he rose, held out a hand, she gaped at him. "Drive?"

"Drive you home." Seeing her in speechless shock was, he thought, nearly as satisfying as . . . No, not even close to as satisfying, he admitted. But it was precisely the reaction he'd hoped for.

He pulled her to her feet, then bent down to pick up her file and her flowers. "Don't want to forget these."

She recalculated on the drive home. He assumed, correctly, she thought, that she wouldn't stay with him at the cottage. And he'd decided, also correctly, that in order to complete the seduction, he would need to maneuver her into her own bed.

And that, Mia thought as she leaned back to watch the stars, was exactly where she wanted him.

Since he'd gone to so much trouble, and it had been sweet of him, she would let him . . . persuade her. Once they'd had sex, her mind and her body would be back on an even keel.

When they pulled up at her house, she felt fully in control of the situation. "It was a lovely evening. Absolutely lovely." The look she sent him was as warm as her voice as he walked with her to the door. "Thanks again for the flowers."

"You're welcome."

At the door, with her wind chimes singing, and the lamplight glowing against the windows, he ran his hands up her arms, down again. "Come out with me again. I'll rent a boat, and we can spend a lazy day on the water. Swim."

"Maybe."

He cupped her face in his hands, tangled them in her hair as he kissed her. Going deeper when she made a quiet sound of pleasure. When she pressed invitingly against him, he reached behind her, opened the door.

"Better go in," he murmured against her mouth.

"Yes. Better." Nearly dizzy with need, she stepped into the house, and turning, caressed his cheek.

He thought she looked like a siren.

"I'll call you." With a hand that he considered admirably steady, he pulled the door closed between them.

They had, he thought as he walked to the car, just had their first official date in eleven years. And it had been a doozy.

# Fifteen

Sneaky bastard. No one had managed to get her so churned up since . . . Well, Mia admitted, no one had managed to get her so churned up since Sam Logan.

And he was better at it now.

Then again, she was better at banking her sexual urges than she'd once been.

She'd had lovers over the years, but they'd been few and far between. As time had passed, she discovered that while she enjoyed the casual flirtation, she very rarely felt satisfied or content after having a man in her bed.

So, she'd stopped at flirtations.

It was something she considered a practical rather than an emotional decision. The energy and power she might have channeled into that area of physicality had gone, instead, into her craft. There was no doubt in her mind that she was a better witch for the period of self-imposed celibacy.

There was no reason whatsoever why she couldn't apply the same habit now.

Since Sam hadn't been in her bed for more than two weeks, it seemed the most logical choice.

In any case, she was much too busy to worry about Sam, or sex, or just why he wasn't following through on any of that maddening foreplay.

"You didn't have to come back for this," she said to Nell as she rearranged the café tables.

"I wanted to come back. I'm as excited about the signing tomorrow as you are. I'll get the chair for that."

"No, you won't. No lifting. Period." As she set the chairs herself, Mia kicked the one Ripley was slouched in. "You could get off your ass and help."

"Hey, you don't pay me. I'm just hanging out here so I don't have to hang out at home while this male-bonding barbecue ritual is going on. I hope to hell Mac doesn't blow something up."

"It's a charcoal grill," Nell reminded her. "Charcoal doesn't explode."

"You don't know my guy like I know my guy."

"Between the three of them, they should be able to get it going and grill some steaks." The image of Zack grilling burgers on their own deck flashed in Nell's mind. And made her shudder. "But God help your poor kitchen."

"Least of my worries." Ripley crossed her feet at the ankles, legs stretched out, and watched in amusement as Mia continued to change the table arrangement.

"Now that one there?" She jerked her thumb toward Mia. "She's got plenty of worries. See the line she gets between her eyebrows? Means she's feeling bitchy."

"I don't have a line between my eyebrows." And vanity had Mia smoothing it out. "Nor am I feeling bitchy. Slightly stressed, perhaps."

"Which is why the barbecue's such a good idea." Nell walked over to the display table and began to toy with a design for the featured author's book. "You'll relax, have an evening with friends, and be clearheaded for tomorrow. I'm glad Sam thought of it."

"He's always thinking," Mia concluded,

but Ripley and Nell could hear the underlying edge to her statement.

"So, how did you like the concert on the beach the other night?" Ripley asked her.

"It was fine."

"And the moonlight sail after the fireworks on the Fourth?"

"Dandy."

"See?" Ripley nodded toward Nell. "Told you she was feeling bitchy."

"I am *not* feeling bitchy." Mia set down a chair with an ill-tempered little slap. "Are you looking for a fight?"

"Nope, I'm looking for a beer," Ripley replied, and sauntered into the café kitchen to help herself.

"It's going to be a wonderful event, Mia." Ready to soothe, Nell continued to stack books. "It'll be beautiful when you get the flowers in here tomorrow. And the refreshments are completely under control. Wait until you see the cake."

"I'm not worried about the flowers, or the refreshments."

"When you see how many customers start lining up, you'll feel better."

"I'm not worried about the customers, or not any more than I should be." Mia dropped into a chair. "For once, Ripley is right. I am feeling bitchy."

"Is that a confession?" Ripley asked as she came out with her beer.

"Oh, shut up." Mia dragged her hands through her hair. "He's using sex. Or rather using the lack of sex to keep me edgy. Candlelight picnics. Moonlight sails. Long walks. He sends flowers every couple of days."

"But no sex?"

Mia leveled a look at Ripley. "There's considerable foreplay," Mia snapped. "Then he dumps me at my front door and walks off. The next day I get flowers. He calls every day. And twice I've gone home and found a little gift at the front door. A pot of rosemary trained in the shape of a heart, a little pottery dragon. When we're out, he's absolutely charming."

"The bastard!" Ripley slammed her hand on the table. "Hanging's too good for him."

"He's using sex," Mia complained.

"No, he's not." With a dreamy smile, Nell brushed a hand over Mia's hair. "Sex has nothing to do with it. He's using romance. He's courting you."

"He is not."

"Flowers, candlelight, long walks, thoughtful little gifts." Nell ticked the list off on her fingers. "Time and attention. That spells courtship to me."

"Sam and I passed by the courtship stage a number of years ago. And that courtship didn't include flowers and little gifts."

"Maybe he's trying to make up for that."

"He doesn't have to make up for anything. I don't *want* him making up for anything." Jittery, she got to her feet, walked over to shut the terrace doors. "He doesn't want the traditional package any more than I do. Now. He just wants . . ."

And that was the trouble, Mia realized. She had no clear idea what he wanted this time around either.

"He's got you scared," Ripley said quietly.

"He doesn't. He absolutely does not."

"He never scared you before. You always had your course plotted."

"It's still plotted. I know what I'm doing. I know where I'm going. That hasn't changed." Even as she said it, she felt a sly chill whisper over her skin.

"Mia." There was both sympathy and patience in Nell's voice. "Are you still in love with him?"

"Do you think I'd risk letting him into my heart again? That I'd risk that not knowing the cost?" Steadier now, Mia crossed over to finish the display. "I know my responsibility to this island, its people, to my gift. Love, for me, is an absolute. I couldn't survive it again. And I have to survive to fulfill my destiny."

"And if he *is* your destiny?"

"I thought that once. I was wrong. When the time comes, the circle will hold."

At the house on the bluff, three men watched the flames spurt from the charcoal grill with the same intense fascination as the cavemen watched their tribal fire.

"Going good," Zack commented, and nodded at Sam. "See? I told you we could do it with good old Yankee know-how. We didn't need any hocus-pocus crap."

"Good old Yankee know-how," Sam drawled. "An entire bag of charcoal and a half gallon of lighter fluid."

"I can't help it if his grill's defective."

"This is a brand-new grill," Mac protested. "This is its virgin run."

"Which is why it needs the hot flame. Has to be cured." Zack tipped back his beer.

Mac looked on sadly as the inside of his shiny red grill blackened. "If this sucker melts, Ripley's going to kill me."

"It's goddamn cast iron." Zack gave it a little boot with his foot. "Speaking of Rip, where the hell are they?"

"They're on their way," Sam replied as Zack frowned at him. "A little hocus-pocus crap. I like knowing where Mia is. Since Mister Science here clued us in on those readings around her house, I've been keeping tuned to her."

"She finds out, she'll kick *your* ass," Zack pointed out.

"She won't find out. She doesn't see clearly when it comes to me. She doesn't want to, and it's damn hard getting Mia to do anything she doesn't want."

"How are things, you know, going between you?"

Sam studied Mac as he drank. "Is that personal or professional interest?"

"I guess you could say it's both."

"Fair enough. I like the way things are going. Can't say I mind keeping her guessing. She's a hell of a lot more complicated than she used to be, and it's interesting—more than I figured—getting to know all the twists and turns."

Zack scratched his chin. "You're not going to start talking about mature relationships and exploring your inner couple or any of that shit, are you?"

"Shh . . . here they come." Mac gestured toward the slash of headlights on the shell road. "Let's act like we know what we're doing."

Lucy, who'd been sprawled over the deck, leaped to attention and flew down the steps inches ahead of Mulder.

"Pretty women," Zack said. "A couple of good dogs and some steaks. Damn good deal."

The steaks were charred, the potatoes slightly underdone, but appetites were keen enough. They ate on the deck, by the strong glow of candles and the backwash of light from the living room, where music pumped out of the stereo.

When Sam lifted a bottle of wine to fill Mia's nearly empty glass, she shook her head, laid her hand over the bowl. "No, I'm driving. And I need a clear mind for tomorrow."

"I'll come by in the morning, give you a hand with the setup."

"No need. Most of it's done, and we have plenty of time tomorrow. I already have thirty-eight pre-sold copies of the hardcover, with orders still coming in, and nearly that many of her backlist set aside. She's going to be very busy tomorrow. I imagine she'll . . ."

Mia trailed off as she caught the look on Nell's face. Her body tensed, and she rose half out of her chair. "Nell."

"The baby moved." The expression of shock and astonishment turned to wonder. "I felt the baby. A fluttering inside me." She laughed, pressed a hand to her belly. "So quick and strong. Zack." She grabbed his hand, pressed it against her. "Our baby moved."

"Do you need to lie down?"

"No." She leaped up, tugged his hand. "I need to dance."

"You need to dance."

"Yes! Dance with me." She threw her

arms around his neck. "We'll dance with Jonah."

"We don't know it's a boy." Swamped with love, Zack wrapped his arms around her waist, drew her up to her toes and held tight. "Might just as easily be a girl. Then it's Rebecca."

"Uh-oh. They're getting sappy." Before it rubbed off, Ripley got up, pointed at Mac. "You're dancing."

"Somebody's going to get hurt," Mac muttered.

Sam watched the entertainment for a moment, then laid a hand on Mia's. "We used to be good at this."

"Hmmm?"

She was staring at Nell, her face wistful and so totally unguarded that seeing it was like a fist to his heart. Tears sparkled on her lashes. What he saw in them was love, and longing.

"Dancing." Holding her hand, he stood. "We used to be good at it. Let's see if we still are."

Following impulse, he pulled her down the steps to the bluff. Then he spun her out to arm's length, whipped her back.

Her arm hooked smoothly around his neck, her body fit to his.

"Oh, yeah." He slid his hands down to her hips and began to sway with her. "We're still good."

It had been a long time, but she hadn't forgotten his moves, his rhythm. And she remembered as well the sheer pleasure of moving with him to music. Giving herself to it, she kicked off her shoes. Sand flew under their feet as they turned, dipped, and spun.

Dancing had always been a kind of joyful and somehow innocent mating ritual between them. Bursts of energy. Coordination. Anticipation.

She stopped hearing the music with only her ears. She heard it in the quick pressure of his hand on her back, the grip of his fingers on hers, the whirl of her own body.

When he lifted her off her feet, she threw her head back and laughed. Then she linked her arms around his neck, for the first time in more than a decade, in an embrace that was sheer and simple affection.

The applause and whistles exploding from the deck had her shifting her head, leaving her cheek resting against his temple as she caught her breath.

"Told you they were show-offs." Ripley elbowed Mac, but she was grinning.

"Hey, we don't have to take this abuse. Come on!" Holding Mia's hand, Sam dashed down the beach steps so that Mia had to run to keep up.

"Slow down! You'll break our necks!"

"I'll catch you." To prove it, he hauled her up, spun her in circles. "How about a swim?"

"No!"

"Okay, we'll dance instead." He set her on her feet, pulling her close and tight against him. The slow, seductive strains of "Sea of Love" flowed into the air, over the beach.

"That's an old one," she remarked.

"Classic," he corrected. "Change of pace."

He buried his face in her hair as they circled in the sand. Her heart was a steady beat against his. Their legs brushed as she rose on her toes, sliding with him until they formed one shadow in the moonlight.

He remembered, so much, that the shapes and sounds of all the memories whispered and blurred in his brain. "Do they still have dances in the high school gym?"

"Yes."

"Do kids still sneak outside to neck?"

"Probably."

"Let's pretend." He turned his head, skimming his lips along her jaw before they met hers. "Come back with me."

Before she understood, could think to resist, she found herself spinning. They were no longer dancing on the sand, but wrapped together in the shadows of the high school gym while a crisp fall breeze blew the scents of aging leaves and blooming mums around them.

Music pumped out of the building, a rebel crash of drums and guitars. Her hands rushed over the cool, worn leather of his jacket, into the silky warmth of his hair.

His body was slimmer, his mouth less skilled, but, oh, how hers responded.

The torch of love burned blinding bright inside her.

She whispered his name, mindlessly. And offered everything.

It was the ache swelling inside her, throbbing like a wound, that snapped her back.

Breath heaving, she shoved him away. "Damn you. Damn you! That wasn't fair."

"No. I'm sorry." His head was spinning.

For a moment he could still smell the crispness of autumn in the humid press of summer air. "No, it wasn't fair. I wasn't thinking. Don't walk away." He pressed his fingers to his temples as she turned from him.

He hadn't planned it, and would have found some way to stop the impulse that had taken them back into what they'd been. How could he have known what it would be like to have her love him like that again? To feel that absolute purity of emotion from her?

To know he'd tossed it away, and might never, never have it again.

When he steadied himself she was standing at the edge of the water, hugging herself and staring out at the night.

"Mia." He went to her, but didn't touch her. One of them, he was certain, would break if he did. "I have no excuse, no way to apologize for that kind of manipulation. I can only tell you I didn't intend to do it."

"You hurt me, Sam."

"I know." And myself, he thought. More than I could have realized.

"Time can't be erased. And it shouldn't be." She turned to him now, her face pale against the night. "I don't want to go back to that girl, or that boy. I don't want to give up what I've made of myself."

"I wouldn't change a thing of what you've made of yourself. You're the most astonishing woman I've ever known."

"Words are easy."

"No, they're not. Some of them have never been easy for me. Mia—"

But when he reached out, she turned away again. Then froze as she saw the pale blue light spilling out of the cave. "Stop it. You go too far."

He saw it too, and did touch her now so she would feel, and believe him. "I'm not doing it. Wait here."

He set her behind him, then strode quickly toward the cave, stopping only when he stood at the opening, washed in the light. He heard her step beside him, but said nothing as they both looked inside.

The light in the cave was soft and blue, the shadows deep and still as wells. In that light were two people. Images carved like statues out of the light itself.

Then they breathed.

The man was beautiful. The sleek muscles of his long, naked body gleamed with water. His hair was glossy black, spilling damp and straight over his shoulders as he stretched on his side in a deep sleep.

The woman was beautiful. Tall and slender in her dark cloak, she stood looking down at him. The hood was tossed back so the fiery curls of her hair tumbled free to her waist.

In her arms, she held a pelt, black as midnight and still wet from the sea.

When she turned, Mia saw what seemed to be her own face, with the skin glowing as if a thousand candles were alight beneath it.

"Love," the one who had been Fire said, "is not always wise." She walked toward them, cradling the pelt like a child. "It has no conditions, and no regrets." She rubbed her cheek against the pelt as she stepped out of the cave. "Time is shorter than you think."

Mia lifted a hand—a gesture of comfort and command. "Mother?" The one who was Fire stopped, and her beauty shimmered when she smiled.

"Daughter."

"I will not fail you."

"It is not for me." She traced her fingers

along Mia's cheek, and Mia felt a line of warmth. "Take care not to fail yourself. You're more than I was."

She looked back into the cave. "You forget, too often, that he is in you as well." Hugging the pelt she turned back until her eyes met Sam's. "And me in you."

She walked away across the sand. "It watches, in the dark." And vanished like smoke.

The light in the cave winked out.

"I can smell her." Mia cupped her hands in the air as if it were water, and brought it to her face. "Lavender and rosemary. You saw her amulet?"

He lifted the disk of silver and sunstone that Mia wore on a linked chain. "This one. The same way I looked at her face, and saw this one," he said, lifting Mia's chin.

"I have a lot to think about." She started to step away, but her gaze was drawn up. As she watched, an inky haze blurred the bright edges of the moon.

"Trouble's coming," she whispered, seconds before they heard the growl.

Fog spilled in from the sea, crawled up the sand. The wolf, the pentagram a white flash against its black body, waded into the mist and bared its teeth.

For the second time, Sam pushed Mia behind him. His body blocked hers like a shield. "Go. Now. Get to the house."

"I won't run from this." She stepped to the side, into clear view, and watched the wolf track her. With no time to wait for her circle, she began the spell alone.

"Air that swirls and spins, arise, build to wind that screams and cries. Tremble earth beneath the sea, walls of water build for me!"

She speared her hands up, through the gale that spewed around her. Her hair blew out, wild ropes of red. And at the shout of her voice, the quiet waves of the cove boiled up, higher, higher with each crash.

The world roared.

"Rage and thrash and whirl for me, air and earth and rising sea. Flames within my blood that churns, I conjure from you a circle that burns. Now you that crawled out of the mire, come if you dare, and face my fire!"

A ball of lightning hurled out of the sky, blazing like a comet on its violent arc. An instant before it crashed into the land, she saw the black wolf curl itself back into the fog.

"Coward," she called out, riding wildly on the whip of her own power.

"Mia." Sam's voice was rock steady. "Can you turn it back?"

"I just did."

"No, baby. The wave."

"Ah." She studied the wall of water, a full twenty feet high now and sweeping closer while the jaws of wind snapped vicious teeth. She held out her arms, targeted her energy down them like sighting down the barrel of a gun. Then flung it outward.

The wave collapsed into a shower of silver drops. The cool rain of them washed to shore, over her hair and skin as she twisted her fisted hand and gathered back the spinning wind.

The night was once more clear as glass, the breeze playful as a faerie.

She threw back her head, gulping in air while the heat of power streamed through her blood. "Well, yes, that gave him a taste, didn't it?"

Sam was still gripping her shoulder, as he had been since she'd stepped out from behind him. "How long have you been doing that spell?"

"Actually, that was the first time I put it all together. I have to say"—she blew out a laughing breath—"it was better than sex."

Hearing the shouts and running feet from above on the bluff, she turned to reassure her friends.

"Are you sure you're all right?"

Mia grabbed one of Nell's stroking hands. "I'm fine."

"Well, I could use a drink." Ripley popped open a beer, turned to Mia. "You?"

"No, thanks." She already felt wonderfully, gloriously drunk.

"Some lemonade for the little mother." Ripley poured a glass. "Sit down or something, Nell. You're making me twitchy."

"I think we should go down and see what they're doing."

"Oh, let them play with their toys." Restless, Ripley paced the deck. Mac and the other men had hauled equipment down to the beach. Even now she could hear the beeps and mechanical squeals.

"That was a pretty big spell there, Glenda. How did it feel?"

Mia's lips curved, slow and smug.

"Figured. Even linking last minute and adding a push, I got a nice rush. Always leaves me wanting more, though."

"Zack's going to get very lucky later." Nell laughed, then immediately stopped herself. "How can we stand around here laughing about sex? That was terrifying. Mia, we couldn't get down to you. Your wind came up like a tornado."

"A nice summer breeze wouldn't have done it. And you did get to me. I felt you." With her hands braced on the rail, she leaned out, her face lifted to the sky. "It was like a thousand hearts beating inside me. A thousand voices in my head. And every cell, every muscle, every drop of blood was so alive. When it looked at me." She whirled back. "When it looked at me, it was afraid."

"Maybe it's finished," Nell said.

Mia shook her head. "No, not yet."

"Whether it's done or not, I've got to say one thing." Ripley tipped back her beer. "I didn't know you had that much, and I've known you all your life. And seeing what I saw tonight, I've got a better handle on why you've always been so picky and careful. That's a lot of firepower to cart around."

"Is that a compliment?"

"It's an observation. With a warning tagged on. Wait for us next time. Okay." She gathered up three more beers. "Playtime's over. Let's go see what Mac and his pals have come up with."

On the beach, Mac had sensors and monitors scattered, cables strewed everywhere. He sat on the ground hammering away at the keyboard of his laptop.

Hauling the equipment down, carting it to where Mac wanted it, had helped. But Sam needed to do something physical and sweaty to take the edge off.

"Look, this is all really cool stuff, but what the hell is it doing?"

"Measuring. Triangulating. Documenting." Mac tapped more keys, squinted behind his glasses at a near monitor. "Wish I'd gotten to a damn camera. Best estimate on that wave's twenty feet. But that's just eyeballing it from up above."

"Twenty's conservative," Sam said mildly. "And that's eyeballing it from down below."

"Um. Ah." Mac peered at the readout on his thermometer. "Give me your best guess at ambient temperature at the center here during the climax of the event."

Sam shot a look at Zack, who just shrugged. "Ambient temperature? Jesus. It got hot."

"But was it a dry heat?" Zack asked and made Sam laugh.

"Makes a difference." Mac shoved up his glasses and frowned. "The ambients around the negative energy flow dip. It gets cold. In trying to reconstruct and calculate the ion clash and the dominant direction of force, I need reasonable estimates of the ambients."

"It got hot," Sam said again. "Damn it, I'm a witch, not a meteorologist."

"Very funny. Now take that sensor and get me a reading where her fireball hit. Hey. Wow!" As one of his machines began to hum like a beehive, he scrambled up, barely missed snagging his foot on a cable. He made a dash for it just as the women came down the beach steps.

"Oh. Should've known." He nodded,

crouched down to get a better look at the readings.

"I'm going to take a look at the cave," Nell informed Mac. "I want to help if I can."

He grunted, then crooked a finger at Mia. Amused at him, she strolled closer, then stopped when he held up a hand.

"Whoa, baby," he said. "Look at this, just look. It's phenomenal. Are you doing any internal spells? Do you have anything working, actively working, in another area?"

"Not at the moment. Why?"

"Your readings are spiking. They're all over the place, and all the way up the scale. You always have a high level, even at rest, but this is a big surge. Hold on. I want to measure your vital signs."

He took her blood pressure, her body temperature, her heart rate. He was studying the readout on her brain wave patterns when the rest of the group gathered around them.

"How do you do it?" Mac's voice was quiet now, and sober.

Mia leaned toward him. Mimicking his tone, she pretended innocence. "Do what, Mac?"

"The level of energy pumping around inside you right now would have most people bouncing off the walls. But your vitals are well within normal range. You've been sitting here, calm as ice, for ten minutes."

"Exquisite control. Now, this has been a delightful and entertaining evening, but I really have to go." She rose, one smooth movement of grace, and brushed the sand from her skirts. "I have a busy day tomorrow."

"Why don't you stay here in the guest room?"

"You don't have to worry about me, Mac."

"It's not finished."

"No, it's not finished. But it's done for tonight."

# Sixteen

She didn't sleep, nor had she expected to. Instead, she put the bubbling energy to good use. She worked on kitchen magic, put together some pocket charms. She polished furniture, scrubbed floors, then gave herself a manicure.

At dawn, she was in the gardens, selecting and clipping the flowers she wanted for store decoration.

When she arrived at Café Book at eight, her energy level showed no signs of waning.

Nell, dependable as sunrise, arrived at nine, loaded with supplies.

"You look incredible," Nell said as Mia helped her transport boxes and containers.

"I feel incredible. It's going to be a good day."

"Mia." Nell set the cake box on the refreshment table. "I trust you. But it's just not like you to be so casual about what happened last night. That level of magic, that scope—"

"Was like having a dragon by the tail," Mia finished. "I take what happened very seriously. I have to ride this wave, little sister. Physically, I really don't have a choice. It doesn't mean I'm not aware, or that I'm glib, or that I don't know that what's coming is more potent yet."

A dragon by the tail? Nell thought. More like a herd of them. "I saw what you were able to call last night. I felt the edge of it whip through me. Just the edge, and it was staggering. Now you're setting up for a book signing as if it's the most important thing you have to do."

"Today it is." She took one of Nell's apple fritters from a box. "Can't seem to get enough to eat. It's a matter of routing the energy, which I imagine you did, very skillfully, with Zack last night." She smiled a little as she bit into the pastry. "I've had a lot of practice finding ways other than sex to route mine. You could serve canapés off my kitchen floor this morning."

"I thought you and Sam would leave to-gether."

"So did I." Thoughtfully, Mia licked sugar from her finger. "Apparently he had other things to do."

"After you left, Mac took readings from Sam. Sam didn't like it. Zack had to insult him into it. You know, the way men do."

"Questioning the size and stamina of his penis."

"Basically. And calling him Mary."

"Ah, yes." Mia chuckled and nibbled. "Always effective."

"Sam's readings were nearly as high as yours."

Still ravenous, Mia contemplated another fritter. "Really?"

"Mac's theory, or one of them, is that Sam was at ground zero and absorbed some of the energy flying around. Now, of course, he wants to wait a few days and then get readings from Sam for comparison. His standard levels and so on."

Mia gave in, took the second pastry, and told herself she'd do an extra hour of yoga later. "Sam wouldn't care for that."

"No, he didn't like it. But my impression is

he's going to cooperate. Mac's very persuasive, and he used you."

"Me?"

"Any data are essential, every scrap of information goes into the whole and helps—don't get mad at this—protect you."

Mia brushed sugar from her fingertips, admired the slick coral polish on her nails. "Did I give anyone the impression last night that I needed protection?"

"They're men," Nell said simply, and restored Mia's good humor.

"Can't live with them, can't turn them into jackasses."

With preparations at Café Book well under control, Mia went down to meet the ten o'clock ferry. She noted that Pete Stubens's dog had gotten off the leash again and was racing around the docks with the remains of some unfortunate, and very dead, fish hanging out of his mouth.

She spotted Carl Macey's boat at the dock and imagined that he and his crew would be unloading a fresher, more appetizing catch.

She toyed with wandering over and asking him to set aside some of it for her. There was little doubt that by the end of the day her appetite would be just as keen as it was now.

"Hi, Miz Devlin." Dennis Ripley skidded his bike to a halt inches in front of the open toes of Mia's Pradas.

"Hi, Mister Ripley."

The boy grinned, as he always did. Growing like a weed, Mia thought, and well into the gangly-arms-and-awkward-elbows stage. In a couple of years, she mused, he'd be zipping along in some secondhand car instead of on his bike.

And the idea made her sigh.

"My mom's coming to your store today to see that writer lady."

"I'm glad to hear it."

"My aunt Pat works at the hotel, and she says they've got a fancy room for her, with a whirlpool tub and a TV set in the bathroom."

"Is that so?"

"She says writers make lots of money and live high on the hog."

"I imagine some do."

"Like Stephen King. His books are cool.

Maybe I'll write a book and you can sell it in your store."

"Then we'll both get rich." She pulled down the bill of his ball cap and made him laugh.

"I'd rather play for the Red Sox, though. Gotta go."

He shot off, whistling for Pete's dog, who raced after him. Mia turned to watch them, and there stood Sam.

Neither spoke for a moment, but the air seemed to snap.

"Hi, Miz Devlin."

"Hi, Mister Logan."

"Excuse me a minute." He slid his arms around her, gripped the back of her dress in a fist, and crushed his mouth down on hers.

And the air seemed to sizzle.

"I didn't get around to doing that last night."

"Today works." Her lips vibrated from the heat of him.

She shifted away, a test of will with the energy bubbling inside her, and watched the ferry chug its way toward the dock. "Ferry's on time."

"We need to talk about last night."

"Yes, we need to talk about a number of things. But not today."

"Tomorrow, then. We should both be a little less . . . distracted."

"Is that a euphemism?" Mia asked, amusing herself, and stepped forward as the ferry docked.

A black sedan eased down the gangplank, steered to the side. Before the driver could walk around to open the door, a pretty blonde popped out of the backseat.

She gave a laughing shout, then rushed forward and all but jumped into Sam's arms. The kiss was audible, an extended *mmmmm!* with a quick popping sound at the end.

"God! It's good to see you! How did you manage to get better-looking? I can't believe I'm here on your island. Just thinking about it's gotten me through a week of book tour wars. Let's have another kiss."

Oh, yes, let's, Mia thought dryly as she watched the exchange. Caroline Trump was as attractive as her book jacket photo. A swing of sunny blond hair curved around a pretty elfin face, warmed by honey-brown eyes and dominated by a shapely pink mouth. A mouth that, Mia noted, was currently fused to Sam's.

She had the young, perky build of a high school cheerleader, though her bio put her at thirty-six.

The bio had neglected to mention that she and Sam Logan had been lovers.

"Tell me everything you've been up to," Caroline demanded. "I can't wait to see your hotel. There has to be time for you to show me around this place. It's great! The book signing will probably be a dud—God knows why they schedule in these little holes-in-the-wall—so I can cut out early. We'll go to the beach."

"You still talk too much." Sam eased her back, giving her shoulders a squeeze. "Welcome to Three Sisters. Caroline, this is Mia Devlin, the owner of Café Book."

"Oops." Caroline turned her cheerful smile on Mia. "I do talk too much. Just run on and on. I didn't mean it about the signing." She took Mia's hand, pumped. "I'm just all wired up. Haven't seen Sexy here for over six months, and I've had about a gallon of coffee already this morning. I really appreciate you having me."

"It's our pleasure," Mia said in a voice so smooth it made Sam wince. She drew her hand free of Caroline's grip. "I hope the trip from the mainland was pleasant."

"It was great. I—"

"Then I'll just add my welcome to Sam's, and let you go so you can settle in. If there's anything you need, you can reach me at Café Book. Sam," she said with a regal nod and walked away.

"Oh, ouch." Caroline rapped a fist against her forehead. "I'm such a moron. Brilliant author-bookseller relations."

"Don't worry about it," Sam told her. He would. "Let's get you settled at the hotel. I think you're going to like your suite."

An hour later, Sam braved the sting of hellfire and walked into Café Book.

"Upstairs," Lulu called out as she busily rang up sales. "And she's on a tear."

He found her giving instructions to the part-time clerk at the auxiliary checkout counter.

She didn't look like a woman on a tear, he

thought, but like a coolly efficient business owner taking care of details. But then, Lulu knew her all too well.

She moved away to replenish stock that customers had already taken from her area display. "Is our VIP settling in?"

"Yes, she's changing. I'm going back shortly to take her to lunch."

"I hope our little signing doesn't interfere too much with the social aspects of your reunion."

"Can we take this somewhere a little more private?"

"I'm afraid not." She turned, beaming a professional smile as a woman took another book off the display. "Be sure to fill out the form for our prize drawings. We'll be pulling names throughout the event," she told the woman. "As you can see," she said to Sam, "I'm too busy dealing with my pesky event in my little hole-in-the-wall to chat with you."

"She didn't mean to insult you, Mia."

"Not to my face, in any case. There's no need for you to explain your *friend* to me. On any level."

"I was going to suggest you join us for lunch." He didn't flinch at the long, slow stare she aimed at him. "Give her a chance to smooth over the awkward first impression."

"Not only would it take more than lunch to manage that, but I don't have the time or the inclination. And I certainly don't intend to be part of any little ménage à trois, however civilized."

Okay, he thought. First things first. "Caroline and I haven't been involved in that way for a long time. And I don't appreciate having to explain something like that in the middle of the damn store."

She nudged him aside so that she could speak to a group of tourists who were currently goggling. "Good morning. I hope you'll be staying for our event this afternoon." She picked up a book to show them. "Miss Trump will be here to discuss and sign her latest."

By the time she finished her pitch and had the customers browsing the paperback display, he was gone.

"Dud, my butt," Mia murmured.

---

"I'm going to be so charming she's going to forget I ever had my foot in my mouth."

"Stop obsessing, Caroline."

"I can't." She poked at her Cobb salad. "And it'll hurt my feelings if you've forgotten that about me. Obsession is like breathing for me. I'm going to win her over before I'm finished. You'll see."

"Eat your lunch."

"I'm nervous. She made me nervous. God, Sam! I couldn't stop babbling."

"You always babble." He nudged the coffee aside, nudged up her salad bowl.

"No, I chatter. Babbling's different. She's the one, isn't she?"

"The one what?"

"The one you were always hung up on." With her head angled to the side, Caroline studied him. "I always knew there was *the one*, even when we were together."

"Yes, she's the one. How's Mike doing?"

"Ah." She wiggled her fingers so she could see the glint of her wedding ring. It was still new. And though it was the second she'd worn, she was determined that this one would stick. "He's great. Misses me when I'm on tour—which is good for my ego. I'm going to have to bring him back here for a vacation. It's wonderful. And," she added, "you changed the subject to distract me. You don't want to talk about Mia Devlin."

"You look wonderful, Caroline. Happy, successful. I really enjoyed your new book."

"Okay, we won't talk about her. You're really not coming back to New York?"

"No, I'm not coming back."

"Well." She glanced around the dining room. "You've got a hell of a place here."

She studied the portrait of the three women, turned a questioning glance at Sam. But when he simply continued to eat, she tossed her napkin on the table. "I've got to get over there and make her love me or I'm not going to be able to settle down."

"I don't believe I've ever seen you settled down." But he rose, signaled to the waiter. "You've got time for a little walk around the village."

"No, let's just do it. I'll go over to sign stock now and look around later."

He led her through the lobby and out onto the sidewalk.

"Terrific building," she said, scanning Café Book. She squared her shoulders, sucked in a breath. "Okay, let's do it."

"She's not going to claw you, Caroline." He waited for a break in the traffic, guided her across the street. "She wants this event to be successful as much as you do."

"Brother, you don't know females." Caroline stepped inside, blinked. "Wow! What a place! Dream bookstore. And I'm everywhere. Jesus, Sam, it's packed. I can't believe I called this place rinky-dink."

"You didn't. Your term was 'hole-in-the-wall.' "

"Right. Right. Did I mention I was a moron?"

"Yes, I think you did. Lulu, this is Caroline Trump."

"Glad to have you." Lulu bagged up a sale, stuck out her hand. "I've been ringing up your books like they were going out of style. I read the new one last week. It had a good punch."

"Thanks. I love the store." She turned in a circle. "I want to live here. Oh! Look at those candles. Sam, I need ten minutes."

When she dashed off, he leaned back, watching fondly as she whipped through the aisles. It took fifteen minutes, but he managed to head her upstairs.

"Well, you made Lulu like you," he commented.

"That was just a side benefit. Her stock is

so smart—not just the selection of books, which is impressive, but the sidelines too. Class all the way. And look at this."

She stopped at the top of the stairs, dazzled.

The crowd was already thick. The café tables were packed, as were the rows of chairs. Over the hum of conversation, she heard Mia's smooth voice announce her name and the time of the event.

"It's a wonder she didn't kick me out," Caroline murmured. "There must be a hundred people up here."

"Since you're determined to feel lousy about it, I'll tell you she worked her butt off. Look, just pass on what you think to your publicist. Getting other authors to Café Book will go a long way toward prying your foot out of your mouth."

"Consider it done. Okay, here she comes." Caroline boosted up her smile and walked in Mia's direction.

"You have the most incredible store. And I want to know if there's anything I can do to make up for being a jerk."

"Don't give it another thought. Can I get you something to drink, a bite to eat? We're very proud of our café."

"Got any hemlock?"

Mia put a hand on her shoulder. "Oh, it could be arranged."

"Why don't I settle for a diet Coke, and you can put me to work."

"I have a number of pre-sells, if you'd like to take care of them before the event. It will give you more beach time. I'll show you into the stockroom, set you up. Pam," Mia called to the woman waiting tables. "Would you bring Ms. Trump a diet Coke? We'll be in the stockroom. Sam, if you're staying, you might want to find a seat. Just this way, Ms. Trump."

"Caroline, please. I've done enough of these to know how much time and effort go into hosting a signing. I want to thank you."

"We're thrilled to have you."

Caroline followed Mia into the stockroom. She'd also seen enough behind-the-scenes action in bookstores to recognize ruthless organization.

"I've flapped the copies at title page," Mia began. "If that's not your preference, I'll change them."

Caroline moistened her lips. "These are all pre-sold?"

"Yes. Fifty-three at last count. Those that

require personalizing—I was told you'd personalize?"

"Sure. No problem."

"They're labeled with Post-its. Your publicist indicated this is the brand of pen—"

"Just stop a second." Caroline dumped her briefcase, sat down at a stool at the counter. "I've never sold over a hundred new titles at a signing."

"You're about to break your record."

"I see that. Just as I see you have the pen I like, and that there were pink roses, my favorite, on the signing table."

"Wait till you see the cake."

"Cake?" Caroline seemed flabbergasted. "You have cake? You sent me bubble bath and candles, and were at the ferry to meet me."

"As I said, we're thrilled to have you."

"Not finished yet. Your store, which is amazing, by the way, is full of people, and an unbelievable number of them are holding my books. And you hate me because I said something careless, rude, and stupid."

"No. I was *annoyed* with you because you said something careless, rude, and stupid. But I don't hate you for it." Mia moved to the door to take the soft drink from Pam.

"And because I was once involved, romantically, with Sam."

"Yes." Her tone pleasant, Mia offered the drink. "Naturally I hate you for that."

"And that's fair." Caroline sipped her soft drink. "But since Sam and I haven't been anything but friends for more than four years, and I'm happily married. . . ." She wiggled the fingers of her left hand. "*And,* since he's hung up on you, who happen to be beautiful, smart, younger than I am, and who has those really fabulous shoes, I get to hate you more."

Mia considered her for a moment. "That seems entirely reasonable." She handed Caroline a pen. "I'll open these for you."

Four hours later, Mia was in her office tallying figures. When the publisher called on Monday for a follow-up on the event, she was going to knock their socks off.

Nell came in, dropped into a chair, and patted the belly she was sure had started to round. "That was great. That was outstanding. That was exhausting."

"I noticed that even with free refreshments, the café did a brisk business."

"Tell me about it." Nell yawned hugely. "Did you want to do totals?"

"We'll wait until closing for those. However, I do have the totals for the Trump books that sold during her appearance."

"And they are?"

"New title, including pre-solds? Two hundred and twelve. Paper backlist, also including pre-solds? Three hundred and three."

"No wonder she walked out of here looking shell-shocked. Congratulations, Mia. She was terrific, wasn't she? Funny and warm during the book discussion. I really liked her."

"Yes." Mia tapped a pen on the edge of her desk. "So did I. She used to be involved with Sam."

"Oh." Nell straightened in the chair. "Oh."

"After meeting her, it's easy to see why he was attracted. She's very clever, urban, energetic. I'm not jealous."

"I didn't say a word."

"I'm not jealous," Mia repeated. "I just wish I hadn't liked her quite so much."

"Why don't you come home with me? We'll sit around, talk about men, and eat hot fudge sundaes."

"I've already gone way over my sugar intake for the day, which is probably why I'm still edgy. You go on. I've got to finish here. Then I'm going home to sleep for twelve hours."

"If you change your mind, I have homemade fudge sauce." Nell pushed herself to her feet. "You did an amazing job, Mia."

"We did. We did a stupendous job."

She turned back to her keyboard and worked until six. Sticking to practical tasks gave her mind the chance to circle and circle and consider. And it gave her the opportunity to admit that the buzz still vibrating through her wasn't going to quiet on its own.

Given the alternatives to select from, she saw no reason not to choose the one that appealed most.

Sam stripped down to cutoffs and considered the cartons of leftover takeout Chinese in his refrigerator. He was, as he had been all day, famished. He thought he might order in a pizza, or a side of beef to top off the egg rolls and pork fried rice.

He was relieved that Caroline had turned down his invitation to dinner. As fond as he was of her, his brain just couldn't handle an evening of struggling to concentrate on conversation.

Not after the day he'd put in. Or the night before it.

He'd swum for an hour, hard, after he helped Zack haul all the equipment back to the house on the bluff. Then he'd swung by the hotel on the way home and let himself into the health club. He'd worked out another hour, doing what he could to burn off the edge. He'd done fifty laps in the hotel pool, taken a frigid shower.

And hadn't slept all night.

After the signing, he'd taken Caroline back to the hotel, where she'd claimed she was going to take a long bubble bath. He'd used the health club again, worked up a heavy sweat. Showered. Spent an hour swimming.

And his system was still careening.

He disliked sleep inducements, even of his own making, but he thought, after he ate, that that was the only solution left.

The only practical solution, he corrected. The more satisfying one would be to find Mia, drag her off somewhere, rip off her clothes, and pump out the energy in wild, crazy sex.

Which would take him right back to square one of his plan to cement a bond with her outside of wild, crazy sex.

He wasn't sure his overworked system could take either.

He'd settle for pizza.

He closed the refrigerator and turned toward the phone. And when he saw her at the back door, his entire body clenched like a fist.

Served him right, he thought grimly, for trying to tame his raging hormones by tuning her out for a few hours.

But his expression was as easy and pleasant as hers as he crossed to the door.

"Didn't expect to see you. I thought you'd be somewhere with your feet up and a drink in your hand."

"I hope you don't mind me dropping by."

"Not at all." He opened the screen door and willed himself to behave.

"I brought you a present." She held out a box, prettily wrapped in dark blue foil and topped with an elaborate white bow. "From the owner of Café Book to the owner of the Magick Inn." She came in, making sure her body brushed his lightly as she passed.

And she felt the quick tremor.

"A gift."

"To thank you for your part in making today happen. It was an enormous success for all involved."

"Caroline was nearly staggering by the time she got to her room. It takes a lot to wear her out."

"I'm sure you'd know," Mia countered.

"She's married. We're friends. That's it."

"Touchy." She clucked her tongue. "Why don't you offer me a drink, and have one yourself?"

"Fine." He got out a bottle of wine, yanked out the stopper. "I had a damn life the last decade, Mia. I assume you did, too."

"Naturally. Would you like me to parade some of my lovers for you?" Helpfully, she took glasses out of the cupboard. The searing look he shot her pleased her enormously.

He'd be easier, and more fun to seduce, if his temper was up.

"I don't want to hear about them. And I didn't parade Caroline."

"No, but you didn't tell me beforehand, either. It made it awkward and irritating. But I've decided to forgive you."

"Well, golly. Thanks."

"Now you're annoyed. Why don't I pour that, and you can open your present? We'll see if it puts you in a better mood."

"Rapping your head against the wall might put me in a better mood."

"But you're much too civilized for that."

"Don't go to the bank on it." But he pulled off the top of the box. And pulled out a wind chime made of foolish brass frogs.

"I found it whimsical, which suits the cottage. And apt, as I had a lovely fantasy going about how I turned you into one of these for a few days." She tapped a frog, sent it dancing and singing against its brothers. Then picked up her wine.

"It's very . . . unique. Whenever I see it, I'll think of you."

"There's a hook just outside the kitchen. Why don't you hang it, see how it looks there?"

Obliging her, he stepped outside, looped it over the empty hook.

"You smell of the sea," she told him, trailing a fingertip down the center of his bare back.

"I've been swimming."

"Did it help?"

"No."

"I could." She leaned against him, nibbled at his shoulder. "Why don't we help each other?"

"Because then it's all about sex."

"What's wrong with sex?"

She was clouding his senses. Woman's magic. He turned, gripped her arms. "We used to have more. I want more again."

"We're both old enough to know we don't get everything we want. So we take what there is." She spread her hands over his chest, felt surprise when he stepped back. "You want me, I want you. Why complicate it?"

"It's always been complicated, Mia."

"So we simplify. I need a release from what happened last night. So do you."

"We need to talk about what happened last night."

"You're a real fan of talking lately." She tossed back her hair. "Nell has this notion that you're courting me."

A muscle jumped in his cheek. "That's not a word I'd use. I'd say 'dating.' I've been dating you."

"In that case—" She crossed her arms, slid the straps of her dress from her shoulders. And let it slither to the floor. "We've dated long enough."

# Seventeen

He'd have sworn the world stopped. For one rushing moment there was no sound, no movement. There was nothing but Mia, tall and curved and beautiful. All alabaster and fire, she wore only a slim silver chain that nestled a moonstone between her breasts and an anklet made up of tiny Celtic knots above shoes that were no more than a trio of narrow straps and stiletto heels.

His mouth watered.

"You want me." Her voice was a low feline purr. "Your body aches as mine does. Your blood's as hot."

"Wanting you has always been the easy part."

She stepped to him. "Then this should be a snap." She ran her hands up his torso, over his chest. "You're trembling." Easing closer, she rubbed her lips over his shoulder, over muscles that were tensed rock-hard. "So am I."

His hands flexed, fisted. "This is your answer?"

"I don't need an answer when I don't have a question." She lifted her head until their eyes met. "I have needs, just as you do. Desires, hot and restless inside me. As you do. We can both take what we need, and harm no one."

She leaned in, nipped sharply at his bottom lip. "Let's take a walk in the woods."

When he jerked her hard against him, her face lit with triumph. A quick, laughing moan escaped when he swung her into his arms. The moment of victory was hot and sweet.

"Here," he said. "In this house. In my bed."

Needs bubbling inside her clouded her mind, only for an instant. But an instant was enough to have him striding through the kitchen before she struggled. "No, not here."

"It can't be all your way."

"I won't be with you here." The minute she hit the bed, she rolled, but he pinned her.

"Yes, you will."

She fought him. Pure instinct had her bucking under him, straining against his hold. She could smell the lavender she'd planted outside the window, and the sweetness of it tore at her heart.

She hadn't come for sweetness, nor for intimacy. She had come for sex.

She gathered herself, reached for composure and derision. "All you've proved is that you have superior strength."

"Yeah. That's the breaks," he said. Her voice might have been cold, but the heat was pumping off her skin. "I'm not letting you go this time, Mia. Considering the mood we're both in, you fighting me is only going to make this better. So, fight me." He yanked her arms over her head. "I don't want it easy. And I don't want it fast."

He handcuffed her wrists and used his mouth on her.

She continued to struggle, because he was right. She could damn him for it, but he was right. The underlying threat of violence added a slippery thrill that fed the reckless need inside her. She could hate herself for wanting that, for the part of her that reveled in being overpowered, undone, taken. But she couldn't deny it.

He ravished, his mouth assaulting her body. The little war had her skin springing with sweat and her senses tangling into one mass of molten pleasure. Her body twisted, arched, but he simply found new spots to torture and entice.

The energy that burned inside her whipped to flash point, ripped a cry from her throat as he drove her to the first brutal climax with his mouth alone.

And that quick and glorious release only fueled a hunger for more.

He felt her body quake, heard her breath catch. Beneath his lips her pulse beat like fury. Her flesh was damp and fragrant, erotically hot and slick. Knowing that she fought them both only added to the vicious passion surging through his blood.

He rode it, recklessly, until they were both quivering.

When his mouth conquered hers, the kiss was a kind of madness. There was no thought, no room for reason. In a war of lips and tongues and teeth, they fed on each other. When he felt her fly a second time, he released her hands to take more.

They branded each other, rolling restlessly over the bed in a search for dominance and more pleasure. The air went thick, and the sun streaming through the windows turned to gilt.

She rose over him. Craving her, he reared up, clamping his mouth over her breast. Drawing her in like breath.

She lost herself in the frenzy of sensation. Gave herself to that feral need to take and be taken. Here there was only desperation, and the one man who could make her feel it. The glory of those animal urges, the mindless wonder of being alive raced inside her.

Time quickened, then sprinted past her, as the storm inside her broke yet again.

Breathless, still spinning, she wrapped herself around him, holding on as if for her life. Her heart quaked, and threatened to break open.

She heard his harsh murmurs as his body slid over hers, as his lips skittered over her face, her throat. She shook her head, quick denial, as the Gaelic stroked her aching heart.

Light, warm and blue, pulsed from him.

"No. Don't."

He couldn't stop. What they'd brought to each other sapped his control. The need to complete the intimacy was raw and open in him.

*"A ghra. A amhain."* My love. My only. The words tumbled out of him without design. His power shimmered, seeking its mate even as his body craved. But when he brushed his lips over her cheek, tasted tears, he squeezed his eyes shut.

"I'm sorry." His breath ragged, he buried his face in her hair. "Just a minute. Give me a minute."

He fought for control, to pull the magic back inside him. Whatever they were or had been to each other, he had no right to force her to share that part of herself.

She felt him quiver as he struggled to pull it in. It would hurt him, she knew. A deep and physical aching that came from denying the blood and starving the soul.

Still, he held her while he locked himself away. Held her while she listened to his breath tear out against the pain of it.

She couldn't bear it, for either of them.

She lifted his head, looked into his eyes. And gave him her magic. "Share with me," she said, drawing him down into the kiss. "Share all."

Her light was gilded red against his deepening blue. The brilliant thrill flooded her, swamped her as their powers entwined and merged. And merged, streamed inside them both. She let herself fly on it, rose to him as he filled her.

There was a rush like the wind, a stream of sound like a hundred harpstrings plucked at once. The air swelled. All she was, and all he was, laid open.

The air shimmered, light against light building to a radiant glow. Even as he moved in her, long, slow thrusts that savored the gift, he took her hands. Linked fingers curled tight and sparks swirled from them to dance in the air.

As they climbed, the light brightened, building, building toward a flash that burst like lightning. And on that burst, he met her mouth with his, and flew with her.

He nuzzled at the curve of her shoulder, rubbed his cheek to hers, whispering soft and foolish endearments. His power continued to whisper inside her as well. Her body felt unbearably soft. And though her heart continued to pound, she knew its beat was no longer for her alone.

What had she done?

She'd stripped aside, by her own will, the last of her defenses. She had given him all she was, taken all he was.

She had let herself love him again.

Stupid, she thought. Stupid, careless, and dangerous.

Even knowing it, she could lie here with his weight pressing against her and want to gather him close and cling to the dreamy echoes of what they'd shared.

She had to get away, clear her head of him. And consider what to do next.

She lifted a hand to his shoulder, intending to nudge him away. But her fingers slid into his hair.

"Mia." His voice was thick and sleepy. "*Allaina*. So soft, so lovely. Stay with me tonight. Wake with me tomorrow."

Her heart trembled, but when she spoke her voice was brisk and even. "You're speaking Gaelic."

"Hmm?"

"You're speaking in Gaelic." Now she did give his shoulder a little nudge. "Which means you're about to fall asleep on top of me."

"No, I'm not." He braced himself on his elbows so he could gaze down at her. "You make my head spin." He dropped a kiss on her forehead, then the tip of her nose. "I'm glad you dropped by."

It was hard to resist the easy affection. "So am I. But I have to go now."

"Uh-uh." Idly toying with her hair, he studied her face. "I'm afraid I can't allow that. And if you try, I'm going to have to get rough with you again. You know you liked it."

"Please." She pushed at him, tried to slither free.

"You really liked it." Leaning down, he lightly bit her shoulder.

"Maybe, under this limited set of circumstances, I found it . . . arousing. I needed an outlet for the excess energy that last night's spell worked up in me."

"Tell me about it." He caught her chin in his hand. "I mean that. I want you to tell me about it. But right now, I'm starving. Aren't you starving? I've got leftover Chinese takeout."

"Yummy. But—"

"Mia, we need to talk."

"Talk isn't the usual activity when we're lying naked in bed and you're still inside me."

"There is that." He slid his hands under her hips, lifted them. Slid deeper into her. "Tell me you'll stay."

Her breath caught. "I'm not—"

"I want to watch you climb again." He kneaded her hips, his thrusts slow and steady. "Just let me watch you."

He left her no choice. He exploited her weakness, drained her will with a ruthless tenderness.

He watched her surrender, to him, to herself, to the rise of sensation. And when she crested—one long wave—it rippled through him. And he lifted her, wrapped her close.

"Stay."

With a sigh, she rested her head on his shoulder. "I could eat."

They made quick work of the Chinese, then scavenged for more. By the time they were digging into a box of dry cereal, the edge was off. Sam took a last handful of puffed rice.

"Strong magic and good sex. Nothing like it to sharpen the appetite."

"I had two muffins, a sandwich, cake, and

a bowl of rotini. And that was before the sex. Give me that." She took the box from him and dug in.

"It was a potent spell."

"Now that we've very efficiently cleaned out my kitchen of all edible products, let's take that walk in the woods."

"It's getting late, Sam."

"Yeah, it is." He took her hand. "And we both know it." He glanced down at her bare feet. "Since I don't see how you can walk anywhere in those shoes you had on, maybe we should head to the beach instead of the woods. Easier on your feet."

"I'm used to walking barefoot in the woods." It was best, she thought, to deal with it. As long as they were talking, or eating, or seducing each other, she wouldn't have to think about loving him. Or what she would do about it.

"You want me to explain the spell, and I'm not sure I can."

"I don't want the nuts and bolts." He drew her across the lawn toward the shadows and the path. "But I'd like to know, first, how long you've known you had that kind of power."

"I'm not sure I did—not exactly. Felt," she

continued. "As if there was a switch inside waiting for me to flip it."

"It's not that simple."

"No, it's not." She could smell the trees and the sea. And on such a night, she thought, you could smell the stars. A cool brush along the senses. "I've worked on it, studied, practiced. I've gathered myself. You understand that."

"I also understand that to pull that out the way you did the other night, without any real preparation, is beyond anything I've experienced."

"I've been preparing all my life." And in the last decade, she thought, it's been my one and only love. "Still I couldn't finish it. It wasn't quite enough." Determination toughened her voice. "But I will finish it."

"That's where you and I have a problem. What you did was dangerous, for you. It didn't have to be."

"The risk was minimal."

"If you'd told me what you could do, what you'd obviously planned to do, given the opportunity, I could have been prepared. I could have helped. But you don't want my help."

She said nothing as they passed the little

stream where foxglove nodded on the banks. "It's been a long time since I considered having your help."

"I've been back for over two months, Mia."

"And were gone over ten years. I learned to do a great deal without you in that length of time. Without anyone," she added, "as Ripley cut herself off from me and what we shared during the same period. I've taken what I was given and honed it, built it."

"That's right, you have. I wonder if you would have if I'd stayed."

She rounded on him, her temper quicker than it might have been, as the same thought had come to her. "Is that a new rationalization? A new reason for what you did?"

"No." He met her fury with utter calm. "My reasons for leaving were completely selfish. It doesn't seem to change the results. You're stronger than you would have been."

"Should I thank you for it?" She angled her head. "Maybe I should. Maybe it's time for me to acknowledge that your leaving was the best thing for both of us. I saw you as the beginning and end of my life, and everything in between. But you weren't. I lived without you. And whether you stay or go, I'll continue to live, to work. To be. I can enjoy you now without illusions. It's a nice bonus to share myself with someone who understands power and who expects nothing in return but pleasure for pleasure."

It rubbed at his temper, as he supposed she'd intended it to. "Don't thank me too soon. You wondered why I'd maneuvered you into dating. I needed to show you, and maybe to prove to myself, that there's more than sex between us."

"Of course there is." Calm again, she began to walk. "There's magic, a shared history. And though I didn't initially believe it, a shared love of the island. We have mutual friends."

"We were friends once."

"We're friendly now." She breathed in deeply. "How do people live without the sea close? How do they breathe?"

"Mia." He touched the tips of her hair. "When we made love, I didn't intend to ask you to share magic with me. It wasn't calculated."

"I know that." Though she stopped walking, she kept her back to him.

"Why did you let me?"

"Because you would've stopped. It meant something to me that you would've stopped when I asked. And, I suppose, because I've missed it. Sharing power excites and fulfills."

"Was there no one else in all these years?"

"You've no right to ask me that."

"No, I don't. So instead I'll tell you what you don't ask me. There was no one but you. Never anyone but you in that way."

"It doesn't matter."

"If it doesn't," he said, taking her arm before she could move away, "then you should be able to listen. I never got over you, and if I was with another woman, it was never the way it was between us. Every one of them deserved better than I could give. I couldn't give them better, because none of them were you."

"There's no need for this," she began.

"I need it. I've loved you all my life. No spell, no incantation, no act of will has ever been able to change that for me."

Her heart stumbled in her chest. It took all of her strength to balance it again. "But you tried."

"I tried. With women, with work, with travel. Not loving you is beyond my power."

"Do you think, Sam, that even if it were only my own heart at risk, I could pour it into your hands again?"

"Then just take mine. I'm not doing anything else with it."

"I can't. I don't know how much of what I feel is an echo of what was. How much mixed with that is anger. More," she said, turning back to him, "I don't know how much of what you believe you feel is real. Everything's at stake now, and clouded emotions are dangerous."

"My emotions aren't clouded. They were, for a long time."

"Now mine are. And I've learned to step back from them. I care about you. The link's too strong for that to be otherwise. But I don't want to be in love with you again, Sam. And that's my choice. If you can't accept that, then we need to stay away from each other."

"I can accept that it's your choice, for now. But I'm going to do everything I can to change your mind."

She threw up her hands in frustration. "By

sending me flowers, going on picnics? Those are frills, trappings."

"Those are romance."

"I don't *want* romance."

"Deal with it. I was too young and stupid to give it to you once. I'm older and smarter now. There was a time when it was hard for me to tell you I loved you. Didn't come naturally off my tongue. And it sure as hell wasn't a phrase that was bandied about in my house."

"I don't want you to tell me."

"You always said it first." He saw the surprise on her face. "You never realized that, did you? I was never able to say it to you, unless you'd said it. Times change. People change. Some people take longer than others. I realize I've been waiting, Mia, maneuvering again, so you'd say it first. Easier for me that way. You used to make things too damn easy for me."

"Fortunately, that's changed. Now I have to go. It's late."

"Yeah, it's late. I love you, Mia. I love you. I don't mind saying it a few hundred times until you believe it."

It hurt to hear it. A quick, pinching pain.

She used that pain to keep her heart cool and her voice even. "You gave me words before, Sam. We gave each other words. They weren't enough. I can't give you what you want."

She ran down the path, away from him.

"Won't give me," he replied. "Yet."

She didn't stop until she got to her car. Didn't go into the house for her shoes, or think about them. She thought only of driving away, driving fast until her mind settled again.

She had let herself love him again. Or rather, her heart had turned on her when she'd been vulnerable. But that was her problem, and one she would deal with.

Rationally, reasonably, if loving him were the right choice, it wouldn't make her so unhappy.

If hearing him say he loved her was the solution, how could it have been like a blow to the heart?

She would not become a victim of her own emotions, not a second time. She wouldn't throw herself mindlessly into love, putting herself and everything that mattered to her at risk.

Balance, she told herself, and clear thinking. They were essential when one was contemplating a life-and-death decision. Maybe it was time to take a few days off, regroup. She'd been spreading herself too thin, she decided. She needed to be with herself.

Alone.

"What the hell do you mean she's gone?" Annoyed at being roused out of sleep before eight-thirty, on a Sunday, on the *only* day that week she could sleep in, Ripley scowled at the phone.

"She's off the island." A pulse was pounding in Sam's throat, making speech almost painful. "Where did she go?"

"I don't know. Christ." She sat up in bed, scrubbed her hand over her face. "I'm not even awake. How do you know she went off-island? Maybe she's just out for a walk or a drive."

He knew, Sam thought, because he'd tuned in to her. And the snapping of the connection had awakened him. Next time, he thought grimly, he wouldn't limit the link to the island.

"I just know. I was with her last night. She didn't say anything about plans on the mainland."

"Well, she doesn't keep me as her social secretary. Did you have a fight or something?"

"No, we didn't have a fight." What they'd had could never be boiled down to such an elemental word. "If you have any idea where she's gone—"

"I don't." But the worry in his voice got through. "Listen, ask Lulu. Mia wouldn't go anywhere without letting her know. She probably just went over to do some shopping or something and—" Scowling, Ripley held the phone out and listened to the dial tone. "Well, goodbye to you, too."

He didn't bother with the phone this time, but jumped in his car and drove to Lulu's. He barely noticed that she'd changed the paint from the pumpkin orange he remembered from his boyhood to a wild purple. He knocked on the front door.

"You got two seconds to tell me why you woke me up out of a dream where I was dancing with Charles Bronson and we were both naked. Otherwise, I'm kicking your—"

"Where's Mia?" he snapped.

He slapped a hand on the door before she could slam it in his face. "Just tell me she's okay."

"Why shouldn't she be?"

"Did she tell you where she was going?"

"If she did, I'm not telling you." She could sense his anger and his fear. "You try any hocus-pocus on me, and I'll not only kick your ass, I'll mop the floor with it. Now back off."

Disgusted with himself, he stepped back. When the door slammed he just sat on the porch steps and rested his head in his hands.

Had he driven her away? Was it some kind of ugly joke fate continued to play on them that one of them would love so much that the other was compelled to flee?

It didn't matter, he told himself. Not now. All that mattered now was that she was safe.

When he heard the door open again, he stayed where he was.

"You don't have to tell me where she is, what she's doing, or why she left. I just need to know that she's all right."

"Any reason you know of she shouldn't be?"

"I upset her last night."

With a sniff, Lulu marched over and gave him a quick boot with her bare foot. "I should've figured it. What did you do?"

"I told her I loved her."

Behind his back, Lulu pursed her lips. "What did she have to say to that?"

"That she didn't want to hear it, basically."

"She's a sensible woman," Lulu said, then immediately felt nasty. More nasty than she was comfortable with. "She's taking a few days off, that's all. On the mainland—shopping, getting pampered. Do her good to decompress, if you ask me. She's been working 'round the clock."

"Okay." He rubbed his hands on the thighs of his jeans, then turned to face her. "Okay. Thanks."

"Did you tell her you loved her to mess with her head?"

"I told her I loved her because I do. Messing with her head was just a side benefit."

"I don't know why the hell I always liked you."

Sam was shocked. "You did?"

"If I hadn't, I'd have peeled the skin off your face for putting hands on my baby. Well, I'm up," she said and buried both hands in her disordered mop of hair to scratch her head. "You might as well come in and have some coffee."

Too intrigued to refuse, he followed her into the kitchen. "I always wondered why you didn't live at the cliff house."

"First off, because I couldn't stand those pompous, self-absorbed Devlins." She dug coffee out of a canister shaped like a piglet. "Didn't mind spending a few days there when they were off on one of their trips, but when they were at home, I needed a place of my own. Otherwise, I might have smothered them both in their sleep."

"When did they leave—for good?"

"Few months after you did."

"After . . . but she was nineteen."

"Just shy of her twentieth birthday. They headed off to—who the hell cares. Came back once or twice during that year, for form, if you ask me. Mia hit twenty-one, and that was over. Guess they figured their job was done."

"They never did their job," Sam stated. "You did."

"That's right. She's been mine since her grandmother put her in my arms. She's still mine." She shot him a challenging look over her shoulder.

"I know it. I'm glad of it."

"Maybe you've got some sense in that pea brain of yours after all." She poured water from a cherry-red kettle into the coffeemaker. "Anyway, after they moved off-island, Mia asked if I didn't want to come up and live with her. Plenty of room. But I like my place, and she likes being up there on her own."

She studied him while the coffeemaker burped and grumbled. "You thinking of trying to convince her to let you move up there with her?"

"Ah . . . I hadn't thought quite that far ahead."

"Don't change much, do you? Always dance back from the sticking point."

"And what would the sticking point be?"

"That girl," she said and drilled a finger into his chest. "*My* girl. She wants marriage, and she wants babies. She wants a man she can share her whole life with, thick and thin, and not one who gets pale when the word *marriage* comes up in conversation. Like you're doing now."

"Marriage isn't the only serious commitment—"

"You think you can bullshit her with that, or are you just bullshitting yourself?"

"A number of people make and keep a bond without a legal ceremony. Mia and I are hardly traditionalists."

Lulu's skewering stare made him feel like a teenager again, bringing Mia home after curfew. "But in any case, I haven't given the matter a great deal of thought. At this point she's not even comfortable with me telling her I'm in love with her."

"That's a real fine speech. Full of hot air, but it sounded almost pretty."

"What's so important about marriage?" he demanded. "You're divorced."

"Got me there." Amused, she got out two cheerful yellow mugs. "Funny thing about life. You just can't get a guarantee with it.

You pays your money, you takes your choice."

"Yeah." Depressed all over again, Sam took the mug. "I've certainly heard that one before."

# Eighteen

She'd intended to relax, shop, indulge in a day at a spa or salon. She'd intended to do as little thinking as possible for three days and three nights. To focus on her own emotional and physical well-being.

She had not intended to take the time and effort to gain admittance into the federal facility where Evan Remington was being held.

But since she had done so, she could rationalize the decision. Time was growing short. If fate was leading her to Remington, she would follow the path. She was in no real danger, and there was the possibility, however slight, that something good could come out of the visit.

She didn't question the fact that she was able to set up a meeting with him with relatively little trouble. There were powers at work that scoffed at the tangled red tape of bureaucracy. And she was part of them.

She faced him across a wide counter split down the center by a barricade of thick, reinforced glass. Mia picked up the phone that would link them, as he did.

"Mr. Remington. Do you remember me?"

"Whore," he hissed.

"Yes, I see you do. And that the months you've spent in here haven't improved your disposition."

"I'll be out soon."

"Is that what he tells you?" She leaned a little closer. "He lies."

A muscle began to twitch in his cheek. "I'll be out soon," he repeated. "And you'll be dead."

"We've beaten him twice. And only a few nights ago he ran from me with his tail between his legs. Has he told you that?"

"I know what's going to happen. I've seen it. I know you'll all die screaming. Can you see it?"

For a moment she could, reflected on the glass between them. The dark, boiling storm, the rips of lightning, the swirl of roaring wind as the sea opened like a hungry mouth and swallowed the island whole.

"He shows you his desire, but not reality."

"I'll have Helen." His voice went dreamy, like a child repeating a rhyme. "She'll crawl back to me. She'll pay for her deception, her betrayal."

"Nell's beyond you. Look at me. At me," she demanded. She wouldn't allow even his thoughts to touch Nell now. "There's only me to deal with. He's using you, Evan. As he would a puppet, or a vicious little dog. He uses your illness, your anger. He'll destroy you with it. I can help you."

"He'll fuck you before he kills you. Want a preview?"

It happened fast. Pain ripped through her breasts as if claws had dug into her flesh. A spear of ice jabbed with one hard thrust between her legs. She didn't cry out, though a scream of rage and horror spewed into her throat. Instead she drew her power down like armor. Punched it out like a fist.

Remington's head snapped back, and his eyes went wide with shock.

"He uses," she said calmly. "You pay. Did you think threats and ploys would make me tremble? I am of the Three. What works in me is beyond your scope. I can help you. I can save you from the horror he will bring you. If you'll trust me and help yourself, I can close you off from him. I can shield you so that he can't use or harm you."

"Why?"

"To save myself and what I love, I would save you."

He inched closer to the glass. She could hear his raspy breathing over the receiver. For a moment true pity stirred in her.

"Mia Devlin." He licked his lips, then they spread into a wide, mad smile. "You'll burn! Burn the witch!" He cackled even as the guard rushed over to restrain him. "I'll watch while you die screaming."

Though Remington dropped the phone when the guard dragged him away, she heard his wild laughter long after the door slammed and locked behind him.

The laughter, she thought, of the damned.

Sam had a meeting with his accountant. Revenue was up, but so were expenses and overhead. The Magick Inn was operating in the red for the first time in thirty years, but as Sam saw it that would change. He'd booked two conventions for the fall, and with the winter holiday package he was putting together, he expected to recoup some of the loss over that historically slow reservation period.

Until that time he could, and would, continue to plow his own money into the hotel.

If the hotel, and the island, went down in a matter of weeks, it wouldn't be because of lack of faith on his part.

Where the hell was she? Couldn't she have waited to go off on some shopping spree until after their lives, their fates, their futures were more secure?

How many pairs of shoes did the woman need, for God's sake?

It was just an excuse to get away from him, he thought. He'd told her he loved her, and she'd run like a rabbit. Things got a little bit sticky, and instead of staying put and dealing with it, she'd bolted to the mainland and . . .

He stopped, scowled down at his own half-finished signature on the correspondence in front of him.

"Moron," he muttered.

"I beg your pardon?"

"Nothing." He shook his head at his assistant and completed his signature. "Check on the winter brochures, Mrs. Farley," he told her as he signed the next letter. "I want to be certain that the corrections are made before the end of the month. I want to meet with the head of sales tomorrow. Find me the time."

She flipped through his calendar. "You're free at eleven, and at two."

"Eleven."

"And send a memo to Housekeeping re . . . How long have you been married?"

"You want to know how long the housekeeping staff has been married?"

"No, Mrs. Farley. How long have you been married?"

"Thirty-nine years last February."

"Thirty-nine years. How do you do it?"

Mrs. Farley laid her pad down, took off her glasses. "I could say it's a bit like alcoholism. One day at a time."

"I never thought of it like that. Marriage as an addiction."

"Certainly as a condition. It's also a job that requires attention and work, cooperation and creativity."

"That doesn't sound particularly romantic."

"There's nothing more romantic than going through life, with all of its spins, with someone you love. Someone who loves and understands you. Someone who'll be there for the big bouquets. Children, grandchildren, a new house, a well-earned promotion. And for the weeds. Illness, a burned dinner, a bad day at work."

"There are people who get used to taking care of the bouquets and the weeds alone."

"I admire independence. The world would be a stronger place if we were all capable of handling life on our own. But being capable of it doesn't mean being unable to share and depend on someone else. It shouldn't mean being unwilling to. That's the romance."

"I never saw my parents share much more than an affection for Italian designers and a box at the opera."

"That's a shame for them, isn't it? Some people don't know how to give love, or how to ask for it."

"Sometimes the answer's no."

"And sometimes it isn't." The faint edge of irritation worked into her voice. "Some people expect things to fall into their lap. Oh, they might work a bit for it. I'll just shake this tree, and if I shake it long enough that pretty red apple will plop right into my hand. Never occurs to them that they might have to climb the damn tree, fall out a couple of times, get some scrapes and bruises before they get to that apple. Because if the apple's worth wanting, it's worth risking a broken neck."

On a huff, she got to her feet. "I need to type up this memo."

He was so surprised when she strode out of his office and shut the door smartly, he didn't call her back to tell her he'd never dictated the memo.

"Look what happens when I have a conversation about marriage," he thought aloud. "My assistant bites my head off. And I know how to climb a damn tree. I've climbed plenty of trees."

And right now, he felt as if he were hanging by his fingertips from a very unstable branch. And the prettiest apple was still just out of his reach.

He picked up a file, intending to bury his

frustrations in work. And a light went on inside him.

Mia was back on the Sisters.

She'd called Lulu from the ferry and had gotten an update on bookstore business, and on island news. As she'd asked Lulu to come up to the house that evening to fill in the gaps, there was no need to drop by work. Tomorrow was soon enough to face the pile of phone messages and the backlog generated over her three-day absence.

She'd called Ripley as well, and Nell. Since she thought the best way to pass on the details of her meeting with Remington was during a civilized meal at her own house the following evening, she needed to drop by Island Market for some supplies.

She'd yet to call Sam.

She would call him. She wheeled her cart over to the produce section and stared at the arugula. As soon as she figured out how to handle him, and what had been said between them, she'd call him.

Life ran more smoothly with a clear-cut, but flexible, plan.

"Still shopping?"

And sometimes, Mia realized as she turned and looked at Sam, fate wasn't content to hang back until the plan was formulated and refined.

"I consider shopping a work in progress." She selected lettuce, contemplated the Roma tomatoes. "It's an odd time of day to see a businessman in the market."

"I'm out of milk."

"I'm quite sure you won't find it in produce."

"I'm thinking about getting an apple. A pretty red apple."

She continued to select items for a salad. "The plums look good today."

"Sometimes only one thing will do." He let his fingers tangle in her hair. "Did you enjoy your time away?"

"It was . . . productive." Because he made her feel uneasy, she wheeled into dairy. "I found a nice little Wicca shop. They had a wonderful selection of bell jars."

"You can never have too many."

"My sentiments," she agreed, and picked up a quart of milk.

"Thanks." He took it from her, tucked it under his arm. "Why don't you have dinner with me tonight? You can tell me about your trip."

He wasn't behaving the way she'd anticipated. There was no flare of temper over her abrupt departure, no demands to know where she'd been, what she'd been doing. As a result, she felt guilty and small.

Damn clever of him.

"Actually, Lulu's coming up tonight so that we can deal with some store business. But I'm having a little dinner party tomorrow. I was going to call you." She put a small wheel of Brie in her cart. "I've some things to discuss with everyone. Will seven o'clock work for you?"

"Sure."

He leaned in, cupping her cheek with his free hand, laying his lips on hers. Softly, warmly, lingering over the kiss until it shifted from the casual to something more suited to the dark.

"I love you, Mia." His fingers skimmed over her cheek before he stepped back. "See you tomorrow."

She stood where she was, her hands vised on the handle of the cart, as he strolled away with a quart of milk under his arm.

For years, so many years of her life, she'd

have given everything to have him look at her in the way he'd just done, to tell her he loved her, in just that way.

Now that he had, why should it be so hard?

Why should it make her want to weep?

Lulu got behind the wheel of her battered and beloved orange VW bug. Since the night she'd taken the unexpected swim, she'd felt safe, solid, secure.

She didn't know what charms Ripley and Nell had conjured up, but they were working like—well, charms. Whatever you wanted to call the thing that was hovering over the island, her girls were going to screw it to the wall.

Still, she felt better knowing Mia was back on-island, tucked into the cliff house, getting back to her routine. And though it had been a pill to swallow, she felt more at ease about Mia since she had Sam fretting over her.

The boy'd been an idiot, she decided as she drove through the village with the classic sounds of Pink Floyd blasting through the speakers. But he'd been young. She'd done plenty of stupid things when she was young.

Every one of them had led her here. She supposed, if she was going to be fair, everything Sam had done had led him right back to the Sisters, and Mia.

Not that she was finished giving him grief, but she would dispense it in smaller doses now.

Only one thing mattered, and that was Mia's happiness. If Sam Logan was the answer to that, then he was going to damn well come up to the mark.

If she had to kick him up to it.

The idea made her grin wickedly as she started up the cliff road. And was oblivious to the mist that rose and rolled behind her.

When the music turned to a hiss of static, she glanced down at the radio, slapped irritably at the little tape player installed under it.

"Damn it, you better not eat *The Wall*, you cheap bastard."

The response, a long, deep howl through the speaker, had her hands jerking on the wheel. The car shuddered around her as the fog poured, cold as death, through her open windows.

Yelping, she hit the brakes first, an automatic response as her vision was obscured. Instead of stopping, the little car speeded up, its cheerful rubber band pinging now a machine gun's *rat-a-tat*. Under her hands the wheel vibrated, iced, and began to spin on its own. Though it felt like a slick and frozen snake, she gripped it, hard, and yanked. The scream of the tires echoed her own as she caught a glimpse of the edge of the cliff.

In front of her the windshield became a starburst. Ice crackling over ice. Then the stars went black.

The spoon Mia was using to stir sauce for the pasta she'd made for Lulu clattered out of her numb hand. As it bounced to the floor, the vision shrieked through her head, all sound and fury. Her throat tightened as if a hand had squeezed it as she whirled away from the stove and ran.

She flew out of the house, blind with panic, racing to the road on foot. From her hilltop view, she saw the filthy mist spewing behind the little orange car on the road below, and was running, running when she saw the car spin out of control and toward the cliff.

"No, no, no!" Fear blanked her mind, rolled sick in her stomach. "Help me. Help me." She chanted it over and over as she struggled to find her power through the sheer wall of terror.

All she had, everything she was, she gathered. And heaved the magic inside her toward the car as it crashed into the guardrail and flipped like a toy tossed by a child's angry hand.

"Hold, hold." Oh, God, she couldn't *think*. "Blow air, come wind, a bridge to form. Hold her safe, keep her from harm. Please, please," she chanted. "A net, a bridge, a steady wall, keep her from that terrible fall."

Panting, her vision blurred with tears, she ran the last yards to where the car teetered on the broken guardrail, over the drop to the rocks below. "It will not have what's dear to me. As I will, so mote it be."

Her voice broke as she reached the rail. "Lulu!"

The car balanced precariously on its roof, seesawing on the crushed rail. The wind she'd conjured blew the hair back from her face as she climbed over the rail.

"Don't touch it!"

Small rocks and clumps of earth spilled off the unstable edge when she spun around at the shout. Sam leaped out of his car.

"I don't know how long it can hold. I feel it slipping, inside me."

"You can hold it." He pushed his way through the wind, climbed the rail until he, too, stood on the narrow edge. "Focus. You have to focus. I'll get her out."

"No. She's mine."

"That's the point." He spent a desperate moment to take Mia's arms, shake her. The car could go at any minute, he knew. And so could the edge where they stood. "Exactly. Hold it. You're the only one strong enough to do it. Step over the rail."

"I won't lose her!" Mia shouted. "Or you."

Her legs trembled as she climbed over the rail. Her hands shook as she lifted them. And she saw the fog begin to rise again. Saw the dark shape of the wolf forming from it.

Her body stilled. Fury spiked inside her and stabbed away the fear. "You won't have her." The hand she flung out was rock-steady now. She faced the wolf, bore the weight of the magic she called on her shoulders. "You may have me, that's up to fate. But by all I am, all I have, you won't take her."

It snarled and started toward her. It could take her life now, she thought, and so be it. Her magic would hold. She risked a glance at Sam and saw, with inner horror, that he was easing a bleeding and unconscious Lulu out of the car. And the car tipped and swayed.

With a last push, she left herself open and defenseless, shoving everything toward the cliffs.

And the wolf bunched to leap.

As he charged, energy shot into her, out from her. It struck him like a lightning bolt. With a furious howl, he vanished into the fog.

"Didn't count on my sisters, did you? You bastard."

The wind sucked away the mist, and she saw both Ripley and Nell spring out of their cars before she turned to run toward Sam.

He had Lulu in his arms. The edge of the ground crumbled under his feet and sent him stumbling forward as a chunk of the ledge rained down to the sea. Mia reached out, grabbed him as the car overbalanced and tumbled over the cliffs. He was struggling back over the rail when the gas tank exploded.

"She's alive," he managed.

"I know." She kissed Lulu's white cheek, laid a hand on her heart. "We'll take her to the clinic."

Outside the emergency clinic, where the air was quiet and the breeze balmy, Nell tended the cuts on Mia's feet.

"Got six million pair of shoes," Ripley stated while she paced, restless as a cat. "And you run barefoot over broken glass."

"Yes. Silly, isn't it?" She hadn't felt the glass slice into her feet when she'd run to the wrecked car. Under Nell's gentle healing, she felt no pain now.

"You can fall apart." Ripley's tone gentled, and she laid a hand on Mia's shoulder. "You're entitled."

"I don't need to, but thanks. She's going to be all right." Mia did close her eyes for a moment, waited until she felt steadier. "I looked at her injuries. She'll be unhappy and very pissed off about her car, but she'll be all right. I never considered, never thought she could be harmed this way. Used this way."

"Harm her, harm you," Ripley said. "That's what Mac . . ." She trailed off. Winced.

"Mac? What do you mean?" Despite Nell's protest, Mia got to her feet. She caught a glimmer, turned white as a sheet. "Something happened before. The beach." Furious, she grabbed Ripley's arms. "What happened?"

"Don't blame her. Blame all of us." Nell rose, ranged herself with Ripley. "She didn't want you to know, and we agreed."

"Know what?" Sam asked as he walked up with a tray of takeout coffee.

"How dare you keep anything to do with Lulu from me." She swung around to him, ready to bite.

"He didn't know," Nell interrupted. "We didn't tell him either."

Ripley told them now, said it all fast. And watched Mia's pale cheeks bloom with ripe temper. "She might've been killed. I left her! I left her and went to the mainland. Do you think I'd have done that if I'd known she was a target? You had no right, no right to exclude me from this."

"I'm sorry." Nell lifted her hands, let them fall. "We did what we thought was best. We were wrong."

"Not so wrong. You're going to have to deal with it, Mia," Sam added when she turned to him. "You nearly lost on the cliff road tonight because you divided your energy. Divided hell. You dumped it out and all but left yourself empty."

"Do you think I'd give less than my life to protect her, or anyone I loved?"

"No, I don't." He touched her cheek, and when she jerked away he simply moved in and took her face firmly in his hands. "And neither does she. Isn't she entitled to think of you?"

"I can't talk about this now. I need to be with her." She stepped away, walked to the door. But stopped when she opened it. "Thank you for what you did," she said to Sam. "I'll never forget it."

Later, while Mia sat beside Lulu's hospital bed, Ripley and Nell slipped into the room. For a time, there was nothing but silence.

"They want to keep her until tomorrow,"

Mia said at length. "Because of the concussion. She wasn't happy about it, but she's weak enough that she couldn't put up much of a fight. The arm . . ." She had to take a moment to steady her voice. "It's a clean break. She'll be in a cast a few weeks, but it'll be fine."

"Mia," Nell began. "We're so sorry."

"No." Mia shook her head, kept her eyes on Lulu's bruised face. "I'm calmer now, and I've thought it through. I understand what you did, and why. I don't agree. We're a circle, and we must value and respect that—and each other. But I also know how stubborn and persuasive she is."

Lulu's eyelids fluttered, and her voice was thin and raspy. "Don't talk about me like I'm not here."

"Just be quiet," Mia ordered. "I'm not speaking to you." But she took the hand Lulu held out. "Thank God you'll have to buy a new car. That mini monstrosity is finally dead."

"I'm gonna find me another one just like it."

"There couldn't be another one like it." But if there was, Mia thought, she would find it for her.

"Don't give these girls or their guys a hard time," Lulu mumbled. She opened one of her blackened eyes, closed it again because her vision was blurry. "Did what I told them to do. Respected their elders."

"I'm not angry with them. Just you." Mia pressed her lips to the back of Lulu's hand. "Go on home," she said to her sisters. "Tell your husbands I won't be turning them into toads anytime in the near future."

"We'll come back in the morning." Nell moved to the bed, laid a kiss on Lulu's forehead. "I love you."

"Don't get sloppy. Just a few bumps."

"Too bad." Her voice a bit thick, Ripley leaned over the bedrail and kissed Lulu's cheek. "Because I love you, too, even though you're really short and ugly."

With a weak cackle, Lulu freed her good hand from Nell's grasp and waved them off. "Go away. Buncha chattering females."

When they'd gone, Lulu shifted in her bed.

"Pain?" Mia asked.

"Can't get comfortable."

"Here." Rising, Mia trailed her fingers over Lulu's face, down her casted arm. She murmured softly as she stroked, until Lulu sighed.

"Better'n drugs. Feel floaty now. Brings back memories."

Relieved, Mia sat again. "Go to sleep now, Lu."

"Will. You go home. No point you sitting here watching me snore."

"Yes, as soon as you sleep."

But she sat while Lulu slept, kept watch in the dim light.

And she was there, keeping watch, when Lulu woke in the morning.

"You didn't have to come early."

"Zack needs to bring the patrol car." Nell helped Mia set the table and admired the lovely old china. "This time of year, there's no telling if he'll get called in for something. And I wanted to see Lulu."

"It took guilt, temper, and threats to get her to agree to spend a couple of days in one of the guest rooms. You'd think I was putting her in prison."

"She likes her own space," Nell said.

"She can have it back when she's steadier."

Nell brushed a hand over Mia's hair. "How are you?"

"I'm fine." The long night's vigil had given her plenty of time to think. To plan.

"I'd hoped I'd get here early enough to give you a hand. Not that you need it."

She studied the dining room, with its flowers and candles already in place. The windows were open wide to summer.

"You can check my fricassee," Mia said as she draped an arm over Nell's shoulders. The gesture, the easy warmth of it, erased any remnants of tension between them.

"From the smell, it's perfect." When they were in the kitchen, Nell removed the lid while Mia poured two tall glasses of iced tea. "Everything's perfect."

"Well, the weather's not cooperating." Restless, Mia moved to the door, pushed open the screen and breathed in the wind. "We'll have rain after sunset. A pity. We won't be able to have coffee in the garden. Still, my morning glories have grown a foot in the last three days. Maybe the rain will tease out the blooms."

She turned back to find Nell staring at her. "What?"

"Oh, Mia, I wish you'd tell me what else is troubling you. I hate seeing you look sad."

"Do I? I'm not." She stepped outside, looked up at the sky. "I'd rather a storm than rain. We haven't had enough storms this summer. It's as if they're building up and waiting for one big blow. I want to stand on my cliffs and meet the lightning."

She reached back, covered Nell's hand. "I'm not sad, just unsettled. What happened to Lulu shook me, on the most primal of levels. And now something inside me is waiting, building, like those storms. I know what I have to do. What I will do, but I can't see what's coming. It's frustrating for me to know, and not to see."

"Maybe you're looking in the wrong place. Mia, I know what's between you and Sam. I can feel it when I'm within ten feet of you. When I fell in love with Zack and was pulled in all those directions, you were there for me. Why won't you let me do the same for you?"

"I depend on you."

"To a point. Then you step back over this line, and it's only you who can cross it. And you step over it more often since Sam came back to the Sisters."

"Then I'd have to say he has upset the balance."

"Upset your balance," Nell corrected, and waited for Mia to turn. "Are you in love with him?"

"A part of me was born loving him. I closed that part off. I had no choice."

"And that's the problem, isn't it? The not knowing if you should open it up again or keep it closed."

"I made a mistake once, and he left. I can't afford to make a mistake again, whether he stays or goes."

"You don't believe he'll stay."

"It's not a matter of believing. It's a matter of considering every possibility. If I open myself to him again, completely, what happens if he does go? I can't risk that. Not just for myself, but for all of us. Love isn't a simple thing, you know that. It's not a flower to be picked on a whim."

"No, it's not a simple thing. But believing you can control it, mold its shape, plot its direction? That you *have* to do that? That's a mistake."

"I don't want to love him again." Her

voice, always so smooth, so sure, trembled. "I don't want it. I put those dreams aside. I don't need them now. I'm afraid to take them out again."

Saying nothing, Nell slipped her arms around Mia, drew her close.

"I'm not who I was when I loved him."

"Neither of you is. What you feel now matters most."

"My feelings aren't any clearer than my vision. Before it ends, I'll do whatever needs to be done." She sighed. "I'm not used to having a shoulder to cry on."

"The shoulders are there. You're just not used to leaning."

"Maybe you're right." She closed her eyes, let herself focus on Nell and the life glowing inside her. "I can see you, little sister," she murmured. "I can see you sitting in an old wooden rocker, in a room soft with candleglow. There's a baby at your breast, and its hair is soft as down and bright as sunlight. When I see you like that, I have such hope. Such courage."

She drew back, pressed a kiss to Nell's forehead. "Your child will be safe. That I know." She heard the sound of her front door slamming.

"That would be Ripley," Mia said dryly. "Not only doesn't she bother to knock, but she can't resist slamming a door. I'm going to take a tray up to Lulu. Then I think we'll have drinks and appetizers in the garden, while the weather holds."

As Mia moved inside to greet her guests, Nell thought how typical it had been. She'd begun by offering comfort, and Mia had ended by giving comfort to her.

"So then this joker says, 'But, Officer, I wasn't stealing the cooler full of beer. I was just moving it.' " Ripley forked up more fricassee. "When I pointed out that that didn't explain how come he had Budweiser on his breath and three empty beer cans lying beside him in the sand, he said maybe somebody drank the beer while he was sleeping. I guess somebody poured beer into him, too, because he was half trashed and it was only three in the afternoon."

"How'd you handle it?" Zack asked her.

"Fined him for drinking in a restricted area, and littering. Cut him a break on lifting the cooler since the guys he'd lifted it from didn't want any hassles. Seeing as they'd had a cooler of beer in a restricted area to begin with."

"Imagine that." Sam shook his head. "Drinking beer on the beach."

"Rules is rules," Ripley stated adamantly.

"Absolutely. None of us ever snuck a six-pack onto the beach."

"I recall somebody copping a bottle of his father's best scotch." Zack grinned. "And how he generously shared it with his pals. Who proceeded to get toasted."

"Speak for yourself." Ripley wagged her fork. "One pull of that stuff was enough for me. Talk about foul."

"Such a girl," her brother said.

"That may be, but I'm not the one who got creamed when we got home."

"True enough. I was eighteen," Zack recalled, "and Mom still skinned my butt."

"Then she skinned mine." The memory made Sam wince. "Jesus, that woman could terrorize me. No matter what you did, she knew about it before you'd finished doing it. And if she didn't, she'd get it out of you. She'd just stare at your face and pick away until you'd beg to confess."

"That's how it's going to be with my kids.

They won't have a prayer." Ripley slanted Mac a smug look as he laid his hand over hers.

It flashed into Mia, fast and bright. "You're pregnant."

"Hey." Ripley lifted her water glass. "Nell's not the only one who can get knocked up."

"A baby!" Nell leaped out of her chair, danced around the table to throw her arms around Ripley's neck. "This is wonderful! What a way to announce it."

"I've been working on that story and segue since this afternoon."

"How about that?" With a grin a mile wide and a voice that wasn't quite steady, Zack moved over to tug Ripley's long ponytail. "I'm going to be an uncle."

"You've got a couple of months to practice being a daddy first."

Amid the jokes and congratulations, Mia rose. She walked to Ripley, running her hands up and down Ripley's arms as she, too, got to her feet. Then Mia simply drew her in. Drew her close. Held her tight.

Emotion flooded Ripley's throat, and she turned her face into Mia's hair.

"There are two," Mia whispered.

"Two?" Ripley's jaw dropped. "Two?" It was all she could say as she pulled back. "You mean..." Staggered, she stared down at her flat belly. "Man."

"Two what?" In the process of drinking the wine Sam had poured into his glass for a toast, Mac smiled over at his wife. Gradually the shock on her face trickled through. "Two? Twins? We've got two in there? I need to sit down."

"You need to sit down?"

"Right. We need to sit down." Mac sat, pulled her onto his lap. "Two for one. That's so cool."

"They'll be safe. I can see it." Mia leaned over, kissed Mac's cheeks. "Go on in the living room, be comfortable. I'll bring coffee. Tea for the mothers. Ripley, you'll want to cut back on the caffeine."

"Something's wrong," Sam commented when Mia walked into the kitchen. "Something more than Lulu's weighing on her."

"She gets worked up about babies." With her hand on her stomach, Ripley tried to imagine two.

"It's more than that. I'll give her a hand with the coffee."

When he stepped into the kitchen she

was standing in the open back door, watching the soft summer rain fall on her gardens.

"I want to help you."

"It's no trouble."

He moved to her. "I'm not talking about the coffee. I want to help you."

"You have." She took his hand, gripped it hard for a moment. "You risked your life yesterday for someone I love. You trusted me to hold you, and her, safe so you could help her."

"I did the only thing that could be done."

"The only thing you could do, Sam. Being you."

"Let's leave that. I want to help with what's bothering you now."

"You can't. Not now, in any case. This is my battle, and now there's more at stake than ever. Everything that matters to me is inside this house tonight. And it's there, out there, wanting. Can you feel it?" she whispered. "Just beyond my circle. Pressing, shifting. Waiting."

"Yes. I don't want you staying here alone."

When she started to move away, he took her firmly by the shoulders, turned her. "Mia, whatever you think or feel or want from me, you're too smart to push aside the power I can add to yours. Are you certain that either of us could have saved Lulu alone?"

"No." She let out a breath. "No, I'm not."

"If you don't want me with you, I'll sleep in one of the guest rooms, or the goddamn sofa. You've got your dragon to guard you—and a broken arm wouldn't stop her. This isn't about me trying to get into your bed."

"I know. Let me think about it. We have other things to discuss tonight."

She could think all she liked, he decided as she walked away to finish the coffee. He was staying with her, even if he had to sleep outside in his car.

She served coffee and slices of cream cake. Then she did something Nell hadn't seen her do in the time they'd known each other.

Mia drew the drapes and closed out the night.

"It watches." Mia's voice was calm as she walked the room, lighting more candles. "Or tries to. My gesture was meant to be rude and dismissive. A petty slap. Petty," she continued as she sat and picked up her own coffee, "but satisfying. I owe it more than a petty slap for harming Lulu."

And she would give it more. Much more.

"I have to say, the timing of this is poor. We should be celebrating Ripley and Mac's news. And we will."

She was like a queen, Sam thought. A warrior queen addressing her troops. He wasn't sure how he felt about the image. But as he focused on her, narrowed his vision on her, his belly did a queasy roll.

"Where did you go, Mia? When you left the island, where did you go?"

He saw from the quick race of surprise over her face that he'd caught her off guard. And because he had, he reached through that narrow chink and pulled out more. Pulled out enough to have him pushing to his feet.

"Remington? You went to see Remington?"

"Yes." She sipped her coffee, gathered her thoughts while the emotions in the room bulleted and careened around her.

"Oh, that's fine. That's just fine!" At the explosion from Ripley, Mia looked over at her coolly. "You're the one who's always haranguing me about being cautious, controlled. About being prepared."

"That's right. And I was. I wasn't careless or foolish."

"And I am?"

Mia lifted her shoulders in an elegant little shrug. "I'd use the word *reckless,* which you tend to be. Going to see him was a calculated risk, one that needed to be taken."

"You had the nerve to ream us last night for not coming clean about Lulu, then you keep this to yourself."

"Hardly," Mia said smoothly. "I'm telling you what I did, and what happened. Freely."

"You shouldn't have gone alone." Nell's voice was quiet, and all the more effective for it. "You had no right to go alone."

"I disagree. Remington's feelings toward you would have prevented any possible discussion. Ripley's temper would have very likely forced a confrontation then and there. Of the three of us, I'm most able to deal with him, and I have more need at this point to do so."

"There are four of us," Sam reminded everyone.

"There are fucking six of us." He'd said

nothing to this point, but now Zack got to his feet. "You're going to start remembering there are six of us," Zack ordered Mia. "I don't care if you can shoot lightning out of your goddamn fingertips. There are six of us in this."

"Zack."

"Be quiet," he snapped at Nell and had her gaping at him.

"You think because there're two of us in this room who can't whistle up the wind or pull down the moon or whatever the hell you call it, we're just going to sit on our hands. I've got as much at stake as you do, Mia. And I'm still the sheriff on Three Sisters."

"I come from them, the same as you do." Mac drew Mia's considering gaze to him. "I don't have what you have, but I've spent most of my life studying it. Cutting us out this way is not only insulting, it's arrogant."

"Just one more way to prove you don't need anyone else."

She made herself look directly at Sam. "That wasn't my intention. I'm sorry if that was the result. I'm sorry," she repeated, lifting her hands to encompass everyone in the room. "I wouldn't have gone to see him if I hadn't been certain I could deal with him.

At that time and under those circumstances."

"Never wrong, are you?" Sam shot out.

"Oh, I've been wrong." Because the coffee lay bitter on her tongue, she set the cup aside. "But I wasn't wrong about this. He couldn't harm me." She shut off the memory of claws and cold. "Remington is being used, and his hate, his madness, is a powerful tool. There was a chance I could reach him, that with his cooperation I could close him off, shut down that source of energy. He's a conduit," she said, looking to Mac for verification. "Shut off the valve, so to speak, and the power weakens."

"It's a valid theory."

"Screw theories. What happened?" Ripley demanded.

"He's too far gone. He believes the lies, the promises. And he's damned himself. But that's a weakness, that hunger to bring pain and misery. The singularity of that purpose is innately flawed. In the end it'll destroy itself. But I think we can, and should, move that process along. After what happened yesterday, we must move it along. I won't take any chances with Lulu, and as long as it can't get to me, it will try for her."

"I think you're right about that," Mac put in. "Your feelings for her would be seen as a weakness. An Achilles' heel."

"Then we act sooner—because it's not a weakness. It's another weapon."

"A preemptive strike?" Sam suggested.

"In a manner of speaking," Mia nodded. "An offensive move rather than defensive. I've been thinking about it for some time. I know, without doubt now, that his power builds over time. There was more when I faced off with it yesterday. Why should we wait until September, give him that much more time to gather strength against us? With you and Ripley and Nell, we have the four elements represented. We have new life, a new circle inside the old—three children who carry the old blood—waiting to be born. That's powerful magic. A banishing spell with full ritual."

"The legend calls for something else," he reminded her. "It calls for you to make a choice."

"I'm aware of that. I'm aware of all the interpretations, all the nuances. All the risks and sacrifices. Our circle isn't broken, as theirs was. Our power isn't diminished, as theirs was." Her voice went steely. "By hurting Lulu it has only given me more reason to finish it, by whatever means necessary. My part comes when it comes. And a banishing ritual would be a hell of a distraction—and very possibly put an end to things. Mac?"

"You'll need the full moon," Mac added, his brow furrowing as he calculated. "That doesn't give you much time."

Mia only smiled, but it was fierce and it was cold. "We've had three hundred years."

# Nineteen

"What didn't you tell the others?"

"There's nothing more to tell." Mia sat at her dressing table, brushing her hair. She knew Sam wouldn't go, and there was no point arguing.

Fruitless battles wasted energy. She intended to conserve hers for when it mattered most.

"If you thought a banishing spell would turn the tide, you'd have tried one before."

"You weren't here before."

"I've been here since May. And will there ever come a time when you don't throw that in my face?"

"You're right." She set her brush aside, rose to open the balcony doors to the sound of rain. "It's annoying and repetitive of me. And it was more effective before I forgave you."

"Have you, Mia?"

The rain was warm, wonderfully soft. And still, she longed for the storm.

"I've spent some time looking back, trying to see those two young people objectively. The girl was so wrapped up in the boy, and in her visions of what she wanted their life to be, she couldn't see he wasn't ready. It wasn't that she ignored it, or overlooked it." Mia had searched her heart on that one point. "But that she really couldn't see it. She assumed he loved as she loved, wanted what she wanted, and she never looked beyond that. What happened to them was as much her fault as his."

"No, it wasn't."

"All right. Maybe not quite as much hers, because she was as honest as she knew how to be and he wasn't. But she wasn't blameless. She held too tight. Maybe, maybe because she wasn't any more ready than he was. She just wanted to be. She was so lonely in her house on the cliff, so desperately hungry for love."

"Mia."

"You shouldn't interrupt when I'm forgiving you. I don't intend to make a habit of it. It's so weak, and so typical, to blame one's parents for the flaws and the failures of a life. And a woman of thirty should certainly have come around to making her own flaws and failures—and triumphs."

She had thought about that, too, very long and very hard in her time away. "But for the sake of that young girl, we'll point the finger. She was young enough to deserve to assign the blame somewhere else."

She walked back to the dressing table, absently opened a little cobalt pot, dipped her fingers in and rubbed the cream over her hands. "They never loved me. That's sad and that's painful, but more, they never cared that I loved them. So what was I to do with all that love just burning inside me? There was Lulu, thank the goddess. But I had so much more to give. And there you were. Poor sad-looking Sam. I heaped my love on you until you must have felt buried in it."

"I wanted you to love me. I needed it. And you."

"But not so I had us settled in a little cottage with three children and the faithful family dog." She said it lightly, though it cost her to dismiss that sweet and pretty image. "I can't blame you for that. I can still blame you for the way you ended it—so abrupt, so harsh. But even that . . . You were very young."

"I'll regret for the rest of my life the way I ended it. Regret that the only way I thought I could save myself was to hurt you."

"Youth is often cruel."

"I was. I told you I was done with you and this place. That I wouldn't be trapped anymore. That I wasn't coming back. I wasn't ever coming back. You just looked at me, with tears running down your face. You so rarely cry. It panicked me, so I was only more cruel. I'm sorry for it."

"I believe you are. I'd like to think that eventually we could put that part of our life where it belongs. In the past."

"I need to tell you why I waited so long to come back."

She retreated without moving a step. "That's the past, too."

"No, I want you to know that when I said I wasn't coming back, I meant it. That need to be away, to breathe some other air, pushed me through those first years. Every time I thought of you, waking or sleeping, I slammed the door shut. Then one day I found myself standing in that cave on the west coast of Ireland."

He wandered to her dressing table, picked up her brush. Just turned it over and over in his hand. "Everything I felt for you, the joy of it, the fear of it, came rushing back into me. But I wasn't a boy anymore, and those feelings weren't a boy's."

He set her brush down, looked at her. "And I knew I was coming back. That was five years ago, Mia."

It left her shaken, caused her to carefully control her thoughts, her voice. "You took your time."

"I wasn't coming back, to you, to this island, the way I'd left. Thaddeus Logan's son. That Logan boy. I'd carried that around like a goddamn chain around my neck, and I was going to break it. I needed to make something of myself. For me. And for you. No, let me finish," he said when she started to speak. "You had all the dreams before, all the goals, all the answers. Now I had my own. The hotel isn't just a piece of real estate to me."

"I know that."

"Maybe you do." He nodded. "Maybe you

would. It was mine, always, part symbol, part passion. I needed to prove I was coming back here with more than a name and a birthright. I started to come back countless times in the last five years, and every time I did, something stopped me. I don't know if it was my own doing or a shove from fate. But I do know that before this, it wasn't my time."

"You always had more than a name and a birthright. But maybe you could never see it before."

"That brings us to now."

"Now, I need time to consider if the step I take is my own, or a shove from fate. You're welcome to sleep here. I need to check on Lulu. Then I want to spend some time up in the tower before I go to bed."

Frustration pushed through him again, had him balling his fists in his pockets. "I'm asking for a chance to prove to you that you can trust me again, that you can love me again. I want you to live with me, be with me knowing that whatever else I might do or not do, I'll never deliberately hurt you again. You're not giving me a lot of room."

"I can promise you this. After the full moon, after the ritual, that will change. I don't want to be at odds with you. We can't afford to be."

"There's something else." He took her arm as she started past him. "There's more."

"I can't give it to you now." Her fingers itched to push his hand off her arm before he pushed too hard, saw too much. Timing, she thought, would be an essential element. She resisted, and met his gaze levelly. "You want me to trust and believe in you. Then you have to trust and believe in me."

"I will, if you'll promise me you won't do anything that could put you in jeopardy, without your circle, without me."

"When it comes to the sticking point, I'll need my circle. That includes you."

"All right." If that was all, he would settle for it. For now. "Can I use your library?"

"Help yourself."

When she was sure Lulu was sleeping comfortably, Mia went up to the widow's walk to stand outside in the soft rain. She could see, from that height, everything that was hers. And the dark that pressed against her borders, breathing cold against her warmth so the steam rose up in fitful spurts.

Almost absently, she lifted a hand sky-ward, let the power tremble up her arm. She plucked a lightning bolt out of the night, hurled it like a lance through a puff of steam.

Then she spun away and slipped inside, into her tower.

She cast the circle, lighted candles and incense. She would seek a vision, but wanted no whisper of it to leak outside that ring. What was in her heart and mind could be used against her, and against those she loved.

She ate the herbs, drank from the chalice, and kneeling in the circle, at the center of a pentagram, she cleared her mind. She opened her third eye.

The storm that she had sensed burst over the island, and despite the gales of wind, the land was blanketed in a thin gray fog. The sea lashed at the base of her cliffs as she flew over them, through the driving rain, the strikes of lightning, and over the fog that spread and thickened.

In the clearing at the heart of the Sisters was her circle. Their hands were linked, and hers with them. The greedy fog licked and lapped at the edges of the ring, but crept no further.

Safe, she thought as she knelt in her tower. Safe and strong.

She could feel the rumble of the earth below, the rumble of the sky above. And her own heartbeat where she knelt, and where she saw herself.

They called, in turn. Earth, air, water, fire. Power was rich. Rising up, streaking out. Though it tore at the fog, those mists reknit themselves. Out of them stalked the wolf that bore her mark.

When it leaped, she was alone on her cliffs. She saw the red eyes burning. She heard her own voice cry out—despair and triumph—as she wrapped her arms around it. And took it with her off the cliffs.

As she fell she saw the moon, full and white, break through the storm and, with the fire of stars, shine over the island.

In her tower, she knelt on the floor, her eyes blurred with visions, her heart pounding.

"You give me this only to take it away? Is there a price for the gift, after all? You would have let the innocent be harmed, the mother of my heart? Does it all come down to blood?"

She slid to the floor, curled in the circle.

For the first and last time in her life, she cursed the gift.

"She's holding something back." Sam paced the kitchen in the house where he'd grown up. "I know it."

"Maybe she is." Mac pushed through the documents spread over the kitchen table. They'd been his breakfast companion until Sam had shown up. "Something started bugging me last night, but I can't put my finger on it. I've been going through everything I have on Three Sisters: the island, the women, the descendants. I've read over my own ancestor's journal. I feel like I'm missing something. Some angle. Some, what was the word Mia used? *Interpretation*."

Sam pushed the bag he'd brought with him over the table. "You can add these to your research pile, at least until she realizes I pulled them out of her library."

"I've been meaning to get to these anyway." Carefully, reverently, Mac took an old and scarred leather book out of the bag. "Mia gave me the go-ahead to scour her books."

"Then we'll use that when she gets pissy about me hauling them over here. I'm going to talk to Zack." Sam jingled change in his pockets and paced again. "The Todds have been on the island as long as anyone can remember, and he's had his finger on the pulse of things all along. Maybe if I can think of the right questions, he'll have the right answers."

"We've got just over a week until the full moon."

"Start cramming, Professor." Sam checked his watch. "I've got to get to work. You come up with anything, let me know."

Mac grunted his assent, already absorbed in the first book.

Instead of going to his car, Sam followed the urge and walked down to the beach, heading toward the cave.

There had always been something pulling him there, even before Mia. As a little boy he'd slipped away from his mother or his nanny and wandered there. Even if it had been only to curl up and sleep. He could still remember the time—he had been only three—when the police had been called to search for him. Zack's father had rooted him out, scooping him out of a dream where he'd slept in the arms of a beautiful woman with red hair and gray eyes.

She'd sung to him in Gaelic, a story-song about a handsome silkie who had loved a witch, then had left her for the sea.

He'd understood her words, and the language of her song had become his own.

When he was older, he and his friends had played inside the cave, used it as a fort, a submarine, a den of thieves. Still, he'd often gone in alone, sneaking out of the house after bedtime to stretch out on the floor, make a fire with a thought, and watch the flames play on the walls.

As he'd grown from child to boy, the woman had come to his dreams less often, and less clearly. But he'd seen her in Mia. The two images had blurred in his mind until there had been only Mia.

He stepped into the cave and could smell her. No, he corrected, fascinated. He could smell them both. The soft, herbal scent of the woman who had sung to him, and the deeper, richer scent of the woman he loved.

Mother, Mia had called her the night they'd seen her carry the pelt from this place. With the warmth of affection, the formality of respect, she had addressed the vision as though they had met many times before.

He supposed, though she'd never told him—even when she had seemed to tell him everything—that they had.

He crouched, studying the smooth cave floor where he had seen the man curled in sleep.

"You had my face," he said aloud. "Just as she had Mia's. Once I let myself believe that meant we weren't supposed to be together. It was one of my many excuses. You left. I left. But I came back."

He shifted, reading the words he had carved into the stone so long ago. As he read, he reached under his shirt to pull out the chain he wore. His foot tapped against something and sent it clinking against the stone.

With one hand closed around the ring he wore on the chain, he picked up its mate.

The smaller ring was badly tarnished, but he could feel the carving that circled it. The same Celtic knot pattern that circled the one he'd found in the cave on the west coast of Ireland. The same pattern as the design Mia had etched under the promise he'd carved in stone.

Gently, he closed his fingers over the ring and brought out a dimly remembered spell suited to housewives. When he opened his hand again, the little ring gleamed silver.

He studied it for a long time, then slid it onto the chain with its mate.

In her office, Mia printed out e-mail orders, set them aside to fill, then efficiently began on the paperwork generated during her brief absence. She'd used the backlog as a legitimate excuse to leave the house early. Though, she recalled, Sam hadn't seemed eager to keep her around.

By nine, she'd made considerable progress, and stopped to make her first phone call. She needed to see her lawyer at the first opportunity and make a few adjustments to her will.

She told herself she wasn't being fatalistic, just practical.

From her satchel she took some of the personal papers she'd brought from home. Her partnership agreement with Nell in

Three Sisters Catering was in order. But she intended to leave Ripley her share, should anything happen.

She thought Nell would appreciate that.

As the will stood now, the bookstore went outright to Lulu, but she'd decided to change that and designate a percentage to Nell. Lulu, she had no doubt, would approve.

And she intended to start a small trust fund for her sisters' children, including the deed for the yellow cottage. It was something she would do in any case.

She would leave her library to Mac, as he would make the best use of it. For Zack there was her star collection, and her great-grandfather's watch.

It was the sort of thing one left to a brother.

She would leave the house to Sam. She could trust him to preserve it, to see that her garden was tended. And to guard the heart of the island.

She put the papers in her bottom drawer, locked it. She didn't intend for any of these arrangements to be necessary anytime soon. But she strongly believed in being prepared.

She gathered up the printouts, took them downstairs to fill the orders. And she got on with the day, and her life.

"Something is just not right."

"Yeah," Ripley agreed. "There are too many people on the beach, and half of them are idiots."

"Seriously, Ripley. I'm really worried about Mia. We only have a couple of days before the full moon."

"I know what day of the month it is. Look at that guy there, on the Mickey Mouse towel. Frying like a fish in a pan. Bet he's from Indiana or someplace and hasn't seen a beach before. Give me a minute here."

She marched across the sand, nudged the brilliantly pink man with her toe. Nell waited, shifting from foot to foot while Ripley launched into her lecture, pointed skyward, leaned down and poked a finger in the man's shoulder, as if testing doneness.

As she marched back, the man dug out sunscreen and began slathering it on.

"My public service for the week. Now, about Mia—"

"She's too calm. She's breezing along like it's business as usual. She came to the book club meeting last night. She's in there right now checking inventory. We're doing the biggest spell I've ever done in a matter of days, and she just pats me on the head and tells me it'll be fine."

"She's always had ice water for blood. What's new?"

"Ripley."

"All right, all right." With a huff of breath, Ripley marched along the seawall to finish her beach patrol. "I'm worried, too. Satisfied? And if I wasn't, Mac's twitchy enough for both of us. He's buried himself in research, spends hours making notes. He thinks Mia has something going on that she's not telling us."

"So do I."

"That makes three of us. I don't know what the hell we're supposed to do about it."

"Zack and I have talked about it. We could confront her. All of us, at one time."

"What, like an intervention? Come on. You couldn't crack that woman with a sledgehammer. I wish I didn't like that about her."

"I had another idea. I thought that between the two of us, we could . . . well, if we were linked, we could get through this shield she's thrown up and see what she's thinking."

"You're talking about prying into her private thoughts, against her express wishes?"

"Yes. Forget I said it. It's rude and intrusive and sneaky."

"Yeah, that's why I like it. Great idea. I can take an hour . . ." She checked her watch. "Right now. Your place is closer."

Twenty minutes later, Ripley lay back on the floor of Nell's living room, panting and sweating. "God! She is such a bitch. You've got to admire that."

"It's like trying to cut through concrete with a toothpick." Nell swiped her forearm over her brow. "It shouldn't be this hard."

"She figured we might try it. She was ready for us. Man, she is good. And she's got something to hide." Ripley wiped her damp palms on her slacks. "Now I'm seriously worried. Let's tap Sam."

"We can't. Whatever she's protecting probably has to do with him. It wouldn't be right. Ripley, she loves him."

Staring at the ceiling, Ripley tapped her fingers over her stomach. "If that's her choice—"

"She hasn't made her choice. At least that she's letting on. She loves him, but as far as I can tell, it isn't making her happy."

"She never could be simple. You know what I think? I think she's going to go for it during the banishment spell. A double whammy. She's already made her decision, Nell. She doesn't do anything spur of the moment."

"Ripley, she said our babies would be safe."

"That's right."

"She never said she would be."

Sam loosened his tie as he watched Mac circle the outside of the cottage with one of his handheld gadgets. Every so often, Mac would detour, crouch, mutter.

"He puts on a real show, doesn't he?" At Sam's side, Ripley rocked back on her heels. "Since Mac's big production, he's been doing this check at our place, and at Lulu's, twice a day."

"What's all this about, Rip?" Sam had come straight from one meeting into what appeared to be another. Zack and Nell were

due any minute. "Why are we doing whatever it is we're going to be doing without
Mia?"

"This is Mac's deal. I've only got pieces of
it." She cocked her head as Mac started
back toward them. "Okay, Dr. Booke, what's
the story?"

"You keep this place tight," he said to
Sam. "Good job."

"Thanks, Doc. Now what the hell is this
about?"

"Let's wait for the others. I've got to get
some stuff out of the car. Is Mia expecting
you anytime soon?"

"I don't punch a time clock." Noting the
easy humor that passed between his friends
at the statement, Sam set his teeth. "Look,
she'll be on her way home shortly. Lulu, who
must've passed stubbornness on to Mia
through osmosis, has moved back to her
own place. I don't like Mia being alone for
long."

"We'll get you off to play house," Ripley
began, then saw the icy temper on Sam's
face. "Hey, hey. Easy, Sam. We're on the
same team, remember?"

"It's hot out here." With that, Sam turned
and strode into the house.

"Edgy," Ripley said as he passed.

"Who isn't? Here come Nell and Zack. Let's get started."

Within ten minutes, Sam found his little cottage taken over. Nell, obviously anticipating the state of his supplies, had brought cookies and a cooler of iced tea. She managed to set it all up like a party even as Mac spread his notes and books over the table.

"Nell, would you sit down?" Zack tugged her toward a chair. "Get the kid off his feet for five minutes."

"Hey, I've got double." Ripley boosted herself onto the kitchen counter, snagged a cookie. "So, I'll start. Nell and I decided to do a little spying yesterday—"

"It wasn't spying."

"It would've been," Ripley said, "if we'd pulled it off. But we couldn't. Mia's totally blocked. She's got herself locked up like a vault."

"And you think this is news?" Sam asked.

"She's got something going on in that prissy brain of hers that she doesn't want anyone to know," Ripley continued. "It's irritating, but more, it's got us worried."

"She's worked out what she's going to do."

"I think you're right about that," Mac said to Sam. "The other night when we were together, she said something about knowing all the aspects, the interpretations. It got me thinking. On the surface, it's pretty cut and dried. Her task, let's call it, deals with love. Love without boundaries. We can take that to mean she's meant to love that way, or to let go, freely, of an attachment that restricted her. Sorry," he added.

"We've been through this before."

"Yeah, but what seems cut and dried rarely is. The first sister, her counterpart, trapped the man she loved. You take a silkie's pelt, you bind him to the land and to you. They had a life together, a family. But his feelings for her were a result of magic, not free will. When he found his pelt, he reverted, left her."

"He couldn't stay," Sam put in.

"No argument. Now, a possible interpretation is that Mia is required to *find* a love without boundaries. One that comes to her without qualification or magic. That just is what it is."

"I'm in love with her. I've told her."

"She has to believe you." Zack laid a hand on Sam's shoulder. "And either accept or let you go."

"But that's not the only interpretation. You need to follow along here." Mac picked up one of the old books, opened it to a section he had marked.

"This is a history of the island, written in the early seventeen hundreds, that used documents I've never seen. If Mia has those documents, you didn't get them from the library."

"She wouldn't keep them there." Worry clouded Sam's gaze. "She'd probably have them in her tower."

"I'd like to see them, but for our purposes, this is enough. It goes into the legend in some detail," Mac continued. "I'm going to hit the highlights."

He adjusted his glasses, skimmed down the yellowed page. " 'By magic it was formed, by magic it will thrive or perish. So the choices of the circle deem life or death, one times three. Blood of their blood, hand of their hand. The three who live must face the dark, each to her own.

" 'And Air must find her courage. To turn

from what would destroy her or to stand against it.' You did both," Mac said to Nell. " 'When she will see herself, give herself for what she loves, the circle is unbroken. So Earth will seek her justice, without blade or lance. To shed no blood but her own in defense of what she is, and all she loves.' "

Ripley turned her hand palm up and studied the thin scar that slashed across it. "I guess we pulled that one off."

"You had a choice." Mac turned to her. "More of a choice than we'd realized. 'And when her justice is meted with compassion, the circle is unbroken. Thus Fire must look into her heart, open it and leave it bare. To see love with no boundaries and offer for what she holds dear, life. When her heart is free, the circle is unbroken. The power of the Three will join, will hold. Four elements rise and end the Dark.' "

"Sacrifice? Her *life*?" Sam surged forward. "She can sacrifice her life?"

"Hang on." Zack clamped his hands on Sam's shoulders. "Is that how you're reading this, Mac?"

"You could interpret this that any one of them could have given her life, for the others. For us. For courage, for justice, for love.

This book came out of Mia's library, so it's an option she's aware of. The question is, is it one she would consider?"

"Yes." Pale now, Nell looked at Ripley. "We all would have."

Ripley nodded. "If she thinks it's the only way. But she wouldn't." Uneasy, she pushed herself off the counter. "She would pit her power against anyone or anything."

"It's not enough." Sam fisted his hands as if he could clamp the fury and fear inside them. "Not close to enough. I'm not standing back while she considers dying to save a few square miles of dirt. We're going to put a stop to this."

"You know better." As her nerves built, Ripley yanked off her cap. "You can't stop what's been in motion for centuries. I tried, and it ran right over me."

"Your life's not on the line, is it?"

If she'd seen only anger, she might have snapped back at him. But she saw fear as well. "What do you say we both take it out on Mia after this is done?"

"Deal." He gave her shoulders a squeeze, then dropped his hands. "There's no point in confronting her about this: We won't budge her. Dragging her bodily off the island won't change anything. The last step has to be taken, and it's best that it be taken here. It's meant to be taken here. With all of us."

"Center of power," Mac agreed. "Her center, her circle. Her power's the most refined, and it's the strongest. But that leads me to conclude that what's going to come against her will build its power to match."

"There are more of us now," Nell pointed out. She reached out a hand for her husband's, laid the other on her belly. "Linked, our energy is formidable."

"There are other sources of power." Sam nodded as the idea formed. "We use them. All of them."

His mind was clear, his thoughts controlled when he walked into the house on the cliff. Mia wasn't the only one who could block.

He found her in the garden, calmly sipping a glass of wine while a butterfly fluttered in the palm of her outstretched hand.

"Now that's a picture," he said as he kissed the top of her head, then sat across from her. "How was your day?"

She said nothing for a moment, studied his face, sipped her wine. What was inside her yearned under the steel of her will. "Busy, productive. Yours?"

"The same. Some kid stuck his head through the iron pickets on one of the balconies. He took it pretty well, but his mother screamed the roof off and wanted us to cut through. As there was no way I was damaging a centuries-old rail, I was about to flick him free with a quick spell. The housekeeper beat me to it. Slathered his head with baby oil and popped him out like a cork."

She smiled, and was obliging enough to hand him her wine for a sip. But her eyes were watchful, wary. "I imagine he enjoyed the entire thing. Sam, I noticed some of my books are missing from the library."

"Mmm?" He held out a finger so the butterfly on her palm flew gracefully to him, perched. "You said I could use the library."

"Where are the books?"

He passed the wine and the butterfly back to her. "I spent some time looking through some of them, thinking I might find some fresh angle on this whole business."

"Oh." A chill shivered around her heart. "And?"

"Never claimed to be a scholar," he said with a shrug. "I mentioned it to Mac in passing, and he asked if he could borrow them. I didn't think you'd mind."

"I'd prefer that the books stay in the house."

"Oh. Well, I'll get them back. You know, sitting out here with you like this feels . . . perfect. And every time I look at you, my heart rolls over in my chest. That feels perfect, too. I love you, Mia."

Her lashes lowered. "I should do something about dinner."

When she rose, he took her hand. "I'll help you." He kept his fingers linked with hers as he got to his feet. "There's no need for you to do all the work."

Don't touch me, she thought. Not yet. Not now. "I'm better . . . in the kitchen, by myself."

"Make room," he suggested. "I'm not going anywhere."

# Twenty

He had something on his mind, Mia was sure of it. He was too damn pleasant, attentive, considerate. If she hadn't known better, she might have wondered if someone had put a good-nature spell on him.

As ridiculous as it was, even to herself, she preferred him with his edge on. At least then she knew what to expect.

Still she didn't have the time to dig below the surface, couldn't risk him digging below hers. And had she the time, she couldn't spare the energy. She was stockpiling power like blue-chip stocks.

She was resolved, she was prepared, and she was as confident as she could manage. When nerves trickled in, she used them. When doubts crept close, she swept them aside.

On the day of the full moon, she rose at dawn. She'd wanted, almost painfully wanted, to roll over into Sam, and his warmth. Just to have his arms come around her as they sometimes did in sleep. They'd done nothing but sleep together, in the most innocent sense, since the night in the cottage.

He hadn't questioned her on this, nor had he tried to seduce her. The fact that she found his cooperation mildly insulting only caused her to become annoyed with herself.

It had been she who, more than once, had nearly turned to him in the night, when her mind was soft with dreams and her body aching with needs.

But on this most vital of mornings, she left him sleeping and stood on her cliffs. Here she gathered fire from the rising sun, and strength from the crashing sea.

Arms spread, she drank power, and gave thanks for the gift.

When she turned, she saw him on the bedroom balcony, watching her. Their gazes locked, and held. Light sparked between them. With her hair blowing in the wind, she walked back to the house, and ignored the black-edged fog crawling along the edges of her world.

She went to the bookstore for her own peace of mind. It was something she'd built through sweat and dreams. Despite her broken arm, Lulu was back to manning the counter. Since there'd been no stopping her, Mia hadn't bother to argue.

And she had to admit, the work—and the visits from neighbors and friends—seemed to keep Lulu in good spirits.

Still, Mia had hoped she would ease back to work rather than leaping.

Because business was unusually brisk, she didn't have the opportunity she'd wanted to spend time with Lulu—to fuss over her without seeming to fuss. But it seemed that every second person who lived on the island found a reason to stop in and spend time with her.

By noon the café was jammed, and she couldn't pass by without someone calling her over for a word.

To escape long enough to catch her

breath, Mia slipped into the kitchen, snagged a bottle of water from the refrigerator.

"Hester Birmingham just told me Ben and Jerry's ice cream is on special this week."

"Two of my favorite men," Nell responded as she built a grilled chicken and Brie sandwich to go with the soup special.

"She was pretty damn intense about it. I thought she'd burst into tears any minute."

"Some of us take our ice cream seriously. Why don't I get some? We can make sundaes tonight . . . after."

"Fine. I'm glad you're not worried about tonight." Mia walked over to give Nell's back a quick rub. "You have everything you need. Tomorrow, it'll be over. No shadows."

"I believe that. But you have to let me worry about you a little."

"Little sister." Mia rested her cheek on Nell's hair, just for a moment. "I love you. Now I'm going to get out of here. I still have things I need to do, and all I'm getting accomplished here today is socializing. I'll see you tonight."

As she hurried out, Nell closed her eyes. And prayed.

It wasn't, Mia discovered, a simple matter to leave. By the time she managed to get to her office, retrieve the papers she'd locked there, and make her way downstairs, an hour had been eaten up.

"Lulu. Two minutes," she said, gesturing to the back room.

"I'm busy here."

"Two minutes," Mia repeated and went inside.

"I don't have time to lollygag, and I don't need another break." With her face scrunched in disapproval, Lulu clomped into the room. Her cast was covered with colorful signatures, and a few lewd illustrations. "I've got customers."

"So I see. I'm sorry, I need to go home."

"It's the middle of the damn day. Might remind you, I'm down to one arm instead of my usual six."

"I'm sorry." A well of emotion rose in her throat, thickened her voice before she could swallow it again. This was the woman who'd been mother, father, friend. The only constant in her life other than her own gift. And more precious than magic.

"You sick or something?" Lulu demanded.

"No. No, I'm fine. We can close the store for the rest of the day. I don't want you to overdo."

"I'll be damned if we're closing. If you want to play hooky, go ahead. I'm not a damned invalid, and I know how to run the shop."

"I know. I'll make it up to you."

"Damn right you will. I'll take an afternoon off next week, and you can stay in the trenches."

"That's a deal. Thanks." Careful of the broken arm, Mia hugged her, then unable to help herself, pressed her face into Lulu's hair. "Thank you."

"If I'd known you'd get so worked up about it, I'd have taken two afternoons off. Go on if you're going."

"I love you, Lu. I'm going."

She hitched her satchel on her shoulder and, rushing out, didn't see the tears swim into Lulu's eyes or hear her sniff them back.

And when she was sure Mia wouldn't hear, she whispered, "Blessed be, baby girl."

"Everything in order, Mrs. Farley?"

"It is."

Sam nodded. "I appreciate your help. I'm

going to have to leave matters in your capable hands."

"Sir . . . Sam," she amended. "You were an interesting boy, and a good one, all in all. You're a better man."

"I—" Words failed him. "Thank you. I have to get home."

"Have a good evening."

"It's going to be one for the books," he predicted as he walked out of his office.

There were things he needed at the cottage. Tools of his own that he hadn't taken to Mia's. He packed them—his oldest athame and ritual sword, the old jar where he kept his sea salt. He changed into a dark shirt and jeans, deciding to take the black robe with him rather than driving in it. He wrapped a favored wand in silk.

All of this he placed in a carved wooden box that had been in his family for generations.

Rather than an amulet or pendant, he wore the two silver rings on a chain.

Before he walked to his car, he stopped to look back at the house, and the woods that ran beside it. His protection would hold. He refused to believe otherwise.

He could feel the simmer of his own

power as he crossed the edge of his charm and stepped clear of it into the street.

The force struck him, a full body blow that lifted him off his feet, sent him flying back. His body slammed into the ground, and a thousand black stars spun inside his head.

"It'll take you an hour to set up all this equipment," Ripley complained as Mac loaded the last of it into the back of his Land Rover.

"No, it won't."

"You always say that."

"I probably won't need it all, but I'm not taking any chances. This promises to be one of the biggest paranormal events in recorded history. There." He slammed the cargo door. "Ready?"

"I've been ready. Let's get—"

He watched, stupefied, as her eyes rolled back in her head and her hands clawed at her own throat while she choked for breath.

Nell waited while Zack put the bag holding her tools in the car. "This is going to work,"

she told him. "Mia's been working toward this all her life."

"Doesn't hurt to have backup."

"No, and Sam's idea wasn't just brilliant, it speaks to the purpose of the island as well."

He hefted the cooler holding the ice cream and the makings for sundaes. "I believe that. But it gives me some trouble knowing Remington's gone catatonic. My contact said it was like pulling a switch. He just went blank."

"He's being used. I can feel sorry for him, opening himself to what will, without question, destroy him."

"What's in him wants you, Nell."

"No." She touched Zack's arm. The man who'd once been her husband, and her terror, held no more fear for her. "What's in him now wants everything, and Mia most of all."

She started to turn to the car door, then with a shocked cry, doubled over.

"What is it? Nell?"

"Cramps. God, the baby!"

"Hold on. Just hold on." He swept her into his arms, fighting against panic as he saw the pain on her face. "I'll get you to the doctor. It's going to be okay."

"No, no, no." Pressing her face into his shoulder, she struggled against both pain and terror. "Wait. Just wait."

"Not for a second." He yanked open the door, would have set her inside, but she clung like a burr.

"It's not real. It's not real. Mia said the baby would be safe. She was sure of it. This is *not* real." She dug down, found the power beneath the fear. "It's an illusion, to keep us away. To keep us from making the circle." She let out a long, shaky breath, and when she looked at Zack again, her skin glowed.

"It's a lie," she said. "We have to get to Mia."

She went to her cliffs first, stood with her robe, white as the moon that had yet to rise, billowing. She could feel the dark pressing, its edge ice-cold, blade-sharp.

She watched, calm, as the fog rolled in over the sea and began, foot by foot, to spread over the island.

However fiercely she'd guarded her thoughts, it understood one point. Tonight was the battle for all.

"So mote it be," she murmured, and turning away, walked into the long shadows and dying light of the forest.

The fog closed around her. Cold and full of whispers. It made her want to run. She could feel it, horrid little fingers tickling along her skin. A kind of tease.

She heard the long, low howl of a wolf, and the sound was almost a laugh. Panic leaked through her shield of will as the fog crept hideously beneath the skirt of her robe.

On a sound of disgust, she slapped at it, driving it back from the path, though she knew she scattered some of her carefully hoarded energy in doing so.

Her pulse raging, she walked to the clearing. To the heart, to wait for her circle.

It would not be so easy, she thought, and pulled her emotions back. She imagined them, bright and dark, coalescing into one narrow beam buried in her heart. Not so easy to harm what she loved, to use that love to destroy.

She would protect. And she would win.

Nell came first, running through the woods with Zack to throw her arms around Mia. "You're all right!"

"Yes." Gently Mia drew Nell back. "What happened?"

"It tried to stop us. Mia, it's very close."

"I know." She took both of Nell's hands. Gripped tight. "You and yours won't be harmed. We need to start. The sun's nearly set."

She released Nell, opened her arms, and the candles she had set around the clearing burst into light. "It wants the dark," she said, then turned as Ripley stepped into the clearing.

"The son of a bitch thought he could scare me away." She laid down her bag of tools as Mac hauled in the first load of his equipment. "It's time we showed the bastard who he's dealing with."

"I could use a hand with some of my stuff," Mac said.

"You don't have much time," Mia told him.

"Time enough." Sam walked in, hefting one of Mac's monitors and his own carved box.

Mia crossed to him, touched a fingertip to the corner of his mouth. "You're bleeding."

"Sucker punched me." He wiped at the blood with the back of his hand. "I owe him one."

"Then let's fight." Ripley reached into her bag and drew out her ritual sword.

For the first time in days, Mia laughed and meant it. "You never change. This place is sacred. It is the heart. Circle within circle within circle protects all from cold and dark. Here where stood the sisters three I will meet my destiny."

As she spoke, she walked the edges of the clearing, her bare feet inches from the bubbling fog.

"Once this circle has been cast, the bond we form will ever last."

"That's not the opening for the banishing ritual," Sam said, but she ignored him and continued.

"The setting sun gives me its fire, and the moon will rise higher and higher." She picked up a jar and spread a ring of sea salt around the husbands of her sisters. "One is three and three is one, through our blood the web was spun. What is dark and wears my mark will bear it for eternity. As I will, so mote it be."

She lifted her arms and called the thunder. "Cast the next circle," she said, and looked at Sam. "I know what I'm doing."

"So do I."

Mac studied his gauges as the circle was cast. "As far as I can follow this, by casting this outer circle, around the clearing, by herself, she's focusing the negative force on her. Even when she's linked with the others, she's the target."

"Sam called that one," Zack replied.

"That's right. She circled us with the sea salt as a second defense. Her plan is for us to stay inside the protective ring, whatever happens."

"In a pig's eye," Zack stated.

"You got that right, too. Power's building." He could feel it.

Around the circle, light shimmered, deep gold. With the tips of blades, each scribed their symbols in the ground. The first chant rose with the moon.

"Air and earth and fire and water, mother to son, and son to daughter. Through our blood we claim the right to call the power from the night. Under the light of the Moon of Mead, we ask to be given what we need. We seek the light, we seek the sight."

Nell lifted her arms. "From Air I come, of Air I call. I bring the wind to rise and fall. To sweep away what seeks to harm, I bring to bear all magic, all charm. I am Air and she is me. As I will, so mote it be."

And while the wind rose up to roar, Ripley lifted her arms. "From Earth I come, of Earth I entreat. Quake and quiver below my feet. The dark what's mine will swallow, and none his fall will follow. I am Earth and she is me. As I will, so mote it be."

The earth trembled.

"From Water I come." Sam spread his arms high. "Of Water I cry. Pour from the sea, flood from the sky. To wash clean this isle of light and protect it from the hound of night. I am Water, and he is me. As I will, so mote it be."

As the rain lashed them, Mia threw back her head. "From Fire I come, of Fire I yearn. Spark and flame and cleanly burn. To purge this beast who hunts for blood, and from him shield what I have loved. I am Fire, and she is me. As I will, so mote it be."

Lightning flamed across the sky, spewed up from the ground. It roared in the air and sparked like diamonds on the rain.

The storm broke like a fury, spinning a whirlwind out from the clearing and through the forest.

"My equipment can't measure it," Mac called out over the explosions of thunder. "I can't get a clear reading."

Beside him, Zack drew his weapon. "You don't need one. It's howling. The wolf. And it's getting closer."

Within the circle, the four linked hands. With the moon beaming like a beacon through the storm, Mia drew Nell's hand over to Sam's. And made them three.

"Twice the Three have stopped your breath. I alone am left to test. Tonight I stand and challenge you. Come from the dark and do what you will do. My fate within my own hands rests. Which one of us will meet our death? You have come to your last hour. Come and face this witch's power."

She stepped through the fire of her own making, and out of the circle.

The black wolf formed out of the fog and snarled at the edge of the clearing. Even as she moved forward, Sam lifted his ritual sword. A wild blue light speared from the tip as he spun out, using his body to shield hers.

"No." A trickle of panic cut through her fierce control, and the light around the clearing wavered. "This isn't yours."

"You're mine. I'll go to hell with him before he hurts you. Get back in the circle."

She stared at him, and even as the wolf took the first testing step into the clearing, her panic receded. Her power built from the heart, and spread through her.

"I won't lose," she said quietly. "I can't." With her destiny bright in her mind, she ran from the clearing with the wolf leaping after her.

It would end where she chose to end it. Of that she was certain. She flew through the woods, the heat of her body cutting through the icy fog that covered ground and path and stung the swirling air. What pursued her screamed with greed. She knew every twist of the path, every rise of the earth, and ran through the storm-wracked night, an arrow with the target already in sight.

She broke out of the woods and raced unerringly for the cliffs rising slick and black from the stinking mist. Gathering, she hurled power behind her to gain the time she needed, and heard the cry of pain and outrage. And felt, beneath it, the sly pleasure.

She was beyond her circle. Separated and alone. And standing now on the cliffs where the one who was Fire had made her last choice. Behind her was the roaring sea, below her the unforgiving rocks.

*Trapped.* She heard the whisper in her head. *Stand, and be ripped to pieces. Step back, step off, and escape.*

Breathless from the run and what was building inside her, she inched back. Wind snatched at the wet hem of her robe, and the slippery rocks beneath her trembled and shook.

The island was coated with fog, smothered with its weight. But that she'd anticipated. She saw one clear circle at the edge of the village where the light beamed like a thousand candles. That she hadn't anticipated, nor the rush of energy that streamed from it, and into her like love.

She wrapped it close, shielded it with her own power, and watched the wolf climb slowly up the cliffs.

Stalk me, she thought. Yes, come closer. I've waited for this all my life.

It bared its teeth and rose, like a man, on its hind legs. *Fear me. For I am your death. I bring you pain.*

A black bolt spilled out of the sky and scorched the rock at her feet. She inched back and saw the triumph gleam in those red eyes.

"I'm not done," she said coolly, and hurled a stream of fire at him.

It was what Sam saw when he tore out of the trees. Mia standing on the edge of the cliff, her white robe shining like silver, her hair flying in the wind, while the monstrous black form rose over her. Fire burst around them, and smoke spewed thick. Out of the turbulent sky, spears of light fell like flaming rain.

His cry was more of fury than fear as, with his sword sizzling like lightning, he charged the cliffs.

Now! she thought, and whirled on the rocks as if she stood in a ballroom. "On this night I rejoice and make my choice. He chooses me, and I choose him." She flung out her arms, baring her heart. "This light no force has power to dim. My heart is his, and his for me. And this is our joined destiny. My death I'd give for theirs to spare," she shouted, her voice like thunder as the others spilled out of the woods. "For those I love all would I dare. Three hundred years to end this strife, by these words: I choose love." She clamped her hand over Sam's as he leaped up beside her. "I choose life."

The wolf form shuddered into a man. The faces of him, legion, shifted and melted into each other. Her mark scored them all. "You save this place, but not yourself." His breath spewed out, rotted and foul. "You'll go with me."

It leaped, and Sam's sword, bright as water, swung out. "Her mark. And my mark." As it cleaved, the form spilled into a mist that slithered over the rocks like snakes.

"Bullies never play fair," Mia said as the mist hissed and spit and crawled toward her feet. Power, a steady stream of white, burned in her. "It's for me to finish."

"Then finish it," Sam told her.

She tossed aside all shields, opened all locks. The power that had pulsed inside her burst free so that she stood aflame under the ravaged sky. "By all I am, by all I'll be, I hurl the darkness back at thee. With courage, justice, hand, and heart I finish what my blood did start. Now you taste the fear most dire, as you face my righteous fire."

She stretched out her arm, and in her cupped fingers a ball of flame formed. "Your fate is wrought by the sisters three. As we will, so mote it be."

For Lulu, she thought. And for all the other innocents.

She hurled the ball into the mists. They burned, writhing. Burned as they spilled over the edge of the cliffs and fell howling into the sea.

"Drown in hell." Sam's voice echoed. "Die in the dark. Burn eternally with my woman's mark. Your force is crushed by this vast sea."

"As we will," Mia said, turning to him.

"So mote it be." He stepped back, drew her with him. "Come away from the edge, Mia."

"But it's a lovely view." She laughed, a full-throated, joyous sound and lifted her face to the sky, where stars burst out of the clouds. The moon sailed, a white ship on a calm sea. "God, what a feeling. You'll have questions," she said. "I need a minute first, with Nell and Ripley."

"Go ahead."

She walked down the cliffs and into the arms of her sisters.

Later, she left the others in her kitchen and went out into the garden with Sam. "It may be hard for you to understand why I didn't share everything I intended with you, with all of you. It wasn't arrogance, it was—"

The words clogged in her throat when he spun her into his arms, held her crushed against him.

"Necessary," she managed.

"Just don't talk for a minute. Just—Mia." He buried his face in her hair, rocking, chanting soft words, wild words in Gaelic. Then just as abruptly, he yanked her away, gave her one hard shake. "Necessary, my ass. Necessary to rip the heart out of my chest? Do you know what it was like to see you standing on the edge of that cliff, with that *thing* coming at you?"

"Yes." She framed his face in her hands. "Yes. It was the only way, Sam. The only way I knew to be sure. To end it without harm to anyone."

"Answer me one question. Look straight at me when you answer it. Would you have sacrificed yourself?"

"No." When his eyes narrowed, she kept hers level. "Risking one's life is different from sacrificing it. Did I risk it, yes, I did. Clearheadedly, because I'm a practical woman with a healthy appreciation for life. I risked it for the only real mother I've ever known. For this place and the people on it. For them," she said, gesturing toward the house. "For the children to come from them. For you. For us. But I intended to live, and as you can see, I did."

"You planned to leave the circle that way. You planned to take it to the cliffs. Alone."

"It was meant to end there. I'd prepared in every way I knew how, considered every possibility. And still I missed one that you didn't. When I looked down from the cliffs and saw that circle of light. . . . Sam." Swamped with love, she leaned into him. "When I felt that strength, that love and faith sweeping up and into me, it was the greatest gift. Who knows what would have happened without it? You did that. By asking for help when I didn't think of it."

"Islanders stick together. Spread the word to a few people—"

"And word spreads to a few more," she finished. "And they gathered around the cottage and in the woods tonight. All those hearts and minds turned toward me."

She pressed her hands between her breasts where that song still sang. "Strong magic. You have to understand," she continued, easing back, "I couldn't tell you, any of you. I couldn't allow myself to open even that much, take the chance that what was in my own mind and heart would be read by what we were going to fight. I had to wait until everything was in place."

"I'm working on that, Mia, but this wasn't your fight. It was ours."

"I wasn't sure of that. I wanted to be, but I wasn't sure until you stepped out of the circle in front of me. And what you felt for me . . . telling me you love me paled with feeling it burst out of you in that one moment. I knew you'd come after me. I knew then, without question, that we had to finish it together. I need to tell you . . ."

She shook her head, stepped away from him until she was sure the words would be there. "I loved you once, so much. But my love was twined around my own needs and wants and wishes. A girl's love, that has borders. When you were gone, I made myself lock that love away. I couldn't survive with it alive inside me. Then you came back."

She turned to him. "It hurt to look at you. As I said, I'm a practical woman, and I dislike pain. I dealt with that. I wanted you, but

I didn't have to unlock that love to have you. So I thought." She brushed his hair from his forehead. "So I wished. But the lock wouldn't hold, and that love spilled out. It was different than it had been, but I didn't see, didn't want to see. Because looking hurt again. Every time you told me you loved me, it was a knife in my heart."

"Mia—"

"No. I'll finish. The night we sat out here in the garden, with the butterfly? Before you came I'd been trying to settle my mind, once and for all. To reason it all out, to prepare myself. You sat, and you smiled at me, and everything inside me shifted. As if it had only been waiting for that one moment, that one look. When you told me you loved me, it didn't hurt. It didn't hurt at all. Do you know how it made me feel?"

"No." He skimmed his knuckles over her cheek. "Tell me."

"Happy. Down-in-the-gut happy. Sam." She ran her hands down his arms, couldn't stop touching him. "What I felt for you then, and now, and always will isn't a girl's love. It bloomed out of that, but it's new. It doesn't need fantasies or wishes. If you go—"

"I'm not—"

"If you go again, what I feel for you won't change or be locked away. I had to know that, without a shadow of doubt. I'll cherish it, and what we made together. I know you love me, and that's enough."

"Do you think I'd leave you now?"

"That's not the point." Flying on her own heart, she stepped back, turned in a circle. "The point is, I love you enough to let you go. That I won't wonder or worry, or look at you with that shadow on my heart. I love you enough to be with you. To live with you. With no regrets, no conditions."

"Come here, will you? Right here," he said pointing in front of him.

She nodded and walked to him. "Close enough?"

"Do you see these?" He lifted the chain so that the rings were in her line of vision.

"What are they? They're beautiful." She reached out to touch, and her breath caught at the warmth and the light that pulsed from them. "Their rings," she whispered. "Hers and his."

"I found his in that cave I told you about, in Ireland. And hers just a matter of days ago, here. In our cave. Can you see what's carved on them, and inside them?"

She traced her finger over the Celtic symbols and read, as her heart began to thud, the Gaelic inside the circles.

He slid the chain over his head, took the smaller ring off. "This is yours."

All the power that still surged inside her seemed to pause. As if a million breaths were held. "Why are you giving it to me?"

"Because he couldn't keep the promise. But I will. I want to make it to you. I want you to make it to me. Now, and again when you marry me. And every day after that. I want to say it to you every time one of our children is born."

Her gaze flew up to his. "Children."

"I had a vision," he began, and brushed the first tear away with his fingertip as it spilled down her cheek. "You were working in the garden in the very early spring. The leaves were just a green haze, and the sun was soft and yellow. When I came out to you, you stood up. You were so beautiful, Mia. More beautiful than I've ever seen you. You were full with our child. I put my hand on you, over it, and felt it move. Felt that life we'd made just . . . surge. So impatient to be born. I had no idea."

He took her face in his hands. "No idea

what that would mean. No idea that I could want, so much, everything I saw and felt in that one slice of time. Make a life with me, Mia. Our life, and what comes from it."

"I thought the magic was done for the night. Yes." She pressed her lips to his cheek. "Yes." And to the other. "To everything," she said, laughing now as her lips found his.

He circled her once, then took her right hand. "That's the wrong finger," she told him.

"You can't wear it on the left until we're married. Let's be a little traditional. And since we are, though I think people who've been in love all their lives should have a very short engagement . . ."

He opened his hand, and where her tear had lain was a slice of light. Grinning at her, he tossed it high, and stars fountained from it, raining down like little sparks of flame.

"A symbol," he said, plucking one of the lights from the air. "A promise. I'll give you the stars, Mia." Turning his hand over, he offered her a circle ringed with diamonds clear as water, bright as fire.

"I'll take them. And you. Oh, and you, Sam." She held out her hand, absorbing the thrill as he slipped the pledge onto her finger. And there it glittered. "What magic we'll make!"

"Let's start now."

Laughing with her, he lifted her off her feet and danced her around a garden bursting with flowers.

And their stars shimmered brilliant against the dark.